HUNTER BROWN

and the Eye Of Ends

THE MILLER BROTHERS

Warner Press™

CONNECT • EQUIP • INSPIRE

Once again, the Miller Broth
As Hunter Brown meets up
father and rid himself of a tra
hooked in Hunter's latest adv
fantasy, you should like this b
Hannah Davis

The Miller Brothers' world
imagination and immersing yo
conclusion left me in awe.
Brock Eastman, author of The Quest for Truth series.

This is the best book of the series. I could not put it down.
Aidan Ray

Wow! Hunter Brown 3—this is the one I've been waiting for! The first two were very good but this one definitely tops them! One, because the whole book is the climax; and two, it answered all the questions I had. Did I add that the "Eye of Ends" is a very cool title!"
Jonathan Carter

Reading this book with my son was a pleasure—a masterful mix of adventure and teachable moments. It was great to find so many of our favorite characters from previous Hunter Brown books are back, and there are plenty of intriguing new characters as well for readers to enjoy. My only complaint is that this story is so skillfully woven together we had a summer full of late mealtimes, simply because we couldn't put it down!"
Debbie Collins, teacher and mother of two

I literally would have devoured this book if it were possible.
Michael Collins (age 10)

Hunter Brown and the Eye of Ends had me enthralled from beginning to end. The plot was filled with twists and turns that kept me guessing in every chapter, along with characters who made me alternately glare at the book in frustration, or grin with joy. I loved reading all three of these books.
Mary Cooley, Age 14

I knew an epic conclusion was coming, but this surpassed all expectations. This tear-jerking, heart-moving, spine-tingling tale was so worth the wait. Trying to put it down was like trying to remove the Bloodstone without help from Aviad: IMPOSSIBLE!!!!

Marie (Bladebearer), Age 19

Ever since I received the first Hunter Brown book as a Christmas present, these books have stayed on my favorites list and *Hunter Brown and the Eye of Ends* is no exception. With an original plot filled with excitement, *Hunter Brown and the Eye of Ends* is dripping with Christian analogies that reveal deep meanings and lessons that are important to know and remember. With a good pace and mysteries to be solved around every corner, Hunter Brown will hold you to the end and leave you wanting to begin again.

Rachel Harris, age 20

Eye of Ends is the kind of book I wish existed when I was young. Colorful writing, engaging characters, and an intriguing plot make this a stellar conclusion to Hunter Brown's riveting adventures.

James L. Rubart bestselling author of Rooms and Book of Days

As a director, I dig through countless stories before finding anything that will hold my attention. The Eye of Ends grabbed my imagination and wouldn't let go. With the book's twists and turns, the Miller Bros have woven together an image-rich story that any director would long to create. The Eye of Ends brings the Codebearers series to its rightful epic conclusion. I love this story.

Darren Thomas, Producer/Director
Working Element, LLC

Dedicated to

Dad

You are a model of courage,

strength, creativity and love.

Thank you for being a hero

we can look up to.

The Codebearers Series™ 3: Hunter Brown and the Eye of Ends

Published by Warner Press, Inc, Anderson, IN 46012
Warner Press and "WP" logo is a trademark of Warner Press, Inc.

ISBN-13:978-1-59317-400-2

Editors: Karen Rhodes, Robin Fogle, Arthur Kelly
Creative Director: Curtis D. Corzine

Library of Congress Cataloging-in-Publication Data

Miller, Christopher, 1976-
    Hunter Brown and the eye of ends / The Miller Brothers [Christopher and Allan Miller]. -- 1st ed.
        p. cm. -- (The Codebearers series ; 3)
    Summary: Having lost his memory, Hunter returns from Solandria with no knowledge of his last visit, and he must try to piece together the growing puzzle of his past under the constant surveillance of an intimidating detective who is more than what he seems.
    ISBN 978-1-59317-400-2 (alk. paper)
    [1. Magic--Fiction. 2. Memory--Fiction. 3. Space and time--Fiction. 4. Books and reading--Fiction. 5. Adventure and adventurers--Fiction.] I. Miller, Allan, 1978- II. Title.
    PZ7.M61255Hty 2011
    [Fic]--dc22
                                        2010044174

75665018080

Printed in Canada
2011 – First Edition

www.warnerpress.org

www.codebearers.com
The Codebearers Series™
Lumination Studios

ACKNOWLEDGEMENTS:

There are books you write and then there are books that write you.
So much life has happened during our penning of the third Hunter Brown
adventure, so many people have given of themselves to see us through to the end.
For this we are forever grateful. To our friends and family who hung in there with
us when life seemed to be getting the better of us...we simply say thank you.

For our dear friends at Warner Press. Eric, Regina, Karen, Robin, Curt, Mike
and Gwynne—Phew, we made it...again!

To our fans who have waited forever-and-a-day to hold this book.
Well, what are you waiting for? The adventure awaits!
May this story bless you as much as it has blessed us.

To that "penguin" guy Lance (aka RocketSnail). Your words of encouragement
and your interest in our work has been an inspiration.

Jared—We rejoice that God has put you in our lives. Our friendship runs much
deeper than ink and paper, but it is great to finally be working together.
Thank you for blessing us with the brilliant brushstrokes of a masterful artist.
Your talent is inspiring.

A very special thanks goes out to the Collins family, without whom we can only say
this book would not have been completed. God has used you in mighty ways
in our lives. Your love for us in action was worth more than any words could say.
Be blessed by this the fruit of your labor. 1 John 3:18

Lastly, may our Lord Jesus Christ, the Sovereign God, find favor in the work
of our hands. May this book be a sacrifice that is pleasing in your sight.
Thank you for giving us a reason to write and our hope for a future.

CONTENTS

CHAPTER I

ONE FALSE MOVE

"It's too quiet, Nowaii," the hooded figure spoke gently to the saddled creature beneath him, stroking its neck. Moonlight glimmered against the iridescent tones of the large bird's magnificent feathers. Bird and rider sat perched at the cliff's edge, waiting.

The man's breath hung in the cold night air. "No wind tonight."

Nowaii cocked his head toward his rider and blinked a massive yellow eye in silent acknowledgement. His master did not note the conditions just for a pleasant flight. His concern was with his fellow Codebearer fighters on the ground, attempting to quietly take up their positions even now, somewhere amidst the tangled woods far below. If they were to have any success executing their daring attack on the enemy this night, they would need more than just the cover of darkness and forest trees—they would need the element of sur-

I

prise. As it stood, just one false move—a snapped twig or carelessly drawn breath—could bring their whole mission crashing down on top of them…with deadly consequences.

"What was Aviad thinking? If it were left to me, I would have called it off. He risks too much."

The rider stared off into the distance where the flickering of torchlight could be seen in the fallen city of Direse. Three days ago, it was a city at peace. Two days ago the Shadow forces had invaded and seized their latest stronghold. Tonight, the Resistance would set it free…or die trying.

To Aviad's credit, his plan was a bold move. Never before had the Resistance countered so quickly and decisively. The Shadow would have no reason to suspect them, a fact the Resistance leader's daring plan depended on.

And what if it fails? the rider wondered to himself.

Perhaps he should have thought of this more, but he had been eager for the chance to prove himself, looking for an opportunity to stand out from the crowd. This mission offered that opportunity. How well he performed his role tonight would make all the difference for his future advancement.

Turning his thoughts back to the task at hand, the rider shook his head to clear his mind. Regardless of what doubts he might form now, the fact remained that other men out there tonight were depending on him to do his part.

And I must count on the Author to do his, the rider reminded himself, lifting his eyes skyward.

He watched as a bank of heavy clouds finally settled in front of the moon, smudging out the shadows it cast below. It was time.

"Via, Veritas, Vita," whispered the rider.

With a mighty flap, the mystical Thunderbird launched itself and rider out over the forested expanse below.

"Eh? What's this?" grunted a lone Shadow sentry, tilting his pig-shaped head skyward. From his high tower post he typically paid attention to things below him, but a small speck of movement from above had caught his eye, though more out of curiosity than actual concern. He squinted, trying to make out the odd shape drifting down toward him. Was it a bat…a bird? Couldn't be. There were no wings. Yet it was gliding, no, racing down at him now…and with alarming speed!

Suddenly, a pair of flashing talons sprang out from the empty sky, locked around the guard's head and with a powerful twist, finished off the sentry before a struggle could occur.

A hooded figure dropped seemingly from out of nowhere to land crouched next to the now motionless body.

"Good work, Nowaii," the man whispered his praise to the nearly invisible bird. In a rippling effect, the bird reversed the natural cloaking effect of its feathers to reveal its massive frame once again.

"Keep low and wait here until my signal." He made a motion with his hands to indicate the same.

Taking hold of the Veritas Sword on his belt, the rider cautiously peered over the edge of the tower they had landed on. It was the highest point of the city. If his intelligence was right, the presiding Shadow lord would be quartered somewhere below. From the calm activity of the other sentries scattered across the four towers and outer walls, no one had witnessed their intrusion. Everything was going as planned.

****

"Are the troops in position?" a commanding, scarlet-caped form asked with a snarl. He did not bother to turn or look up when asking the question. Rather, he remained hunched over a desk, preoccupied with examining a collection of peculiar documents.

"Yes, Lord Bledynn. They await your command," the reporting Shadow first officer, Geptun, replied. Looking decidedly like a pig-faced troll, Geptun stood a good two feet taller (two and a half if you didn't count the added height of the goblin's spiked helmet) than his accompanying second officer, a short, rotund goblin.

"Good," Bledynn replied coolly, leaving it at that.

Sensing his desired dismissal, the first officer turned to leave and then hesitated for just a moment.

"What is it?" Bledynn asked in an irritated tone.

"Well, my lord, there have not been any reported sightings of enemy movement. I was beginning to wonder if perhaps you were mistaken…if we should consider…."

Before he could finish, Lord Bledynn roared, overturning the desk and scattering his papers as he swung violently around to clamp a clawed hand around his surprised officer's throat.

"*Never…question…my powers!*"

Tightening his grip, Bledynn dragged the gasping Geptun closer toward his snarling teeth. The officer winced painfully, though less from his onsetting suffocation than from the absolute terror of being forced to look upon the fearsome sight.

Coarse grey hair covered the Shadow lord's muscular body, bristling angrily about his thick neck. His fiery red eyes burned with intensity. He was no man, but a Vulvynn, a ferocious wolf-like beast in a man's form, and likely would have been the last thing Geptun ever saw were it not for the old man who suddenly stepped forward from a shadowed corner.

Slowly the robed elder knelt, his long grey beard touching the floor as he gathered up the displaced papers. "Might I propose to you, O excellent lord," his voice was as deep and calm as a wide river, "that not all have been given the gift of such great insight as yours." Rising to his feet, with bowed head he presented the stack of drawings back to Bledynn.

The approach of the wisened advisor seemed to calm the enraged leader enough to finally release the near-unconscious Geptun, letting him fall to the stone floor, a gasping, coughing heap.

Snatching the drawing from the top of the offered stack, Bledynn allowed his own crazed breathing to slow as he traced the odd string of lines scrawled across the parchment with one of his long, crooked claws.

Eyes still fixed on the cryptic art, Bledynn addressed his wheezing officer once again. "Tonomis is right. You doubt because you have not seen as I have. Allow me to ease your anxiety." Bledynn held the paper out for Geptun and the second officer to see.

"This," Bledynn said, waving broadly with his free hand, "is the future. With my own hand, I have drawn that which Fate itself revealed to me."

From the bewildered expressions on the Shadow officers' faces, they both thought the ugly, twisted mess of ink looked just like an ugly, twisted mess of ink. Wisely they chose to keep their observations to themselves.

The Vulvynn lord continued, "Armed with this intelligence, I have been able to anticipate each and every move the Codebearers have made, leading up to tonight. In fact, the only reason I even bothered to take over this pathetic stink-hole of a city was because I *knew* the Resistance would follow us here, an opportune time for them to corner and contain my forces within these walls, no doubt." Bledynn traced his claw over a particular line that when looked at just right, could be construed to resemble the distinct five-towered silhouette of the city of Direse.

Bledynn's face twisted into a cruel smile. "It is almost sad, isn't it? The Resistance foolishly believe they'll actually surprise me with their clever attack. Too bad for them I will always be one move ahead." Bledynn laughed aloud just thinking of the brilliance of the plan he had put into motion. He had discovered the existence of two underground escape tunnels, a closely guarded secret that only a few living Dieresiens even had knowledge of. And by simply assigning a few Shadow to "greet" those privileged few at the tunnel exits during their siege, Bledynn had made quite certain that the secret had died with them.

"When the Resistance attacks tonight, and they will," Bledynn continued, pausing to glare at his first officer, "you will do exactly as I planned. Those inside the walls will stage an adequate, but weaker defense. When the Codebearers advance, you will remind them why it is so important to always watch one's back. On my command, our forces will swarm out from the tunnels to overwhelm and crush their futile attack from behind!"

He snatched another drawing from his advisor, Tonomis, and displayed this next mess of wild, almost jubilant, lines proudly. "See? Look upon our sweeping victory! This is the glorious triumph that awaits my army tonight!" Looking down at Geptun, Bledynn's face suddenly darkened once more. His voice was no longer exuberant, but cold. "That is, assuming faithless, weak-minded leaders such as you, my worrisome Geptun, do not foul it up."

At this suggestion, Geptun promptly knelt, his bruised throat croaking out a feeble apology. "You are right, my lord…. Forgive me for doubting you and your…" he forced himself to say it, "art. It will never happen again!"

"Precisely," Bledynn agreed, unsheathing his curved sword and taking a menacing step forward to make an example of the creature. "So let me make certain it doesn't."

There was nothing the helpless first officer could do to defend himself against the swift, powerful down-stroke of Bledynn's blade. Using a clawed foot, Bledynn pushed the still kneeling, now headless, body to the ground. Hooking the former first officer's medallion by its neck strap with the tip of his sullied sword, he flicked it unceremoniously toward the terrified second officer. "Consider yourself promoted."

The trembling goblin accepted the ribbon, stumbling awkwardly down to one knee. "I l-live to serve you, L-lord Bledynn. Whatever you command, I will...."

"You will return to the tunnels," Bledynn interrupted, not wasting time. "Continue to await my signal and relay my expectations of unwavering confidence throughout the ranks. There must be no weak links, first officer..." Bledynn's red eyes squinted down at the stocky goblin, trying unsuccessfully to remember his name.

"Zeeb, your greatness."

"Of course," Bledynn said with a grunt and waved his dismissal.

Zeeb sprang quickly to his feet, stepping over his fallen comrade, and hurried out on his assigned task, glad to finally be out of Bledynn's presence.

The advisor, Tonomis, was the first to speak into the ensuing silence. "Might I remind you, Lord Bledynn, that you are not the first to wield the power of the Eye? As you know full well, many have killed to obtain what you hold. You would be wise to guard its secrets more judiciously."

Bledynn growled, clutching protectively at a leather pouch strapped to his breastplate. He shot an angry look over his shoulder at his advisor. "Keep your lectures, old one, unless it is your intent to outlive your usefulness," he said threateningly, turning to impose his intimidating frame on the much smaller, feeble man.

Tonomis did not flinch. Nor did he give even a hint of concern as he observed a flicker of movement from somewhere in the shadows of the room behind Bledynn.

"Perhaps it is not I who have outlived my purpose," replied the aged advisor, letting Bledynn's precious drawings drop carelessly to the ground and lifting his eyes to meet his lord's in defiance, "but you."

The enraged Vulvynn took another step forward, raising his clawed hand to strike. Without warning, a sudden flash of green light shot straight out from Bledynn's chest as a sword's blade ran him through. He arched his back and roared in pain, his stunned face awash in the unexpected glow. Just as quickly, the blade of light disappeared and the once proud leader fell forward, landing amidst the pile of his haphazard drawings, now greedily soaking up his blood.

"How…" he asked, "did I not see?" As the life slowly drained from his angry, confused eyes, he searched the lines one last time for an answer that would never come.

His master vanquished, Tonomis now found himself face-to-face with the Codebearer assassin, his Veritas Sword lit and aimed to strike him down with its next stroke.

"Tell me where these tunnels are that Bledynn spoke of," the warrior demanded.

Tonomis remained calm, studying his attacker carefully before answering. "Bledynn may have acted like a blind fool at times, but his drawings have always tracked the Resistance flawlessly. This can only mean one thing: you are not here as part of the Resistance attack. On whose authority did you come?"

"I ask the questions," the warrior deflected, though his worried expression was answer enough. Thrusting his sword blade short of the old man's neck, he again demanded, "The tunnels—where are they?"

Directing the warrior with his eyes toward a map hanging from a nearby wall, Tonomis replied, "You'll find them marked on the map, but that is not what you are truly looking for."

Ignoring the comment, the warrior moved to the map, all the while keeping his sword tip trained on the old man. He quickly noted the tunnel exits Bledynn had identified, then tore the map from the wall and stuffed it into his belt.

Tonomis made no move to flee, but watched patiently with great interest as the rogue warrior strode back toward him.

Holding his hands peacefully out at his sides, Tonomis said, "Permit me to offer some helpful advice before you kill me."

"Why should you?"

"I have lived long enough to recognize greatness when I see it."

This interested the warrior who chose to momentarily stay his attack. "Speak," he said, pointing the sword near Tonomis' throat.

"It is clear to me that you are both foolish and impulsive."

Irritated by his words, the warrior started to object, but Tonomis raised his hand and continued, "Yet, what you lack in knowledge, you make up for in zeal. You had ambition, took a great risk, and tonight you proved to be the right man for the job. Whether sanctioned or not, your actions have single-handedly eliminated a powerful Shadow lord and now the intelligence you have gained will undoubtedly deliver the Resistance from the Shadow's deadly ambush. A sure promotion is in order, if ever one was." The crafty old man watched with a suppressed smile as he hinted at the hero's true motivation. "You have done well for yourself," Tonomis continued, "but you can do better—much better. And I can show you how...if you would allow yourself to learn from me."

"Learn from you?" the Codebearer said with disgust. "You are one of them! A Shadow. I should not even let you live."

Tonomis smiled. He knew the Codebearer's threat was hollow. "I am not Shadow; however, even if I were, you have already determined not to kill me. Why?"

Unsettled, the warrior looked away, allowing his Veritas blade to fade as he did. "Because, it is my choice," he said.

"So it is," Tonomis replied. "And that is why you and I are very much the same."

The warrior cast him a wary look. "In what way?"

"We are both men who reserve the right to carve our own destinies. After all, why should anyone command your fate, especially when it is yours to control?" At this, Tonomis directed the warrior's eyes to the lifeless body of Bledynn, pointing to the peculiar leather pouch the Shadow lord had strapped to his breastplate, the better to guard it. "The Eye of Ends. As you have killed Bledynn, you are now its rightful master."

The warrior stared questioningly at Tonomis, then back down at the common-looking pouch, imagining what must be inside, debating his decision. Before he could decide, the sound of approaching footsteps caused him to spin around. He turned just in time to see the surprised face of First Officer Zeeb, as he entered the room. Shocked to see his lord sprawled out on the ground in front of him, the stout goblin could not decide fast enough what to do—attack the intruder or run for help.

Seeing the Codebearer's Veritas Sword flash to life, he made the decision to run. It was too late. A brilliant arc of green light sliced through the air from the Veritas Sword and caught him in his retreat. Zeeb tumbled forward, bouncing down the flight of stairs that curled from the tower room. When he came to a stop ten steps later, he groped at his left leg and howled in pain. Horrified to see his leg was no longer with him, the squealing goblin fainted. Even so, the damage had been done. Shouts from Shadow guards who had heard the commotion came from the corridor below.

Realizing he had let the old man intefere with the immediacy of his mission, the Codebearer strode back to where Tonomis still stood. "Clever game, old one. You almost had me, didn't you? But tonight, the victory belongs to the Resistance."

He turned quickly and walked over to the window, whistling for his ride, the Thunderbird Nowaii. As he climbed up to the windowsill, he faltered, looking back toward Bledynn and his pouch. Jumping down, he raced back and sliced the pouch free with his sword.

"I'll take it," he offered in explanation, "but only because the Resistance cannot afford to have it in the wrong hands."

"Certainly," Tonomis said with a slow nod.

Leaping back to the windowsill, the warrior quickly dropped out of sight only to rise up and away on the invisible wings of his Thunderbird.

From the tower's highest window, the old man watched his unassuming protégé race against time to save the Resistance. He smiled. Everything was going according to plan.

CHAPTER 2
A SPARK OF HOPE

At first, there was nothing. I was alone, surrounded by a deep and impenetrable blackness. Whether awake or asleep, I could not say. The only thing I knew for certain was that I was alive. I had a presence in this space, as empty as it was, and for that I was grateful. But I could not feel my own form, let alone see it.

No memory…no sounds…only darkness, complete and terrifying. For what seemed to be an eternity, I waited for something… anything…to happen. Eventually, something did.

A tiny spark of light appeared, piercing the heart of the blackness like a distant star in an endless midnight. It began as the smallest of specks, drifting haphazardly through the air like an ember carried by the winds of a raging fire. Gliding back and forth, the glowing speck found its way closer to the center of my vision. I could not look away. All I could think of was the spark. There was nothing else.

"Hunter, can you hear me?" the spark whispered. The voice was sweet and feminine, a warm blanket in the emptiness of space. There was something familiar about it as well, something I couldn't quite recognize, but knew that I should.

"Can you hear me?" it asked again.

I wanted to say "yes" but no words formed. I had no voice. For that matter, I couldn't tell if I even had a mouth—a fact that suddenly caused me to wonder. *What had I become? Where had I gone?*

"Don't worry. You can't speak here," said the ember, confirming what I had already discovered. "But I can hear you just the same," it added, as if reading my mind.

Where am I? I thought, strangely at ease with the speck that could read my mind.

"You have been taken by the Shadow; you are in hibernation. When you wake, things will be different. You have to remember how it was before."

Before what?

"Remember the Fire. Remember the marks. Remember…me."

What fire? Who are you? How do you know my name?

The ember flashed in response, spinning itself into a small flame, which quickly grew and stretched into a raging cyclone of fire. The heat from the inferno blasted through my unseen skin. I wanted to run but there was nowhere to go. The spinning cyclone slowed itself and began to settle into the shape of a person. It was the form of a girl, the figure of someone I recognized immediately, even through the flame.

Hope!

"Yes, it's me," she answered. "I've come to set you free."

As she spoke, Hope moved closer, becoming less flame and more flesh with every step, until at last her metamorphosis was complete. It was Hope all right, though I had never seen her look quite like this before—regal and majestic, a princess of light. She was wrapped in a long, flowing silk gown that faded from bright red to light orange at the hem. A golden band rested on her head like a crown, holding her wavy brown hair in place. Though she was no longer flame, her presence still glowed in a way that warmed the deepest parts of my being. I felt at peace as long as she was near. I wanted to reach out…to touch her…to see if she was for real. But without form I was helpless to even smile back. Somehow, she knew this and smiled in return.

"It's okay, it's really me. I'm alive, Hunter. The Author saved me. The Shadow want you to forget, you know."

Forget what?

She pointed near her heart, where the mark of the three-tongued flame glowed just above the neckline of her gown.

"The Fire has fallen. Its power is for all who call on the Author's name. Do you remember?"

I…don't know, I thought, staring blankly at the mark.

"Yes, you do. You must. It is what unites us—all of us, Hunter. It is the Author's spirit, his breath of life."

Hope reached out and took my unseen hands in her own. I had held her hand once before, but this felt different. Her touch was full of a deep and wonderful magic that ignited my very soul. Until that moment, I hadn't realized how cold I was. Compared to her warmth, I felt as though I were frozen solid. Now my chilled heart began to melt. I was winter and she was the spring.

Slowly, one by one, my senses began to return and with them my form appeared as well. But even as my own body began to appear, Hope's began to fade away in an invisible exchange.

Remember me. Remember the marks. Remember the Fire. Her voice echoed through my mind, repeating her warning. The sound grew fainter until she vanished from sight. My heart began to beat, pounding in my chest like a caged animal looking for a way to escape.

"Hope, don't go!" I shouted out loud, hearing myself for the first time. It was no use; she was already gone. Nothing more than a memory—a memory I was determined *not* to forget, no matter what.

A moment later, I would.

CHAPTER 3

FORGOTTEN THINGS

"**I** think he's waking up. Hurry!" shouted a voice that sounded vaguely like Emily, my sister. The only difference was this one sounded eager, almost excited to see me, which meant it couldn't possibly be her. Could it? I cracked open my eyes and found that surprisingly, it *was*. Before I could ask what planet I was on, Mom pounced into view.

"Hunter, sweetie, you *are* awake! How are you feeling? Are you all right?" Her voice was frantic; her eyes, blackened with tear-streaked mascara, searched my own for the answers. She brushed my shaggy blond hair out of my eyes and clutched tightly to one of my hands.

"Yeah, Mom, I'm fine. A little dizzy but…." My gaze shifted across an unfamiliar room. I was tucked in a slim bed with an oxygen mask strapped uncomfortably to my face. The walls were a horrid shade of drab pink and a small TV, tuned to the evening news, hung from the ceiling just over the foot of the bed.

"Where am I?" I asked.

"You're in the hospital, honey. You were rushed here by ambulance about an hour ago, remember?"

"Ambulance?" I asked, searching my mind for any sliver of memory that matched her description. Nothing came up.

Keep in mind that I've never been good at waking up quickly. Even under normal circumstances, I have difficulty remembering basic things in the morning. But this wasn't morning, and I wasn't anywhere that I was supposed to be.

Strangely, I felt as though I had just awakened, like a bear, from a deep hibernation. I had absolutely no idea what day it was or how long I had been sleeping.

"What happened? Why am I here?"

"You were in a…" Emily started to say, but Mom jumped in over her with a stern look.

"The doctor said we shouldn't tell you. He wants you to remember on your own."

Sitting up, I closed my eyes and gave my head a good shake in hopes of clearing space for my absent memories to reappear. It didn't work; all I got was a headache. My balance was off.

"You better lie down," said Mom gently, noticing my unsteadiness. "The nurse should be here any minute."

As if on cue, a nurse scurried into the room. She said nothing at all but went straight to work, checking my vitals in preparation for the doctor's arrival, which came only a moment later. He was a rather stout man with thick black eyebrows and a mustache to match. His whiskers, as thick as a hairbrush, were the kind meant to be noticed first.

There was nothing tidy about the man. His tie hung loose, his collar was unbuttoned, and his face looked like it hadn't been shaved in several days. In one hand he carried a clipboard of curled up, mismatched papers; in the other he held a tall cup of coffee, which he sipped mid-stride. The white jacket he wore was speckled with coffee stains, evidence that he wasn't particularly good at multi-tasking.

He swished his most recent sip around in his mouth for a moment, wiggling his eyebrows up and down in delight before swallowing. When at last he arrived at my bedside, he set the cup down on a tray table and the mustache began to talk.

"Well now, if it isn't our little sleeping beauty. How are you feeling, young sir?" he asked, extending his free hand in an awkward greeting. His voice was a bit crackly and low, but loaded with charisma and seemed friendly enough. I could tell he was the kind of guy that rarely slowed down, even without coffee. The night shift caffeine had clearly put him into overdrive.

"Fine, I guess," I answered, accepting his firm handshake, which was much stronger than necessary.

"Good, good," said the man. "I'm Dr. Trent by the way, but you can call me Dr. T. Everyone else does."

I managed to catch a glimpse of the nurse, rolling her eyes as she moved toward the door. Clearly the nickname was one he had chosen for himself.

"So what's your name, son?" he continued.

"You mean you don't know my name?" I asked warily, a bit shocked that a doctor wouldn't know such things about his patient.

"Don't be silly. Of course I know your name. Says it right here on the chart. The question is, do *you* know it?"

"Hunter," I said, deciding that he meant it as a test of my memory and not really a question after all. "My name is Hunter."

"And is there a last name with that, Mr. Hunter?"

"Brown."

"That's the right answer, all right," the doctor said with a satisfied smile. He pulled a pencil from behind his ear and marked something on his clipboard. "High-five!" he shouted, raising his hand for a celebratory slap. I obliged him, but couldn't help but wonder if he treated all his patients like this during the night shift. His reaction was equally troubling.

"Whoa, easy there, kiddo. I need that hand for your surgery, you know."

My jaw dropped. "Sur...surgery? Nobody said anything about any surgery."

"Ha! Gotcha! Had you worried for a sec, didn't I? No, no, no, you won't need surgery; just checking to make sure you were listening. I can put a check in *that* box now too," he said, marking the clipboard again. From where I sat I couldn't see his paper, but I was willing to bet it was randomly placed. I hadn't known Dr. T very long, but I knew enough to realize he was possibly off his rocker. After all, there's a fine line between trying to have fun and complete insanity. I was beginning to think he had already crossed that line.

"Listen, Hunter, I've got a series of quick questions I'm going to shoot at you, and you're going to give me your best answer, okay?"

I shrugged my shoulders and nodded.

"Okay then," Dr. T said, clearing his throat and posing his first question in a serious tone. "What was the last thing you remember doing?"

"Slapping your hand," I said. Somewhere in the corner of the room, Emily stifled a chuckle. The doctor stared blankly at his clipboard, blinking for a moment before catching on to the absurdity of the question.

"Right, of course. *Touché*," he said. If he smiled at all, the mustache kept it well-hidden. "I meant the last thing you remember *before* coming to the hospital. Just close your eyes and blurt out the first thing you see. Anything will do. Go on!"

I closed my eyes and started imagining what it was that I had done earlier that night. All at once an image came to mind.

"The fair," I nearly shouted. "We were at the fairgrounds."

"Good, good! It's a start. What happened at the fair?"

With my eyes still closed I recounted my evening for him exactly as I remembered it.

"I was waiting to meet up with my friends, Stretch and Stubbs, but they didn't show. Trista came and invited me to hang out with her. That's when we bumped into this new kid, Rob, who was being chased by Cranton."

"So this Cranton was a friend of yours then?" the doctor asked.

"No, I don't think he's anyone's friend, not really. He just likes to pick on people for the most part. Anyway, he started chasing all three of us. We were racing through the crowds, trying to get away, and had to hide behind a hay pile in one of the livestock barns. He almost found us but…but…something happened…I can't remember what. We ended up running to the Sky Cars and the lights went out…and…we fell…."

"You fell? You mean you fell out of the Sky Car?" Dr. T asked.

"No, the whole Sky Car just fell off the cable. But…something happened and…."

"Yes, yes, go on, what happened next?" Dr. T asked, leaning forward in eager anticipation.

"We started to fly away. That's the last thing I remember," I explained, realizing how utterly absurd it sounded.

"Fly away?" both the doctor and Mom said at once.

"Yes, one minute we were falling and the next we were flying."

"In the gondola?" the doctor asked.

"Yes, the whole thing just floated up into the air," I answered.

"But where did it take you? And how?"

I didn't know. Something had happened...something important, but I couldn't recall exactly what it was. I knew it was there, but the answer lay hidden behind a black cloud. I opened my eyes.

"I don't know...that's where my memory ends," I answered.

"Hunter, this isn't the time for joking around!" Mom said sternly.

"I'm not, I swear it happened just like that. Ask Rob or Trista!"

The doctor held up a hand.

"It's okay, Ms. Brown. In fact, it's fairly common, considering the circumstances, to have his memory be...a bit sketchy. I have no doubt that what Hunter is telling us is truly what he sees." With that he turned and asked, "I am curious though, if you had to guess, what time would you say this happened?"

"Around nine o'clock."

"And you said this Rob kid was with you and the girl...uh... Trista?"

"Yeah, why?"

Dr. T didn't answer at first; instead he jotted a few notes down on his clipboard before addressing me again.

"Son," said the doctor at last, "I haven't heard any reports of a Sky Car falling, but you were involved in a very serious accident—a fire to be exact. We just want to make sure that everyone else involved has been accounted for and treated. You're very lucky to be alive."

"But I don't remember a fire at the fair," I said, turning to my mom and Emily for reassurance that I wasn't insane.

"No, sweetie, the fire was at your school," Mom said, feeling free to speak of the incident now that the doctor had started the conversation.

"But I wasn't at the school; I was at the fair. How come I don't remember any of this?"

Mom looked to Dr. T, who did his best to explain. "Even though you didn't sustain any major injuries, you likely inhaled a lot of toxic smoke. We don't know for sure yet, but I believe there were a substantial amount of chemicals mixed in the flames. It's the most likely reason your memory isn't completely...shall we say... intact. But don't worry; your memory will be replaced in time. For now, however, you'll just...."

"Replaced? Don't you mean returned?"

"Yes, that's what I said; it will return in time."

It wasn't what he said and I knew it, but there was no point in arguing with him about it now. It would only prolong his visit... and my confusion.

"Other than your temporary memory loss, I'd say you're a pretty healthy boy. Still, I'd like to keep you overnight for observation. We'll have you out of here by noon tomorrow. Sound good?"

"Yes," I answered, still trying to remember anything about a fire.

Mom was smiling, clearly happy to hear that everything was going to be fine. The doctor gathered up his coffee and headed for the door. Before he left the room, he motioned for Mom to come near and whispered something to her. Whatever he said caused her face to lose its glow.

"What was that about?" I asked after he was gone.

"It was nothing. The doctor just wants me to keep an eye on you, that's all," Mom said. I could tell she was lying, trying to protect me from something. *But what?*

"Oh hey, look," Emily interrupted, gesturing toward the television, which had been left on in the background. "The school fire made the news!"

She pointed the remote toward the TV and raised the volume.

We quickly turned our attention to the broadcast as a smartly dressed field reporter gave the update, live from the scene. In the background floodlights lit up the now blackened south wall of Destiny Hills High School. A ladder hose continued to douse the building in a preventative stream of water.

The story focused on what few facts they had. The school had been broken into after hours by what appeared to be more than one vandal. At precisely 10:48 P.M. emergency crews were alerted by a 911-call that a fire was spreading through the south wing of the school. At least two teens escaped the scene and were taken to a local hospital where they were being treated for minor injuries. Another person of interest was being held for questioning at the police station; no names were being released. Whether the fire was an arson attempt or childish prank gone wrong had yet to be determined.

At this point, the report cut away to a previously filmed interview with the lead detective on the case, Arthur Vogler. The intimidating, bald, African-American man wore his mirrored sunglasses throughout the interview. I wondered what he had to hide.

"I can assure you that the Destiny Hills Police Department is treating this investigation with the utmost seriousness. It is a crime against our school and our community and we intend to make sure that everyone involved in this reprehensible act is brought to justice."

I had a sudden cold feeling at the back of my neck as Detective Vogler ended his interview. He almost seemed to be glaring straight through the camera and into my soul. I wouldn't call the feeling fear, exactly, but it wasn't a pleasant feeling at all. I knew for certain that I was one of the teens that would soon be meeting this giant.

Mom gripped my hand tightly. Emily's eyes darted to my face, and then quickly away. They knew something.

"Well, that's enough of that for one night," said Mom. Emily was already a step ahead of her, pointing the remote at the screen and killing the broadcast before it finished.

"He's coming here, isn't he?" I asked Mom nervously.

"Who's coming?"

"Vogler. You know, the detective on the news."

Mom was never good at keeping secrets. She looked down and nodded slightly. I could tell she was bothered by it too, perhaps even more than I was. After all, she had no way of knowing if I was to blame for the fire or not. Come to think of it, neither did I.

"He'll be here first thing in the morning," she answered, an awkward pause filling the room before she continued. "The doctor recommended they put it off until after your memory returned, but he said Vogler was very persistent. He wanted to meet you as soon as possible despite your condition. I'm sure it will be nothing, just a simple introduction to get to know you."

"Right, he looks like the type who could use another friend," I said with a smirk.

Mom frowned at the remark, but held her tongue. I could tell she wanted to scold me for it, but this was neither the time nor the place.

"Just promise me you'll be on your best behavior when he does come," she said at last. "No goofing off. The last thing we need is to give them further reason to suspect you. After all, it's not like you've had the perfect record at school lately. It would be easy to…" Mom stopped short, not wanting to complete the thought out loud.

"Don't worry, Mom," I replied. "I might not remember what happened, but I wouldn't set the school on fire. You know that, right?"

Mom nodded. "I know that and you know that but it's *them* I'm afraid of. I only hope someone else can shed some light on what happened."

Mom was right, of course. Since I had no memory of what actually happened, the detective would be relying primarily on the testimony of the others involved in the incident, which made me wonder.

"Who else was there?" I asked.

"Just Trista..." Emily answered. *Trista was good. She was a friend.* But then Emily finished her sentence. "...and Cranton."

"Cranton!" I shouted, catching the attention of the nurses in the hallway.

"Hunter, not so loud," Mom hushed. I tried to keep my cool, but this was not good news.

"You don't understand. Cranton hates me. He takes pride in inventing new ways to pick on guys like me." My stomach sank. There was no way Cranton would take the fall for something he could pin on someone else...especially with the possibility of juvenile detention at stake. For all I knew, Cranton had planned the whole thing to begin with. It was probably his twisted way of getting even with me for the prank I'd pulled on him the previous year.

In an effort to calm my anxiety, Mom leaned over and planted a gentle kiss on my forehead.

"Hey, weren't you the one who just told *me* not to worry?" she said. "Look, I'm sure everything is going to be fine. We all just need to get some rest and let the morning worry about itself."

"I wish Dad could be here," I said, almost unintentionally. It had been a long time since I had risked broaching the subject of Dad. So much went unsaid between Mom and me lately. With the busyness of her schedule, trying to play the role of both mother and father, she carried a lot of stress on her shoulders. We kids knew this and we knew our role was not to burden her with questions that would add more stress than necessary. Even now as I said it, I could tell the words had re-opened a deep wound. Her smile faded and a fresh set of tears pooled in her eyes.

"I know, Hunter," she sighed. "Sometimes I do too. We all miss him, but we have to accept that he's…he's just gone. We're on our own now. You're my main man, right?" She messed up my moppy blond hair a bit in a playful attempt to lighten the mood. I nodded back, silently agreeing that we would once again avoid the subject.

With that she stood up and moved toward the door. Emily followed.

"Mom," I called out before the door closed.

"Yes," she answered, turning toward me once more.

"I love you." It was another one of the things we had not said lately.

"I love you too, Hunter. Try and get some sleep. Visiting hours start at eight, and I promise I'll be the first one in line," said Mom, closing the door behind her.

But I couldn't sleep. Not with so many unanswered questions swirling through my mind. I wanted desperately to know what I had forgotten, but there were too many missing pieces, too many lost memories.

The more I thought about it, the more I became convinced that something *had* happened at the fair, right after the gondola fell. Something important. Something big.

CHAPTER 4
THE NEW PLAN

A black fog blanketed the Underworld, providing the perfect cover for evil to lurk, an impenetrable curtain of eternal night. Throughout history, the world above had seen many changes. But for ages untold, the fog had remained untouched, undisturbed and unsearched. This ancient and undying guardian was a barrier between the world of the living and the world of the dead.

Silently, a tall determined figure cut through the haze across the desolate landscape. He came alone, and yet…he wasn't really alone. There was the fog. There had always been the fog. Nothing escaped its touch in this place.

In spite of the bone-chilling blackness, the wanderer continued across the ashen floor, undeterred by the evil of the place. His hooded, black cloak billowed behind him as he moved with a swift, uncanny sense of direction. Black on black, his motions blended with the space around him. Were it not for a hint of light emanating from the stone atop his gnarled walking staff, the darkness would have been complete. As it was, the faint glow was more than enough. He knew his way. His path was set.

The emptiness appeared to guide him, full of dark magic and untold secrets. Out of the abyss of darkness, a single jagged white stone emerged, jutting up from the parched ground like a crooked, decaying tooth. There was a mark on its surface, a gruesome double §, the mark of the Shadow. The traveler approached the stone without fear.

He wasn't being followed, but he glanced over his shoulder a time or two before continuing further. When his attention returned to the stone, he stooped low and touched the mark with something barely recognizable as a hand—a mass of scar tissue, gnarled, boney and dead. Almost immediately, a soft wind began to blow. The traveler backed away in anticipation of what was to come.

The first movement was subtle, as sand and small bits of rock began moving away from the stone on all sides. Layer by layer the sand peeled back, dropping to expose more of the stone buried beneath the surface. The supernatural excavation quickened until a long trench was formed by the unseen force. Giant mounds of ash rose on two sides of the stone in a sort of reverse landslide. When the last of the ground swells stopped and the movement had settled, the visitor looked over the completed structure that had been revealed beneath the ground.

Before him stood a monolithic structure in the shape of a serpentine head. The mouth was gaping wide open. Remaining bits of sand and dirt toppled down from the face of the statue like miniature waterfalls, cascading from the gaping mouth and fangs like venom. Beyond the jaws, a pair of giant doors sealed the statue's throat, daring those who entered to be swallowed whole. Unafraid, he started his approach down the trench toward the underground entrance.

Here, amidst the deepest blackness, hidden from all living things, the most secret of Shadow strongholds remained as it had for ages—known by name as Death's Den, and rightly so, for nothing living had ever passed through its gates and survived. The Den was home to only the darkest of spirits and the souls of the damned. Here the very spirit of Sceleris, the first of the Fallen, resided.

The traveler stopped at the entrance and knelt in acknowledgement of an ancient phrase etched over the doorway. He had no need to read it; he knew it well.

BOW THE KNEE TO ENTER YE
WHERE THE LIVING CANNOT BE

With a slow and mighty groan the massive doors cracked open, granting entrance at last. As Death's doors opened, a green aura gloomed out from the statue's throat, highlighting the traveler's face beneath its black hood.

He appeared to be sixteen at most, a boy with light blond hair, which dangled in his face from time to time. He had a rugged look of youthful adventure and mischievousness about him. If you passed him on a city street, you might think he had his whole life before him...but this was no ordinary boy. In fact, he was no boy at all.

As he marched into the gaping mouth of the stone serpent, his features shifted to that of his true nature. His skin shriveled and darkened against his boney skull, and his black eyes disappeared entirely, leaving gaping holes where they once had been. He reached up and pulled a white skull mask down over his face.

He was a feared warrior, a mighty leader among the Shadow. His eyes were as black as midnight and his heart was darker still.

He had been known by many names over the years but the title of Venator suited him best, a title bestowed on him by none other than Sceleris himself. He was the embodiment of sin, the hunter of souls and the right-hand man to Sceleris alone. At least, that is how he thought of himself.

His mission was to work on behalf of his spirit-lord in order to stop the Codebearers' rise to power. Unfortunately, his job had become more difficult of late. He had been charged with the task of harvesting the soul of a boy, targeted by his master as a threat. He had performed this simple job on countless souls before, but this one refused to cooperate. Despite his best efforts to mislead him, something would always manage to save the boy at the last possible moment. It was exasperating to say the least.

A new strategy was needed, which was likely the purpose of his being called here. Any number of goblins, dispirits, deceivers, gorewings and foul creatures were at Venator's disposal. But today he came alone. It was a rare honor for any Shadow warrior to be called into Sceleris' presence and he wished to share it with no one. This meeting was for him and him alone.

The doors slammed shut behind him, sealing off the world of the living for good. Venator didn't look back; he marched forward, descending down the Dragon's Throat—a long arched hallway lit only by a distant light somewhere in the belly of the fortress. The eerie green light that spilled up was accompanied by a warm breeze and the echoed sound of a million tortured souls far below.

Eventually, the hall opened to a large cavernous chamber with a luminous green lake. A series of stepping stones bridged the gap between his side of the room and the island throne in the center of the space, where Sceleris waited. Sceleris, a giant ghostly serpent, wrapped himself around the arms and legs of the chiseled throne. The spirit-bound form of Sceleris watched Venator with expectant eyes. Venator froze in place at the sight. Even after all these years, being in the presence of his master was a frightening ordeal.

"Come closssser," the serpent hissed.

Venator's confidence waned. There was something in his master's voice, something he didn't like. He crossed the stones, stopping only briefly to take note of the millions of souls who now haunted the waters of the lake below. Day and night, the tormented screams of lost souls could be heard rising from the surface of the water, serving as a fearsome reminder of the power Sceleris held over those who dwelled in the Veil. They were so easy to manipulate, so willing to follow the Shadow's whispers, even to the very gate of death itself. And make no mistake, the ending was always the same.

The futility of their resistance to serving the Shadow was proven in the finality of their inevitable plunge into the eternal prison below. No matter how good they pretended to be in life, all of them ended up here—every last one. Well, nearly every last one; there was an exception—one glaring exception. It was clearly a mistake, and one Venator hoped to correct himself.

Upon reaching the island throne, Venator bowed low before his master.

"Arissssse, Venator, we have much to dissscuss about Hunter Brown."

"Yes, of course, Master," Venator said, stumbling over his next words with uncertainty. "I…I have failed you, I know. It's just that the boy…well…his belief is stronger than I had expected. He still has not let go of Hope; he won't let her die. Even now she lives."

"His beliefsss do not concern me," Sceleris hissed. "It issss more than that. You sssseem to have underesssstimated his place in the greater ssssscheme. Time is running short, and you have not done what I have asssked. I have no time for gamesss."

"He has become harder to sway, my lord. Ever since that cursed Aviad destroyed the Bloodstone, the bond between us has all but vanished."

Even the mere mention of the word "Bloodstone" caused Venator's burned hand to twitch. The power of the united halves had ruined him, melting his arm like butter and leaving a permanent scar where once his fingers had moved. The loss would have been worth it if the boy had died; at least then the Bloodstone would be theirs. But he had been tricked, and had killed the Author's son in place of the boy. He tried to clinch his fist, but it didn't clinch anymore.

"This isss precisssely why I have assigned the boy to another," Sceleris explained, "sssssomeone I believe to be more capable of handling thissss matter." As he said it, a stream of inky black fluid wound its way out from behind Sceleris' throne. The ooze gathered together in a pool on the rocky floor, where the black blob of a figure rose out of it. The featureless silhouette of the shape-shifting Shadow was as black as night and as large as an ox.

"I...I don't understand, Master. I assure you I can handle the boy myself," Venator found himself pleading. Suddenly, he no longer wished he had come alone. The conversation was starting to take an unexpected turn.

"It isss too late for that," said Sceleris. "A new plan is already in motion. The boy issss no longer your problem."

Venator's confusion quickly turned to anger. How could Sceleris move forward with another plan behind his back? Despite his recent failure, Venator had been flawless in his service to the serpent. He could think of no one more loyal and trustworthy than himself. The faceless blob in front of him certainly didn't deserve the honor of such a task. He was far too unpredictable...too volatile to be trusted.

"I hesitate to remind you, Master," Venator attempted, "but

this…this *thing* has failed before. How can you bring it back? How can you trust one of them?"

"Tonomissss has ssserved hisss purpossse. He will finish thissss, I have no doubt. He will find the Eye; he will ressstore the Bloodssssstone and once it is accomplished, I will erasssse Hope myself. The Author's sssstory hasss come to its end. A new sssstory will begin…mine."

Blazing red eyes appeared in the space where the black form's head could have been. Venator saw this and he shuddered. They were Sceleris' eyes, burning with the very fire that burned in his soul. How Tonomis had come to rise again was beyond Venator's knowing, but one thing was clear: this thing now held the serpent's power and his confidence. If Venator wanted any part in bringing about the end and earning an eternal place of honor with his master, he had to find a way back into the plan. After all he had gone through to see Hunter Brown stopped, he couldn't just stand here and let another take his place in the eleventh hour. He had to think of something, and quickly.

"Please, Master, allow me to help. After all, I have insight about the boy that could be helpful. I have a lifetime of experience that could prove invaluable to us all. The bond we once shared may be broken but I still know him better than any other."

"Don't worry, Venator. I have not forgotten you," Sceleris said. "I am sssure you will be useful. Assss you have ssssaid, I do not intend to leave all of your knowledge behind. There issss a role for you in my plan as well."

This was good news to Venator. A broad smile of relief crossed his face and he breathed easier for the first time since the conversation had begun.

"Thank you, Master," Venator said, bowing in humble reverence. His plea had worked; he was still needed. "I won't disappoint you."

"No...you won't," Sceleris replied, his eyes burning even brighter than before. The eyes in the black blob glowed hotter as well. Without a word passing between them, the inky creature dissolved into a pool on the floor and moved quickly toward Venator. Venator noticed the movement in time to step back from the pool before it could touch him. All at once it became clear...he wasn't needed at all.

Venator tried to run away from the thing, but the bridge of stones that had once allowed him to cross the green lake of souls had lowered beneath the surface. He was trapped on the island with nowhere to go.

"Master? Please," Venator begged, falling to his knees once more, "don't do this."

Sceleris said nothing as the black ink pooled itself around Venator completely, inching inward toward him. The first edge of it touched the hem of his robe and then his feet, bonding with his skin and spreading up and over his entire body in a heartbeat. With a final scream, Venator was buried in the blackness and he was no more. The ink fell back into a pool and rose again into the shape of the featureless figure, which stepped back toward Sceleris' throne, leaving Venator's white skull mask alone on the floor. The knowledge that was once Venator's now belonged to Tonomis.

"I am...ready," Tonomis said in a low voice.

"I know," Sceleris said. "This time, we will not fail."

"No, we won't," Tonomis said with the confidence of one who had already seen what was to come. "I have been there, and I know how the story...ends."

CHAPTER 5

VOGLER IS WATCHING

"**M**ind if I…sit?" asked the mammoth, standing at the foot of my bed. His voice was low and powerful like a roar of thunder. Vogler had arrived early this morning, too early in fact. The clock overhead read seven o'clock. Mom wouldn't arrive for nearly another hour. Visiting hours weren't until eight. Apparently, for Vogler the front desk had made an exception.

There was little doubt why. The man was nothing short of massive and had no trouble getting his way. The badge he carried gave him authority to do what he wanted, but I was willing to bet it was rarely used. His sheer size alone would be convincing enough, in most cases.

Vogler was dressed the way I expected a detective might dress, only more colorful. He was wearing a black trench coat, but where the coat hung open his personality showed through. His tweed vest, slacks and dress shirt were all a dark shade of purple. He wore a tie as well, which oddly enough was golden yellow. Despite the boldness of his color choices, they seemed to work very well on him.

He carried a black leather briefcase, the hard-case kind with snapping locks. In a way he looked like a retired NFL linebacker who had gone into business, or the mob, or even worse…politics.

I motioned to one of the chairs beside my bed and watched as the man settled into it. In doing so, he managed to make it look half the size it should have been. Once comfortable, Vogler carefully placed his briefcase on the seat beside him. He ceremoniously brushed the rain off each of his shoulders and turned to look at me through the same mirrored glasses he had worn on TV the night before. This time I could see my own reflection in them—what he saw in me was what I worried about. Somehow, I sensed he knew more than he should.

I sat in silence, waiting for the storm of questions to hit. Instead, he said nothing. He just sat there, staring at me, his hands folded in front of his lips.

Time passed slowly, each tick of the clock marking another awkward second between us. I had spent half the night preparing myself for the questions he might ask. For starters there would be the basics about where I was and what I experienced the previous night, things I still couldn't remember. Certainly he would want to know about my encounters with Cranton; that was a given. Then there would be questions about my recent incident with my teacher, Mr. Tanner. No doubt Principal Strickland had filled him in on that one and my previous year of pranks as well. My record wasn't exactly clean.

A full minute passed and not a single word was exchanged between us. I cleared my throat and decided to be the first to break the silence.

"So, have you got any good leads yet?" I asked. My boldness surprised me. Even before the words left my mouth, I regretted starting the conversation with them. Vogler seemed unfazed by my approach and answered right away.

"Oh, it's too early for that, but I'm sure we'll find someone. I always get my man," he said. It was a clear challenge, one I hadn't missed. There was no doubt he was here to nail me; any word I spoke from here forward would be used against me. I decided instead to keep silent. As awkward as it was, I would be better off if I didn't open my big mouth. His next statement, however, threw me for a loop.

"You might have trouble believing this, Hunter, but I came here today because I'm concerned about you. I'm concerned for your family, and for the…shall we say…precarious situation you have found yourself in."

Vogler leaned back in his chair. Its tired springs let out a long whimpering groan from the unjust punishment he was putting them through.

"I'm willing to offer protection, if you want it," he said.

"Protection?" I asked. Of all the ways I had imagined this conversation going, this wasn't anywhere close.

Vogler's bald, black head nodded in a silent reply.

"Protection from what?"

"You tell me," Vogler replied. "Have you noticed anything strange happening lately? Things you can't easily explain?"

Where should I start? I wondered to myself. The past few days had been a series of unexplainable events: the stalker in black who attacked me at school, the eyes in Mrs. Sheppard's crystal ball, the appearance of Boojum, the flying gondola, and the school fire I couldn't remember. The unexplainable had become the norm ever since I discovered the Author's Writ. Yes, my life was far from usual.

The question was, could Vogler be trusted with this information or was he just playing the "good cop" role to get me to open up. Either way, it was better to play it safe.

"Depends on what you consider strange," I answered. It wasn't a lie, but it wasn't exactly an answer either.

Vogler furrowed his brow. "Do flying gondolas seem…normal to you?"

"I guess not," I said. How did he know about that already? Dr. T must have informed him—so much for patient confidentiality.

"Let me put it as plainly as I can. On the surface you fit the bill of "troubled teen" nicely—a boy with a missing father, a prankster looking to get even with his childhood rival, a below-average student who's had a recent fallout with your best friend, attacking your teacher with a…a mop."

I cringed at the last statement. The way he said it made me sound so pathetic. It definitely wasn't one of my better moments. One thing was for sure, Vogler had done his homework. I felt like a bug under a microscope must feel.

"This case could be closed tomorrow if I wanted it to be. Just another story for the talking heads on the evening news, but that's what bothers me most of all. It's too perfect, too…easy."

Vogler's chair snapped upright as the giant abruptly leaned forward and started to crack his knuckles one-handed. One by one, each finger popped under the strength of his thumb. Then I noticed a curious tattoo on the back of his hand, the symbol of an eye.

"Why are you telling me all of this?" I asked, still watching him pop his fingers.

"Because I believe there is more to it than this. Cranton said there was someone else in the basement. My guess is you are hiding something, Hunter, something you weren't supposed to know about and I intend to find out exactly what…it…is."

He stood up at once, casting a shadow that nearly filled my room. Under his shadow a cold feeling shot up my spine, the same feeling I had the other night when watching him on TV.

"I have something for you," he said mysteriously. Turning around he unlatched his briefcase and pulled out my trusty grey backpack. It was considerably smushed from having been stuffed into his case. Apparently, he hadn't wanted to be seen carrying it or something. Probably would have ruined the image he projected.

Vogler dropped the pack onto the foot of my bed. Something clanged inside. It was a sound I hadn't expected to hear.

"We recovered it in the school parking lot. I found the contents to be…shall we say…enlightening."

"Oh," I answered, glancing down at the bag and trying to recall anything that would have made a noise like that. The corner of a bright yellow Boojum bar wrapper sticking out of the front pocket caught my eye. It reminded me of the furry little blue-eyed creature that had ransacked my house. I had stuffed him in my backpack and taken him to the fair in hopes of proving to Stretch that Solandria was real…only it was Trista and Rob who saw him instead. Trista had given the little critter the name Boojum because of his appetite for the tasteless snack food they were handing out at the fair that night. I could only imagine the look on the detectives' faces when they opened the bag and Boojum began squealing the way he did. But the bag was too flat to contain him now and it didn't explain away the mysterious clanging sound I had heard.

"Just remember," Vogler repeated before I could think of an explanation, "I'll be watching. You have my card if you ever need…a friend."

He nodded toward the nightstand beside me where I spotted his business card. I hadn't seen him place it down, but it was there nonetheless. When I looked up again Vogler had already snatched up his briefcase and disappeared behind the curtain that blocked the doorway.

Alone at last I snatched up my pack and rummaged through it. In a rush of excitement, I dumped the contents onto my lap. There was the odd assortment of random pens and scraps of paper of course, but what fell first had been the source of the sound—two gleaming Veritas Sword hilts.

One of them I recognized almost immediately; it had been mine during my visit to Solandria at the start of the summer. I had often wished it had returned home to Destiny with me. Now, here it was. I picked it up and swung it lightly through the air. It felt good.

Wondering if the blade would work the same for me here in Destiny as it did in Solandria, I held the hilt a safe distance away and began to dwell on the words of the Author's Writ.

"For the Way of Truth and Life," I whispered.

The once absent blade began to glow just above the hilt as it had in Solandria not so long ago. I smiled, tightened my grip and let the familiar surge of energy rush down the blade, through my hands and up my arms. The blade and its bearer were one; the bond was complete. For the briefest of moments all was well, but then everything went wrong.

Skreeeeee!

A deafening wail echoed through the room, causing a powerful pounding pressure in my skull. At first, I thought it was an alarm of some kind but then I realized that it sounded as if it were coming from inside my head. Imagine the wail of a thousand shrieking Halloween ghost effect CD's amped up to twenty on the volume dial and you'll be close to what I was experiencing. Dropping the sword, I covered my ears in hopes of quieting the horrendous tone. Somehow, it only made it worse.

Skreeeeeeeeeeeeeeeeee!

The blade disappeared before it hit the bed, leaving the hilt empty, but the sound…the horrible deafening racket, persisted a few moments longer. I clinched my eyes shut in pain, expecting my head to explode at any moment.

A flash of seemingly unrelated images rushed through my mind like the replay of a long forgotten dream. There was an image of a man with a blackened face and gleaming silver eyes, a giant worm with razor-sharp teeth, a man's head trapped in a glass ball, and a glimpse of Hope reclined and hovering over a stone altar. The images flew by so fast I could hardly keep up with them. As quickly as they came, the images disappeared and the sound faded away.

When at last the sound subsided, I opened my eyes and stared at the sword hilt, laying on my lap. Had I done something wrong? Perhaps using the blade in Solandria was different from here in the Veil. One thing was for sure, I wasn't about to try it again.

My eyes fell on the second sword. The hilt of this Veritas Sword was slightly different. It was darker than most swords I had seen. The Author's mark, the emblem of the Codebearer, was etched in the center of the hilt just as on my own, but it appeared altered. Another marking caught my eye, letters etched into the bottom of the hilt. I held the sword so the engraved lettering caught the light in just the right way. The letters spelled a name.

Caleb Brown

I gasped in disbelief. Could this really be my father's Veritas Sword? The Codebearers had said he had been to Solandria, that he had been a great Codebearer warrior. This was proof that what they had said was true.

How either of the swords came to be in my backpack remained a mystery. The odds were good that Vogler had something to do with it. If so, he knew much more than he was letting on.

I snatched up Vogler's card from the nightstand and looked it over. The front seemed perfectly normal: Destiny Hills Police Department logo, his name and phone number, the basic information you might expect. The back of the card was printed in solid black ink with the exception of a single white symbol in the upper right corner, the symbol of an open eye—the same one he had tattooed on his hand.

I'll be watching, he had said.

I shuddered at the thought. Something was wrong about this man. There was just something I didn't like.

CHAPTER 6
WHAT MOM SAID

When your life is spinning out of control, the little things can keep you grounded. Today, chocolate pudding was my anchor.

When Mom found out that Vogler had been to the hospital before visiting hours, she was furious. None of the nurses on duty seemed to know anything about it. As we left the hospital, she vowed to get to the bottom of it. The car ride home was a tense one. Mom wanted to know everything he had asked. I did my best to tell her, but found it impossible to explain how intimidating he was, how cold I felt every time he looked at me.

On the way home Mom stopped by the grocery store to stock up on my favorite comfort foods. It was part of her plan to help me recover. We had just arrived home and had hardly walked through our front door when Mom pulled a pudding cup from one of the many grocery sacks on the counter. She tossed me a spoon and insisted I go make myself comfortable on the couch while she pulled dinner together. I didn't complain. After all "Mom knows best," right?

Dropping my backpack on the couch, I flopped down next to it and stretched out, pudding cup in hand. It felt good to be back. Looking around the room, I was reminded of the bizarre chain of events that had taken place only a couple of days ago. Boojum had left his mark on the room to be sure. I picked up the couch's sole surviving throw pillow and stuck a finger into one of its fresh holes.

I wonder where the fur ball went? I thought to myself. When the fuzzy blue pest had popped into my life unexpectedly, he nearly destroyed the entire house in his quest to fill his insatiable appetite. Our family aquarium was shy one fish as well; Emily's favorite blue one was no longer with us. Boojum had made sure of that. I managed to blame a neighborhood cat for the mess and the fish, but I still felt guilty about all the lying I had done to keep him a secret.

At the time, the thought of keeping a secret pet seemed like a good idea. After all, he looked cool, could go invisible on command and genuinely seemed to like me. Plus, he was the proof I needed to convince my best friend, Stretch, of the existence of Solandria.

In a way, I half expected him to show up at any moment, begging for my pudding cup. He didn't.

It was probably for the best anyway; he was a horrible roommate. His freakish aversion to direct light was more than a nuisance; it was downright dangerous at times. After wrecking the house he completely destroyed my bedroom and continued his trouble-making ways at the fairgrounds too. The details were somewhat fuzzy, but I did remember chasing the little monster around the fair, trying to retrieve something he'd taken from Rob.

"You know, Emily's bringing Trista over for dinner tonight," Mom called out from the kitchen. I heard the oven door open and shut and the beeps of a digital timer being set. "I heard the two of you were hanging out at the fair together Friday night. She's a nice girl, don't you think?" Mom said with a hint of teasing in her voice.

"Real subtle, Mom," I protested.

"What? I was just asking. Just making an observation."

"Well, it's not like that okay? She's Emily's friend."

"So? Your father was best friends with Uncle Jim in high school when we met."

"I didn't know that," I said, glad to be turning the attention from me and my feelings, back to Mom.

"Yeah well, there's a lot about your father and me that you don't know."

"Okay, ew, Mom. I think you should just stop right there," I said.

Mom rolled her eyes and chuckled. "Nothing like that you goof. All I'm saying is not to overlook somebody simply because of your sister, okay? Besides, a little bit of friendship might be exactly what you need to take your mind off things."

"Point taken, can we talk about something else now? I'm trying to...you know, heal here."

Part of me wanted the conversation to end there, but the other part of me was interested in seeing where it might go. While it was technically true that Emily and Trista had struck up a friendship first at the beginning of the school year, Trista was actually in my grade and had been acting pretty friendly toward me too.

I had convinced myself it was just her upbeat, energetic person-ality that made her friendly to everyone—that there was nothing special about the attention she had shown me. But, for some reason

I couldn't shake the weird feeling that she and I knew each other better than just passing acquaintances.

Finished in the kitchen, Mom walked into the room with her own pudding cup and waved her spoon at me. "Scoot over," she said.

I swung my feet off the couch to make space for her, hoping the whole Trista thing was behind us.

She let herself sink low into the couch, took a bite of pudding and released a long-reserved sigh. No doubt, the last few days had been as traumatic for her as they had for me…maybe more so. Setting the remaining pudding aside, she turned to me.

"I don't know if you remember or not, but you and I had a date to talk today."

"We did?" I replied. Truth be told, I hadn't remembered until she brought it up, but now I was acutely aware of the tense moment we'd shared just before she sent me off to the Destiny Fair. Friday had been a bad day—before my alleged involvement in the school fire. Apparently, I owed Mom some explanations.

"If you are up for it," Mom said, "I'd like to take some time now to talk over what's been troubling you lately."

"Sure…" I offered hesitantly, "I can try."

Ever since my first trip to Solandria through the Author's Writ, Mom had grown increasingly agitated whenever I brought up the subject. I tried to brace myself for more of the same.

Mom surprised me by saying, "Before we start, Hunter, I owe you an apology. I've been thinking things over and realize now that I've been coming up short for you lately."

"Mom, you don't need to…" I tried to interject, but she persisted.

"No. I mean it. You clearly have been going through a lot and the truth is I haven't been willing to listen, I mean really listen. I'd like to do that now."

I was stunned. "I'm not sure where to start," I said.

"How about starting with where you found this?"

She reached down and lifted a heavy, leather-bound book from beside the couch. It was the Author's Writ, a book unlike any other. The Writ was a portal to the hidden world of Solandria and each time I saw it served as a reminder that there was more to life than what my eyes could see. Apparently, Mom had been in my room and brought the book down during my overnight stay at the hospital. There was something strange about the Writ Mom was holding; its binding was falling apart in places I hadn't remembered. The brown leather was soft and the golden markings were the same, but the book looked as if it had aged a hundred years overnight. I marked it down to one of the other things I couldn't accurately remember. The list was growing longer by the minute.

"I'm not sure you'd believe me if I told you," I said.

"Try me," Mom answered. Her patient expression told me she was serious. "You might be surprised."

I took a deep breath and then launched into my unbelievable tale while Mom, true to her word, listened intently to the whole story. I told of how the book pulled me across the Veil into Solandria, and of my training as a Codebearer, using a Veritas Sword to fight with the Resistance against the Shadow. Finally, I told her of my quest to end the Bloodstone's curse, which ultimately led me back home to Destiny after the Author rewrote my life. As much as I wanted to leave it at that, I still had to tell her about what happened at school with the mysterious stalker who stole my backpack, and my mop assault on Mr. Tanner, which led to a visit with Principal Strickland and an afterschool counseling session with Ms. Sheppard.

When I had finished, Mom said, "It might come as a surprise to you, but I have heard most of this before, not from you, but from your father."

I was shocked.

"Dad told you about Solandria?" I asked. While it was true that my experience in Solandria had revealed some clues of my dad's involvement there, I had never heard my mother talk about it before.

"I know," Mom said, hanging her head. "It was a mistake for me not to tell you before. I can see that now. But I was just so afraid."

"Afraid of what?" I questioned her.

"That I'd lose you to…whatever all this is about, just like I lost your father."

"Mom, what do you mean?" I asked with growing concern in my voice. "Is Dad lost in Solandria?"

"No, no," Mom answered quickly. "Well, I guess perhaps in a way he is. Who's to say where he really is now? The point is, for the last year before he left, he started getting mixed up in this crazy book. He gradually got more and more obsessed with it until he and I rarely talked anymore. It's like he became a stranger in our house."

I remembered that feeling well. Dad had been largely absent from our family events, leading up to his eventual disappearance. More than once Emily came home crying from a softball or swimming meet because Dad hadn't shown up.

"But how come I never saw the book, or heard Dad talk about Solandria?" I asked.

"Because I wouldn't let him," Mom snapped. She always was one to stand her ground with Dad. Apparently, this time was no exception. "That stuff never came home. And the more intense he got about it, the more convinced I was that you and Emily needed to be protected from it." She reached over and squeezed my shoulder reassuringly. "I know it sounds awful, Hunter, but in some ways I felt relieved when he finally left us. I could finally let my guard down again…. But then," she looked back at the Author's Writ resting between us, "you found it."

"It found me, Mom," I corrected her.

She gave me a worried look. I could tell she was still tense about the whole thing.

"Well," she said bravely, "I'm certainly not going to make the mistake of forcing you to believe or not believe something because I say so. With my luck, I'd just push you away, but can I at least say that I'm really concerned for you? Please be careful with this. I don't..." her voice quavered a bit, at the memory of what my father had done. "I just really don't want to lose you."

"You're not going to lose me," I tried to reassure her. "Not like that. I'm not going anywhere." I hugged her close as she wiped her eyes. I couldn't help but think how strange it must be for her to know so much about the Codebearers, the Shadow, Solandria, yet still not really *know* it as being real. That's when the sobering thought struck me: what if she never did find that understanding? What if *I* lost *her*?

I determined right then and there not to let that happen. Not if I could do something to prevent it.

"Mom," I said tentatively, but with a sense of urgency, "I don't know what Dad talked about or showed you, but would you let me show you how the book works?"

She started to shake her head, "I don't know, Hunter. I'm not sure I want to set you up for the disappointment."

"No, really Mom. It's not that big of a deal," I said, flipping open the book. How could she ignore it if she saw for herself? She watched curiously as I flipped past blank page after blank page of the Author's Writ. That's when I remembered.

"I forgot; you can only see the words when you use the key." I snapped the book shut and pointed to the keyhole on the hinged latch. "I've got the key somewhere up in my bedroom," I said, jumping to my feet and laying the book back on the floor. "I'll be right back."

Mom chuckled, saying, "Then I guess I better plan on eating dinner alone. You do realize that your room is still torn apart from last night's fiasco, don't you?"

I cringed just thinking about the mess Boojum had left in his wake after he nearly set himself on fire. Finding the key up there would be like finding a needle in a haystack—make that two haystacks.

"Hold on," I said, suddenly thinking of another option. I scooped up my backpack, unzipped it and then reached in. "Did Dad ever show you one of these?" I asked her as I withdrew my gold Veritas Sword hilt, holding it out for her to see.

Her eyes widened as her fingers ran over the polished metal and leather-wrapped handle. Touching the engraved triple *V* mark at its center she asked, "Where on earth did you get this, Hunter? You're not taking metal shop this year at school, are you?" She knew better than to ask that—I'd never been good with Popsicle stick crafts let alone mastering wood or metalwork.

"It's the real thing, Mom. Go ahead, hold it," I said, placing it into her hand.

Gawking at its solid feel and weight she assessed, "A replica like this had to cost…well, more than anything you've ever saved up. Where'd you get the money for this?"

"It's not a replica. It's an actual Veritas Sword—my sword. It was given to me during my training with the Codebearers in Solandria. It really works too! Here, let me show you." I took the bladeless sword from my mother and stood in the most impressive pose I could manage. I had to fight back a smile as I imagined the look on Mom's face when she saw the blade of light for the first time. This was the moment I had been waiting all summer to share with somebody back home in Destiny, the proof that Solandria was real.

With both hands firmly gripping the hilt, I recited a passage from the Author's Writ, saying, "*I will walk by fire and not be...* Aaaagh!"

Skreeeeeeeeeeeeeee!

Instantly, I dropped the sword and reached for my head, pressing hard on both sides, trying to stop the horrendous, mind-numbing squeal that was surging through my brain. With eyes tightly shut, I saw flashes of more, seemingly unrelated images race through my head: a giant turtle, water pipes, fire. When I opened my eyes I saw Mom holding her ears as well, only for a different reason.

"Not the fish sticks!" she shouted, as she leaped off the couch and ran into the kitchen. The painful sound in my ears slowly faded to the equally annoying, but less painful sound of the kitchen smoke detector. The smell of smoke told me all I needed to know. Dinner was done...and, unfortunately, so was our conversation.

Chapter 7

Girl Trouble

The smoke detector and I have an unspoken understanding... we hate each other. It's not that I don't respect the thing; it's just that it doesn't know when to shut up.

The smoke detector was still screaming for its life when I yanked it down from the ceiling and stepped out on the porch with a screwdriver. Removing the batteries was the only way I had been able to successfully quiet the screamer in the past. It was time once again for open heart surgery.

After fighting with the screw on the battery case for far too long, I finally gave up and chucked the howling device out into the front yard. It landed on the sidewalk with a whimpering chirp and continued crying as it rolled to a stop beside the mailbox and the black boot of a girl I'd never seen before.

Nonchalantly, she bent down, picked up the alarm and pressed a red button on the back. Like a baby in the arms of its mother, the alarm went quiet immediately.

"Sure, do it for the girl," I muttered to myself as I shuffled out to retrieve the little brat.

The girl standing there was attractive and stylish, but not in your traditional "girly" way. There was a look of toughness about her—not the "bad girl" kind of tough, but more of the sassy kind. She looked like she had a lot of fun and didn't care too much about the "in crowd." My sister, Emily, would have hated her, which made me all the more interested.

The first thing I noticed about her was her eyes: one green and one blue, but both outlined in dark eye shadow. She wore dark blue jeans, which were torn in all the right places, and a white form-fitting tank top layered with a short wool sweater that looked like a tiger had torn it to shreds. Her hair was black, pulled back in short pigtails and covered with a white bandana.

"Violence isn't always the answer, you know," she said, holding the tortured smoke detector out to me.

"He started it," I said, not really wanting the dumb thing back.

She raised a neatly plucked eyebrow and narrowed her eyes curiously, but she didn't walk away as I thought she would. She seemed to expect something more from me.

"Thanks," I said, realizing I hadn't said it before.

"Mmmm," she answered, bobbing her head in acknowledgement but still not leaving.

Intrigued by her boldness I decided to find out more about her. Fighting my nervousness, I searched for something intelligent... something cool to say.

"So, you from around here often?" I said, stumbling over my words. The girl smirked, amused at my slip up. It was a curse I had to live with—the king of bad first impressions. Already, I could feel my ears turning red.

"A few streets over, actually," she replied as she whipped a post-marked envelope from her back pocket. "We're '2012' same as you. Mailman must have mixed up his delivery."

"Oh, right. Thanks again," I said, taking the envelope but not looking at it.

"Just doin' my civil duty, Mr. Brown," she said, finally walking away. She was already a few steps past the driveway. I'd have to move fast if I wanted to keep things going.

"Wait. How do you know my name?" I called out to her.

She spun around and shouted back with a feisty smile, "It's on the letter!"

Oh, duh! I thought to myself.

I wanted to ask her name, but I couldn't think of a way without sounding as interested as I was. Just then a noisy car with peeling blue paint pulled into the driveway between us, ending any chance for more conversation. Emily was home.

"Later," the girl called back, sparing a casual wave good-bye as she strode off. I let my gaze linger as she disappeared around the corner.

Moments later Emily, track star that she is, came sprinting across the yard with her cell phone at the ready. She'd apparently seen the smoke coming from the kitchen window.

"Meatloaf?" she asked.

"Fish sticks," I replied.

She sighed, pressing a few buttons on her phone. "What'll it be, teriyaki or pizza?"

As if she needed to ask....

"Pizza," I replied automatically.

Emily pressed the speed dial and launched through the front door to help Mom with the aftermath. I glanced back to where the girl had just disappeared, hoping to catch sight of her once more.

"Did ya lose something?" Trista asked coyly, walking up behind me. In all the commotion, I had almost forgotten she was coming over for dinner.

"No," I said, feeling a bit nervous. I held the smoke detector out in front of me. "Just putting old Smokey to sleep."

"I see," Trista answered in a clearly suspicious tone. She folded her arms with a playfully jealous look. "So....who's the girl?"

I tried not to sound too interested when I explained that I hadn't gotten her name. "I don't know. Just some neighbor, I guess," I said, waving the letter in my hand. "She gave me this."

"Ooo, let's see," Trista snatched it out of my hands before I could take a look at it. She quickly handed it back with a bored look on her face when she realized it wasn't a personal note. It was addressed to me from Destiny Public Library of all places. That counted as a first. I didn't even have a library card.

Satisfied with the explanation, Trista went back to her usual smiling self as we walked toward the house. We reached the porch and decided to wait for things inside to settle down before heading in. Trista flipped her blonde, pink-highlighted hair back over her shoulders and pulled herself up onto the railing. She looked cute, in that "sister's best friend" kind of way.

"So, did you tell them about what we did?" she asked.

"What we did?" I replied. I had no clue what she was talking about. "What do you mean?"

"You know," she said with a bit of sass in her sparkling green eyes. "Going to Solandria and everything!"

I couldn't believe what I was hearing.

"Hang on," I said, holding a hand up. "I thought you didn't believe in Solandria."

"Yeah, but that was before we went there, duh!"

"You and me? Together?" I asked.

"And Rob," Trista added, starting to sound worried. "Don't you remember?"

I shrugged my shoulders.

"Hunter, what's wrong with you? You're acting like the whole thing never happened."

Suddenly, I felt sick to my stomach. Not remembering thirty minutes is one thing, but missing an *entire trip* to Solandria. Why didn't I remember that? What was going on?

"I wish I knew," I finally said, resting my elbows against the porch rail and gazing into the early evening sky. "Last thing I remember before waking up at the hospital was getting into the Sky Car ride and then our gondola flew away."

A lone raven flew overhead and I watched curiously as it circled down, finally landing on our mailbox. The large black bird cocked its head every which way as if looking for something lost. *You and me both, buddy,* I thought to myself.

The bird seemed content to stay and listen while Trista tried her best to reignite the memories in me, telling me of how the Shadow had chased me, Rob and her through the fairgrounds; of our journey to Solandria in the flying gondola; of the Consuming Fire and its seven marks; of the ruthless assassin Xaul and our race to rescue Hope. It was a fantastic tale. Apparently the raven's friends thought so too, because soon there were a handful of black birds quietly roosting along my fence and in my yard.

Although I knew I should believe Trista's accounts were the truth, the fact remained that they were someone else's memories.

"Still nothing?" Trista said, noting my look of frustration.

I shook my head slowly, absentmindedly fingering Hope's medallion beneath my T-shirt.

"Here," Trista said, determined to win me over. "Have a look at this." She pulled down part of her shirt collar, revealing her left collarbone. "See the mark? I got it in Solandria. It was the mark of the Flame."

I blinked. Besides a few scattered freckles, her skin looked perfectly clear to me.

"I don't see anything," I remarked.

"Really?" Trista looked shocked and tried hard to tilt her head just right so she could see what I evidently couldn't. She even checked the other collar, just in case. "I swear it was there just this morning after my shower."

I shrugged my shoulders again, and gave her an "I have no idea what you're talking about" look. Realizing the mark was no longer there, Trista started to panic. Then, unexpectedly, her panic turned to anger.

"Oh, I get it. This whole thing is one of your pranks, isn't it?"

"No, I swear," I said shaking my head. She seemed unconvinced.

"What did you do, slip me some kind of crazy juice to make me think I'd been to another world with you? Wait a minute, that's it! You started talking about Solandria and then..." her eyes lit up. "The Boojum bar! You put something in the Boojum bar, didn't you?"

"No, I..." I started to say, but by now Trista had gotten herself more worked up than I had ever seen her.

"I can't believe I fell for it. I even made a fool of myself in front of the police. They all had a good laugh at me when I told them about the flying gondola. Even my family thinks I'm crazy and it's all *your* fault. Grrrrr...." She punched me in the arm. "I can't believe I let you talk me into this whole thing."

Things were not going well. She hopped down from the porch rail and started to walk away, but I caught her arm. She almost slapped me again, but I grabbed her wrist before she could connect.

"Trista, will you stop for a minute!" I said firmly, trying to calm her down before releasing her wrist. "I believe you. It's just that I'm missing a lot of my memory right now, more than even I know, apparently, and I can't change the fact that your memories aren't my own. Something happened to me."

Trista's breathing eased slowly as I spoke. I relaxed my hold on her wrist.

"Are you okay?" I asked. Trista took a deep breath and nodded her head a few times.

"Are *we* okay?" I rephrased the question.

She started to cry. Sniffling, she leaned into me, unable to hold back the emotions. Unsure how to proceed I put my arms around her, holding her close.

"I'm sorry, Hunter. I just feel so alone, you know. I wanted…no I *needed* you to tell me what we experienced was real because nobody believes me. I thought for sure you'd understand. I'm frustrated."

"Trust me. I might not remember, but I do understand. That's how I felt last time I went to Solandria. Stretch went with me, but he doesn't have a clue that he did."

We stood silently, holding each other for a moment. Then she pulled away and dabbed her eyes with her shirtsleeve.

"What did you think of Vogler?" I asked.

"Who?" she answered, looking somewhat confused.

"Big. Bald. Black. Detective."

"Oh right, the guy they interviewed on TV? I never met with him, just with a couple of regular cops at the scene."

"Well, with any luck, you won't ever have the *privilege*," I said with added sarcasm.

"He's really that bad?" Trista asked, still sniffling from her cry.

I nodded emphatically. "Worse. He gave me the creeps."

Upon hearing this, the raven perched on my mailbox bristled its feathers and cawed angrily; clearly he agreed with me too.

"What do you mean, creeps?"

"I don't know exactly; I can't explain it but I just felt like he knew way too much about me. About us."

"But he's a cop. Isn't that like, his job?"

I shrugged my shoulders.

"I guess so, he's just weird that's all."

A second car pulled into the driveway, causing the birds to finally fly away. An illuminated "Flying Pie Pizza" sign sat atop the car's roof. Dinner was served.

"Listen," Trista said, sounding much more upbeat but still looking like she had just cried. "I'm going to track down Rob at school tomorrow. Maybe hearing some of it from him will help sort things out."

I nodded, knowing I could use all the help I could get. Trista went inside to clean up as the pizza man approached the front porch. I asked him to wait and carried the smoke detector inside in search of Mom's purse. Emily stopped me short.

"Hunter! Why was Trista crying? What did you do?"

Ugh! Why did girls have to be so much trouble!

That's when old Smokey decided to go haywire again. Annoyed, I chucked him back out the front door onto the front lawn and decided to leave him there.

Tucking the library letter deep in my back pocket, I brushed right past Emily and headed in for pizza. Whatever the letter was about, it could certainly wait until dinner was over.

CHAPTER 8
LIBRARY GAMES

Visiting libraries can be hazardous to your life; I should know, I nearly lost mine trying to avoid late fees.

The next morning when I stepped into the newly renovated public library, I found myself awestruck by the sheer size of the place. Everything about it was different than I had expected. From the modern design of the slanted ceiling, the giant wall of windows, the sculpted columns and the rows of computer workstations, everything felt new and fresh. The centerpiece of the polished cement floor was an inlaid design of an open book placed over a globe and compass. The words that encircled the design read: *A World Awaits Within a Book.*

"If only they knew how true that is," I muttered to myself as I crossed over the design.

Not being a bookish person myself, I hadn't made a point of visiting the library on my own. Of course, without a library card there had never been a need to, which made the late fees all the more perplexing. How can you have a late fee if you've never checked out a book in your life? I was about to find out.

"Can I help you, sir?" a hushed voice asked from behind the counter. The line of people ahead of me had disappeared and it was my turn. Stepping forward, I found the voice belonged to a tall, slender, young man with a reddish goatee, rectangular glasses and a button on his pocket that read, "Head Librarian." He was a far cry from the small silver-haired lady I had imagined would work here.

"Actually," I answered, "I got a letter about a late fee for a book that I haven't checked out and I was hoping you could help clear it up for me." I dropped my backpack off my shoulder, letting it fall onto the floor with a *thud*. I dug through the large pocket in search of the notice I had received in the mail. It was tucked behind the Author's Writ, lying atop my Veritas Sword. I slipped the letter across the desk and waited. The librarian picked it up and glanced over the information.

"I'd be glad to help. When did you last use the account?"

"Well, that's the trouble; I haven't got one," I answered. "I've never actually had a library card, which is why I was surprised when I received this bill."

The clerk went to work typing in the account number that was displayed on the late fee sheet.

"Your name is Hunter Brown, right?"

"Yes, it is, but…"

"Do you live at 2012 King Street?" he said, cutting me off.

"Yes, but…"

"Then your account is active. Is it possible that someone else has used your card, or that you've misplaced it perhaps?"

"No, I don't have a card—I never have. I don't even know anything about this book."

The librarian raised his eyebrow and pursed his lips in thought. A moment later his fingers flew across the keyboard again, typing at a feverish rate, presumably to pull up further information.

"Our records show your account was just opened two weeks ago. Is this your signature?"

He turned the computer screen to face me. I couldn't believe what I was seeing. All the account information was mine, including my own sloppy signature.

"Yes, but I just don't remember getting the card."

"I can print you a new one if you'd like," the clerk offered, trying his best to be helpful, but clearly confused.

"No thanks," I answered. "The main problem isn't my account, anyway, it's the fact that I don't have the book. I don't remember checking it out."

"Oh, I see," said the librarian in a rather grim tone. "Well, in that case the best I can do is to make a note on your account. If the book does show up in our system again, we can always credit your account, otherwise you'll have to purchase the book, I'm afraid."

"How much would that be?" I asked.

"In this case the book is a very rare hardcover edition. It could be as much as eighty dollars."

"Eighty dollars!" I blurted out in a much louder voice than I had intended. My voice carried across the room and echoed from the arched expanse overhead, disturbing readers nearby. The clerk frowned and answered with a decidedly lower tone.

"Look, I'm sorry but like I said, that's all I can do. You can always check the shelves upstairs. It's possible the computer made a mistake. Find the book and I can reverse the charges."

The librarian handed me a scrap of paper with a sequence of letters and numbers on it. He then pointed to a broad stairway that led up to the second floor before promptly turning his attention to the next person in line. I was left to navigate the maze of books alone, with a cryptic code written on paper to guide me. Fifteen minutes later I had found my way to what seemed to be the correct aisle—the third shelf to the left of the stairway marked 1500-1600.

Three times I walked the length of the aisle, and three times I came up empty-handed. I threw up my hands in frustration and was about to give up when a short red-haired girl about five years old bounced into view. There was a sizeable gap where her front teeth used to be, and she was wearing purple-rimmed glasses to match her outfit.

"You look lost. Are ya lost?" she asked in one of those obnoxious little kid voices.

"No, I'm just trying to find a book, that's all," I answered.

"You're not very good at it, are you?" she said in a blunt way that only kids can get away with.

"I'm browsing," I said awkwardly.

"Butcha been down the same row lots of times. I was watching you from the other side of the shelf. What's on the paper?"

"A number I got at the front desk. It's supposed to help me find a book or something."

The girl eyed me with a sympathetic look.

"Oh boy. You need help. You sure you don't want me to show you, 'cause I'm really good at finding stuff and I'm smart too. My mommy says I know too much."

I'll bet that's not all she says about you, I thought to myself. But before I could brush her off again, it occurred to me that she might actually be right.

"You know what? Fine. If you can find this book I'll give you a quarter," I said, handing the paper to her.

She eyed the paper, contemplated the offer for a moment, then raised her eyebrow with a mischievous grin.

"A quarter can't buy nothin' anymore; make it a dollar."

"A dollar? What are you, an extortionist?"

"I don't know what that means, but I know you need me and I'm worth more than a quarter."

This kid was something else—a regular businesswoman in kindergarten. I shuddered to think of what she would be like by the time she was twenty. She'd probably own half the city by then.

"Fine, a dollar. But I'm not paying you until you find the book."

"No problem, this is gonna be easy," she said greedily. With an eager smile she examined the numbers and silently mouthed each one as she read them. Then, in a moment of recognition her face lit up.

"It's right over here…. C'mon, follow me." She led me up and down aisle after aisle, skipping and giggling all the way. At times we circled back across the same aisles until it became clear that this was actually some kind of game for her.

Just when I was about to forget it, she shouted, "Here it is, mister…. See?"

"But this is where we started!" I said, realizing we were standing in the exact same place as before.

"I know," she answered with a goofy smile. "I told ya you were lost!"

"Right," I said slowly, suddenly realizing I had just been duped by a little girl. Good thing my friends weren't here or I'd never live it down.

"The book should be right up there somewhere," she explained, pointing to a shelf too high for her to reach. Looking up, I immediately caught sight of a pair of books that were placed backwards, their spines facing in. Sandwiched between the two misplaced titles was a green hardcover book. It was about an inch thick with gold embossing on the side. To my surprise the label on the spine of the book matched the number sequence the librarian had handed me. Retrieving the book from the shelf, I examined the cover and title, which read:

THE WATCHERS: MYTH OR MYSTERY
Simon Ot

"Wow, that's a boring kind of book to be reading," the little girl said. "I'll bet it doesn't even have any pictures in it. Why do you want a book without pictures? Are you boring or something?"

"I guess," I answered still staring at the cover. It was a strange title to be sure, but what I was more interested in was the symbol that accompanied the title, an open eye. It matched the one I had seen tattooed on Vogler's hand and printed on the back of his card. In a snap, the thought occurred to me that Vogler could have been the one who set up my library account. He certainly had all my information and more than enough authority to pull off something like that. The question was, why would he want to?

"Ahem," the little girl interrupted, her hand outstretched with her palm facing up. "The dollar?"

"Oh, right…how could I forget?" I said, digging in my pocket for change. I came up empty. The girl gave me an angry glare. Before I could explain myself, a nervous-looking woman ran up the aisle and saved me.

"There you are, Sabrina," the flustered woman with a strong Spanish accent said as she approached us. She took the little girl by the arm and began to scold her. "I've been looking all over for you. You know better than to run off like that!"

"But Mama," Sabrina replied, "this guy owes me a dollar. I helped him find a book and…."

"I don't want to hear it! You're in trouble, *chica*."

Sabrina folded her arms in an agitated *humph*.

It struck me as slightly odd that she would call the woman her mother. After all, the little girl was fair-skinned with red hair; her mother was exactly the opposite: tanned skin, jet black hair.

The mother turned her attention to me and offered an embarrassed apology. "Sorry for the trouble. I hope she wasn't too annoying. She can get a bit…excited at times."

I explained how she had been a big help, and with a pleasant smile the woman snatched the little girl away in a hurry, leaving me alone with the mysterious book in hand. Sabrina shot a look of pure hatred my way, motioning a finger across her throat in a clear threat. If she wasn't so small, I might have been genuinely frightened of her.

Boo-dwe-oop.

The book in my hand let out a gargled, digital sound. The muffled ring seemed to be coming from somewhere within the pages. Flipping the cover open, I discovered the book was a fake. The pages were missing; the edges were there but the center had been hollowed out. What remained was a perfect compartment for hiding things. A curved black device was nestled inside the book, its smooth display backlit with bright blue letters that read DESI. Below the letters, two digital buttons offered me a choice: *Accept* or *Ignore.*

I picked up the device and pressed *Accept.* A voice spoke.

"Took you long enough," the voice said in a playfully urgent tone. It sounded like a girl close to my age. In a way she sounded strangely familiar, though I couldn't figure out why.

"Excuse me?" I answered. "Do I know you? Who is this?"

"You need to get out of there," the girl said authoritatively.

"Why, is this some kind of prank?" I asked. "Who is this!" I demanded in hopes of a direct response. The voice didn't say.

"I'll explain later. You're in trouble. You need to focus on what

I'm about to say. Vogler is coming. He wants to take you into custody. He's entering the building as we speak. If you want to save your life you will run."

"Run? Are you kidding? I'm not running from the cops. That's... like...illegal, isn't it?"

"He's not a cop, he's a Watcher. And it's only illegal if they catch you trying. Do you want that to happen?"

I glanced back at the book title in my hand. The caller knew something about Watchers and apparently Vogler was one of them. Considering the tattoo that made sense, only I hadn't a clue what a Watcher was exactly.

"What's a Watcher? Are you a Watcher?"

"You ask too many questions," the voice said, sounding a bit annoyed. "Listen, the main thing is to get you out. Vogler is in the building. See for yourself."

With a soft *bleep*, a hidden screen behind the polished face of the device brightened to display a closed-circuit video stream of the library interior. The angle of the shot was positioned somewhere across the room, high above the bookshelves. It zoomed in on the front doors as the detective entered. In the video he pushed open the glass door, took a quick glance in either direction and approached the main desk.

Curious to see if the feed was indeed live, I moved to the railing and glanced over the edge. Vogler was down there all right, and he was discussing something with the clerk. The man behind the counter gestured upstairs as he had done for me. Quicker than lightning, I ducked down in hopes of remaining unseen.

"He's...he's coming up!" I gasped.

"Yes, I know. Now, are you going to listen to me or are you going to take your chances with the man in black?"

"How do I know I can trust you?"

"You don't…but if you do as I say, I promise to help."

It didn't take long to make up my mind. I was just starting to piece my life together. The last thing I wanted was to be in custody. I decided to side with the voice on the phone.

"What do I do?"

"From now on don't talk, just do as I say. Move one aisle over and head to the middle of the bookshelf… keep low to the ground and wait for my word." Doing as I was told, I crawled around the bookshelf I had just finished searching and fell to my stomach. Angling my head just right, I could see through stacks of books to the staircase. Moments later, Vogler's bald head bobbed into view, rising up the stairs with each step.

"Remember, stay put and don't make a sound," the voice said. I held my breath as the detective topped the stairs and turned my way. With the confidence of a cat, Vogler headed for the exact aisle where the Watcher book had been kept. What he didn't know was that on the opposite side of the same bookshelf, I was watching him, keeping as low to the floor as I could.

His polished black shoes came to a stop directly in front of my face. After a brief pause, he shuffled to the right then back to the left. He was searching for something he wasn't finding. The thought crossed my mind that he might be looking for the book I was holding.

"Hmmm," he breathed, intrigued by what he found or couldn't find. A breathless two minutes later, Vogler turned and walked away. Once he was a safe distance from me, I let out a deep sigh of relief and gasped for air.

"Go to the other end of the aisle now," said the girl in the devise. This time the urgency in her voice was understood. She didn't have to ask twice, I was already on my way. As Vogler moved toward the outer end of the aisle, I countered his move on the inner side.

I turned the corner and flattened myself against the width of the bookshelf. For the next several minutes I held my place in silence as Vogler scanned down each of the remaining aisles, one-by-one.

Eventually, he gave up the search as a bad job. His next move was to the edge of the railing where he could look out over the lower level of the library. His eyes, still hidden behind the reflective lenses, were no doubt searching the faces of those below…searching for clues…searching for me.

The voice in the device spoke up once more.

"Listen, we're running out of time. There's a group of chairs and reading tables near the wall to your right. It's where the second-story emergency exit is located. It's out in the open, but if you hurry you might make it."

"Might?" I half-whispered, wondering how it was she expected me to take a chance on a word like *might*. "Can't we just wait it out until Vogler is gone?"

"Shush!" the voice answered, clearly upset that I had broken silence without permission. I couldn't tell for sure if he had heard me, but Vogler cocked his head slightly to the right. I flattened myself against the endcap once more just in case. He didn't look fully but I sensed that even though his back was turned his attention was somehow aimed this way.

"That was close!" she scolded. "I'm only going to say this once and then I'm hanging up. Outside the emergency exit, you'll find a ladder behind the door. Climb up to the roof. You have sixty seconds before I leave without you…fifty-nine…fifty-eight…."

Bleep.

Just like that the call ended as abruptly as it had begun.

The logic of her suggestion was more than questionable; it was entirely absurd. Running for the exit meant walking right into plain view. Besides, there was sure to be an alarm on the door. If I somehow managed to arrive unseen, the alarm would be sure to draw everyone's attention. Vogler would be on me like a rat on cheese.

With no time to think, I checked around the corner of the bookshelf once more. To my surprise, Vogler was gone from his perch at the railing. But where was he now? I eased my way to the end of the aisle and glanced both directions. Nothing, just the briefest glimpse of movement down the stairs. With any luck he was leaving.

With Vogler out of the picture, my attention quickly returned to the emergency exit at the end of the aisle. It was less than fifty feet away, directly in front of me. Too easy. Alarm or not, I couldn't leave this stone unturned. I needed to know more about the Watchers, and the girl on the device seemed the only one capable of telling me. I made up my mind, I would trust the voice and go for it.

Slinging my backpack over my shoulder, I headed for the exit with a determined pace, only glancing once over my shoulder to see if anyone was watching. All was clear until I turned back around. I found myself on a one-way collision course with Vogler himself. How he had done it was anyone's guess, one moment he was missing—the next he seemed to appear out of thin air.

There was no time to slow my pace. I slammed into him like he was a brick wall. I tried to brace myself for impact but nothing could prepare me for the strength of this man's frame. I stumbled backward, steadying myself before I fell over. *So much for escaping unnoticed.*

"I was hoping I'd run into you," Vogler said coldly, seeming to eye the book under my arm. "What do you have there?"

"It's nothing, just a book," I answered, standing up quickly and tucking the book further under my arm. He was blocking my path to the emergency exit like a safety guards the end zone. If I wanted to escape, I'd have to get creative. I needed a Plan B.

"Let me see it," he demanded, holding out his humongous hand. I shook my head.

"Listen, Hunter, don't be afraid. I'm trying to help you, remember? Now, hand it over."

Out of the corner of my eye, I spotted the little girl, Sabrina. Her flustered mother was pushing a stroller and waiting anxiously by the elevator door. With a friendly *ding* the door slid open and they began loading inside. Even after the stroller was loaded, the elevator looked large enough to accommodate me, if I had enough time to make it before the doors closed. I would have to be quick. I could make it. I would have to.

In a rush, I tore down the aisle that led to the elevator. Vogler stood in shock, apparently not expecting me to run. He gathered his wits and started to give chase. I was only halfway down the aisle when the elevator doors began to close. The little girl's eyes widened as she realized I was coming straight at her. Her mother pulled her aside in a hurry. If I was going to make it through without triggering the doors to reopen, I'd have to think skinny. Miraculously, I slipped through with inches to spare.

Vogler was too late. He tried to stop the door with his arm but came up short. My timing had worked perfectly. Only now I had to worry about getting out at the bottom before Vogler made it down the stairs. Breathing hard now, I looked over at the mother and daughter who were staring at me in slack-jawed silence.

"Let me guess," Sabrina said slowly. "You owe him a dollar too?"

"I guess they take late fees pretty seriously around here," I answered, feeling a bit awkward.

"Is everything okay?" the woman asked, sounding genuinely concerned. "Should we call for help?"

"No, I just need to run as fast as I can when the doors open. So if you can make sure to stand clear, I'll…." Then I noticed the elevator hadn't moved. My only hope was to beat Vogler to the ground floor, but this was not helping.

"Why aren't we moving?" I asked nervously. "Is it always this slow?"

Sabrina shook her head and pointed toward the buttons.

"You never pushed one. It was my turn to do it too, but you jumped in before I could."

She was right, none of the buttons were lit. This was good. By now Vogler would be halfway down the stairs already. I could still make it to the emergency exit in time. I pressed the number two button and the elevator door slid open immediately. As expected, Vogler was gone.

Stepping out, I turned around and gave the confused family some advice. "If you meet a large angry man at the bottom of the elevator, tell him Hunter says 'hi.'"

The doors shut on a pair of frightened faces. I felt bad sending them down to meet Vogler. I wondered what he'd do when he realized I've given him the slip.

As I pushed open the emergency exit, a loud siren and bright flashing lights overhead alerted the entire library to what I'd done. Stepping out into the light of day, I found myself standing on a metal platform. A slim staircase headed down to the sidewalk below. Just as the voice had explained, I spotted a ladder mounted to the side of the building and hidden behind the door. I started to climb.

I had just about reached the top of the ladder when Vogler barged through the doorway below. Without looking up, he dashed for the stairs to catch up to me. He would have completely gone off track too if it weren't for one silly mistake.

I dropped the book.

CHAPTER 9

GHOST RIDING

With nowhere to go but up, I finished my climb. Thanks to the dropped book, Vogler was already starting up the ladder behind me. At most, I had thirty seconds to find a new hiding place. As it turned out, I wouldn't have to.

"For a second there, I thought you'd stood me up," a familiar voice shouted from across the rooftop. The voice from the device belonged to the same girl who had delivered my mail the other night and silenced Mr. Smokey.

"You? What are you doing here?" I asked, somewhat in shock.

"What? Did you have a rooftop date with someone else?"

"No, I'm glad it's you, I just…didn't expect…up here."

She looked me over and raised an eyebrow.

"Here, give me that," she demanded, snatching the sleek device out of my hand and wrapping it around my wrist. Somehow, the seemingly solid device changed shape in her hands, morphing from a phone to a watch with an incredibly large screen. I noticed she was wearing a similar device as well.

"Wear it like this; it keeps your hands free," she said.

"Whoa, how did you…?"

"It's not important. Name's Desi, but we'll have to save the small talk for later. Looks like you've got a babysitter we need to ditch," she said just as the first of Vogler's hands reached over the top of the ladder.

Pulling my arm, she led me across the rooftop. The back wall of the library was shared with Cavinaugh's hardware store. Beyond that a series of rooftops continued down the street as part of the revitalized "old town" of Destiny. The properties were built fairly close together, only ten feet between them.

As we neared the end of the first rooftop, Desi released her grip and leaped across the ten-foot-gap. I stopped short, uncertain I could make the jump with my backpack. I pulled it off and tossed it across to Desi.

"Hurry up!" she shouted.

I wasn't usually one to back down from a challenge, especially in front of a girl, but this was ridiculous. At least at school when you practiced trying to outjump your friends, it wasn't over a two-story drop. A mistake here would mean a long fall to a quick end.

"STOP!" Vogler growled from over my shoulder. He was still a distance away, but was gaining quickly with long powerful strides.

With a running start I fixed my gaze on Desi and put everything I had into making the jump. Surprisingly, I crossed the ten-foot gap with ease and landed on the other side. Desi reached for my hand once more and together we continued across the rooftops. Glancing back over my shoulder, I watched as Vogler neared the gap. He made no effort to jump. In fact it almost looked like he had run straight across the gap as if it didn't exist at all. Watcher or not, whatever he was, I was beginning to be frightened.

We came to a second gap, but this time Desi slowed to a stop and stepped up on the ledge.

"See you below," she said, dropping over the side of the building. She planned the fall perfectly, landing in a pile of trash bags in the dumpster below. She climbed out of the dumpster and waved up at me, encouraging me to do the same.

"I'm going to regret this," I muttered to myself as I stepped up for the dive. I tossed my backpack down first and took one last look over my shoulder at Vogler who was closing in quickly.

"Don't do it!" he shouted as I fell back.

The fall was quick and the landing was less painful than I expected. One of the bags had split open after Desi's jump and bits of popcorn packing material puffed into the air. She had clearly planned our escape to the last detail. Desi was already waiting with a gift by the time I retrieved my backpack and crawled out.

"Here, put this on," she said, tossing a white cycling helmet at me like one might toss a basketball to a friend. I caught it despite the fact that I wasn't prepared. From out of the shadows Desi wheeled over a sleek white motorcycle. I had never seen anything like it. The wheels had no spokes, just open space where a tire hub should have been. The word *Ghost* was written in glowing neon lights that continued down the sides. Desi mounted the bike and fired up the engine, which sounded less like a bike and more like a small jet engine.

Thweeee.

"This is yours?" I gawked.

"It belongs to my uncle. Get on, and hold on...tight," she shouted over the whirring hum. I cinched the straps of my backpack on my shoulders and straddled the back of the bike, wrapping my arms around Desi's waist. Before we could drive off, something large landed beside us. Vogler.

He too had made the jump, only he hadn't bothered landing in the dumpster as we had done. The fall should have killed the man, but he rose to his full stature, seemingly unaffected by it. For the first time, I saw something glisten in his hands, a silver pistol, which I assumed was loaded. Things were getting tense.

Desi didn't wait; she pulled the throttle and the *Ghost* lurched forward like a shot out of a cannon. Looking back, I spotted Vogler's mirrored gaze watching us race away. I couldn't be sure but I thought I saw him vanish before we rounded the corner onto the main road. *Just a trick of the eye,* I told myself. *People don't vanish.* But deep down, I couldn't shake the feeling that was growing in me. Vogler was no ordinary person.

Hoooooooooooooonk!

The angry sounds of traffic pulled my attention once more. A disgruntled driver shouted something out his window as Desi flew past him, and for good reason. Her driving could only be described as impulsive. She rarely slowed, often running through red lights, aggressively passing between lanes and even drove on the wrong side of the road now and then. I held on for dear life.

"Can we slow down?" I begged.

"No," Desi answered. "You aren't safe in Destiny...not any-more."

"Not safe? It's your driving that's not safe," I said, as we rounded a corner far too quickly. "Where are we going anyway?"

"To see my uncle. He's kind of an authority on the Watchers. Wrote a book on it, actually."

"Let me guess, *Myth* or *Mystery*, right?"

Desi nodded.

"The letter from the library was a setup, wasn't it?"

"You just figured that out?" she said jokingly. "It was the only way I could get you a message without Vogler knowing. He's been listening to your phone calls and monitoring your e-mail. I knew you never went to the library so I figured it would be the easiest way to get your attention."

"How?" I asked.

"How what?"

"How do you know that I never go to the library? In fact, how do you know so much about me when I know absolutely nothing about you?" The question had been nagging at the corners of my mind ever since the library. It wasn't much fun being the only one left in the dark. Having lost some of my memory was difficult enough, stuff like this just added to my confusion.

"I told you, my uncle has been studying the Watchers' moves for years. They've had their eye on you, so he did his research. He sent me to find you."

"But I still don't understand why they're watching me."

"I'll let him explain. We're almost there. Hang on, this is going to get bumpy," she said.

Almost like an afterthought, she cut across three lanes of traffic and slipped down into the train yard. I couldn't decide if she truly was this bad a driver or if she just liked watching me squirm— probably a bit of both.

A series of warning signs flew past that read: *No Trespassing, Authorized Personnel Only, Stay Off the Tracks*. Not that Desi noticed. Before I could argue the point, we were driving up on the train tracks, headed straight for the gaping mouth of a black tunnel.

"Are you sure this is safe?"

"Safe? There's no fun in safe." She said this as if it were supposed to be funny, or witty or something. When it's your life on the line, the humor gets lost.

The neon lights of the bike lit the tunnel wall with a ghostly ring of blue. Sounds of trains rattling on the rails nearby echoed off the walls of the tunnel. The tunnels kept splitting into multiple lines, making it difficult to tell which way we were heading. I tried to keep count in case we got lost and needed to turn back. So far we had a right, a left, two rights and a center track where the track split in three.

More than once we were barely missed by speeding trains that were far too close for my comfort. I could feel the vibration in my chest, like an electronic body massage chair stuck on high speed. The sooner this ride was over, the better.

Desi's final turn was down a shortened tunnel ending in a solid rock wall. The track wasn't finished, but she didn't seem to care.

"It's a dead end!" I shouted, just in case she wasn't paying attention.

"I know. Just hold on," she commanded, increasing her speed as we approached the end of the line.

"Are you crazy?" I shouted. "We'll be killed!"

"No, we won't. Trust me," she replied still speeding up.

I didn't trust her at all, but I also was out of options. Falling off the bike would only kill me quicker, and maybe in a more painful way. I had to take a chance that she knew what she was doing. At the last possible moment, Desi flipped a switch near her thumb and the entire tunnel around us vanished in a ring of blue.

Next thing I knew, we were driving down a similar tunnel, except the train tracks had been replaced by smooth asphalt and there were lights overhead.

"What just happened?" I gasped, patting my chest and counting all my body parts. "We should be dead. You don't just drive into a rock wall at 80 miles an hour and live to tell about it."

"It's called *ghosting*. We skipped through space to avoid the wall," she pointed her thumb over her shoulder and I looked back at where we had just come from. Sure enough the backside of the rock wall was safely behind us.

"You can do that?" I asked, both a little concerned and impressed at the same time.

"We just did. Think of it like skipping rocks across the surface of a pond…only between dimensions. My uncle's idea."

I couldn't quite grasp the concept but it sounded cool.

"Is your uncle a genius or something?" I asked, thinking of Stretch and how much he'd love to figure out this kind of thing.

"Something like that. Welcome to the Underground, Hunter," Desi said as we slowed to the end of the tunnel. We entered a brightly lit room roughly the size of a football field, only round. High overhead, the entire ceiling was backlit—a single canopy of light. It gave the impression of daylight even though we were well underground. At the base of a rock feature, water fell into a small pond. Tropical plants of all sizes grew from the walls, giving the space an atrium look.

Dozens of vehicles lined the circumference of the room, parked in perfect order. Desi circled to the right and found a parking space beside another *Ghost*, this one black. The kickstand automatically dropped and we dismounted. Desi took our helmets and placed them on a nearby shelf.

"Whoa, what happened there?" I asked, pointing to the back half of a third *Ghost* bike sticking out of the wall in front of us. It was embedded at an awkward angle, a good foot above the ground.

"*Ghosting* accident," she said nonchalantly. "Someone bumped the switch when they were getting on their *Ghost*. Luckily, they hadn't sat down yet or they'd have gone with it…."

"You mean we could have been permanently stuck in that rock wall back there?"

"No, we cleared the jump by ten feet at least."

Just then, a mousy little man, wearing a blue jumpsuit, scurried across the room to where we stood. He spoke with nervous excitement and carried a formerly red handkerchief that was now almost grey with grime. A name patch on his coveralls said "Tweez," which was either his nickname or a bad joke, since his black eyebrows were a single, scruffy line.

"Desi, thank goodness she's back! Please, please, tell me. How did her first solo go? Is she all in one piece? Is she safe? Is she sound?" the man asked.

At first I found his speech curious, talking about Desi in the third person. When he walked straight past us and began examining the bike, I realized it wasn't Desi he was talking about. It was the bike.

Desi answered, "Uh…good, you know, steering is a little tight but…uh…other than that…."

"Tight? Tight? How can she be tight, I just calibrated this morning. Unless…hmmmm…" the man pursed his lips and let his thoughts run away with him. He pulled a wrench from his back pocket and was partially disassembling the machine before our very eyes. For the time being, he forgot we were even there.

"Come on," Desi said with a mischievous grin. "I'll show you around."

We passed eight vehicles on the way to the next corridor. All of them were very expensive: a Rolls Royce, a black Porsche Carrara, two BMWs, and a handful of concept cars that I didn't recognize off-hand. Not to mention the two *Ghost* bikes we had just left behind, and the one in the wall too.

"I wouldn't have pegged you as a car collector," I smiled.

"Oh no, not me. These are my uncles," she clarified; then added, "but don't tell Tweez. He thinks they're his."

The first door we came to was flanked by a pair of guards, a man and a woman. They were both wearing white uniforms and black sunglasses.

"He's with me," Desi said nonchalantly as we approached the door. They nodded as we passed between them.

Desi explained that her uncle was an inventor who loved experimenting in new technology. He had developed the concept for the *Ghost* based on extensive study of snarks, who could also pass through walls. She said this as we passed a room full of the caged creatures. The room was mostly dark, but dozens of glowing blue eyes stared back through the glass, assuring us that they were still there and likely up to no good. I couldn't help but think of Boojum and smile. Despite all the trouble he caused, I couldn't dismiss the fact that he could be a lot of fun too.

The tour continued; the underground hideout turned out to be an underground compound of some kind. Each room had its own purpose. A handful of people scurried about in an attempt to keep up with the daily chores. None of them made eye contact. It was one of the most amazing hideouts I could have imagined.

One thing was missing however; there were no doors to the outside world. Being underground it made perfect sense, but it also gave me an uneasy feeling. It meant there was no exit...no way out.

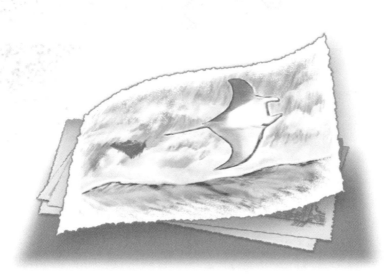

CHAPTER 10

THE EYE OF ENDS

Desi left me in a fascinating room while she went in search of her uncle. I sank into one of two leather chairs that were placed in front of a giant oak desk and let my eyes wander the room. It was a comfortable space with the kind of warm lighting that could soothe you to sleep if there wasn't so much to look at. Overhead, the dome-shaped ceiling was like an indoor observatory. Painted midnight blue, it sparkled with fiber-optic starlight. In the center of the dome a mechanical solar system orbited the soft glow of an orb-shaped light meant to be the sun.

A room-length bookshelf loaded with hundreds of books lined the back wall. Antique maps and charts framed the remaining walls. I recognized a few DaVinci sketches as well—after all he was one of Dad's favorite inventors. I especially liked DaVinci's knack for writing things in reverse. An unfinished chess game was set up on a table between my chair and the one across from me. From the looks of things, white was winning.

At the center of the room, directly under the sun, sat a large ornate oak desk. The surface was clean and organized—a place for everything. Even the one loose pen left on the desk was positioned in a perfectly straight line. The room looked like it had been prepared for a museum—with one exception. A second desk, more of a drafting table actually, sat in the back corner of the room. I hadn't noticed it until now because it was partially blocked by a potted palm tree. This desk held a sloppy pile of sketches, pencils, brushes and crumpled up papers.

Only a few of the charcoal sketches could be seen from this distance but they were really quite good. The first was a picture of an eagle soaring over a sparkling white city at night. The second sketch was a bit more surreal, featuring a manta ray floating through the sky. But it was the third and final sketch that made me pause. It was unlike the others, a still-life picture of a grandfather clock. In the picture the hands on the clock face were approaching the eleventh hour, but there was something different about the clock. Instead of numbers on its face, it had symbols.

Could it be Aviad's clock? I wondered.

In a rush, I hurried over for a closer look. Sure enough the clock in the picture looked almost identical to the one Aviad kept in his bookshop. Only there was something different. The symbols didn't look at all familiar to me. They were similar in design, but certainly not the same as the ones I had seen before on the clock and on the back of my Author's Writ. I took note of it and glanced over the other drawings once more.

On second glance I noticed I had misinterpreted the other two drawings. The first was not of an eagle at all; it was a Thunderbird with the shadowy silhouette of a man riding on its back. And even though I had never seen the manta ray creatures before, the second drawing had a few floating shards of land in the distant clouds. This could only mean one thing: whoever had drawn these pictures had been to Solandria.

"Solandria," I whispered aloud. In many ways the place seemed like a far-away dream. It was odd to know that I had been there only a few days ago and yet had no memory to show for it. What Trista had told me about my visit sounded so amazing, but none of it felt real. I sighed, suddenly realizing how Stretch must have felt. He probably wanted to believe what I was saying, but without memories to match my own it was impossible.

"Impressive, isn't it?" a short, smartly dressed man asked. He had entered the room so quietly I wasn't even aware he was there. Embarrassed, I backed away from the desk.

"I'm sorry, I…I didn't mean to pry…" I began to say.

"Not at all, dear boy," said the man, a pipe clinched tightly between his teeth. He appeared to be nearing sixty, and spoke with the formal accent one only gets from living overseas. He was a rugged, good-looking man for his age, with a spirit of adventure in his tanned face. His long white hair was neatly combed back, his beard short, trimmed and peppered with patches of dark grey. Desi slipped in behind the man, who I assumed was her uncle.

Removing the pipe from his lips, he said, "It is an honor to cross paths at last, Hunter. You don't know how long I've been waiting for this day."

"It's a pleasure, Mr.…uh…." Halfway through my greeting, I realized I couldn't remember his name. I had seen it on the book cover at the library, but already it had slipped my mind.

"Oh, never mind the mister part. Simon's the name, simply Simon." We shook hands in a warm greeting.

"Anyway, I'm sorry for all the excitement," Simon confessed.

"Desi's driving didn't alarm you, I hope?"

"No, she's…a great driver," I replied, casting a sideways glance in her direction. Desi smirked and mouthed the word "liar" as she leaned against the doorframe.

"Are these yours?" I asked, pointing to the charcoal drawings beside me.

"Oh heavens no. I haven't an ounce of artistic blood in me—not for lack of trying mind you. I'm more of a collector, you might say. I find art to be an illuminating expression of one's soul." He man-uevered toward the desk and started shuffling through the pictures to find others lower in the pile. "Actually, I'm glad you've noticed them; they are part of the reason I've been looking for you."

"The pictures?"

"Yes, but I'm getting ahead of myself. Nasty habit of mine, do forgive me." He cleared his throat and waved a hand at Desi to shut the door behind us. Whatever he was about to say next was meant for the three of us alone. Desi did as she was told, then slumped into one of the chairs beside me.

The man raised his pipe and took a few lingering puffs in si-lence. The smell of the smoke was like the fragrance of the juniper tree in our neighbor's front yard.

"I assume that Desi has told you why you're here?"

"Actually, we didn't really have time to talk," I answered, glanc-ing between the two of them. "She told me the Watchers are after me and that I might be in trouble."

"Indeed," Simon said grimly. "How much do you know about the Watchers?"

"Nothing really, except that Vogler is one of them, I think."

"Yes, and a very persistent one at that. He will not rest until he gets what he is after, something he believes you can help him find."

"Which is what exactly?" I asked, hoping to get to the reason for the chaos of the past few days.

"This is where you must take a leap of faith with me, Hunter. There are many legends and half-truths surrounding the Watchers' very existence. Some say they are simply exaggerations of historical figures; some claim they are keepers of a secret that will one day bring an end to all things, and of course many deny they exist at all. I myself have reason to believe some of the legends are actually true and that the Watchers are indeed alive and well today. Actually, the oldest and most reliable accounts come from the Author's Writ itself. I will share with you what I have come to learn through my research, but ultimately, you must choose what *you* believe is true."

He emphasized this last statement by pulling the pipe from his mouth and poking the stem of it in the air at me. Simon raised an eyebrow in thought, carefully considering where he should start his explanation. With years of research to cover, he would only touch on the essentials.

"Long before the Author wrote the story of our world, he created another where radiant beings of light called Shining Ones, lived in harmony with each other and the written world around them. Among them were an elite class known as the Watchers. The first Watchers were simply guardians—keepers of the Author's most sacred treasures. One of the most precious and powerful possessions in the storehouse was a relic known as the Eye of Ends."

As he spoke, Simon retrieved a copy of his own book from the bookshelf, and flipped quickly through the pages to an illustration somewhere in the opening chapters. It was an ancient graphic of three tall, faceless figures, each standing guard around what looked to be a circular object with a symbol etched in its center. It was the Watchers' symbol—an eye.

Simon continued, "The Eye of Ends is a looking glass created by the Author himself from a polished, petrified cross-section of the first tree of Solandria—the Living Tree. As you may already know, this tree was once the source of life for our world. Because the Bloodstone was embedded within the tree itself, the Living Tree was said to retain the entire story of our world within its rings: past, present and future."

"You mean, it can predict the future?" I asked. Simon fixed his gaze right on me, searching my eyes with his own.

"Not predict, Hunter, reveal…reflect. As far as the Author is concerned, the future of this world is already written. The Eye merely reveals to mortals what the Author has already determined will be."

He let the idea of the artifact sink in before continuing.

"After the Bloodstone was stolen and its curse shattered the shards of Solandria, the Author removed what remained of the tree and created the Eye of Ends, placing it under the guardianship of the Watchers. Throughout history only a very few people have been granted the privilege of using the Eye of Ends, but never were they allowed to look directly upon it."

"How do they use it then?"

"The Watchers brought the Eye to chosen individuals while they slept. The soul of the sleeper would awaken in a Maze of Rings where the Watcher would reveal a vision that the sleeper was meant to see. The visions are revealed through dreams—dreams that were meant to serve as warnings of things to come."

"Wait a minute," I said. "If the Watchers are working for the Author, then wouldn't that make them good?"

"Some, but not all Watchers still serve the Author. In fact, one of the Watchers who vowed to protect the Eye betrayed him and stole it," Simon explained.

"Let me guess…Vogler?" I asked.

Simon nodded. "He appears in many forms and goes by many names both in Solandria and the Veil. Vogler is one, but his given name is Tonomis."

"But why would he do that? Why would he steal the Eye for himself?" I asked.

"As a Watcher he was not allowed to see the visions of the Eye himself. That honor was reserved for select mortals and the Author, of course. Over time, Vogler came to suspect the Author's intentions for the story's end were not as good as he had once believed. When he was alone, Vogler stole the Eye and hid with it in Solandria, hoping to discover for himself what the coming end would be. In using the Eye he broke his vow and became imprisoned inside the Maze of Rings."

"So, how did he escape?" I asked.

"What makes you think he did?" Simon asked.

"Well, I just assumed since Vogler is free he found a way out."

"He did not find any way out; rather a way found him. For countless ages the Eye of Ends remained lost in Solandria, deep in the forests of Solone, until one day a goblin by the name of Volias happened upon it. The mortal's touch awakened the Eye's power and his soul joined the Watcher in the Maze of Rings. The Watcher led Volias to a vision in the rings as he had done for so many mortals in ages past. When Volias awakened from the Maze, Vogler somehow returned with him. He was free. Still, he could not quench his thirst for more of the Eye's knowledge. He asked the goblin about the vision he'd been given and found the goblin had no memory of it, except for the single picture he sketched for the Watcher. It was the image of a lightning bolt, striking the tree outside his village. The very next night, the exact tree was struck."

"The Watcher stayed with the goblin, promising him great power if he would continue to use the Eye. They entered the Maze of Rings several times together, each time with the same results.

The goblin returned with a single image from his visions and would sketch it for the Watcher to see."

"Of course, power of this kind is hard to keep quiet. Volias was careless and bragged about his gift to his friends. He sold the images for vast wealth. But, when one of his friends learned the source of his visions, he stabbed Volias in the back and took the Eye from him. Volias died and when he did the Eye bound itself to the one who had slain him, Gargamas, a young recruit in the Shadow army."

"Vogler followed the Eye and helped Gargamas learn how to use it. Like the former owner, Gargamas could remember only a single image when he returned. Gargamas rose in the Shadow ranks until he too was slain by another Shadow warrior. And so the cycle continued for ages. Every time the previous owner was killed, a new owner would be mentored by the Watcher."

"That's an interesting story, but it still doesn't explain why the Watcher would be looking for me. I don't have the Eye. I didn't even know anything about it until today."

"No…but someone close to you did."

"Who?" I asked.

"Some time ago the Eye of Ends changed hands again. This time, a lone Codebearer killed a Shadow lord in battle—Lord Bledynn, a Vulvynn, who unbeknownst to the Codebearer was also the current keeper of the Eye. As before, the relic passed into the killer's hands. That man was your father, Caleb Brown."

"My…my father?" I asked, stumbling over the words. I searched Desi's face for answers. She simply smiled knowingly and nodded my attention back to Simon. "My father had the Eye of Ends? How do you know?"

"Because these are your father's drawings, Hunter," Simon said, pointing to the stack of papers. "All of these and many more document what he saw in the Maze of Rings." Taking new interest in the drawings, I began flipping through them. The three on top were by far the tamest images in the collection. Most of the others were disturbing and dark: a village being burned to the ground, a shard of land cracking in two beneath a giant fist, a figure falling headlong into the black clouds of the Void. Then, I came to an image that nearly made my heart stop. The picture was of Aviad and me, his hand plunged into my chest where the Bloodstone once was. Dad must have seen this in the Maze of Rings...in the Eye of Ends.

"I can't believe he was here...in Destiny all this time and he never told me," I said. "Why wouldn't he have tried to reach us?"

"He was afraid for you, Hunter—afraid for his family."

"Afraid? Of what?"

Simon raised a knowing eyebrow and the answer hit me before he could speak again.

"Oh, right...Vogler," I said, finally piecing things together in my mind.

"Your father and I both served in the Codebearers' ranks; we were like brothers. After your father recovered the Eye, Tonomis or Vogler, as you know him, found your father and trained him to use it just as he had done for other mortals before him. Because of your father's prior knowledge, the Codebearers enjoyed many victories. But all of that changed one day when your father received a vision that disturbed him. He never told me what it was exactly, but he called it the Day of Doom. From that moment forward he was set against Vogler. When Vogler learned what your father had seen, he intended to kill your father but he failed. Your father escaped, taking the Eye with him. He came to me for protection, and for help in protecting the Eye of Ends."

Simon moved to my father's desk where a small leather purse hung from the corner of the chair. He opened the pouch and removed a deep blue cloth that had been folded multiple times. Laying it on the desktop, he began to unfold the cloth, one corner at a time, until it was much larger than I had first imagined. The final corner flipped open to reveal what should have been impossible to fit in that little bag. Hidden magically inside the folded cloth was a polished, black, circular cross-section of petrified wood. It was well over two inches thick and three feet in diameter—far too large to have fit in the leather purse.

The rings rippled out from the center of the ancient wood, where a circular shape that resembled the symbol of the Watchers' eye stared back at me. This was no ordinary object; this was the Eye of Ends.

I held my breath, astonished to know the relic we had just been discussing had been kept in this room all along. In some ways I was afraid of the Eye, of the power it held, the history it represented. I swallowed hard and shuddered at the sight before looking away.

"Where is Dad now? Is he here? Can I see him?" I asked, anxious to be reunited with my father once more.

Desi and Simon exchanged concerned glances, and this time it was Desi who spoke.

"We…we don't know where he is anymore. He disappeared over a year ago when he went in search of something he believed could prevent the Day of Doom from becoming a reality. He never returned. We've been searching for him ever since, and as you've learned, we're not the only ones."

Despite the news that my father was missing, I was encouraged by the thought that I was closer to him than I had been since he left. He was out there somewhere.

"Does Vogler know about the Day of Doom too?" I asked.

Simon spoke up again.

"There is no way to be sure, but even if he doesn't he will still be searching for your father. The Eye of Ends is Vogler's greatest treasure and he believes your father still has it. One thing is certain, wherever your father is, we must find him before Vogler does. That's where you come in. We've hit a dead-end in our search and honestly, we could use your help."

"I'm afraid I don't have much to offer," I said. "It's like you said, Dad kept the family in the dark about his adventures in Solandria. I haven't seen him in over three years."

"I understand," Simon said, sighing. "Frankly, it's one of the reasons I have put off contacting you for so long. I had hoped to honor his wishes to keep you in the dark on the matter; however, the situation has changed. Despite your father's best intentions, Vogler has returned. And he will not hesitate in the least to use your family to get what he wants from your father. I felt it was time to make an exception. You are the only one in your family who has been to Solandria. In some ways, it seems your involvement has been unavoidable, which is what gives me hope that you may indeed know something that even you don't yet realize."

"But I wouldn't know where to start," I said. "I haven't got a clue where my father is."

"Ah, but we do," Simon said eagerly.

Simon produced a shabby piece of paper that looked like it had been torn in half, yanked straight out of a book.

"We found this in your father's research," Simon said, "along with three drawings dated a few days before he disappeared."

The page was blank except for a couple of random scribblings around the edges. They were nothing more than gibberish. The first note read:

NS LNWZR
NRZX STHYJ
JY HTSXZRNRZW
NLSN

"What does this mean?" I asked, hoping Simon might know.

"Just gibberish, as far as I can tell," Simon answered. "There aren't any vowels so it's not scrambled. That's about all we could figure out.

"Before he left, your father made three more drawings. They are the only clues we have as to what he was hoping to accomplish on his mission." Simon passed the pages to me.

I glanced over the images and found the pictures to be very intriguing. The first was not a drawing at all, but rather a series of seemingly meaningless letters jumbled together.

I nodded in agreement and moved to the second drawing. The scenic picture was of a fruit tree, growing near the edge of an unknown Solandrian shard. The image seemed to focus past the tree into the Void beyond it. The skies were an angry swirling storm of clouds where a fleet of incoming Sky Ships approached the land like an aerial navy. The drawing was interesting, but could have been any number of land shards in Solandria. Without more to go on, it would be difficult to tell where it was.

"Before you look at the final image," Simon added, as I began to shift the pages, "I must warn you that it's a bit troubling. Despite what it shows, I feel this is the best clue we have to discovering what happened to your father."

I braced myself for the worst, but nothing could prepare me for what I was about to see. The third drawing was of my father, trapped in the corner of a dungeon cell. In the picture a large shadow loomed over him, a knife raised so that the shadow of it was pointed at my father's throat. The knife itself appeared in the foreground of the image, but only the very edge of the hand that held the knife was visible in the artwork.

I tried not to tear up, thinking about how hard it must have been for him to draw these pictures...to have seen the end that would come to him.

"I know what you are thinking," Simon said in a somber tone. "But keep in mind, if this was your father's final moment, we must focus all our energy on finding the one who killed him. You can bet Vogler is already searching to reunite the Eye with its new master, whoever that may be."

A long moment of silence passed as I stared at the picture. Slowly my sadness turned to bitterness, then to all-out anger at the one who had taken my father from me. I wanted to find him all right, but I wanted to avenge whatever harm he had done to my dad.

"Count me in," I said menacingly.

Simon patted me on the shoulder. "Very good," he said. "I'll have Desi upload the images of your father's drawings to the Symbio devices. That way, you can carry them with you no matter where you are."

Simon folded the Eye back up into the cloth and hid it away again. Then, gathering the pictures, he handed them to Desi. During the transfer, one of the papers slipped out of the pile and fell to the ground. It landed at my feet and I picked it up to hand it to Desi, but the image stopped me dead in my tracks.

It was a picture of my house. In the image, it was late evening and the entire house was covered in hundreds, maybe thousands, of blackbirds. The rooftop and telephone wires that led up to the house were all lined with them as well. But it was the figure walking up to my house that terrified me most. Even from the back, I would recognize the shape of the man anywhere. Black trench coat. Bald head. Broad shoulders. Vogler...and he was carrying a gun. Then I saw something else, something that made the blood drain from my face. In the grass, sitting beside the mailbox, was the smoke detector I had left out overnight in the exact location it appeared in the image. This image was a vision of today.

"I need to go home," I said anxiously.

"You can't," Desi said, sounding almost desperate to keep me. "It's too dangerous out there. Now that Vogler has seen you with me he's going to find you and he's not going to let you go."

"My family is still out there, and they're in danger too. I need to get them out of the house, now."

Simon spoke up with an even voice, "You'd be making a mistake. It's too late for them; you need to focus on finding your father. That's the only thing that matters now."

I couldn't believe what I was hearing. Simon and Desi couldn't just expect me to stand by and wait while the only family I had left was about to be captured, or worse, by Vogler. There was no telling what he might do to them.

"You're wrong," I said, storming out of the room and down the stairs. Desi chased after me. By the time she caught up to me, I was already halfway into the garage. I grabbed a helmet and hopped onto the only *Ghost* that was still in one piece—the black one.

"Hunter, don't be silly. You can't go. You don't even know how to drive."

"I'm sure I can figure it out."

Tweez, who was still busy assembling the white *Ghost*, looked nervously at me mounting the bike and muttered under his breath. "Oh dear, oh dear, dear."

"But what about your dad?" Desi asked.

"I'll be back once I get my family, I promise."

I managed to start the engine and backed the bike up to the

tunnel runway again. Pulling on the throttle, I sped toward the wall just like Desi had, only a little on the slower side just to be careful. When at last I approached the wall of rock, I flipped the switch and disappeared into the train tunnel beyond it.

Chapter 11

Lights On, Nobody's Home

Swimming during a lightning storm, juggling chainsaws, and attempting to eat the cafeteria "chef surprise" are all great ways to get oneself killed. I found a new one to add to the list.

With no training, no license, and no clue what I was doing, I was operating the *Ghost* on pure instinct. Normally, this would be a bad combination for me—tech and impulse—but for some reason, it was working. The bike almost seemed to understand my need to get back home as quickly as possible, directing me to make quick work of retracing the impossibly dark tunnel route back into the open. Once there, I steered the bike up the embankment toward the road.

Boo-dwe-oop! A digital ring chirped from my Symbio wrist device. Its smooth face lit up with the message: *DESI*. I knew what she wanted. She was just going to try to talk me out of going, but my mind was made up. There was no way I was turning back—not while Mom and Emily could be in trouble, not while I could still do something about it. I tapped the *Ignore* option and squeezed the *Ghost's* throttle harder.

The sun was low in the sky when I finally made my cautious turn onto King Street. Long shadows had stretched themselves out across the road, making a checkerboard of dark and light patches to count off my nervous approach.

Remembering the chilling image of the painting, I held my breath, waiting for my house to come into view. There. Both cars were in the driveway. Lights were on. But, no birds, no Vogler....

Yet, I reminded myself, looking nervously toward the sky. It was empty. Still, who was to say how much time I had before he showed up?

I made a wobbly turn into the driveway and lurched up beside the house to park the conspicuous bike around back. My clutch and braking skills, or rather complete lack of them, got the bike to stop, just short of crushing Mom's prized rosebush. Luckily for me, the advanced bike automatically engaged its kickstand to support itself before I dropped it.

Still wearing the helmet, I rushed in through the back door, calling out loudly for anyone to hear. "Mom! Em! You home?"

I flipped up my visor and frantically surveyed the scene. From all appearances, someone was. The small, persistent chirps from the kitchen timer were declaring dinner ready. Emily's favorite radio station played quietly in the background. The table had been set for three.

I took a deep breath, relieved to know they were still here. Re-moving my helmet, I set it down on the counter and shut off the incessant timer.

"What's for dinner?" I called out again, peeking into the oven's glass front. *Meatloaf—extra, extra crispy.* I sighed and twisted the oven knob to off. Not hearing the replies from Mom and Emily that I was expecting, I reached out and switched off the radio. Now the house was quiet, too quiet.

"Mom?"

There was no reply. Something was wrong—I could feel it.

Instinctively, I reached in my backpack for my Veritas Sword, but hesitated when I remembered the painful results of my last two attempts. Thinking better of it, I looked for the next closest weapon. My choices were between a dirty frying pan, or…a mop. I wasn't going there again.

Armed with the frying pan, I approached the basement door and nudged it open. No lights. No movement.

They must be upstairs, I reasoned, trying to avoid an outright panic. The entryway was mostly dark; only a small patch of sunset spilled in through the window strip above our front door. My senses were on overload. Cautiously, I tiptoed toward the stairs.

Suddenly, my foot slipped out from under me. The pan flew from my grip and clattered violently against the tile floor. My face narrowly escaped the same fate when I managed to catch my forward fall with one hand. As soon as I touched the ground, I recoiled. The floor was smeared with something slick and dark.

Horrified, I jumped to my feet and flicked on the lights, fearful of what I would find. The oozing liquid on my hand was red, but it wasn't blood. It was worse—paint. The floor was streaked with it. Sloppy red strokes left a terrifying message: a symbol in the shape of an ever-watching eye.

The Watchers had already been here. And that could only mean one thing: they had my family.

Boo-dwe-oop!

The sound of the Symbio's incoming call snapped me out of my state of shock. This time I chose *Accept.*

Desi's face appeared as a video stream. At first she looked annoyed, but that quickly switched to concern when she saw the fear in my eyes.

"What happened?" she demanded.

"I…I didn't get here fast enough," I stammered, breathing hard. "I've…lost them."

"Hunter. Listen to me. I'm locking in your location now." A small orange light suddenly appeared at the top of the screen. "Stay out of sight. Stay where you are." Her firm tone made it clear that she wasn't asking. "I'm coming."

The Symbio's screen went dark, all except for the orange dot. For now, I was left alone with my swirling thoughts. Heeding Desi's commands, I dropped low to a corner of the entryway that effectively hid me from any window. The waves of questions washed over me.

Why was the Watcher after my family? Was this really all about Dad? What exactly had he gotten us into? Just thinking of that made my fists begin to tighten; I could feel an overwhelming rage welling up in me.

Wasn't leaving us enough? No. Now he rips apart what little family I still had left by dragging us all into his dangerous dealings. Why couldn't he just leave us alone?

In that moment, I truly hated him for what he'd done, for the pain he'd caused. Yet, as quickly as the raging emotions came, they faded; my hands slowly relaxed.

If what Simon said was true about the Author's Eye of Ends and how Dad had been protecting it, how could I hate him for that? If it were true, then his cruel absence from us was only in a noble attempt to protect us too, from the evil that had now found us. Could I fault him for that? Then again, there was still Mom's side of the story to reconcile. Most of her account certainly didn't make Dad out to be anywhere near noble with the stress, and then neglect, he'd given her…and the family.

Somewhere in the middle of these conflicting portraits of mayhem lay the truth. That was what I needed to find before it was too late for Mom and Emily…and if he still lived, Dad too.

From where I sat on the floor, I felt and heard the approaching footsteps crossing the porch before they ever reached the door. Desi had arrived faster than I expected.

I cautiously stood up, peering through the door's eyehole first to make sure it was her. It wasn't. It was Trista. Her hand was still raised to knock when I whipped the door open.

"You shouldn't be here," I hissed, grabbing her wrist and pulling her inside.

"Ouch! Easy," Trista complained. "I tried calling ahead. I just came over to show you this, to help you remember," she said indignantly, reaching to remove the hand-crafted bow slung over her shoulder. I remembered it all right. It was identical to the bow Hope had used in Solandria, but it didn't matter right now. All that mattered was getting us out alive.

I grabbed her by both shoulders and said, "Forget the bow. I'm in bigger trouble."

I stepped back and directed her to the tiled floor with my paint-smeared hand. Trista's eyes went wide when she finally saw the graffiti. Her gaze went from the floor to my hand, before returning to me.

"Uh…no way José," she said. "If you think I'm going to help you clean up one of *your* messes, you're insane."

"No. Not the paint," I groaned in frustration. "They've kidnapped Mom and Em!"

"They? Kidnapped?"

"The Watchers," I answered urgently, pointing back to the symbol. That's when a shadowy movement in one of the living room windows caught my eye. Whatever it was had moved quickly. No sooner had it disappeared than another dark shape followed it, the passing shape of a bird.

Pushing past Trista, I thrust my head out the front door. From every corner of the sky, ravens were dropping down into my yard, blocking the pathway and filling up every open space around my home.

The drawing was coming to life.

"Oh no," I said in whispered dread. "He's coming back for me."

"Who is? What's going on?" Trista asked nervously, looking out over my shoulder. She gasped loudly when she caught site of all the swarming black birds.

"*Caw! Caw!*" A wave of calls now began spreading throughout the flock; they had seen us.

Grabbing Trista's arm, I wrenched her away from the disturbing spectacle and raced down the hallway for the back door.

"We've got to get out of here!" I shouted, "Now!"

IRON SHARPENS IRON

The *Ghost's* engine whirred to life, leaving an angry flurry of ravens in our wake as Trista and I sped from my house. Thankfully, Vogler was nowhere to be seen…yet. Even so, I couldn't shake the feeling that he would find me soon. After all, he had all the resources of the entire Destiny Police Department at his disposal. By now, every cop in the county would be on high alert, looking for a boy on a conspicuously white bike with rimless tires and neon lights. Though I had the black one now, it still was not exactly your perfect getaway vehicle.

Our only chance of remaining unseen was to stay off the main roads and quickly find a safe place to hide. The Underground was my best hope, but without Simon or Desi to help guide me, I'd never be able to navigate the riddle of train tunnels again.

I tried unsuccessfully to reach Desi on my Symbio device, but nothing seemed to work. Eventually, I gave up and Trista and I settled on Plan B, heading to Rob's house. At the fairgrounds, Rob had told us his family were all Codebearers. We needed allies and we needed them fast. I only hoped that the tracking system was still in place and Desi would be able to find me.

Keeping to back roads and alleyways, we wound our way through town toward the address Rob had scribbled out for Trista earlier that day. We soon came to a street lined with single-story ramblers. Each home looked about the same as the others: beige, brown or grey. The only exception was the home that Rob had identified—the only purple house on the block, and quite possibly the entire town, for that matter.

But the color was only the start of the differences. The garage had been replaced by bay windows and a larger addition to the structure had been made in the backyard as well. The fifteen-passenger van parked in the driveway looked like it was twenty years old or more but had been custom painted with the Author's mark boldly displayed on both sides. As if it weren't loud enough, a wooden carved sign hung over the door that read: *The Way of Truth and Life.*

"You sure this is the place?" I asked jokingly as I pulled the bike up the driveway and around the side of the house to hide it from view. Even before we reached the porch, we could hear the rowdy buzz of activity indoors.

Trista rang the doorbell, but she might as well have poked a stick at a beehive. The commotion inside whipped up into an even greater frenzy than before. With shrieks, squeals and pounding footsteps, an apparent stampede of small elephants raced to be the first to answer the door.

The curtains in the narrow side windows were moved aside by little hands as the deadbolt clicked and the door was tugged open as far as its chain lock would allow. A little girl's face squished into the gap and peered out at us through purple-rimmed glasses. As soon as she saw me, her eyes widened and then narrowed.

"You again!" she exclaimed, none too pleased.

It was the precocious, red-haired girl I'd met at the library this morning. Before I could say a word, the door slammed in my face, followed by a shout.

"Mom, it's that weirdo from the library!" Sabrina shouted.

"Wow," Trista laughed, "should I even ask?"

"No," I said, "but you wouldn't happen to have a dollar on you, would you?"

The mother of the house finally managed to shoo away the barricade of kids and answered the door with a diaper in one hand and a dishtowel in the other. I recognized her at once as the woman from the library—tan, short, curly black hair and a slight Hispanic accent. We introduced ourselves as Rob's friends and she invited us into the chaos with a welcoming smile.

At least a half dozen kids were racing through the house, all of them differing in age and ethnicity. None of them looked like the other, but they all were clearly Bungles. How Rob had ever failed to mention being adopted before was beyond me.

"It's really great to finally meet both of you…properly," Mrs. Bungle said after inviting us inside. She gave me an amused smile, clearly not forgetting our memorable encounter at the library. "Rob hasn't stopped talking about you two all weekend, although I'm sure there's more to tell. I hope you can stay for dinner and we can hear your side of the story."

We graciously accepted the offer though I realized I'd have nothing to share. Perhaps hearing Rob's side of the story would reignite some of my memories.

Mrs. Bungle reached down and scooped up her youngest son: a bashful little guy, clinging to her pantleg and a well-loved blanket.

As soon as he was hoisted up, he tenderly leaned his mop of blond hair against her slender shoulder and melted into her embrace as only a child could. It struck me how, despite their obvious differences, they were unquestionably a family.

"I'd apologize for the mess," Mrs. Bungle continued as she artfully kicked aside one of the many wayward toys obstructing the hallway, "but with the Bungles, what you see is what you get. Come on back. I'll show you to the basement—that's where Rob and his dad are."

As we followed her back past the kitchen and family room, Mrs. Bungle gave us a quick introduction to the other Bungle girls and boys who happily looked up from whatever activity they were engaged in to wave. Sabrina was the only one who didn't smile back, preferring to keep her arms crossed in a bitter reminder of the dollar I owed her.

Having reached the door to the basement, Mrs. Bungle yelled down the stairs, "Rob! I'm sending down visitors!"

She stepped aside and motioned us down the low-ceilinged staircase. "I'd take you down myself," she politely offered, "but some of these trouble-makers just can't be trusted to themselves." As if on cue a skirmish between two of the kids suddenly broke out in the other room. Mrs. Bungle smiled, then dutifully snapped her head around to hurry off in the direction of the trouble, her voice trailing as she went, "No, no, Shane. Mommy said no eating Sarah's crayons!"

Trista and I left the happy chaos behind us and headed down into the much quieter basement. The switchback stairs led us out into a surprisingly large recreation room beneath the house. Blue padded panels covered the typical cement basement floor and walls. Except for a row of supporting posts down the middle, the room was wide open.

Looking through the posts towards the back right corner, we could make out two men dressed in martial art uniforms, slowly circling each other in disciplined stances. One of them was a stocky, but powerfully built Asian man (Mr. Bungle, I assumed), dressed in white; the other, suited up in dark red, was Rob. Both were too engrossed in their lesson to notice us watching from the stairway.

"It is written," Mr. Bungle's impressive voice sounded every bit like the measured, authoritative voice of a real sensei, "*His feet will be swift, his strength will not falter…*" Then, in a blur of unnatural speed, he surged toward Rob who deftly countered the move with his own flourish of speed as he recited, "*…whose mind is fixed on truth,*" completing his father's words.

The elder nodded his head in approval and calmly readied for his next attack. Unleashing a powerful sequence of punches and kicks, he began forcing Rob backwards. "It is written: *Every word of the Code has been given for teaching…*"

Rob met each of his teacher's blows with practiced skill, continuing the recitation, "*…for challenging…*"

"*…for correcting…*" Mr. Bungle added.

"*…for training in the Way of Truth,*" Rob finished.

In defending himself, Rob had not noticed how close to the wall he'd allowed himself to be steered. Mr. Bungle didn't hesitate to take the advantage. With an artful swipe of his hands, he suddenly had both of Rob's wrists locked between his own. Pressing in with his full strength, he attempted to pin Rob against the wall.

"It is written: *As physical training increases strength…*"

I could see Rob's arms giving in under the pressure. He couldn't possibly expect to hold off his dad for long, but Rob wasn't giving up that easily. Determined, Rob dug deeper. "*…so hope remembered…*" he grunted, "*…produces endurance!*" Rob ended with a shout, sending his father sliding backwards by some unseen force.

While evident fatigue was showing in Rob, his dad appeared remarkably unaffected, even energized from their match so far. Mr. Bungle reached for his belt and brandished a Veritas Sword. It was unlike any I'd seen before. The transparent, blue blade of light that flashed to life was long, straight cut and thin, curving slightly back at its chiseled tip. The gold forged hilt was longer as well, its handle wrapped with black leather strips to create a diamond pattern where the gold was exposed. Unlike the winged design on mine, the hand guard on his was a much smaller, flat disc atop which rested an artfully sculpted version of the Author's mark. The three, interconnected *V*s curled around the handle, repeating the design on both sides.

Mr. Bungle assumed an attack stance, calling out to Rob, who was still catching his breath, "It is written: *The sword is made ready for the day of battle…*"

Instead of reaching for his own sword, Rob flung a tired hand out in the direction of his father's, "*…but victory comes by the Author's hand.*" The sword was suddenly wrestled out of Mr. Bungle's grip, flying across the room and into Rob's outstretched hand.

Just like that, the tables had been turned. A cocky smile spread across Rob's face. With renewed resolve he made ready his own attack now.

Ever the picture of calm, Mr. Bungle continued unfazed, "*Consider carefully the path of your feet…*"

"*…and your way will be sure!*" Rob shouted, charging at his unarmed father. "Whoa!"

Before he knew what had happened, Rob was airborne, landing hard on his back. His father caught hold of his sword in midair and in one fluid motion spun it around to point down at his fallen opponent's neck.

"How'd you…?" a bewildered Rob began to ask, looking past the blade to his triumphant father.

Mr. Bungle just smiled and held up the corner of a floor mat that he'd yanked out from under Rob's feet a moment earlier. Rob groaned and let his head fall back to the ground, his dreadlocks splaying out in all directions.

"Excellent sparring, son," Mr. Bungle said, relaxing his stance and returning his sword hilt to his belt. He offered one of his strong hands to Rob. "It is written: *As iron sharpens iron...*"

"Yeah, yeah, *we sharpen each other*. I know," Rob said with a hint of attitude, taking his Dad's hand. "But last I checked iron doesn't bruise like I do." He rubbed at a sore spot on his backside.

Mr. Bungle wrapped a friendly arm around Rob's shoulders and broke into a hearty laugh that Trista and I couldn't resist joining. Hearing our laughter, the dueling Bungles finally noticed their audience.

"Hunter? Trista?" Rob said with surprise. A huge smile spread across his face. He didn't waste any time rushing over to welcome us. "Come on in, you guys! This is great! Dad, these are my new friends I was telling you about."

"It is an honor," Mr. Bungle bowed his head twice in our direction. "I have heard many good things about you both. A friend of the Author is a true friend indeed."

Rob looked to be nearly bursting at the seams with pride over being able to present us to his father.

"It's good to meet you too, Mr. Bungle," Trista said.

"Please. You must call me by my name, Kim."

Of all the names I could have imagined for a tough guy like Rob's dad, the name "Kim" was not even on the list. Kim snapped his attention toward me, his thick crop of black hair springing to follow. "My son tells me how well you fight, Hunter. Would you do me the honor of sparring with me?"

"Maybe another time, Dad. I'm sure they came over for other reasons besides running through drills with us," Rob said.

Kim ignored his son, his piercing coal-black eyes pressing me for my own answer.

"Well, actually, Mr. Bung…I mean, Kim," I began, "my sword has been a little out of whack lately. I'm not sure it'd be a good idea to…."

"May I see it?" Kim asked abruptly.

I wasn't about to say no. "Uh, sure."

I took off my backpack and retrieved my sword hilt, careful not to grab the twisted black one. Kim eagerly accepted the sword from me and gave it a thorough inspection, sighting down its every curve and assessing the balance of its weight.

Gripping the handle firmly in his hand, he commanded the blade to life, swishing it expertly through the air.

"The sword is perfect," Kim proclaimed, releasing the blade and offering the hilt back to me with both hands. His intense gaze locked back on me now. "The trouble you speak of will lie elsewhere." I suddenly got the sense that he was mentally turning me over just as he had done with my weapon, inspecting me down to my very soul, if that were possible.

"Produce your blade," he challenged.

I hesitated, fearing the pain that had come before.

"Yes, sir. I would, but there was actually something else I was hoping you could help us with…."

Kim ignored my attempt to talk my way out of his challenge and narrowed his eyes. He glanced over at the bow Trista still carried slung over her shoulder.

"May I?" he inquired.

Trista looked over at Rob. He shrugged his shoulders and silently motioned with his eyes that she hand it over. Lifting the bowstring over her head, she handed the weapon to Mr. Bungle.

Kim gently plucked the string, invoking a pleasant tone from its vibrations. The effect of the note in my head was anything but pleasant. I winced from the momentary discomfort.

Kim noticed and commanded me once again, "Produce your blade."

I jumped. This time his voice had risen to a level of intensity he had not even approached while sparring with Rob. Kim raised the bow and pulled the string back taut, his penetrating eyes still boring into me. I gulped, uncertain of what he intended to do if I failed to follow his order. Breathing deeply, I tightened my grip and tried to draw upon the code I had found so much strength from before: *By fear a man appoints his master,* I repeated to myself.

In that instant an explosion of mind-numbing pain blasted inside my head once again. I dropped my sword and fell to my knees, screaming in agony as more confusing images fired through my brain.

I was aware of Trista and Rob racing to my aid, but Kim shouted for them to stand back before yelling, "*By Truth the Way will be made clear!*"

I looked up through my pain just in time to see Mr. Bungle, bow drawn with its fiery arrow of light pointed straight at my head. There was nothing I could do to stop him. He let go of the string. A streak of light pierced my skull and everything around me disappeared into a brilliant white.

The flash had only lasted a moment, but amazingly, despite being shot point blank, I felt no pain when at last my vision returned. In fact, the excruciating pain felt moments before the shot was fired was completely gone now. In its place was a remarkable flood of memories, rushing back to me in one massive wave. Suddenly, I could remember everything from the fair. I could remember escaping to Solandria in the flying gondola, even the school fire. Every lost and fragmented memory was filing back into place. Finally, things were making perfect sense again…as much as the strange and sometimes inexplicable truth of my post-Solandria life ever could.

"Ew! What is that thing?" Trista shrieked, backing away from me in terror. From the look on his face, Rob's infamous weak stomach was about to make a comeback.

I whipped around and saw what they had found so repulsive: the writhing form of some kind of slimy, oversized centipede. A smoldering hole had been shot through its body. The splattered trail of some of its gooey innards left a streak across the floor.

"That," Mr. Bungle said factually, "was your problem, Hunter. A Quell. It is a Shadow parasite that blocks all recent memory of truth."

This squirming thing had somehow been living inside my head? I felt nauseated, watching its countless legs grope about for its missing host, knowing they were once comfortably wrapped around my brain before Kim's arrow severed their hold. Looking me straight in the eyes, Kim nodded to the disgusting Quell.

"Produce your blade," he said once again in a much friendlier tone.

Needless to say, I didn't hesitate to follow his orders this time. The powerful blade of light coursed effortlessly from my sword and finished off the revolting creature's struggle. Trista was the first to speak up.

"Ohhh-kay. That was just about *the* grossest thing I've ever seen." She shuddered, looking back at my head. "You didn't drink lake water or something, did you?"

"What? No!" I said in protest. "I don't know how it got there, but everything about our mission—I remember it now! The Quell must have been what was blocking my memory and preventing me from using the sword."

"It is true," Mr. Bungle said. "Quell can cause serious problems such as these."

"Man that sucker was big!" Rob said, "I didn't know they could get that size."

"What do you mean?" Trista asked.

"The Writ describes them as being super small—almost germ-like. There are probably millions of them between the four of us here."

Trista looked horrified. Seeing Trista's reaction, he quickly qualified, "Sure, we all contract them, but they can't live very long in anyone who regularly uses the Code of Life. It's like a pesticide with them—kills them off while they're young. You'll be fine."

"So, how do you explain Quell-zilla?" Trista asked skeptically.

"The Black-Eyes," I answered.

The others looked over at me curiously.

"After the fire, when the ambulance took me," I continued, re-living the moment aloud for the first time, "those emergency work-ers who took me weren't real. I saw their eyes—they were black. I mean all black. They had to be Shadow. I don't know where they took me, but it wasn't the hospital. They were talking about a cham-ber, saying they found 'another one' and then…."

"What?" Trista asked breathlessly.

"And then I don't know. They drugged me with something."

"All of that so they could feed your brain to the giant Quell?" Rob asked. "I don't get it."

"Nor do I," Rob's dad said, his brows furrowed in deep thought. "It is no secret that the Shadow are a constant threat to our ways, but I do not consider them as a likely source for this terror. Their methods in the Veil have always been ones of stealth. This type of aggressive assault is too risky, more likely pointing to someone else."

"Someone else like who?" Rob asked.

Trista caught my eye with a knowing look and said, "Tell them about the Watchers and your family."

I took a deep breath. There was so much to tell, but I touched on the highpoints, briefly explaining my encounters with Vogler, his association with the Watchers, and the background Simon and Desi had provided about my missing father being a target.

"And now..." I choked up, "the Watcher, Vogler...he's taken the rest of my family. He's after me too."

Kim sighed. My story had hit a soft spot in his heart and he looked as if he might tear up.

"Family is one of the greatest gifts a man can have. Please, allow us to do all we can to help you in recovering them. You are welcome to stay with us here until your family is found. Have you notified the police of your trouble?"

"No!" I almost shouted. "I mean...you can't. Not the police. They're in on this somehow."

Kim shot a curious glance at me.

"There have been many myths and speculation surrounding the Watchers," Kim said. "While the Writ does confirm the existence of these beings, there is little that is known for certain to validate what you have been told. I would caution against drawing conclusions too soon. The truth will always set you free."

"They took my family tonight!" I almost yelled. "I'm lucky they didn't nab me and Trista too. There's no arguing with that, is there?"

"No," Kim said reservedly, "I suppose not."

The discussion was interrupted when the doorbell rang once more. The commotion upstairs ended in a hush as Sabrina shouted loud enough for all of us to hear—even in the basement.

"Mom, that big, scary black man from the library is at the front door."

"Vogler!" Trista and I said in unison.

Somehow he had managed to find us. There was no escaping this man.

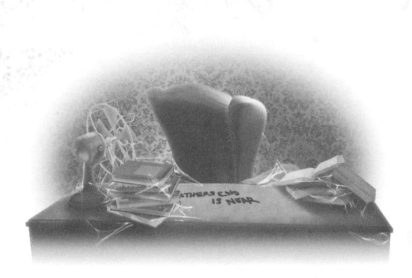

CHAPTER 13

BACK TO THE BOOKSHOP

With each heavy footstep overhead, my heart pounded even louder. Vogler was now inside the house and he wasn't here for supper.

"Dad, what do we do?" Rob asked, looking physically sick.

"Try not to jump to conclusions, kids," Rob's father said. "Confusion will only serve the enemy. We must focus only on what we know. The Author is with us, we have nothing to fear."

His reassurance was cut short by a shriek from upstairs and the shattering of glass. Mrs. Bungle screamed out, "Sabrina, no!"

Kim tried his best to maintain his composure, but his face was an open book. He was worried. His hand moved for his sword.

"Now can we be frightened?" Rob asked.

"Concerned, not frightened," Kim corrected his son. "There is a difference."

Difference or not, there was no avoiding the fact that the threat was real, present and very dangerous. The commotion continued.

"You three stay put while I see what must be done."

Kim darted up into the fray, leaving us alone in the basement to listen and wonder. None of us dared speak.

"Oh no, you don't! This is *my* house," I heard Kim shout at one point, followed by more destruction.

"I've never heard him that mad before," Rob whimpered.

Tap, tap, tap!

The basement window rattled behind us. All three of us jumped at the sound and spun around, expecting Vogler to be there. It was Desi. She had crawled into the window well and was pointing at the latch. Once I explained who she was, Rob unlocked the window and pushed it open.

"This way," Desi whispered. "Hurry!"

I started climbing out, but something caught me by the foot. It was Trista.

"What are you doing?" she asked, pulling at my shoe.

"Escaping," I answered. "It's me he's after. I never should have brought you two into this. It's only causing more trouble."

"Yeah, well, I'm not safe either, not now," Trista said, looking as if she were going to cry. "You can't leave me here!"

She was right. Like it or not, the damage had been done. She and Rob were guilty by association.

"Come with me," I said, reaching a hand out to her. She took it and the two of us slid our way out of the narrow window and onto the lawn. Rob was still left behind.

"You coming?" I called back. He froze, not with fear but determination.

"No, I've got a family to help," he answered. "Go find yours. I'll latch the window from inside to buy you more time."

I nodded my thanks as the window shut between us. Already I could see shadows moving in the stairway behind him. Someone was coming down.

"Follow me," Desi said, mounting her white *Ghost* and firing up the engine. Trista and I ran for the black one and did the same. It was starting to rain outside, and the seat was wet.

Bweeeeeeeeeee!

With a squeal Desi's bike zipped around the house, down the driveway and into the road. We were only six seconds behind, but it was just enough time for Vogler to jump over the front porch railing, run across the lawn and step out into the driveway directly in our path. It was a bold move, but at the speed we were travelling there was no way I was going to stop.

"Hunter, No!" Trista screamed as we neared the inevitable collision with the man.

With the flick of a switch, the bike disappeared and passed through Vogler like water through a hole. Twenty feet later we reappeared in the middle of the road, a little farther than I had planned. There wasn't enough time to adjust for the distance—I hit the curb hard. A cluster of mailboxes skimmed past my left shoulder as the *Ghost* lurched onto the sidewalk and into the neighbor's pristinely kept front lawn. Regaining control, I turned hard right and dug a trench in the moist lawn on the way to the street.

Vogler looked a bit surprised, but quickly recovered and dashed to his black SUV. It couldn't *ghost*, but with the flick of a switch he had other special powers: a Hemi engine, flashing lights and blaring sirens to clear the way.

With Vogler closing the gap, we sped up alongside Desi.

"What's the plan now?" I shouted between us.

"There is none," she answered with a bit more honesty than I had hoped for. "Just try and lose him, anyway we can."

"Oh, is that all," I replied.

"Just follow me, and try to keep up," she said. Leaning forward, she upped the throttle and surged ahead. I swallowed hard and did the same. Trista tightened her grip around my waist.

"I hope you know what you're doing!" she yelled.

So do I, I muttered to myself.

Despite our head start, it didn't take long for Vogler to catch up. What started as a speed race quickly turned into one of agility as we zig-zagged through a maze of streets and alleyways in hopes of shaking him. It didn't work—the man was unshakeable. That's when things got interesting.

In a desperate move, Desi zipped up an off ramp from the freeway heading against the flow of traffic. Before I even had time to process what we had just done, I followed; surprisingly Vogler did as well. At first, Desi kept to the shoulder of the freeway, allowing the rush of oncoming cars to stay to our right. It was well past rush hour and traffic was lighter than normal, but that hardly seemed to matter when driving against it. Everything moved twice as fast. An endless stream of headlights blurred past, adding a "warp speed" effect to the whole experience. That's when Desi did the unthinkable; she pulled off the shoulder and *ghosted* into the heart of traffic.

"She's insane!" I said, shaking my head.

"And yet, you're following her. Look out!" Trista screamed, as a car skidded out of control right toward us. I turned out into the rush of traffic to avoid being hit, but quickly regretted the move. Cars were skidding out left and right as we dodged the oncoming traffic. More than a dozen times we *ghosted* through vehicles to avoid collisions. Two exits up we pulled off the freeway; unbelievably, Vogler did as well. The chase continued back to the streets of Destiny.

"Why don't we just *ghost* through one of the buildings?" I asked Desi when it was safe to pull alongside her again.

"Because we don't know what's on the other side," she answered. "*Ghosting* isn't just for fun. You have to be smart about it."

Could have fooled me, I muttered to myself, remembering the pile-up we had just left on the freeway.

Still, her explanation gave me an idea. Pulling ahead I led the chase to Destiny Hills High School. We zipped across the parking lot, over a curb and headed straight for the gym doors. It was after hours on a Monday night; there wouldn't be any events inside and we could use the school grounds as cover.

We *ghosted* into the gym, slowed to a stop and waited to see what Vogler's next move might be. It also bought us valuable time to talk for a moment.

"He's not going to give up that easily," Desi warned. "He'll loop around and watch for us to exit."

"Yes, but he can't be on both sides of the school at once," I answered. "We can sneak out undetected when he's on the opposite side."

"That hasn't stopped him from finding you before," Trista noted.

"The girl's right," Desi added, ignoring the fact that Trista looked insulted by the title. "You can't hide from Vogler, not in Destiny anyway. What we need is to find your father, and we need to go to Solandria. Do you know how to get there, Hunter?"

I shrugged my shoulders.

"Not really," I answered. "It's always just sort of found me."

"Well, you better sort of find a way soon because Vogler isn't going to wait for you to get an invitation," Desi prodded.

Is that even possible? I wondered to myself. *To find your own way into Solandria?* So far, I had just happened upon it through the Author's Writ and the falling Sky Car. The only problem was that my Author's Writ was at home, and home wasn't exactly the safest place right now. It was probably crawling with cops, investigating the disappearance of my family. Cutting another gondola off the Sky Car ride didn't seem like the best way to get to Solandria either.

That's when it hit me. "The bookshop!" I said.

Desi and Trista just stared blankly at me.

"One of Dad's images was of a clock, one almost identical to the clock in a bookshop downtown," I explained. "The last time I was there the back door led into Solandria."

"It's our best lead so far. So, where is this bookshop?" Desi asked.

"That's the trick," I answered. "Sometimes it's there and other times it's not."

"How is that supposed to help us?" Trista asked.

I told them about how the bookshop had seemed to disappear from between two stores and that I hadn't seen it since.

"It beats sitting around here," Desi decided, firing up her engine.

When the coast was clear we ghosted through the doors again and headed downtown. Vogler was gone. By the time we reached 1421 Lathrop Avenue, the rain had stopped, but the bookshop was nowhere to be found.

"Where did you say the bookstore was again?" Desi asked.

"Right there, between the two stores…only it was wider," I explained. The sewing store and hardware store appeared to have been pinched together over the place where the bookshop had once been. Between the two, a solid brick wall no wider than your average door remained.

"Now what?" Trista wondered.

A sickly moan drew our attention to a bus stop less than a dozen feet away, where a bedraggled old man sat up from the bench. He had been awakened by our arrival but seemed oblivious to our presence. In his hand he held an empty glass bottle, which he lifted to his lips and grumbled at. Though it had nothing left to offer, he still eyed it longingly and muttered to it, unaware that he was not alone. His entire universe centered on that single empty bottle.

Sensing the man was not a threat, Desi dismounted her *Ghost* and walked up to the wall. She felt it with her hand; then wandered to both sides of it, glancing through the shop windows. She scratched her head and looked my way.

"There's unused space here," she observed, pointing to the brick wall. Not much, but more than enough." A mischievous smile swept across her face, and her brown eyes sparkled. "I've got an idea."

Walking her bike to the center of the street, she turned it so it directly faced the brick wall between stores. Then, removing her Symbio device, she attached it to the front of the bike and stood beside it. After a few measured glances between the bike and the wall, Desi flipped the *ghost* button and the white bike disappeared.

Despite the thickness of the brick wall, there was a loud clatter from the other side, the sound of something large toppling in the missing space. The bike had made it through…almost. The final inch of the rear wheel jutted out from the brick wall, still visible.

"Oops!" Desi said with a frown.

The sound of shattered glass turned our attention to the man on the bench again. He was standing now, staring slack-jawed toward Desi. At his feet the remainder of his empty bottle lay in pieces. He rubbed his eyes and gawked back at the place the bike had once been, clearly disturbed by what he had seen. It must have been worse than seeing pink elephants!

Undeterred, Desi hurried back to where Trista and I sat on our bike. "Give me your arm," she demanded, grabbing it before I could ask why. She brought up a digital keypad on the Symbio I was wearing.

"Let's take a little peek inside, shall we?" she said as a video link streamed onto my device from the other side of the wall. The image was a little hazy, a room dimmed by a curtain of swirling dust. Like a remote submarine camera in a deep-sea exploration, the beaming headlamps of the *Ghost* were the only light piercing the darkened dust of the room. As the dust settled and the image cleared, I recognized the space immediately.

"That's it!" I shouted. "Aviad's book shop!"

The place was there, but a mere skeleton of what it once was. The few bookshelves I could see were empty, stripped naked of the books that once graced their shelves. From the looks of things it hadn't been used for quite some time. Despite being abandoned, it was still larger than the wall outside allowed for. I didn't know how, but I knew that the Author's magic was at work.

"It's empty," I said sadly. "I don't understand."

"We're going in," Desi stated, dropping my arm. "It's as safe a place as any and there might still be a way to Solandria in there. Scoot back."

It wasn't a request, she was in a hurry. Desi straddled the black *Ghost* in front of me, taking over command of the bike. Two bodies on the bike were tight, three were downright awkward. My backpack made the whole thing even more difficult to pull off. Struggling to keep the bike balanced, Desi drove us out to the center of the road and then moved forward a full bikes' length to ensure we didn't collide with the other *Ghost*. She aimed for the same spot in the wall where the previous bike had passed through.

"Wait! Are we sure there's enough room in there?" I asked.

"You tell me, Hunter. I've never been there."

I gauged the space mentally and decided that we were okay, but barely.

"Hold on, everyone," Desi said.

Desi tightened her grip on the bike; I held tightly to Desi and Trista clung to my backpack like her life depended on it.

Our sole spectator, the man at the bus stop, watched intently at our odd attempt to share the bike. I gave a quick wave. He raised a hand in acknowledgement. Desi flipped the switch and we vanished from the street, leaving the man to ponder if he should finally give up the bottle.

On the other side of the wall, things were worse than they had looked on the video screen. Our arrival was rough, toppling another bookshelf and causing Trista to fall off the cycle, taking me with her. When the dust finally settled, we removed our helmets and stood up. The air was stale and chalky, with the smell of a room that had not been cleaned in ages.

The front desk was plastered with expired event papers, just like the first time I had visited. The ancient cash register and service bell were still there, but the rest of the room was a tomb—lifeless and cold.

"Aviad's clock is missing," I noticed, pointing to a darkened silhouette on the wall where it once had stood. Sunlight had faded the wallpaper around it, leaving the subtle shape of the grandfather clock on the wall, much like a chalk outline at a murder scene.

I was shocked to find the front door and window on the wall we had just passed through. The window looked out over Lathrop Street and the grubby old man who stood in the middle of the road, examining the place where we had disappeared. It was a surreal feeling to be able to see him through a window we knew didn't exist from the other side.

"What a mess," Trista said, shuffling across the dusty floor. "How long ago did you say you were last here?"

"Four months ago, at the start of summer," I confessed.

"How could it possibly be this dirty already? It looks like it hasn't been touched in over a hundred years."

She was right.

"So, where's this back door to Solandria?" Desi asked.

"In the office," I answered, pointing to the room ahead of us.

"Why don't you and the girl check it out. I'll get the other Symbio," Desi said.

"The girl has a name, you know," Trista asserted. "It's Trista."

"Sorry, I'm Desi. But can't we finish introductions later? We are in kind of a hurry." Trista nodded, though I sensed the two were getting off on the wrong foot.

"Come on, Triss," I said, using the nickname only her friends called her. I grabbed her by the hand and ushered her into the back room.

Aviad's office wasn't in much better shape than the front room. The burgundy chair where he once had sat was turned away from us on the opposite side of the desk so that all we could see was the high back. Despite the dust and cobwebs, I half expected the chair to spin around as it had before, to reveal Aviad smiling broadly. It didn't.

We moved down the hallway to the door at the end, where the once illuminated emergency exit sign was no longer lit. I put my hand against the push-bar of the back door and shoved hard. The door wouldn't budge. Trista and I both tried together, but still the door held shut.

"It's no good," I said. "It's locked."

"What now?" Trista asked.

I shrugged my shoulders, "Maybe there's a key in Aviad's desk."

We made our way back up the hall to Aviad's office to scour his desk for the key, but an object sitting in the dusty chair cut our hunt short. It was a book, an Author's Writ, leaning upright between the seat and the chair back.

"The Author's Writ!" I shouted excitedly, scooping it up. "It's our way out!"

Like my own, this Writ was made of soft leather, but black where mine was brown. It shared all of the same markings as my own. I flipped the book over and examined the Living Tree in the center of the design. As always, a dozen symbols etched themselves into the book around the circle. They were familiar, but the symbols were not the same as the ones on my Writ.

"That's odd," Trista said.

"I know, the symbols are different," I said. "I think I've seen them before though, in one of my father's drawings."

"That's not what I meant…it's the book itself. Why isn't it dusty like the rest of the room?"

Until she mentioned it, I hadn't noticed. Sure enough, there wasn't a single speck of dust on the book, other than on the few edges that had been touching the dusty chair.

"Do you think somebody put it here?" Trista asked.

"I don't know how…unless…."

"Hunter, look!" Trista gasped in fright. She was pointing at Aviad's desktop where five words had been fingered into the dust:

Your Father's End Is Near

The words burned in my soul like an angry fire. Somebody had been here, someone who was no friend of my father's. But who? And how did he know I would be here to read this message? Furthermore, how did he get in here? I looked across the floor, but there were no footprints in the dust other than our own. Whoever had come had been careful to erase his footprints.

"Look on the bright side, Hunter," Trista observed. "At least it means your father IS alive…at least for the moment."

I marveled at Trista's ability to remain upbeat in dreary situations. Leave it to Trista, the "glass-is-half-full" girl, to figure out there was hope hidden in the ominous message. She was absolutely right; if the message was true, my father wasn't dead yet. If I had anything to say about it, whoever was after him would never have the chance to follow up on his threat.

"Any luck with the exit?" Desi called from the front room. Her voice sounded strained. We headed out to see if everything was okay. Desi was lying on a board, which she had placed over a black puddle of oil on the floor beneath the black *Ghost*. Her hands and fingers were coated in the black liquid and smears of it were wiped across her cheek and forehead as well.

"What happened?" I asked.

"One of the boards from the bookshelf punctured the oil pan. I think I've managed to plug it with a pencil eraser." She held up a greasy pencil, minus the rubber end, with a proud grin. "Trouble is, the *Ghost* won't get far without repairs."

She stood up and cleaned her hands on her bandana.

"So, do we have an exit?" she repeated.

We explained how the door was locked, about the Author's Writ and the message in the dust.

"Do you think Vogler could have done it?" I asked.

"Maybe, but why would he leave you the Author's Writ? You said you've seen these symbols before?" Desi asked.

"Yes, in one of my father's drawings, but I'd need to go back to the Underground to see them."

"No, you don't," Desi said. "I've uploaded them into your Symbio so you can access them whenever you want. Come here." She sat sideways on the bicycle and patted the seat beside her. I joined her on the bike and Desi leaned in closely so that we could share the screen on my wrist. Desi took her time showing me the basics of how to use the device before pulling up the pictures on the screen. I could see Trista tense as Desi held my arm in her own.

"I don't feel safe here; we should get going," Trista tried to interrupt as Desi continued to lean in closer.

"Nowhere is safe, Triss," Desi replied. The nickname didn't sit well with Trista this time, not coming from Desi. "Besides, we can't go anywhere until we fix the bike. We need to find a way to Solandria."

Trista rolled her eyes and pretended to look around the room. But her gaze kept returning to me and Desi, sitting far too close for her comfort. Once Desi found Dad's most recent drawings, I quickly identified the one of Aviad's clock. Sure enough, the symbols were identical to those on the book.

"But what does it mean?" I wondered.

"Well, your dad must have seen the symbols. Maybe he left that drawing as a clue to where he was. It might mean we're on the right track."

I pondered the idea. She could be right. What if my dad was leaving clues in his drawings? Maybe all of them were clues that would lead to his location.

"But why wouldn't he just draw the symbols in the picture on the Writ instead of a clock?"

"I don't know," Desi answered. "Maybe because the book could have been anywhere. Maybe he knew that if we saw it on the clock we'd come here."

"Uh, guys," Trista interrupted, "there's something going on outside I think you should see. I think we're being watched."

Desi and I looked out the front window. The dingy man who had been examining the spot where we had vanished was still there, scratching his head at the mystery of it all. He kept looking between the place on the ground and then back at the wall where the bike tire protruded from the wall.

"He's harmless, Triss," I said. "He can't see us either."

"Not, him!" she said forcefully. "THEM!"

She pointed further across the street where there was movement in the shadows on the sidewalk. I squinted, attempting to make out the form of the movement. It wasn't until another shape joined the others that I realized what it was. Ravens.

Hundreds of the black birds lined the sidewalk across the street and perched on the telephone wires. The birds were hopping around on the sidewalk, gathering in droves. But what happened next made even Desi's usually unshakable confidence fade. The birds took to the air and began to circle like vultures in the center of the road around the old man. He swung at the sky, likely thinking it was another of his hallucinations and then he fell to the ground and crawled away from them. The swarm of birds didn't follow the man. Instead, they continued to gather until there were so many circling in the road they looked like a black tornado of wings had touched down in Destiny.

The gathering of birds flocked together so closely they soon became indiscernible from each other. Then, the movement stopped. The birds had become a singular figure. The birds became…Vogler.

CHAPTER 14

A BAD SEED

Vogler could see us, of that I was certain. Even though the window was not visible from the outside, his mirrored glasses seemed to allowed him to see what others couldn't. The cold chills returned and I trembled at the thought of facing him yet again.

Desi didn't waste a moment. No sooner had Vogler formed than she jumped into action. Running to the white *Ghost*, still stuck in the wall, she opened a compartment on the side of it and retrieved two rods. With one rod in each hand, she moved to the door.

"You two, take the bike out the back," Desi commanded.

"But what abou…?" I started to ask.

"It's no good if you're captured, now go!"

"But you'll be killed."

"I can handle myself. Just go!" Desi shouted.

Trista wasted no time following orders. Pulling her bowstring over her shoulder, she took a seat on the back of the cycle and waited for me to drive. I hesitated a moment longer.

Desi closed her eyes and gripped tightly to the two black rods, which lit up at the tips, one orange and one blue. She moved the rods through the air, streaming a trail of light behind each tip like sparklers on the Fourth of July. When she finished her motion, the tails of light did not disappear. Instead, they remained attached to the rods, hanging from the tips like electric whips; orange—long, blue—short. Armed and ready, she set her sights on Vogler, waiting for his first move.

With a bone-shattering yell, Vogler stormed the door, leading with his right shoulder, his gun drawn.

"Hurry, Hunter!" Trista shouted. "He's coming!"

"Go!" Desi shouted again.

This time I obeyed, jumping onto the cycle and firing up the black *Ghost* with an electric whir.

Bweeeeeeeeeeee-cacha-cacha!

The *Ghost* sputtered and choked black smoke into the room before the engine died. This was not good!

Blam!

Vogler slammed into the door, knocking it down like a lineman tackling a child.

"Everybody freeze!" Vogler yelled. Desi was already frozen, standing her ground between Vogler and us.

"You cannot have him," Desi said calmly. "He's with us."

Vogler pointed his silver revolver straight at Desi's head and replied, "There's no way I'm going to let that happen."

Pulling the trigger, a gleaming purple bullet fired its way toward Desi's skull. With her right hand she spun her short blue whip around, creating a protective circle of light, which shielded her from the bullet. At the same moment, she lashed out with the orange whip in an aggressive attack, which Vogler barely evaded. The whip connected with the wall, tearing through it like a knife through butter.

"You're a bad seed, Desi, one I intend to eradicate." Vogler launched himself up overhead and spun around, firing three consecutive rounds at Desi. She deflected the first two with her blue whip and dodged the third by diving to the side. Vogler landed in front of me and would have grabbed my arm if Desi hadn't yelled out, "Duck!"

A flashing line of orange light streamed narrowly overhead, as Trista and I ducked low to the bike. Vogler scrambled backward to avoid being caught by the deadly whip.

"Get out, now!" Desi screamed.

I tried firing up the engine again.

Bweeeee-cacha-cacha! Bweeeeeee!

More black smoke puffed into the air, as the engine struggled to life. The room was beginning to get dark with the fumes. The bike lurched forward toward Aviad's office, but before we could make it out, a bookshelf landed in front of the door between rooms, blocking our escape. With no time to stop, the bike smashed into the shelf and started sputtering again. In the collision, the eraser that Desi had lodged in the oil pan fell loose and we started draining more oil.

"You're not going anywhere!" an enraged Vogler yelled. He had single-handedly thrown the shelf in front of us, blocking our only exit. Desi quickly retaliated, occupying Vogler with a new string of attacks. There wasn't enough room to *ghost* into the next room. We needed to move the shelf.

"You drive!" I shouted at Trista. "I'll clear the way."

Trista nodded and took the handlebars of the bike for the first time. I hopped off the bike and grabbed my Veritas Sword. *"The*

Way of truth will be made clear," I whispered, dwelling on the Code of Life. My Veritas blade gleamed into action as I swung it down across the shelf ahead, severing it in two. The shelving fell apart, allowing Trista to pull the throttle and push through to the other side. I ran after her and jumped onto the back of the bike.

Covering Trista's hands with my own, I turned the bike toward the emergency exit and prepared to *ghost* through it. Before we left, I paused a moment to watch the last of the fight unfold.

I caught a brief glimpse of the struggle between Vogler and Desi through the door between the rooms. The fight had intensified in the last minutes. Flashes of purple and strings of orange and blue lit up the room like fireworks. But when Desi caught a bullet in the foot and fell to the ground, the colorful display came to a sudden end. Vogler raised his revolver at her head and was about to deal his fatal blow. Desi caught my eye and slid her orange whip across the floor, igniting the oil spill beside her in a fiery explosion.

"Noooooooooo!" I shouted, watching Desi and Vogler vanish in the flames. I wanted to stay and see if I could help her, but the trail of oil we had left behind was burning its way to our bike like a snake.

I cranked the throttle and aimed for the exit. The fire was right behind us when I flicked the *ghosting* switch and we felt the pull of the sputtering cycle leap forward. If we were lucky we would make it through the door, but where we would end up was anyone's guess.

CHAPTER 15

MIDDLE OF NOWHERE

The other side of the bookshop door was anything but an escape. With a jolt, our *Ghost* came to an abrupt stop, tossing us over the handlebars onto a searing white sand scape.

The transition from darkness to radiant light was blinding. A full minute passed before I could even think of opening my eyes to face its brilliance. When I did, it wasn't a welcome sight. The mid-day sun reflected off the powder-white sand beneath us in a way that made us feel as if we were words on a blank page. In some ways, perhaps we were. The horizon seemed to be a long way off, if there was one at all.

With the *Ghost* out of oil and lodged in the sand, we were on our own to find shelter from the sun. It was hot…too hot. If we didn't find help soon, we'd become food for whatever creatures lived in this desolate wasteland—if anything could live out here.

"Where do we go?" Trista asked, pulling her sweater off and tying it over her head like a scarf.

Scanning the horizon, I spotted a grey rock formation—cliffs of some kind that seemed within a reasonable walking distance. With any luck we would find some relief, however slight, from the heat of the day. We set off in their direction. Already, I could feel my skin burning. It wouldn't take long before my brain was fried too.

Step by step we inched our way through the sand. The cliffs were nearly twice as far away as we had imagined them to be. A full hour later we reached them, desperate for shelter from the unforgiving sun. I spotted a small cave nestled midway up the side of the cliff that looked deep enough to hold us both, if we could make it up the cliffside.

Despite the odds, we struggled up the steep embankment to the ledge of the cave, pulling ourselves in and collapsing in an exhausted heap. It was a small cave, not big enough to stand up in, but deep and relatively cool. The relief was slight, but welcome. We caught our breath and rested.

"Now what?" Trista sighed after a long moment of silence.

"I have no idea," I answered honestly. "I'm too exhausted to think."

"Me too. What I wouldn't give to be sniffed by a big ol' smelly Scampa right about now," Trista joked, recalling our previous entrance to Solandria.

"Yeah, where are the Thordin brothers when you need them?" I chuckled. "Ven and Zven. What a pair they were, huh?"

Trista smiled fondly at the memory and then, in the best Thordin brother accent she could muster, added, "Don't cha believe none of my brother about being first to find you three," she said, fighting a smile as she spoke. "Twas Godee, my Scampa, that nosed the lot of you first!"

The two of us laughed uncontrollably for a moment at her goofy impression of the two men who had rescued us from the snowbanks.

"You know," I said jokingly, "you sounded just like them. You sure you aren't related? You might even look good in a beard."

"Hey!" Trista complained, slapping me almost immediately in a playful attempt to pretend she was upset. "Watch it, buck-o."

I grabbed her hand to keep her from slapping me again, but didn't let go after she stopped trying. Lying there in the cave on our backs, holding hands, I felt closer to Trista than I had in a long time.

Maybe it was the heat exhaustion; maybe it was part fear of the unknown. Whatever it was, it felt good to be with her again. It was good to remember again. The shared experience we had in Solandria had drawn Trista and me closer to each other, and to the Author.

"Sorry about Desi," Trista said finally, bringing us back to reality. My heart sank a little at the thought of having lost her. Somehow, despite what I saw, I held out hope that maybe she had survived. I let go of Trista's hand.

"Did you like her?" Trista asked.

"What do you mean?" I asked. "Of course I liked her. Why wouldn't I? She was trying to help me…to help us."

"I know, I just…." Trista considered venturing further, but thought better of it. "Never mind."

"What?"

"It's nothing, really," she answered.

Ugh, girls. I thought. *Why can't they just come out and say what they mean?*

"You can't leave me hanging like that," I ventured.

"I dunno; it's complicated, I guess," Trista continued. "I don't want you to think bad of me but, in a weird way...I'm glad she's not with us right now."

"Trista!" I said, feeling suddenly defensive and slightly angry. "How can you say that!"

"I know, I know! See, I told you it was complicated. I don't want her to be dead or anything, I just didn't feel comfortable around her. That's all. She was just controlling and...."

I shook my head. *I can't believe you're jealous*, I thought.

"I'm not jealous," Trista answered my thoughts. "I'm just... protective."

I eyed her suspiciously. Was she even aware of what she was doing? How could she possibly be hearing my thoughts? I quickly decided to change the subject to the situation at hand.

"You want to try and figure out where we are?" I asked, pulling the Author's Writ from my backpack.

"Why not," Trista replied.

I opened the Writ in hopes of locating the holographic map, the one Sam had shown me in the Revealing Room during my first visit to Solandria. The book opened easily but no words appeared on its pages. The book was blank. Once again, I had forgotten my key; without it the book was useless to us. I was about to put the book away when Trista noticed something inside it. There were markings on one of the pages, handwritten notes and randomly drawn circles and lines. Whoever had owned this book had marked things in it, points of reference.

"Listen to this," Trista said, reading one of the notes from the edge of the page. "It says, *The best way to see the future is to make it. Know your end, and the true Author will be revealed.* What does that even mean, 'true Author'?"

"Beats me, I thought there was only one Author," I said.

"Here's another one," Trista continued. "*The circle of seven await fire from heaven.* Mysterious, don't you think? Do you think it has something to do with the Consuming Fire?"

"Could be. The Seven are already marked though; you're one of them, remember?"

Trista nodded, fingering the place on her collar bone where the mark of the three-tongued flame had been made. Surprisingly, it was there again, visible for both of us to see.

"I don't get it," Trista said. "How come you can see it now?"

"Maybe when when we're in Destiny it's hidden," I reasoned. The logic sounded good to me. Trista seemed to agree as well and continued scanning the markings on the page.

"This last one is just a bunch of gibberish; I can't even pronounce it. No vowels." She slid the book between us and pointed to a place on the page where the markings had been made. The random sequence of letters was written above five vertical lines.

RNWWTW WNR
|||||

I wasn't as interested in the note itself as much as I was curious at what Trista had just said about it; no vowels. It was the same observation Simon had made about the letters my dad had written on his final drawings. Could there be a connection?

"What?" Trista asked, noting the curious look that had crept across my face.

"It's just interesting," I explained. "My father wrote a message like this on one of his drawings."

"He did?" Trista asked, wondering why anyone would write such nonsense. "In what language?"

That's when it hit me. It wasn't a language at all. It was a code— a cipher actually. My father loved them almost as much as I did. He had taught me many of them: writing in reverse like DaVinci, using letter substitutions, anagrams and binary coding too. As a kid I had thought they were good fun. We often left secret messages for each other to decipher. It was something of a game between us at the time. It had been a long time, but I was willing to bet the message was a cipher.

"Caesar's cipher!" I exclaimed.

"Excuse me?" Trista asked, having trouble keeping up.

"It's a coding system where letters are replaced with other characters in the alphabet. Here let me show you."

With my hand I brushed the thin layer of sand that blanketed the rock floor evenly across the stone to make a clean slate to write on.

"If I wanted to say 'hi' to someone using a Caesar's cipher, I'd replace each of the letters with another letter a few characters forward. Let's just say we agreed to use a three letter shift. In this case, HI would become KL. See?"

I wrote the word in the sand, then the coded word below it.

H I
K L

"But how do you choose how many letters to skip?" Trista questioned.

"Usually you decide ahead of time," I answered, "but in this case I think whoever wrote this left a message in another kind of code below it."

"You mean, those scratches below it are a code too?" Trista asked, looking at the five vertical lines.

"Numbers actually. Five 1s."

Trista's eyes widened, "So, whoever wrote this message wanted us to rotate the letters five times."

"No," I added, "They aren't tick marks, they're binary."

Trista gave me the look of someone who had just heard a foreign language. "Bi-what?" she asked.

"It's a numbering system that only uses 1s and 0s. Digital devices use it to calculate all kinds of information. It's actually not that much different from the numbering system we normally use…once you get to know it."

"I'm not sure I want to know it," Trista answered.

"Sure you do, it's cool," I said.

Trista shrugged her shoulders as if to say, "If you say so." I took it as her approval for me to continue.

"Our numbering system is based on tens. We call it the decimal system. That just means we have ten numbers that we use to count with: one through nine, plus zero."

Trista nodded, keeping up with me so far.

"Binary is different; it only has two numbers. One and zero."

"So you can't count past one? That's stupid!" she exclaimed.

"No, no. Look," I cleared the sand slate again and started drawing. "The first numbering space in our decimal system is the one's column. It can be anything from one to nine or zero, right?"

Again, Trista nodded.

"Then there's the ten's column and the hundred's column and so on. In binary there are columns as well. But each column can only be a one or a zero. So if I wanted to write zero, I'd write 0, if I wanted to write one I'd write 1."

"Exactly like the decimal system," Trista observed.

"Right, except there's no 2 in binary so if you wanted to write two what would you do?"

Trista stared back blankly, "Beats me."

"You would do the same thing you'd do if you ran out of digits in the decimal system. You'd start another column."

"So two would be 11?" Trista asked

"No, it would be 10. The first column resets itself to zero, just like when we start a new column in our numbering system. Like when we write 10 for example."

"So, how would you write three in binary then?"

"You just add another 1 to the one's column. Three would be 11."

Trista's eyes lit up a little, "I *think* I get it. But it's still weird."

I remembered how hard it was for me to grasp the concept at first too. It had never occurred to me there would be more than one way to count things. In some ways, learning binary was like learning another language—a language with only two digits.

"To read binary you just have to think differently about your number columns," I explained, drawing out the number 11111, which had been written below the coded message. Between each number I drew a line to separate the columns. I wrote the value of the columns below each number, starting from right to left.

"The first column is the one's column, just like in decimal. The second column is the two's column, double the first column. The third column is the four's column, then eight's, then sixteen, then thirty two and so on. See? You just double the previous column value. Add the values together and you'll have your number. If there is a 1 in the column you add that number, if there is a 0 then you don't."

$$1 \quad 1 \quad 1 \quad 1 \quad 1$$
$$16 \quad 8 \quad 4 \quad 2 \quad 1$$

"Okay, so 11 would be two plus one, which is three!"

"Exactly, and 11111 would be…."

"Sixteen, plus eight, plus four, plus two, plus one," Trista said triumphantly, pausing a moment to add it all up in her head. "Thirty one!"

"Right," I said, proud of the fact that I had explained it so well. "So, if my hunch is correct, thirty-one is how many times we shift the letters of the alphabet to decipher the message."

"But there are only twenty-six letters," Trista said hesitantly.

"Right, so twenty-six will bring us back to the same letter and then we continue forward to thirty-one which would be...."

"Five," Trista said with a smirk. "Isn't that what I said to start with?"

I was dumbfounded. Double checking the math, I found that she was indeed right. The number was five.

"Yeah, I guess this was a bad example," I said sheepishly.

"You think? Can we just decode the message already?"

I nodded eagerly. Clearing the sand slate, we wrote out the letters from the message in the Writ. Below each letter, we wrote the character that came five letters after it.

R	N	W	W	T	W		W	N	R
W	S	B	B	Y	R		B	S	W

"Wow," Trista said sarcastically. She was clearly unimpressed with my code-breaking skills. "That's impressive. It makes a whole lot of sense now."

I tried to ignore her and kept to the task at hand.

"I don't get it," I said, holding my chin in thought. Where had I gone wrong? I thought for sure I was on to something but maybe I was simply wanting to find something where there wasn't anything to be found.

"Don't feel too bad, Hunter. Maybe it's just gibberish after all," Trista decided.

"Or," I said, suddenly realizing my mistake, "I solved it backward. Instead of shifting our letters forward five letters, let's go the other way."

Brushing away the bottom row of letters, I rewrote them in place beneath the original message. This time it worked. We had words.

R	N	W	W	T	W		W	N	R
M	I	R	R	O	R		R	I	M

"Okay, I'm actually impressed this time, Hunter," Trista said.

We stared at the phrase for a moment. I was proud of my work. Cracking a code felt like a major accomplishment every time.

"Mirror Rim, huh?" Trista said. "But what does it mean?"

"I have no idea," I said, staring blankly at the words.

"Are you thinking what I'm thinking?" Trista answered.

"Depends on what you're thinking," I answered, wondering if she had already read my mind.

"Do you think this book could have belonged to your father?"

"It's possible," I answered, "and it makes sense too. Whoever left this for us must have found it while searching for him. Maybe they intended for us to decode the messages in it for them."

Then Trista had a terrible thought. "Or maybe they are using the book to throw us off track."

Both options were equally possible. We didn't know enough yet to figure out which was true.

"You said your father had another message like this in his drawings," Trista said. "Can you pull them up on that bracelet Desi gave you?"

"It's a Symbio," I said, correcting her and spinning the device around my wrist, freeing some of the white sand that had lodged itself between the Symbio and my arm.

"Well whatever it is, let's see if it can help us," Trista said.

I looked at the Symbio device and wondered if it would still work here in Solandria…assuming we were in Solandria. Trista's cell phone didn't work the last time we visited, but it had still powered up. The Symbio screen flashed on but there wasn't any service. I slid my fingers across the smooth surface of the screen, which flickered a bit before it lit faintly.

"Well, it's not working perfectly, but I'm in!" I said excitedly. Trista leaned in close beside me as I searched for the folder Desi had shown me on the device. In no time at all I pulled up the image my father had drawn with the cryptic jumble of letters.

NS LNWZR
NRZX STHYJ
JY HTSXZRNRZW
NLSN

"Do you think the same shift would apply to this one?" Trista asked.

"It's worth a shot," I said, clearing the sand once more. "You work from the end of the message and I'll work from the start. That way, we'll finish twice as fast."

Trista agreed and set to work on her half of the mysterious message, whispering each letter as she replaced it. Oddly enough, every letter she wrote was the same as mine.

IN GIRUM
IMUS NOCTE
ET CONSUMIMUR
IGNI

"That's so weird," I gasped.

"What?" Trista wondered, looking at the jumble of letters.

"Well, I just noticed that the letters are the same backwards as they are forwards. The whole sentence would read the same both ways."

"Really?" Trista gawked.

"Yes, I only noticed it because you were whispering each letter as I was writing the same one."

"It's too bad the message doesn't mean anything," Trista noted. "It feels like we're close. Maybe it's another language?"

I agreed, but if it were another language it was unlike any I had ever known. My stomach started to growl. It was time we started focusing on the more important things. We both were hungry, thirsty and tired. If we didn't find some kind of help soon, it wouldn't matter if we solved all the riddles in the world. We'd be dead.

It was midday in Solandria, in the middle of nowhere, but it felt like the middle of the night by Destiny's measure. We needed rest, and it was no good venturing out during the daylight. The heat would only wear us out quicker. Having discussed our options, we decided to sleep until nightfall and scavenge for food during the cooler evening hours.

The cave floor wasn't comfortable, it was hardly even bearable, but it was far better than the blistering heat that awaited us outside. With nothing else to do, I glanced through the drawings on the Symbio device. The last image I studied was the one of my father, cowering in the corner beneath the shadow of a knife.

I had hope my father was still alive—but for how long? If he had seen this vision in the Eye of Ends, it would be only a matter of time before the shadow in the picture found him. The question still remained; could the picture be changed? Was the Eye's vision of the future able to be altered or was it written in stone?

With this terrible thought, I finally drifted to sleep, in the middle of nowhere.

CHAPTER 16

NIGHT LIFE

I awoke peacefully to see a sky, twinkling with diamond-like stars, just outside the cave entrance. The moon was set high in the sky, full and brighter than I had ever known. The white sand of the desert sparkled in the moonlight and was now flowering with bright neon plants that must have been buried beneath the sand during the day. By night, the wasteland had become a wonderland, seeming more like the sandy floor of an underwater crystal lagoon than the desolate place we had known during the day. The night air was comfortable and cool, but not the least bit cold.

The night would be perfect for traveling, with one exception—the sounds. The sounds of the night creatures were many and frightening. A chorus of long haunting moans, growls and squeals carried on the wind like an eerie song. First one voice, then another joined in the unfamiliar tune. The voices seemed to be coming from everywhere at once, though I suspected it was just a trick of the night.

Trista lay beside me, still soundly asleep. I brushed the hair from her face, tucking it neatly behind her ear. She looked so peaceful in the moonlight, angelic even. I hated to wake her, but we had to get going. I had just talked myself into letting her sleep five more minutes, when I heard a sound in the back of the cave. The sound was followed by a shuffling movement. We were not alone.

Crumple, crumple.

"Trista," I whispered, poking her in the side. "Get up."

She moaned and started to stir, stretching and yawning before cracking one eyelid open beneath her furrowed brow. "What is it?"

"Something's there, at the back of the cave," I said, pointing toward where the sounds had come from.

Crumple, crumple.

She heard it too. Rustling sounds. The kind of sounds that made your imagination run wild. Trista didn't need to be told twice. She shot up in an instant and scooted safely behind me. If it were a fearsome creature, I would be her human shield. After all, there was no use in a girl being eaten before a boy. It went against the order of nature—an ancient pecking order set in place by the Author himself.

Part of me liked being her protector, but another part deep inside desperately hoped it didn't come to that. The rustling sounds stopped momentarily. The creature had sensed our movement. I grabbed my sword and brought the blade to light.

"Grab your bow and let's get out of here," I whispered to Trista out of the corner of my mouth. Trista nodded nervously and managed somehow to reach across the cave without leaving the safety of my shield.

"My backpack! Where's my backpack?" I asked, glancing nervously around. Trista didn't know either. My father's Writ was still lying out in the open, but my backpack, which I left beside it, was gone. All of a sudden, something flew out of the blackness of the cave straight at us. Swinging my sword in defense, I nearly sliced my own backpack to pieces before it landed at my feet.

"Who goes there?" I demanded, pointing my sword in the direction from which my pack had been thrown. "Come out and show yourself!"

"Boojum, friends?" came a weak squeaky voice, followed by a pair of gleaming blue eyes. The furry grey creature waddled out from the darkness, dragging his long tail behind him.

"Boojum!" Trista squealed with delight. No longer needing me for protection, Trista clamored across the cave to where Boojum sat and picked him up in a big hug. I couldn't tell for sure, but I thought I spotted a smile of relief on the little runt's face.

"What are you doing way out here?" Trista asked him.

"Special jobs," Boojum answered. "Boojum help."

"Help who?" I asked, wondering what mischief he might be up to now.

"Helping an old friend find you two," a girl's voice, warm and familiar, answered the question from over the ledge behind us. My heart leaped at the sound—spinning around to face the mouth of the cave, I caught sight of a girl hoisting herself over the ledge of the cliff. She was dressed in a loose white poncho and tan leggings, the lower part of her face wrapped behind a white shawl meant to block the sun and sand. Her chocolate brown eyes were all I could see, but it was all I needed. I knew in an instant it was Hope. She wasn't a flame, she wasn't a vision…this time she was real, and every bit as beautiful as I remembered her, perhaps even more so.

Without wasting another moment, I threw my arms around her in a warm embrace—one I had waited far too long to give. Tears welled up in my eyes, and for once I didn't mind one bit. There was no need to act tough with Hope. She and I had been through far too much together to hide my true emotions.

When at last we broke the embrace, I wiped my eyes and introduced Trista for the first time.

"Hope, I want you to meet Trista," I gestured toward her.

Trista and Hope shook hands in a warm greeting.

"I remember you," Hope said. "You came with Hunter—with the Flame, right?"

Trista nodded, continuing to scratch Boojum on the head. He leaned into it, enjoying the attention so much he nearly fell out of her hands when she pulled away.

"If I'm not mistaken, we have something in common," Hope said, revealing the mark of the Flame on her collar bone. Trista showed her mark in return. "That makes us practically sisters then. Maybe between the two of us, we can keep Hunter in line."

Trista smiled. I could tell the two of them were going to hit it off just fine. Trista eyed me knowingly and I wondered if she understood what I was thinking.

"I still can't believe you're really here!" I said excitedly. "How did you find us?"

Hope pointed to Boojum. "That was his job. Snarks have a knack for finding their way back to their owners. It's like a sixth sense."

"I see," I said, wondering if it meant I'd have to keep the little bugger again. Last time, things really hadn't worked out so well.

"Don't worry," Hope explained. "He's been given a specific job to do and then he'll be heading back home to his family. Right, Boojum?"

"Yes, Boojum papa," he explained.

"Awww," Trista fawned over the little guy. "Baby Boojums, how cute is that?"

I shuddered at the thought. Keeping track of one snark was hard enough, let alone a whole litter of the little deviants. Still, I was happy for Boojum. He had been a good friend and had helped me out of some tight jams before.

Trista and I were both thrilled to learn that Hope had not come empty-handed. She had brought water and food as well. Her canteen was filled with the coolest, most refreshing water I had ever tasted. And the simple meal of fruits and nuts was more than enough to satisfy my groaning stomach. With spirits revived, we set to the task of finding our way to safety.

."We're on the Shard of Noc. Though one of the most desolate shards in Solandria, it has its beauty as well. Do you see those lights over there?" Hope asked. I nodded, feeling surprised that I hadn't noticed them before. The horizon to the north was aglow with a peculiar teal light, shooting up into the sky. "That's where the Noctu live and it's where we are heading. They're a very vibrant tribe, but a bit…unpredictable. Just keep in mind, the desert may look beautiful at night, but it is a dangerous beauty. Keep your guard up."

"So, you're coming with us, then?" I asked hopefully.

"Well, you didn't think you'd get rid of me that easily, did you?" Hope said in return. "Besides, I've seen how you fight. You're going to need all the help you can get."

Trista stifled a chuckle at my expense.

"Ouch!" I said. "Looks like the desert isn't the only dangerous beauty I should watch out for tonight."

"Dangerous beauty, huh?" Trista said, rolling her eyes at my comeback. "Is that the best you can come up with?"

"What? I thought it was good. You know the whole play-on-words thing. It was good, right?" I tried to defend myself, but the girls were already heading down the hillside together. Trista waved back without looking. I gathered the remainder of my things, shoved them into my backpack and ventured out of the cave into the wild of the night, following the two giggling girls ahead of me. Already I could tell it was going to be a long trip.

Trista offered to return Hope's bow, but Hope insisted that she keep it as her own. From that moment forward they were practically inseparable. They were becoming the best of friends.

I followed behind, kicking up sand and marching across the desert, surrounded by the most gorgeous and enormous plant life I had ever seen. The leaves of many of the flowers were larger than I was. The blooms spiraled up in the most intricate designs. The colors of the flowers ranged from indigo blues to neon green and everything in between.

As we walked, Hope caught us up on everything that had happened over the several months we were away from Solandria.

Word of the Seven being marked spread like wildfire throughout the Resistance; when Hope returned, so too did the spirits of the Codebearers. Nobody yet knew who had become the seventh one marked. New recruits joined the Resistance every day in such great number it was hard for the instructors to keep up with the training. Sam especially had his hands full.

The biggest challenge now was to maintain unity among the Resistance. That was one of the reasons Hope had been sent to Noc, to strengthen the Noctus' allegiance by healing one of their own.

"So, how will you know who to heal?" I asked.

"I don't know yet," Hope replied. "But I was told by Aviad it would be clear to me and Boojum when we arrived."

"Boojum? He's going to help?"

"He has a role, yes. So, what about you? I was told I would find you but I don't know why you are here."

I explained about the Watcher, about my father and my missing family. Hope listened intently, but didn't say much.

"Just remember," she said, "rescuing your father may not go exactly as you plan it. But if you trust the Author, things will end up right."

I knew fully what she meant. I would never have chosen the path my adventures had taken. Never in a million years would I have expected that letting Hope die could have brought me closer to her. Looking back now, it was almost the best thing that happened to me. I had learned and grown so much since then...but I still had a long way to go. Even so, I couldn't help but believe that rescuing my father would go better.

Eventually, our conversation gave way to a mutual silence. We traveled together across the powdery sands toward the distant lights, unaware that we were being watched by the very sand we walked on.

Trista was the first to notice the eyes popping up from the ground periodically. They were bulbous eyes, glossy and yellow, attached to the tips of thin tendrils, which rose up and sank back into the ground with a puff of sand. The appearance of the eyes became more frequent over time and seemed to move on all sides of us. We picked up the pace in an attempt to lose the thing.

"*Krauk*," the sand thing said in a deep guttural tone.

Boojum scurried up Trista's leg and onto her shoulder, shivering.

"What is that thing?" a frightened Trista asked.

"I'm not sure," Hope replied.

"Well, it's freaking me out."

The googly eyes reappeared not twenty feet from where we stood. This time the eyes raised and lowered more slowly: first the left, then the right eye. Each yellow orb moved independently of the other. In a flash, they disappeared again. There was a rustling underground and the eyes emerged from the sand near our left side.

"*Krauk!*" it repeated.

Fwooosh!

Annoyed, Trista had fired an arrow at the creature, which sank back into the sand before it was hit.

"Go away, will you!" Trista yelled.

"*Krauk*," it taunted back.

"I don't think it can hurt us; it's just curious that's all," I said.

"Well, I don't care," Trista answered. "If I see it again I'm going to shoot it right between the eyes."

"*Krauk*," the sand thing replied.

Furious, Trista readied her bow for the next sign of movement. There was a flash of blue and Trista's bow was yanked from her hands, disappearing into a hole in the sand.

"Did you see that?" Trista screamed. "That thing just ate my bow! Do you think its friendly now?"

"Not so much," I conceded.

With sword ignited I awaited the creature's next appearance. The sand in front of me shuffled as two eyes rose from the ground well within striking distance. With a clean swing, I severed one of the orbs, which fell to the sand, winking and rolling around chaotically. A sinister moan rattled the ground.

"I don't think it liked that," Hope observed.

"Good, it wasn't supposed to," I answered. "Maybe now it will leave us alooooooooo…whoa…."

My last word went unfinished as the sand beneath my feet gave way, caving into a newly formed hole. I leapt to the side to avoid getting sucked under the sand, but a long blue sticky tongue shot out, grabbing me by the foot.

"Help!" I called out, trying my best to swing my sword at the creature's tongue before it could pull me in. It was no use, I couldn't reach it. Turning on my belly, I jammed my Veritas blade into the ground like a stake and hung on for my life. The blade held firm in the ground, but my grip was weakening. The strength of the sticky blue tongue was winning out.

"I can't…hold on…much longer," I grunted, turning my head to where Trista and Hope stood. "Do something!"

Surprisingly, Hope didn't seem to be paying attention at all. Her hands were clasped together, her eyes closed. I couldn't believe it. Here I was holding on for dear life, and she was taking some kind of nap.

"Hope, please!" I shouted.

Her eyes opened again, only this time a piercing fire replaced the once gentle brown. Throwing her hand forward, a stream of fire burst out of her palm toward the creature's tongue. With a whimper the tongue released its grip on my foot and slipped back into the sand, dropping me face first on the ground. The fire disappeared from Hope's eyes and she gasped for breath, as if she had not breathed the entire time she was saving my life.

"How did you do that?" I asked, spitting sand from my mouth.

"A girl's gotta have some secrets," she replied.

A second groan from the sand caused me to jump to my feet. Before I could retrieve my sword from the ground, it was gobbled up by another blue tongue.

The sand shuffled on all sides. A single yellow eye rose in front of us, then a second pair to its right, a third pair behind us and even more to our right. We were being surrounded.

"Gather close everyone," Hope said. "This could get ugly."

Ugly was right. The one-eyed creature poked its whole head out of the ground, showing itself for the first time. It looked mostly like a frog, only much, much bigger and lumpier. It hissed at us, clearly unhappy to have lost an eye and scorched its tongue.

The frog opened its mouth, revealing a dozen razor-sharp teeth around its lips. Just then, a dozen light-tipped spears fell from the sky, showering the ground like rain. Three of the spears hit true to their mark, piercing the creature's skin and causing the other sand frogs to shuffle away in fear. The one-eyed frog let a low desperate groan slip out of its mouth as it breathed its last.

"*Plausee, plausee*," a riotous shout erupted from the desert foliage around us. A dozen powder-white-skinned natives stepped out of hiding, several of them riding on the back of two-legged reptilian raptors. The natives' skin blended perfectly into the white sands and made even me look tan in comparison. For the most part they were human in appearance—shirtless warriors painted in the most intricate neon colors and designs imaginable. Each of the warriors had a different color of hair, brightly painted in neon hues to complement their skin design. Their necks were long—twice, perhaps even three times longer than mine.

"The Noctu," Hope explained in a whisper as they approached. "They speak in the Old Language. You better let me do the talking."

Retrieving their spears, the warriors celebrated the kill and pulled the remainder of the sand frog from the ground. The creature was larger than I had expected. Its body was easily twice the size of the largest walrus I'd ever seen and equally as wrinkled and awkward looking. Its tail stretched out a good six feet from its rump. The mouth was wide and bulging. The skin was spotted with orange and brown. In some ways, it seemed more like an enormous slug than a frog, but either way—it wasn't a pleasant-looking creature.

The tallest of the twelve Noctu approached us with the severed eye of the frog, handing it to me as a gift. His eyes were a brilliant blue and big.

"Thank you," I said as they pulled their spears from the creature.

The man made a motion with his hand as if to suggest that I eat the eye.

"He's kidding, right?" I asked, looking to Hope for advice.

"I don't think so," she said solemnly.

The man pounded his chest with a fist and pointed again to the eye, raising a hand to his mouth.

I shook my head and raised a hand. Hoping the gesture would be received as "Thanks, but no thanks." Instead, the man stiffened, becoming almost indignant that I didn't eat the eye.

"I think you'd better eat it, Hunter," Hope said, looking a little frightened. "We don't want to offend them."

"Seriously, why me?" I asked, looking at the gooey yellow ball in my hand.

"It must be a guy thing," Trista said, trying to be helpful. "You know, male bonding. Pretend it's a hard boiled egg or something."

"Does this *look* like an egg to you?" I replied, holding the yellow eyeball out toward her. Trista turned away, too grossed out to look. "Besides, I hate eggs, especially hard-boiled ones. They're all squishy and…juicy…and…." I shuddered at the thought.

The other Noctu gathered around, their eyes wide with eager anticipation of my first bite. There was no way I was going to get out of it now. I had to suck it up and be a man.

Just hurry up and get it over with, I told myself.

"Oh gross, he's actually going to do it!" Trista squealed, looking away as I lifted the eye to my mouth. The oldest Noctu nodded his encouragement and clinched his teeth. What the natives knew, and I didn't, was that the center of the eye was loaded with a gooey yolk-like paint. The very moment I bit down, the eye exploded like a water balloon, splattering the neon yellow substance all over my mouth, chin and clothes.

The Noctu laughed and cheered at the sight. It was a primitive joke and I was apparently the punch line. The tallest Noctu slapped me on the back in good-natured reconciliation as I spat the yellow paint into the sand. Surprisingly, it didn't taste half bad, almost like a tomato, only sweeter.

"Hunter, you look like a Cheshire cat," Trista giggled, pointing to my mouth. The tips of my fingers were coated with the phosphorous goop, and I could only imagine what my teeth and lips looked like.

The Noctu warrior took what remained of the sand frog's eye from my hand and gathered some goo onto his fingertip. Using his finger as a paintbrush, he drew a series of lines and dots on my forehead. The man finished his art and after a little thought said, "Novitiatus."

"What is that? What did he just say?" I asked Hope.

"He just named you into their tribe. It is their custom to name newcomers. Novitiatus is your new name," she answered.

"That sounds cool; what does it mean?"

"It means Newbie," she said straight-faced.

My excitement faded as Trista stifled a chuckle at my expense. Next, the Noctu leader motioned for Trista to step forward. He reached out to mark her forehead with the neon eye-juice as well. Trista was reluctant at first, but when Hope explained it was part of their tradition, she allowed the man to draw on her forehead, grimacing the whole time. When he finished, the Noctu warrior stooped eye-level with Trista and gazed at her for a long awkward moment. A broad smile lit his face as he gave her a name, "Dit See."

Trista's expression soured as she looked anxiously to Hope for an interpretation. "Please tell me he didn't just call me Ditzy."

"Dit See, actually," Hope answered, disguising a smile behind her hand. "It means Golden One."

It was my turn to laugh.

"Zip it," Trista said, shooting a look of death my way. I zipped.

At last, the Noctu warrior approached Hope; only this time his introduction took a decidedly different tone. "Igni Sola, is good again so to see you," he said in a cheerful voice. The two embraced. Clearly, they knew each other better than Hope had let on.

"Deco oris me," Hope replied. "It is an honor to be with you too, Alti."

"Always you are welcome," Alti replied. "Come and be food with us."

Be food with us? I thought, hoping for our sake it was merely a slip of the tongue. Hope graciously corrected the man in her acceptance of his offer.

"We would be grateful to eat with you; there is much to discuss. I come with a message of great importance from Aviad, a message of healing for one who has fallen."

At the mention of this, the man's eyes lit up, quite literally.

"Yes, yes! The man I know. Fallen from sky. We hurry," the man said. "We must!"

He barked a few commands to the other tribesmen who scurried about to prepare their recent kill for transport. With tribal greetings complete, the Noctu led us toward their desert encampment, dragging the skewered carcass of the sand frog behind.

"So nice of you to tell us that you knew them," I whispered to Hope, replaying the whole encounter in my mind. "You could have spared me the humiliation of the eye thing, you know."

"Yes, but what would have been the fun in that?" Hope answered smugly. "Besides, it's better this way."

"Better how?"

"Better because the Noctu enjoy a good laugh. You'll be one of their favorite people now. A regular celebrity, you might say."

In an hour's time we reached the edge of the village. The rustic cluster of domed huts were scattered beneath a field of giant teal mushrooms. The mushrooms were unlike anything I had ever seen, spiraling up overhead like trees and glowing with a natural light all their own. Despite the late hours, the Noctu village was buzzing with activity. For the Noctu, the coolness of night was day, a necessary lifestyle to avoid the unbearable desert heat. Children ran out to meet us in anticipation of the hunting warriors' return. When they spotted my glowing smile, the children began to laugh and gather around me, pointing at my mouth and pulling on my hand.

It was just as Hope had said; the Noctu were a vibrant people in more ways than one. Boisterous and cheerful people by nature, they radiated a joyful love of life that hardly seemed to match their humble existence. The entire tribe decorated their snow-white skin in colorful and artistic patterns with the glowing paint. The women extended the artwork down their right shoulders, which remained uncovered by the dark blue wool they wrapped around themselves as clothing. The men were shirtless, but wore similar wraps around their waists.

After cleaning up from the journey, we joined the other Noctu warriors and children around a bonfire at the center of the village. The women were already busy preparing the night's supper. A small Noctu child tugged on my shirtsleeve and offered Trista and me our weapons, which apparently had been recovered from the belly of the slain sand frog.

Moments later, Alti returned to the bonfire, leading a man he believed to be the reason for Hope's visit. As he approached, I rubbed my eyes in disbelief. It had to be a trick. The man before us was none other than Xaul…the heartless slayer of the Codebearers, a man who was supposed to be dead.

CHAPTER 17

FROM THE ASHES

Gone were the white hooded uniform and waist-wide belt identifying him as a fierce Xin warrior. No longer did he stretch out his seven-foot frame to tower over me intimidatingly. His silvery eyes were no longer piercing.

Xaul wore a simple Noctu-style tunic now. His broad shoulders were stooped and his head bowed humbly. When his eyes passed over me, they were dull, clouded and lifeless—the helpless eyes of a blind man. Though Xaul may have changed physically, he was still a murderer to me.

I had seen him kill Petrov. I had to watch helplessly as he plunged his sword through Hope. And Xaul would have killed me as well had not the Author intervened and destroyed him in the Consuming Fire. That was the awful end he had deserved. That was the justice I'd witnessed this murderer receive—or so I had thought.

For the Fire to have spared him so that I could share a dinner and friendly conversation with him tonight was inconceivable... but that's exactly what was happening before my eyes.

Led on the arm of a Noctu guide, Xaul took his seat opposite the fire from where I stood. I watched him with silent contempt through the flames, wishing this fire could finish him for good. Trista didn't look much happier with the arrangement, remembering all the harm he'd caused her and our friends as well. As for Hope, she looked surprised, but not upset. That was perhaps the greatest mystery of them all. Yes, the Author had rewritten her; she had a new and greater life now, but how could she look past the evil Xaul had done to her and not hate him?

"Is it true?" Xaul's strained, whispery voice spoke into the night, his ashen eyes wandering aimlessly. "Are you the one sent from the Author?"

"Yes," Hope replied with a steady voice, "I am Hope. I have come to heal you."

The crackling fire sparked suddenly brighter for a moment, as if marking the statement with an exclamation point. Xaul nodded his head in silent acceptance, breathing an emotion-filled sigh of both fear and relief. It was a confrontation he had both longed for and dreaded.

"May it be as the Author has said," Xaul answered. Surprisingly, his tone was a defeated, surrendered one. No longer was he the great Xin warrior. Hope began to stand up, but I grabbed her arm, holding her back.

"What are you doing?" I whispered.

"You'll see," she said confidently, her own eyes spilling over with emotion as she slid my hand from her arm.

I watched in disbelief as she took a step forward and walked untouched through the flames that separated us from Xaul. He inclined his head towards his tender messenger as she knelt and gently gathered both of his charred hands together. Turning them palm up, she curled them to form shallow cups.

"I have come to fulfill the Author's purpose for you," Hope said compassionately, "to raise you up from the ashes."

Having said this, she reached back into the fire and scooped up a pile of hot ash, patiently letting it cool in her hands before pouring the warm, silvery dust into his waiting hands.

"Boojum," Hope called out, "it's time."

"Uh-uh," refused the squeaky voice from somewhere just beyond the firelight's reach. "Light bad."

Hope rolled her eyes, but submitted to his request, passing her hand over the flames till they had lowered to mere embers. "That better?" she asked.

Content with the arrangement, Boojum scampered over and climbed up onto Hope's shoulder, peering curiously down into Xaul's hands..

"Boojum here?" he asked.

Hope nodded the okay. "Just let 'er flow."

Boojum started sucking and snorting, his face twisting and twitching as he forced a thick, wet, gargling sound from the back of his throat. It was disgustingly loud for such a small creature. Children of the Noctu tribe came running over to watch. Hope tried her best to look away.

Unable to see what was transpiring in front of him, Xaul reluctantly asked, "Is it going to…?"

Yes, Boojum was. And Boojum did.

The gooey discharge erupted from his mouth, splattering unceremoniously on top of the gathered ash in Xaul's hand. For a moment all was still except for the slow drip of surplus spittle, oozing through Xaul's fingers. I tried not to laugh, but the absurdity of the situation was too good to be true.

"Boojum good?" the snark's excited blue eyes danced proudly from his handiwork back to Hope.

"Yeah," Hope said feigning a smile, "you did really well, buddy."

Speaking to Xaul now, she did her best to explain. "So, just mash that together till it's a nice paste and then…" she hated to say it, "rub it over your eyes."

Xaul, having willingly gone along with Hope's instructions up to now, stopped to consider the humiliating and unhealthy step he was being asked to take. I could tell he was worried it could be a joke.

"You want me to rub this…glop…on my eyes?" Xaul questioned with a disgusted look on his face.

"Yup," Hope said. "That's the plan."

"What good will that do?" he asked.

"It is the Author's will."

If it were a prank, Hope had planned it perfectly. By now the Noctu parents and elders had gathered with their children to see what their adopted tribesman would do. Resigned to his fate, Xaul shrugged and slathered the sticky mud over his eyelids. I wanted to laugh at how ridiculous the man looked, his eyes smeared with Boojum's spit. I was still gloating at the man's humiliation when he began to shout.

"My eyes…I can see again. I can see!"

I was completely caught offguard. I hadn't expected the prank to actually work. I thought Hope was getting back at the man, not truly healing him. It was a real letdown.

Almost immediately, the Noctu tribe erupted in a spontaneous celebration that was more colorful than their neon paint. *Xaul's sight had been restored!* That was the message on everyone's lips and the reason for every smile. With dancing, singing, feasting and laughter, everyone in the Noctu camp was buzzing with excitement over the miraculous event they'd witnessed from the Author's hand. In recognition of the miracle, their chief held a special ceremony in which they gave Xaul the new name of Xias (it meant "Xin of ash" according to Hope's translation).

It was all very fascinating to watch…from a distance. Trista, Hope and even Boojum let themselves get caught up in the merriment but I had my reasons for sitting this one out. For starters, every minute we wasted here should have been spent searching for my father and rescuing my family. I hadn't come to Solandria to celebrate a criminal who had escaped the punishment he'd deserved. As the party continued, I slipped away to be alone with my thoughts.

Beneath the stars, I pondered the injustice of it all. How could someone as cruel as Xaul be given such a great gift by the Author? It wasn't fair, and I wasn't happy.

Darkness finally gave way to dawn, driving the luminescent plant life back underground and the Noctu back to the shelter of their domed huts. Their "day" had come to an end; it was time to prepare for sleep that would carry them through the heat of a searing, sun-filled "night."

Now that we were finally free from distractions, I was looking forward to getting down to the business of why I came to Solandria in the first place—finding my father.

"I've made arrangements for us to stay in Noctu for the night," Hope said to Trista and me, though by "night" she meant "day."

"Great. Where are we staying?" I asked. Honestly, I would have rather set out in search of my father, but the harsh reality of being burned alive in the scorching sun left me no choice. Instead, I settled on the idea of using "tonight" to formulate our plan with the promise of an early departure in the cooler temperatures of the "morning."

"Sorry for the delay," Xaul said, addressing Hope from behind me. He had snuck up while I wasn't looking to invade our privacy. "I'm so glad you've agreed to stay with me. We have so much to discuss. Come, follow me. My place is just across the camp."

Follow *him?* To *his* place? Hope caught my worried glance and answered the man before I could object.

"Yes. We're looking forward to sharing your company tonight, Xias. I believe it's what the Author intended." Her intentional use of his new name brought a huge smile to his black face; mine was still pale with shock.

Before I could respond, the tall man turned on his heel and led us away with long, exuberant strides through the Noctu encampment to his domed hut. It was all I could do to keep up, kicking and screaming inside the whole way. We reached our destination as the first slivered edge of the blazing sun inched its way over the horizon. Already the temperature was rising, though the day had hardly begun.

Xaul lifted the hut's flapped door and ushered us in. Hope went first, followed quickly by Trista. I, however, was not nearly as trusting or comfortable turning my back on the man. I put one hand on my sword and motioned him in with the other. Xaul understood and entered ahead of me.

Inside, the semi-translucence of the hut's animal skin walls allowed a small measure of sunlight to pass through, lighting up the domed room in a soft orange glow. Grass mats were spread over the sandy desert floor for us to recline on. Xaul sat cross-legged, pouring water into cups made from hollowed-out gourds. He offered them to each of us. Both girls readily accepted. I declined. Suffering from a dry throat was better than accepting hospitality from the man who had killed so many.

Xaul cleared his throat and spoke to the three of us. "I can only imagine what you must be feeling toward me right now. An apology will never fix the wrongs I have inflicted against you, but for what it's worth, I am sorry."

What little composure I'd managed to keep up to this point flew right out the door.

"You're *sorry?*" I scoffed loudly. "You have no right even to *be* sorry! You are supposed to be dead!"

"Hunter!" Hope exclaimed, appalled by my outburst.

"No," Xaul said, intervening. "Let him speak it. I don't deserve my life. It is one thing I know for certain."

Trista tried to smooth things over by saying, "I think it's safe to say we all thought you were dead after the Flame… you know…."

"After it incinerated my pathetic existence?" Xaul suggested.

"Well, I wasn't going to put it *that* way," Trista objected.

No, but I would have, I thought.

A sad smile came to Xaul's face as he reflected on his past. "Of who I was before, there was nothing worth saving. I was hateful, cruel, destructive…." He paused, glancing my way before finishing, "…a murderer and a thief."

I bristled, suddenly feeling robbed that I wasn't the one to deliver the accusation myself. He continued.

"None of this mattered to me at the time. Xin teaching dictated that our wrongs could be 'purified by pain.' So I did what I wanted, whatever evil was necessary, and believed the rituals of fire would cleanse me. But as a wise Codebearer once challenged me, 'No amount of pain—nothing I could do—could ever make me perfect.'" Xaul nodded to me in acknowledgement. "You were right, Hunter."

I shifted uncomfortably beneath his praise. Those were my words, but they were meant to be used against him…not for him.

"I learned that lesson too late," Xaul continued the story. "I pursued and overtook the eternal Flame, believing I would master it. Instead, as you witnessed, the Flame's power overwhelmed and mastered *me*; in the process it consumed every darkened part of my being until I was reduced to…nothing. All that remained was a vast emptiness. Then, into that awful place, a great Voice spoke. I heard it, but being nothing how could I? It sounds crazy, I know."

He was right. It did sound crazy…but not to me. I knew differently. I knew exactly what he meant as only one who had passed through the Author's presence could. In spite of my opposition to Xaul, my heart stirred within me as he related his experience.

"The Voice spoke my name." Xaul closed his eyes now, reliving the memory. "It called to me out of the darkness and carried me toward a single point of light—a candle set upon a desk where a tattered, smudged paper lay next to an inkwell and quill. I recognized the words on the page as my own handwriting. At the top was my name with word after word descending down the page, describing my shameful life.

"If I had been able, I would have looked away, but I couldn't. Instead, I was forced to read each line until I had reached the end. I read how the Flame brought about my deserved destruction.

"As I read the final words, something remarkable happened. The Voice spoke again saying to me, *The seventh of Seven only Fire can name.* Then the quill was lifted out of the inkwell by some invisible hand and its tip dipped into the candle's flame. The flaming tip was touched to my paper, setting it on fire. Amazingly, the blaze did not consume the paper, but only purged the words away until the page was left completely clean and new.

"I know this may sound strange to you," Xaul continued, "but that was the most terrifying moment of all. Those words had represented the last link to the life I had known. Now that they were erased, I was completely finished."

"But you had to know the Author wasn't through with you yet, right?" Trista scrunched her knees up to her chest, eagerly awaiting the rest of the story.

"No," Xaul laughed. "I didn't know anything. But you are right; he wasn't done. Taking up the quill, the invisible hand of the Author dipped it into the candle flame once more and began to write in flaming letters a new chapter he intended for me."

"What did it say?" Trista asked.

"That the Author had chosen me as the 'seventh of Seven.'"

"You!" I blurted out incredulously. "He chose *you*?"

"He did," Xaul nodded humbly, "though I still don't know why. The next thing I remember is falling into the sand of Noc where the Noctu found me just before sunrise, blind and weak. I had been given a second chance at life."

He leaned over and opened a small chest, producing a folded paper from within. He extended it to me saying, "The Author did not send me alone; he left me with this promise so that I might never forget his calling on my life. You may read it if you like."

Trista and Hope leaned in to read over my shoulder as I opened the paper:

> Xaul, my chosen "seventh of Seven,"
> What began as your darkness, I will turn into light.
> Where once you were blind, I will now restore sight.
> I will send you to Noc to discover new dawn, while you learn to find good in what I've rescued from wrong.
> Await my message of hope.
> ~ The Author

I read the letter through twice, not willing to take it at face value. Xaul was the "seventh?" This enemy of everything the Codebearers stood for had become the capstone to the Consuming Fire's prophecy. It didn't add up. How could anyone excuse all the evil he'd done against the Resistance? It wasn't fair. It didn't make sense.

"It was not my choice to be given this chance, Hunter," Xaul said, perceiving my thoughts.

"No," I snapped back. "*Your* choices were to *kill*. You don't deserve this." I angrily threw the letter back at him and stormed out of the hut.

Outside, the blinding sunlight stung my eyes; the rising heat was already stifling but I didn't care. Instead, I was glad to meet something else as hot and angry as I felt inside. Hope slipped from behind the hut's flap and stormed across the sand. She was not happy.

"Hey, what's your problem?" Hope fumed.

"My problem? I'll tell you what my problem is!" I bellowed, flinging my arms over my head in disgust. "I can't do this. I can't sit around and pretend I don't know who he really is."

"Nobody's asking you to. I haven't forgotten either," she replied, "but he's changed. We all can see that; why can't you?"

"Has he? How do you know? How?" I pushed her for an answer.

"You read the Author's letter. Xaul's been rewritten; he's the seventh mark!"

"Yeah, well, he doesn't deserve it," I said. Suddenly, I realized what bothered me most was that the Author chose Xaul over me. Why hadn't I been marked? After all, I was the one who suffered so much to carry the Flame. I felt insulted that the Author had overlooked me after all of my loyalty and sacrifice. Instead, the seventh had been a murderer and enemy of the Codebearers.

Hope nodded, "You think you deserved to be marked instead of Xaul, is that it?"

"Why not? At least I'm not a murderer."

She raised an eyebrow at me, "Oh no? So, Venator had nothing to do with you, huh? And that wasn't your blade that ran me through?"

I flushed, remembering that fateful moment when my Veritas Sword cut through her, all but killing her. It was the darkest moment of my life.

"That's different," I said, rationalizing the thing away. "It was an accident and you know it." But the truth was, Venator, my mirrored self, had killed often throughout his service to the Shadow. Even so, I thought comparing Xaul to me was hardly fair.

"This isn't about me. I'm not saying I'm perfect," I reasoned. "I'm just saying…I did everything the Author asked of me, Hope. I've risked my life for him time and again! I trusted that the Author knew what he was doing. I trusted him even though he never trusted me enough to tell me the whole story…never the whole story!"

Hope reached out for my arm, but I pulled away. Her voice softened as she spoke to me.

"So you're angry with the Author then," Hope said bluntly.

"Maybe I am!" I answered at last, finally being honest with myself.

"It's not a choice between the two of you, Hunter. The Author's story is bigger than any one of us. He has his reasons for Xaul and he has already chosen you. You bear his mark in the deepest fabric of your being. Surely you must know that…."

"But Xaul?" I interrupted. "He spent his entire life as an enemy of the Resistance and now, all of a sudden, I'm supposed to accept him as one of us? As a friend? Doesn't that seem just a bit odd to you? He could cut our throats while we sleep!"

"Look," Hope reasoned, "I'm not defending anything that Xaul did to us…or to me. But, I am willing to accept in faith what the Author has done, what he is making new. You can't forget the steep price the Author paid to save and rewrite your own life. Doesn't it stand to reason that there was a price involved in saving Xaul's life too?"

Her words were sobering. I remembered well Aviad's sacrifice for me when he took the Bloodstone's curse upon himself in my place. If indeed Xaul had been redeemed as he claimed—at what cost, and by whom?

What began as darkness, I will make into light.

Framed by Hope's counsel, the Author's words given to Xaul rang just as true for me now as they did for Xaul. Perhaps he and I were not so different after all.

Still, it didn't mean I had to like the guy.

"I don't trust him," I said flatly. "Xaul, that is...not the Author."

"Fine, but at least give him the chance to earn your trust," she replied. "If not for him, for me...for the Author. *Everything for a purpose,* remember?" she said cheerfully, quoting the words of the Author's Writ.

I nodded in return, begrudgingly conceding the argument.

"Who knows?" Hope said, leading me by the arm. "We might need his help before your adventure is through."

"Stranger things have happened, I guess," I said.

"Oh yeah, like what?"

"Boojum's spit," I chuckled.

"Yeah, that was pretty gross," Hope laughed in response.

She hooked my arm and pulled me back toward the shelter. We re-entered the welcoming shade to find Trista and Xaul engaged in conversation. To my shock, Xaul was holding my father's sword... the one he had used to kill Hope. Trista, being far too trusting, must have retrieved it from my backpack during my absence. Seeing it in his hands made me stiffen a bit more. My memories of crossing blades with this man were still fresh, and I knew how deadly this weapon could be in his hands.

Trista looked excitedly my way and said, "Hunter, I was just

asking Xias about your father's sword and you are not going to believe this! He knows where your father is…or was."

Xias calmly raised my father's sword and offered it back to me.
"I was telling her how this sword came to me long ago, when I was
still a boy. Your father rescued me."

"He did?" I asked, taking the sword from him. "How?"

Xaul recounted the tale.

"As my people were being slaughtered by the Shadow, I ran.
The creatures that came were ferocious, dark and vile. I had never
seen anything like them before or since. They moved swiftly, like a
plague of death from the heart of the Void itself. I was only a boy
of seven at the time—old enough to fight; however, as the crowned
prince of my people I was told to hide. My mother carried me as far
as she could, but she wasn't alone. One of the Shadow creatures had
seen our escape and caught up to us in the hills just beyond the city.
Mother protected me until her final breath.

"I would have died as well if it weren't for your father. He
dropped from the sky out of nowhere, his sword glowing in a fierce
blaze of green flame. Never had I seen a Codebearer fight with such
skill and anger before. He dissolved the creatures at last with a final,
brilliant stroke of his sword.

"I expected more Codebearers to appear, but he was the only
one that day. His Thunderbird landed and together we flew back
to my city in hopes of finding survivors. There were none. By the
time we arrived the Shadow invaders were gone, and the once glorious city was burning to the ground. Each Xin stronghold we visited thereafter told the same story. The Shadow had come to every
shard. In a single day, my people had been annihilated. I was an
orphan, the last of the Xin.

"Your father claimed to have foreseen the danger, but he was
unable to convince the other Codebearer captains to act on his insight. After the slaughter, the Resistance response was to mount

a reconnaissance mission to search for survivors. Your father led that mission; his men were discovered and taken captive. He alone escaped with his life.

"For safety, my existence was kept secret. We hid in the abandoned caves of my people. Only your father knew who I was. He returned from his mission to tell me the news that my family had been slain. The Resistance had failed; they were weak. He knew it, and so did I. He claimed he had business to attend to in Inire. Before he left, he gave me his sword as a promise that he would return. I never saw him again."

Petrov had relayed the sad history of the Xin to us before but hearing it from Xaul himself meant so much more. When he finished we sat in silence, digesting the story for a moment.

"You said my father went to Inire?" I asked, picking up on the name of the shard in Xaul's story.

Xaul nodded, "Yes, but that was long ago."

"You're not thinking of going there, are you?" Trista asked, spotting the curiosity on my face.

"Maybe, it's the only lead we have so far," I answered.

"But just knowing that your father visited Inire at one point isn't enough to go on," Trista replied.

"Even if he's still there, Inire is one of the largest shards in Solandria. We can't very well go tromping across the entire shard in search of clues," said Hope.

"No, I suppose not," I agreed. "I guess I'm just anxious to get started with our mission."

"Who said you haven't already?" Hope asked. "So long as you are following the Author's wishes you are already doing his will."

"Yeah, I know," I answered flippantly, "but I just wanted to make some progress."

Xaul spoke up, "It's like the Noctu always say, *Et Responsum, Imus Nocte*, which in the Old Language means, 'The answers come by night.' That just means sometimes the best thing you can do is sleep on it, and the answer may come to you."

"Hang on a sec," I answered, suddenly curious by the phrasing of the so-called Old Language the Noctu had been using. "Say that phrase again."

Xaul looked a bit surprised by the request. "The answers come by...."

"No, no," I interrupted him. "In the Old Language, say it again in the Old Language, only this time a little slower."

Xaul gladly obliged and repeated the sentence one word at a time, *"Et Responsum, Imus Nocte."*

"There, you see?" I said, repeating the last two words aloud for Trista to hear. *"Imus Nocte,* sound familiar?"

"Not really, should it?" Trista asked.

"Yes, it was in the message we deciphered in the cave, the one from my father's drawings. Remember, the words with no vowels?" I answered.

"Oh yeah, all that gibberish; I remember now," Trista said, her eyes lighting up in sudden remembrance.

I pulled the image up on my Symbio and deciphered the letters in the sand to complete the final phrase. The message read:

IN GIRUM
IMUS NOCTE
ET CONSUMIMUR
IGNI

Xaul read the phrase aloud, "We Enter the Circle by Night and Are Consumed by Fire."

"So it wasn't just a bunch of gibberish, after all," Trista said. "Do you think it has something to do with the Consuming Fire?"

"Probably, but it seems like a random thing to write down," I said, scratching my head. "I don't get it."

"No more random than Mirror Rim," Trista replied in reference to the other phrase we deciphered in the cave.

"I guess not," I said, recalling Dad's notes in the Author's Writ. There was something weird about this phrasing and it wasn't just the meaning of it. He was doing something on purpose; he was trying to be clever, trying to hide a message in it. But what?

One thing was certain; both the phrase in the book and the phrase on the drawing had been written by my dad. I felt closer to Dad every time I solved one of his puzzles. I couldn't help but smile at the memory of him and his goofy binary watch. If it hadn't been for Dad's willingness to train me on how to read binary, I never would have been able to apply the technique for deciphering the messages.

That's when it hit me.

"Wait a minute, that's it!" I shouted at once. "I think I know where to look for more clues. In fact, I've already found our first clue. I've had it all along."

Hope, Trista and Xaul exchanged confused glances, wondering what they had missed.

"How? What do you mean?" Trista ventured, looking rather stunned.

"Belac's castle is in Inire, right?"

"Yeah, so," Trista answered.

"So, it's where I found my father's broken binary watch," I said eagerly. "If his watch was there it's possible some other things might be as well, maybe even my father."

"That's pretty brilliant, Hunter," Trista said in support.

We started making plans to visit Belac's castle. Hope smiled, but it was a weak smile with a thoughtful gaze behind it.

"What's wrong?" I asked her.

"Nothing. It's just...I had a funny feeling, that's all."

"A funny feeling about what?" I asked.

"It was nothing, I'm sure," Hope replied. "I think I'm just tired."

"Me too," Trista added with a yawn.

It was true. The night had been long and full of surprises. We settled onto our mats for rest. No doubt we would need it for the travels ahead. Of course, that was assuming Xaul didn't kill us all in our sleep. His willingness to tell us a story hadn't dampened my awareness that he was still a cold-blooded killer. If I did fall asleep, it would be with one eye open. I managed to keep that up for a whole twenty minutes before my eyelids and the heat got the better of me. Before I knew it, I was dreaming of sand frogs, Shadow creatures and Boojum spit...a strange combination by anyone's standards.

Little did I know, before my dreams ended, things would get a lot stranger.

Chapter 18
Visions and Vanishings

Following a few short knocks, the castle door groaned open for the weary traveler to enter. He welcomed the shelter from the stormy night beyond the castle's barren walls. As he crossed the theshold, a howling wind blew up behind him and the door slammed shut violently on its own. The man startled at the sound and spun around in fright.

"Horrid night," he cursed, setting down his things and fumbling to light a candle in the darkness.

His bones shivered, but only partially from the cold—the other part was from a recent memory he already regretted making. He would never do such a thing again, he promised himself, unconsciously rubbing his hands on his pants to rid them of the blood that wasn't there.

"Hello?" he called out, hearing his echo return four times; the castle was abandoned, just as predicted. The interior of the castle was dark and empty, as good a place as any to be forgotten—much better than a tomb. By daylight things would surely look better. He reassured himself that he was doing the right thing.

Convinced he was alone, he left his things behind and pressed forward down a long hallway in search of a cozier room. As he started down the corridor, he didn't notice a lumbering shadow following him—not his own.

In his searching he came upon a room that seemed to suit his tastes best of all. It was no different from the other rooms except for the window…this room had none. In a hurry, he returned to the entry and gathered up his things, bringing them to the room and shutting the door behind him. He spread out his belongings on the floor before him.

In the jumble of items, he located a black velvet bag, opened it and looked inside. A red light streamed up from the bag, lighting his face in a way that made him look almost maniacal. With a trembling hand he reached down into the sack and produced a glowing crystal roughly the size of his palm. With the glowing stone in hand, he produced a pen and paper and began to draw the room in which he sat. He drew every detail, including himself and his things. When he was done he added something to the drawing, a mirror. Then an amazing thing began to take place. As he drew each line, the mirror in the drawing began to appear against the wall before him. It was a large standing mirror, oval shaped with a simple wooden frame around its edges. What he had drawn had come to be.

When he finished the last stroke of his drawing, he set his paper down and wandered to the mirror. With a sense of pride he examined his creation, pleased with the craftsmanship he had just accomplished. He admired his own reflection for longer than he realized, until he noticed something reflected in the mirror that hadn't been in the room. There was a shape in the corner, a huddled creature of some kind. Spinning around, he examined the actual corner where he had spotted the thing in the mirror. There was nothing there. For a second time he looked into the mirror. Sure enough, the shape was still there…only now it was moving.

"Is someone there?" he called out, scrambling to hide the glowing crystal in its sack once more before it could be discovered. There was no response but his echo. It annoyed him that he sounded so frightened in the echo. It wasn't like him to be that way. He had always been fearless before. But that was before he had seen the vision. Now, all he could think about was what would happen if it were true.

Gathering his courage, he picked up his walking stick and wandered to the corner of the room where the image of the creature had been. He poked his stick into the space, wondering if something invisible were there. Nothing.

Satisfied that it was just a trick of the eye, he turned back toward the mirror and found himself inches away from a creature twice his size and strength. It was carrying a knife and didn't look very pleased with the traveler. Stumbling over his own feet, the traveler toppled to the ground, dropping the bag with the stone for a moment. He snatched it back up again, guarding the object with his very life.

"What have I done?" the man seemed to whimper, but his voice was lost in the roar of the horrible beast that now towered over him. The roar continued through the night but no one could hear it, except for the black birds perched on a lonely evergreen tree.

****

"Hunter, wake up!" the voice said again. This time something poked my side. I sat up in fright, accidentally cracking my head against the nose of the person hovering over me: Desi.

"Ouch," Desi complained, holding her face in her hands. "What did you do that for?"

"I'm sorry, it was an…" I started to reply, then realized who I was talking to. "Desi? What are you doing here?"

My excitement nearly woke Trista who was also still asleep. Xaul and Hope were missing from their beds.

"I came to find you," she said, still cupping her nose behind her hands, "but now I'm starting to regret it. You really know how to make a girl feel welcome, you know that?"

Her face was dirty, and a mess of blood flowed from her nose, which I might have broken.

"Here, lie down," I said, reaching for my backpack and retrieving my sword. In addition to being a weapon, the sword had healing powers in its hilt. She took my place on the mat. I brought the Veritas Sword over and put the hilt of it on her face. Nothing happened. For whatever reason, the wound would not heal with the sword.

"I don't get it; the healing has always worked before," I said, scratching my head.

"Yeah, well, it's okay. I heal pretty quickly anyway," she said, pulling her bandana off of her head and holding it to her nose. Despite her grimy appearance, she didn't have a single scratch on her skin from the explosion the other day.

"Wait a minute. How did you escape the bookshop? I thought I watched you, you know…."

"Got lucky, I guess," she answered. "I blacked out in the explosion and when I woke, I was lying in the rubble behind the front counter. Vogler was gone. I hurried to the back door to try and find you, but it was open. I synced my Symbio signal to yours and stepped through the door and landed in the middle of the desert."

Trista began to stir and seemed a bit shocked at the sight of Desi lying on my mat. I explained the situation and despite her initial reaction, Trista seemed to genuinely warm up to the fact that Desi had returned.

"So," Desi asked, "now that we're here, what's our next move?"

"Belac's castle," I answered, explaining what we had learned earlier in the day. "It's as good a place as any to start looking."

Desi nodded her approval of the plan, and wiped the remaining blood from her nose.

"Hunter, look at this," Trista said, pulling a note from Hope's mat. "It's for you."

The note read:

Hunter,
> *I sense the Author is calling me back. There is something we*
> *may still need in your search for your father. Please wait for me.*
> *I will only be gone a few days. Xias and the Noctu have agreed*
> *to let you stay until I return. Learn from them and let them learn*
> *from you.*
>> *Hope*
> *P.S. Boojum says bye too! I'm taking him back to his family.*

"Well that stinks," I griped, anxious to get out of the camp. The way I figured, the less time we spent with Xaul the better off we were. Two or three days was going to seem like an eternity.

"Maybe it will give us time to figure out some of the other clues," Trista said, always the optimist.

"I've already looked those drawings over a million times. I'm not going to find anything new in…wait a minute…the traveler!" I shouted excitedly. I pulled up the images once more and hurried through them.

Desi turned to look at Trista. Neither of them seemed to have understood what I said.

"The traveler?"

"Yeah, the man in my dreams," I said. "He was searching a castle. There was this creature in the shadows that came after him. It looked just like the one in my father's picture. This one!"

I pointed to the picture my dad had sketched...the one where he was cowering under a shadow in a room with stone walls. The image was nearly identical to the scene from my dream; only in this picture the traveler was my father.

"Okay, so you were dreaming about this picture," Desi said in a practical tone. "That doesn't really tell us anything new."

"No, but the castle in my dream reminded me of Belac's castle, only empty." I pointed back to the screen where the shadow of the beast hovered over my father. "I'm pretty sure this is the same room as the one in my dream."

"How sure?" Trista asked, sounding a bit hesitant.

"There's only one way to find out," I answered. "We go to Belac's castle and look for it."

Trista didn't look too sure.

"But Hope told us to wait for her," Trista said. "We can't just up and leave her behind."

"Why not? She left you," Desi pointed out. "Leave her a note; we might even be back before she is."

"How do you know she won't be coming back with something from the Author for us?" Trista asked.

"How do you know my dream isn't the clue the Author was going to send?" I answered.

Trista started to open her mouth, but stopped short. She had run out of arguments and was somewhat surprised that I would choose to go against Hope's wishes.

"Look," I explained, "if Vogler made it out of the bookshop alive, then we don't have much time anyway. Hope didn't know that

Desi would be here or that I'd have that dream. We have the clues we need…we shouldn't be waiting around."

"I say we vote on it," said Desi. "Those in favor of going to Inire?" Desi's hand shot up first, followed by my own in a meaningless gesture of good faith. All eyes fell on Trista.

Trista raised her hand just to spite Desi. She didn't want to look like the odd one in the group.

"Then it's settled," I said triumphantly. "The only thing to figure out now is how to get there."

As it turned out, the travel arrangements were easier made than I expected. With Xaul's approval, the Noctu offered each of us a Raptor and agreed to lead us to an underground spring where a series of pools served as links to other shards. Each spring was a different color and was marked by a large etched rock to identify the destination that would be found on the other end. Inire's spring was black.

"So, we just jump in then?" I asked, staring at the reflective surface of the pool. In a way, I was scared—frightened of what I might learn about my father on the other side.

The Noctu warrior nodded and pointed down into the spring.

"Let's get going then," said Desi, impulsively diving headlong into the water. She never resurfaced. I was next in line.

"Hunter, wait," Trista said, stealing a moment alone with me. "I just want you to know that I'm glad Desi's not dead, and I'm…I'm sorry for being so…."

"Protective?" I finished her sentence, remembering our conversation in the cave.

"Yeah, that," Trista said shyly. "I know what it's like to have your family torn apart. I have a stepdad."

"I didn't know that," I said, looking at her in a new light.

"I'm not even sure Emily knows it. He's a nice guy and all, but it's not the same as your real dad."

"Why are you telling me this now?" I asked.

"Because I guess I just wanted you to know that I really do care about you...about finding your father." She added the last part, but it wasn't really an effort to hide her emotions. We both knew how we felt about each other. "Anyway, I still like Hope better, but I'm willing to go with Desi if that's what you want."

I nodded and offered her my hand.

"Shall we jump?"

Trista smiled and took my hand in her own for the second time in as many days. She entwined her fingers with mine and squeezed hard. My heart felt lighter than it had before. I wasn't afraid of the other side anymore. As silly as it was, having Trista with me gave me courage.

"Tell me when," said Trista, tightening her grip on Hope's bow with her free hand.

"Deep breath on three," I answered. "One...two...three...
dive."

Together we took the plunge, letting the icy black water swallow us. An invisible current pulled us downward like the suction of a vacuum, then it let go, and we were floating back to the top of the pool once more. *Something must have gone wrong*, I thought. We hadn't gone anywhere at all.

I reached out, breaking the flickering surface with my hand and catching hold of a second hand. It was Desi, but to my surprise, it wasn't water she pulled us out of. It was a sand pit in the middle of a lush jungle.

Coughing and spitting, we lay on the ground to catch our breath. We were completely dry, but covered in sand from head to toe. There was sand in my ears, my nose, my hair...there was sand in places I didn't even know existed.

"Never a dull moment," I said, shaking the gritty, grainy mess from my hair.

"Yes, and if we don't keep moving," Desi warned, "it won't get any duller."

"Why do you say that?" I asked.

"There's something in the woods and I think it's watching us."

Sure enough, twigs were cracking around us and the bushes rustled with life. Desi retrieved the black rods from her back pocket and thrust the orange one in the air. The thing in the bushes ran away, but under the cover of night we couldn't see what it was. Desi retracted the whip and placed it back in her pocket.

"Keep on your guard," Desi commanded. "We need to get moving. Where to, Hunter?"

I pointed in a direction that seemed right, but honestly I had no clue. The forest was thick, black and impossible to navigate without a point of reference to start from.

By night's end, we came to a clearing I recognized at once as Blood Canyon. It was a welcome sight, but also confirmed that we had just wasted half our day walking the wrong way. Belac's castle was a full day's walk back in the opposite direction. Frustrated, we turned around and headed back up the long and treacherous path through the Woods of Indifference. Every step of the way, we were well aware that we were not alone. We were being watched.

CHAPTER 19

CHASING SHADOWS

"O nce bitten, twice shy," they always say, but at the moment I couldn't care less. Sure, having been a prisoner in Belac's castle once before didn't make me exactly *eager* to try it again. At the moment I was so anxious to find out what had happened to my father I didn't much care if I put myself or anyone else, for that matter, in harm's way again.

I was on a mission, and no bug-eyed swamp troll was going to keep me from finding the truth. Not this time.

If the picture proved true and Belac really had killed my father, I was dead certain he was going to pay for his crime. It wasn't that I had revenge on my mind…well, okay, it was a bit of revenge. But there was righteous anger in there too somewhere, I'm sure of it. Besides, it was high time someone put Belac in his place. After all, this wasn't only for me but for all the other boys who had lost their fathers at the tender age of twelve; it was for Stretch and his horrible experience in Solandria; for Mom and Emily who were missing. What all of this had to do with Belac, I'm not exactly sure. But it made sense in my mind and it gave me the motivation I needed to go back to the castle without feeling even the slightest hesitation. "Once bitten, twice the ball of fury" is what I say.

Things were different this time. Desi's fire whips, my Veritas Sword and Trista's bow would be more than a match for a bumbling troll and his club. It was three against one; we had the upper hand. But beyond having mere numbers on our side, I knew a secret that practically guaranteed our success. Like the Noctu, Belac slept during daylight hours…more importantly, he snored.

By snoring I don't just mean that grumbly, snarly sound your uncle makes when he sleeps, but rather an obnoxiously loud, cement mixer snore with the amplitude of a megaphone added in for good measure. If there was anything you could count on from Belac, it was that from dawn til dusk, the grumpy old troll disappeared into his junk heap of a bedroom…and snored. There wasn't a second of the day during my captivity that I didn't hear the beastly sound, echoing throughout the castle.

Our strategy was simple: attack at high noon under the cover of Belac's snore. It was a brilliant plan, and one that couldn't fail, or so I thought.

By daylight, the castle in the swamp looked almost charming, like something out of a fairy tale. Almost, that is, if it weren't for the constant stench of the rotting bog that burned in our nostrils.

"What is that wretched smell?" Desi spat as we approached the last line of tree cover outside the stone fortress. I had forgotten how nauseatingly awful the bubbling bog was.

"It's not the smell of the swamp that should bother you," I replied. "It's what's in it."

"Which is what exactly?" Desi asked.

"You don't want to know," I replied, recalling the giant leeches that had covered my body night after night on my previous visit. The reminder fueled the fire in my stomach again. It was time to get even. As swiftly as we could, we crossed the swamp to the front door. It was locked from the inside.

"It won't budge," I said, shoving my shoulder into it a second time. The first phase of my supposedly perfect plan had come to a crashing halt.

"You weren't exactly expecting a welcoming party, were you?" Desi asked.

Ignoring the comment, I shouldered the door a third time and nearly bruised myself in the process. It was no use; the door wasn't going anywhere.

"What now?" Trista asked, as I stepped away from the door with a slightly embarrassed look on my face. There was no way I was going to admit defeat.

"If at first you don't succeed…" I said, raising my Veritas Sword over my head and preparing to hack my way through the immovable door.

"Whoa there, cowboy," Desi interrupted, stopping my arm mid-swing. "Do you want to wake Belac? We need a better plan."

"Oh, right. Well, maybe there's a back door we can slip in through," I said, feeling good about the suggestion.

"That's not a plan. That's floundering."

The remark smacked my ego full in the face, but I wasn't going to let it get to me. After all, it was my own brilliance that had led us this far. Neither Simon nor Desi had been able to figure out where my father had gone. We were only one door-width away from finding the answers that had eluded us both.

"Floundering or not, I haven't heard any other ideas," I replied.

"Well, there must be some other way in," Trista added.

"There always is," Desi replied confidently, taking control of the situation. "It's just a matter of where…to…look." She backed away from the door a few steps and glanced overhead. "There!" she nearly shouted, pointing to a window on the second story.

"How is that a plan?" I asked, with more than a hint of sarcasm. "It's thirty feet up at least; how are you going to reach it?"

Desi rolled her eyes and held up one of her fire whips. "Stand back and learn," she said, drawing the tail of the blue whip much longer than before. When she was finished, the length of the whip fell to the ground beside her. She gauged the distance and swung the whip overhead, targeting a beam that stuck out from the roof-line just above the window. The tip of the whip wound around the beam tightly and Desi gave it a good tug. It held in place.

"Be back in a minute," she said, using the glowing whip to scale the wall. She crawled through the window and disappeared inside. A few moments later, the front door creaked open and Desi was there. She retrieved the whip rod and retracted the tail into it. Together, the three of us slipped inside Belac's home and closed the door softly behind us.

The dingy interior looked worse than I remembered. The walls were actually growing moss on the inside and the floor looked like it had never been cleaned. But it wasn't the look of the place that bothered me most. It was what we heard…or rather what we didn't hear, that made my heart freeze.

"We have a problem," I whispered. "No snore!"

The absence of Belac's obnoxious snoring could only mean one of two things….

"Maybe he's gone?" Trista asked, sounding somewhat hopeful.

"That, or he knows we're here and he's waiting somewhere," Desi added.

It struck me how different the two girls were. Trista was the eternal optimist, hopeful and trusting to a fault. Desi, on the other hand, was more like a cat, confident and sly, always on the alert and ready for the unexpected to happen. They were a well-matched pair.

"Either way, there's no use wasting time. We'll find out soon enough," I pointed out.

"What's next?" Desi asked, deferring to me, despite the dismal failure of my plan thus far.

"Follow me," I answered, motioning to the left and slinking down the hallway. I wasn't exactly looking forward to the next part of the mission. It meant revisiting one of the darkest moments in my life: Belac's prison.

A collection of iron shackles in various shapes and sizes hung from wooden pegs on the wall outside the prison door. They were the same kind of shackles Belac had used on Stretch and me to ensure we didn't run away. I picked out a pair that seemed large enough to fit Belac himself and imagined the joy I'd feel locking them on *his* wrists for a change.

As we turned to leave, I spotted something through the barred window of the prison door I hadn't even considered a possibility: a prisoner was inside. I'm not sure why but the thought had never occurred to me that Belac might have found another slave to be leech bait. The man in the prison was gaunt and heavily bearded, a mere shadow of the human he once had been. He slept soundly on the stone floor, waiting for the dreaded night to fall when he'd be drug out into the swamp. My heart went out to him; it could have easily been me had the Author not intervened and saved Stretch and me that night. Everything in me wanted to open the door and let him out.

"Not now," Desi whispered, seeing the prisoner. "You can't risk the mission over him. Not until Belac is restrained."

Desi was right; we couldn't wake him. If the prisoner was even half as starved for salvation as I had been, any sign of a rescue and he'd be shouting for joy. That was the last thing we needed with a vicious troll potentially lurking nearby. We needed silence. The rescue would have to wait.

"Stay on your toes. The prisoner means Belac can't have gone far," I said. "He's got to be somewhere."

We returned to the main hall and tiptoed up the stairway toward the room where Belac slept. I ignited my Veritas Sword and motioned to the door. Desi and Trista nodded, armed themselves and prepared for the worse.

With a shove of my hand, the door to Belac's room creaked open, revealing a massive hulking shape in the shadows behind it. At first I figured the shape was Belac, but quickly realized it wasn't moving. It was just a heap of junk, one of many that nearly covered the floor of his room now. We moved gingerly through the precariously stacked piles in hopes of spotting the enormous bed behind them. Unfortunately, the bed was empty.

"He's not here," said Desi. "Do you want to look for clues?"

As much as I did, I knew the better course of action was to contain Belac first…then look for clues.

"We can't afford to be discovered. Let's check the other rooms first. If Belac's here, we need to find him before he finds us. We'll have time to come back later."

The three of us ventured out on our hunt for the troll. Room after bedraggled room turned up no sign of him. The place was a regular pigsty. Each room seemed to be a bigger mess than the previous room, with the exception of one, the library.

The library was surprisingly well kept, not exactly clean, but for Belac it was as close as clean gets. In fact, despite the thick layer of dust that blanketed the room, you might say it was practically pristine. But there was something else about this room, a feeling that something wasn't all that it seemed.

"I guess Belac isn't much of a reader," Trista said, after taking in the state of the room.

"Well, there's a big surprise," I replied smugly, turning back toward the hallway that had led us here. "There are only a few rooms left. Let's go."

"No, wait," Desi said, holding up a hand. "Somebody has been here…recently."

"How can you tell?" I questioned.

She pointed to a stone pillar that curved out from the wall to the left of the doorway. On it, about shoulder height was an iron ring, which hung from a metal plate embedded in the wall. The ring swung out from the wall a bit and held a wooden torch. The torch was still smoldering…. Someone had let it burn out.

"Of course, the torch," I said, nearly kicking myself for having missed it.

"But I don't get it," Trista said, expressing what we were all thinking. "If Belac has been here, then why is it so clean? There aren't even any footprints in the dust."

I scrutinized the room, gazing across the space and down the walls to the floor where the carpet we stood on led up to a bookshelf. That's when it hit me.

"Unless…maybe Belac doesn't think of it as a room at all. Maybe it's more like a hallway to him, a place *between* rooms," I said, suddenly figuring out Belac's secret. "Do you see how the carpet rolls under the bookshelf?"

"Yes," Desi said, her eyes lighting up at the realization. "It's a fake wall. The bookshelf is hiding another room."

The three of us eagerly ran to the bookshelf and went to work searching for a way to open the door.

"There's got to be a trigger of some kind," I said, "a secret book or lever of some sort."

Nothing presented itself. After several minutes of fruitless searching, we were ready to give up.

"Do you think we're overanalyzing it?" Trista ventured to ask.

"What do you mean?" I answered.

"Well, Belac's a troll, right?"

"Yeah, so?" I wondered where she was going with this.

"So, maybe we need to think like a troll thinks."

"How do we do that? Take half our brains out?" Desi asked, smiling at her own joke.

Trista pretended not to notice. "No, but we could try pushing our way in."

Without another word, Trista started pressing against the bookshelf with all her might. Surprisingly, it budged. It was only a half-inch, but it moved. With newfound hope we joined her, pushing together and managing to slide the centermost bookshelf backward a full five feet before it came to a stop against a stone wall. A staircase led down into a lower level of the castle we had yet to explore.

"You'd make a pretty good troll," Desi teased Trista. I could tell from the face Trista made she didn't appreciate the comment much at all.

A cold draft blew up from the blackness at the bottom of the staircase. It was the kind of draft that felt more like a gasp for breath, as if the staircase itself were a gaping mouth that wanted to pull us down its throat. The light of my Veritas Sword seemed to be gobbled up by the darkness of the creepy tunnel.

"Well, I guess we...go down," I said nervously. With wobbly knees I stepped down into the blackness toward the hidden basement. The passage was lined in cobwebs and continued a hundred or more steps down, before ending in a rather small, rectangular room. The room was entirely empty except for a simple wooden stool in the center and a tall, oval-shaped mirror, which seemed vaguely familiar to me.

"Well, that's a let down," Trista said. "All that secrecy for nothing. Who hides a mirror in their basement?"

"What is it?" Desi asked, noticing my attention drifting from the mirror.

"It's the room," I said thoughtfully. "The picture my dad drew of Belac. It happened in this room, in that corner...."

I pointed to the corner I had sensed was the place. The same jagged rock popped out from the wall.

"And that mirror," I said, "I think I've seen it before too, in my dream. A traveler visited a room like this one. He created a black mirror...just by drawing it."

Desi's eyes widened slightly, contemplating the idea.

"What do you mean, 'drawing it'?" Trista asked.

I explained how the traveler in my dream had made the mirror appear, seemingly out of nowhere; how it was almost as if he had *willed* it into being with the help of the crystal stone.

"Scrivening. It's the art of writing into being," Desi said with excitement. "I always thought it was just a myth. Your father had long talked about creating a world of his own—a world where he could escape the fate he saw in the Eye of Ends. Before he went missing, he said he had been studying the art of scrivening. He believed it was possible to create a portal to a new world where he could control the outcome of things."

"How?" I asked.

"By using the power of the Bloodstone," she said, looking me dead in the eye. At the very mention of the word, my jaw tightened and I clutched the place where Aviad had once removed the cursed object from my chest. The Bloodstone had been the source of so much trouble before I couldn't bring myself to believe it existed again.

"But the Bloodstone is gone; Aviad destroyed it," I said. "I saw him do it myself."

"Yes, but your father didn't need to find the original Blood-stone; he only needed to harness the source of its power to make a new one," Desi explained. "He must have found a way."

"How is that even possible?" I asked.

"Well, the Eye of Ends comes from the Living Tree, right?"

"Yeah, so?"

"So, have you ever seen a cross section of a tree?"

"Sure, lots of times."

"Well, the rings of the tree are like a record of the tree's life…its history. According to Simon's research, when you enter the inside of the Eye of Ends there is a Maze of Rings, where the history of our worlds are contained—like a code. Mortals, like your father, must navigate this maze until they come to a dead end. Each dead end reveals another vision. At the very center of the maze—a place known as the Inmost Circle—a pillar of fire rises up to infinite heights. This fire is believed to be from the very stream of the Code of Life…the source that once gave the Living Tree its life and the Bloodstone its power.

"As far as we know, your father is the only one who successfully found his way to the center of the Eye. If what you saw in your vision was true, your father may have learned how to harvest a second Bloodstone from the Code of Life."

"Are you suggesting the traveler in my dreams was really my father?" I asked.

Desi shrugged, "It's a possibility, but whoever it was didn't want this mirror to be found."

I approached the dirty mirror and wiped a layer of dust off its face. As I did, the surface reacted to my touch with a dazzling display of brightly colored lines beneath the glass. It was like finger painting with digital light. The glowing marks only lasted a second or two before fading away, but the effect was impressive.

Trista gawked at the mirror and said, "Can I try? That's cool!"

She was already beside me, drawing random hearts and flowers on the surface of the mirror. Her eyes lit up like a child's with a new toy at Christmas and she drew a pair of glasses and a mustache over the reflection of her face.

A moment later, words began to appear in the colorful ink behind the surface of the mirror, as if someone had written them in from the other side. The words were written backwards and read:

> *My end is my beginning,*
> *my beginning is my end.*
> *Find me in my reflection*
> *beyond the...*

"A riddle?" Desi asked, raising an eyebrow. "Your father loved riddles."

"But this one isn't finished," Trista said.

"That's because the last words of the riddle are the answer, I think," I said. "It's like a password. I think we're supposed to write the answer on the mirror."

"Yes, but what is it a password to?" Desi wondered.

"To finding whoever made this mirror," I said thoughtfully.

"You mean your father?" Trista asked.

I shrugged, but I was thinking the same thing.

"Well, you'd better be sure of the answer before you write it. If your father made this mirror, he likely didn't make it without taking precautions."

"Meaning what?" Trista asked.

"Meaning," Desi answered firmly, "he probably put traps in the room for anyone who didn't answer correctly."

Our eyes darted nervously around, scrutinizing every corner of the space. Suddenly, my imagination got the better of me; nothing could be trusted anymore. The floor could give way, the ceiling might cave in, the room might flood…any number of dismal ends might come to us if we got the answer wrong. There was no way of knowing for sure, but that's what made it all the more nerve-racking.

"Okay, let's think about it for a while," I said in the calmest voice I could muster. My dad had made some pretty difficult riddles for me in the past, but none of them would ever be as important as this one.

I ran through a series of potential answers in my mind.

"What rhymes with *end*?" I asked aloud.

Trista rattled off a long list before I could think of one.

"Send, bend, lend, depend, tend, mend, pretend, ascend, spend, contend, descend, suspend…."

"Whoa, slow down!" I shouted, stopping her short. "Okay, that's like looking for a needle in a haystack. We have to start somewhere else. Let's go back over the first lines; there's got to be a clue there."

I began repeating the riddle aloud a few times in hopes it would help the answer come.

"My end is my beginning…" I said.

"My beginning is my end," Trista continued.

"That's it!" I shouted, in a sudden burst of enthusiasm. "A palindrome."

Trista looked blankly at me.

"A palindrome is a word that can be read two ways: forward and backward. It's kinda like a reflection, only with letters…."

"You mean like the phrase Xaul helped us solve?" Trista said, her eyes lighting up with excitement. "The one where we wrote the same letters down in the cave?"

I nodded.

"So, you think the answer is the word *palindrome*?" Desi asked, not sounding completely convinced.

"*Find me in my reflection, beyond the palindrome*," I said aloud, trying it on for size. "It might be it."

"Yes, but how sure are you? It doesn't even rhyme."

"Well, it doesn't have to rhyme to be a riddle, but still…something doesn't feel quite right."

We sat for several minutes, silently debating different phrases. Everyone had their own opinion of the riddle. There were far too many answers to choose from. Unfortunately, none of them sounded in the least bit right until Trista blurted out something I had forgotten entirely.

"Mirror Rim!" Trista said, at last. "Isn't that the phrase your father wrote in his Writ? It's a palindoo-hicky, or whatever that word is. Isn't it?"

"You're right!" I said excitedly. "Mirror Rim is spelled the same backward and forward."

"And a mirror shows your 'reflection' too," Trista added.

"*Find me in my reflection, beyond the Mirror Rim.* Is that it?" Desi asked.

"It sounds better than anything else I've come up with," I answered. "It's either that or we give up."

We took a vote and agreed to give it a shot. Trista and Desi stepped back toward the stairs just in case our answer was wrong. They would have a chance to escape if a trap presented itself.

When everyone was ready, I wrote the answer to the riddle onto the mirror's surface. I took care to write the letters backwards to match the previous words that appeared above it. As the last letter was completed, the words disappeared and my reflection vanished from the black mirror completely. I backed away from the mirror, wondering if I had gotten it wrong. Then, with a dazzling flash, the mirror lit up with an infinite nest of neon blue rings that made it appear like a tunnel through the wall.

"He did it!" Desi smiled so wide she almost laughed. "He actually did it!"

Now that it was safe, Trista and Desi joined me in front of the tunnel of light.

"So this mirror is a portal to my father's world?" I asked.

"There's only one way to be sure," Desi answered. "You have to pass through it. If this is your father's mirror, he won't be far from the other side."

We decided I should go alone. Desi felt it was best that she and Trista stay behind to guard the mirror from unwanted intruders. After all, Belac couldn't be far, and there was always Vogler. If something went wrong, she would reach me on the Symbio device.

"How do I enter?" I asked.

"Just step through," Desi replied.

I swallowed nervously at the thought and glanced at the tunnel ahead of me in the mirror. After years of wondering, I was perhaps one step away from discovering the mystery of my father's disappearance.

"Hunter, wait," Trista begged. "How do you know it's safe? I mean, how do you know there is even a way to come back? What if you get lost in the mirror like…like your father?"

"The mirror should have two sides," Desi offered. "Pay attention to where it is you arrive. That will also be your way back out."

"Okay then," I said, my heart racing so fast my fingers trembled from the excitement. "I'll be back."

"We'll be waiting," Trista said, wringing her hands nervously in front of her.

Slowly, I approached the mirror, intent on finishing the quest I had begun. I took a deep breath and raised my foot. I stepped into the mirror and time slowed to a crawl until it seemed as if I had frozen in space halfway between the world behind and the world that lay ahead. Though I couldn't move, the lights of the tunnel began to move toward me and past me, slowly at first—then quicker and quicker until they were nothing but a blur of solid light around me.

****

I was frozen now, captured on a brilliant blank canvas of pure white light. Everything my senses perceived felt fresh and new. Words I could not understand began to take voice as whispers all around me. As the cryptic words were spoken, shapes began to form out of thin air like the first, loosely sketched lines, outlining a yet-to-be masterpiece. All at once this budding world burst into life as vibrant colors filled in a new layer of definition. When the sweeping transformation was finally complete, I found myself finishing my original step through the mirror to arrive in a magnificent, glass-domed room.

From its panoramic view, the room appeared to be atop the highest tower of an impressive, modern facility. A lush, rolling landscape stretched off into the distance far below me, warmed beneath the billowing, pink-lit clouds of a soft sunset sky. The view outside was breathtaking.

Inside, however, was an entirely different story—a pack rat's paradise. An infestation of books and loose papers held together what otherwise would have been an unrelated assortment of found items, from the commonplace to the extraordinary. Half of the things, I couldn't even identify, though I supposed that was the function of the notes taped to many of them—an attempt at cataloging the collection. Whatever the intent, the disorderly piles transformed what otherwise could have been a state-of-the-art research lab into a state-of-the-art disaster zone.

Remembering Desi's advice, I checked the wall behind me for the other side of the mirror. I was relieved to see a free-standing mirror set up amongst the junk heaps behind me. This would be my doorway back to Solandria if all went well.

"What is this place?" I marveled aloud, turning slowly to take in the bizarre setting.

"Somewhere you should not be," came the unexpected reply from over my shoulder. Though I hadn't heard the voice since I was twelve, I recognized it in a heartbeat. It was the voice of my father.

CHAPTER 20

MY FATHER'S WORLD

I must have imagined the reunion with my father a million times over. He'd walk up the sidewalk, through the front door and back into our lives, wrapping me up in a great bear hug. All the missing years would be explained, all the hurts forgiven and our family would return to normal once again. I should have learned the lesson by now that we rarely get what we expect.

"Dad?" I whispered, spinning around to scan the room for any sign of him. A head of thick blond hair peeked out from behind a particularly tall stack of books, and I looked into my father's piercing blue eyes for the first time in what felt like a lifetime.

"Son...it's really you!" Dad said, looking as shocked as if he'd just been visited by a ghost from his past. "What are you doing here?"

"Dad!" I shouted, all at once feeling like a child again. Overwhelmed by the emotions, I found myself giving in to the boyish urge to run over and tackle my long-lost father. Whatever obstacles had been stacked between us toppled easily as I raced toward my father; nothing would stop me from reaching him. Unfortunately, "nothing" did.

"Hunter, wait!" Dad warned, raising his arms to halt me.

As I fell forward toward his outstretched arms, I unexpectedly found myself grasping thin air, having somehow passed right through him, crashing awkwardly on the floor. I was stunned.

Dad laughed as he apologized, "Sorry about that. I was trying to tell you that you can't touch me here." Being the one with the bruises, I somehow missed the humor of the situation.

"What do you mean?" I asked, rubbing my shoulder. "Why? What's happened to you?" From where I sat sprawled on the ground, he looked well enough to me—just like I remembered him, only with slightly longer hair than before. He was still standing in the exact spot I'd seen him, so I knew I hadn't missed him. That's when a horrible thought suddenly crashed in on me. I gulped before giving the idea a voice.

"You're not…I mean, are you…?" I couldn't bring myself to suggest it.

"Dead?" Dad finished my words for me. He laughed at this too. "No! Far from it, in fact."

"But, I just *fell* right through you—like you're a ghost," I said in disbelief, picking myself up off the floor. "People don't just walk through each other. It's impossible."

"Yeah, well, that's my fault. I haven't gotten around to building interrelational collisions between humans into my design yet. Being the only one here, it really hasn't been an urgent need. I'm not entirely sure this place can handle it. I wasn't ready for this yet. Everything seems stable but…." His mind started to wander and he acted for a moment as if he forgot I was there.

I stared at him blankly. "I have no idea what you're talking about."

Dad smiled, ignoring my confusion, and took a step back to look me over. "Look at you. You've grown so much," he said, letting out a sigh. "It's so great to see you, son! I never expected to see you again. Not here, anyway. Not yet."

"Dad," I said with growing uncertainty, "where exactly is 'here'?"

"Well you're in… uh," Dad paused awkwardly, searching for a suitable explanation to my question. "Funny. I guess I've been too busy creating this place to think of ever giving it a name. Now that you're here, maybe you can help me choose a name for my world."

My design…creating this place…my world? It took a minute for the full meaning of Dad's collective words to completely sink in.

"Hold on," I said. "You mean to tell me that you *created* all this?" I motioned toward the dream-like world outside the glass dome walls.

"Well…yes," Dad stated plainly. "Of course, not all of it turned out so great to begin with. My first attempts were nothing to write home about, but I've slowly been getting the hang of it."

"The hang of what?"

"Authorship."

"But you can't… I mean, that's not…. How?" I spat out.

Dad smiled back, unfazed by my perceived ignorance. "Just because you've never seen something done before, doesn't mean that it's not possible. Great minds ask the hard questions and don't settle for the easy answers. Like you, Hunter. Finding me should have been next to impossible. Goodness knows I tried hard to make it tough, covering my tracks, setting security points. I don't know how you did it, but somehow you found me. You obviously didn't settle for the easy explanations."

I could feel my dad's evident sense of pride as he exclaimed,

"You're a regular chip off the old block, son!" He started to reach out with a fist to deliver a friendly punch on my shoulder, like he always used to when he was still home. But he stopped short, remembering the gesture couldn't connect with me in this other-world environment.

Sensing I was even more confused than before, Dad tried taking a new approach. Gathering up a collection of drawings from a table, Dad rolled them up and then beckoned for me to follow.

"Walk with me, son. There's something I want to show you."

He didn't have to ask me twice. I readily accepted, eager to learn anything that he might have to share.

"Just watch your step," Dad requested. "Contrary to what you might think, this mess does have a bit of order to it."

I followed in Dad's footsteps as he picked a way through his precarious maze of "organized chaos."

"Let's start with what you already know about Solandria," Dad said as we walked. He nodded toward my belt and the Veritas hilt hanging from its clasp. "You've already been introduced to the Codebearers, I see."

"Yes. Found them—or, I guess they found me—at the end of the last school year," I replied. "At least in Destiny's time, I should say."

"That's right. I forgot about the variable time sync between Solandria and the Veil. To be honest, I still haven't figured out how my world relates back to the others. How long has it been?"

"Too long," I answered, coming to a standstill. "It's been *three* years, Dad…and counting. You left us three years ago."

This news seemed to have a sobering effect on him. He paused for a moment and flashed a weak smile at me. "Has it really been that long?" he said softly. "Of course it has, look at you—you're all grown up now. Practically a man!"

If only it *were* just time lost between us. The pain went so much deeper than that, filling up the awkward silence we found ourselves in.

"What's done is done," Dad abruptly concluded. Turning his head toward our unnamed destination, he pushed on. "You're here and that's what matters now."

It was clearly much more complicated than that but, not knowing what else to say, I kept quiet and fell back in step.

"When you trained with the Resistance, did they teach you anything about the origins of Solandria?" Dad asked.

"Yeah," I forced myself to join in the conversation, pushing aside my conflicting emotions. "I learned about the Code of Life under Captain Samryee, about how *nothing comes from nothing* and all that."

"Samryee, as in Samryee Thordin?" Dad said with surprising interest.

"Yeah. Why?"

Dad smiled and nodded his head knowingly. "Captain Sam... how's that for moving up the ranks?"

"So, it's true then," I said, connecting the dots. "You did serve alongside Sam in the Resistance, didn't you?"

"Yes. With him and a good many others. I remember Sam from the few missions we were on together. He's kind of a hard guy to forget."

I nodded in agreement, feeling my own sense of swelling pride at having confirmed my father's authenticity as a Codebearer. Hadn't Aviad himself said my father was a skilled warrior? An immediate bond began to re-form; I could already imagine the talks we could have swapping our battle stories and braving new adventures together.

Dad's pace had slowed noticeably and I saw a far-off look in his eyes as if he were lost in memories. "So many good people serving with the Resistance…. It's just…bah," he shook his head, letting the thought trail off unfinished.

"Just what, Dad?" I pressed.

"It goes back to what I was saying, Hunter. I think too many people stop asking questions when they feel the answers will be too hard to confront. They want to stay with their comfortable assumptions. I couldn't do that."

I got the sense that what he was saying was somehow related to what the other Codebearers, and more recently Xaul, had alluded to about my father's past—some kind of falling out with the Resistance. With what snippets I had gleaned from their accounts, I had an idea that I would be nosing into a sensitive subject, but I wanted to hear the full story from Dad himself.

Gathering my courage, I asked, "Is that why you left the Resistance?"

My question had as gentle an effect as tossing a cup of cold water into his face. He looked shocked, even hurt by what I'd implied. Whatever fondness he might have momentarily entertained toward his Codebearer days was suddenly washed away to reveal a deep-seated emotional scar.

"We had our differences of opinion. I moved on," Dad said curtly, leaving it at that. "And I'm the better for it."

His fiery expression told me this was as far as he was willing to go for now. Not wanting to press my luck, I followed his cue and dropped the subject.

A moment later, Dad voluntarily added, "What I will say, Hunter, is that *if* I left them, it wasn't to run away like a coward. It took guts to do what I did, to set out in search of the deeper truths *beyond* where the Codebearers' teachings left off. I had a hunch that there was more to the story than what they were willing to discuss. I had a personal responsibility not to ignore the hard questions. That is why I set out on my own…to find the answers.

"But now," Dad said, steering us on to a more cheerful subject, "now I am not alone in my hard-core truth-seeking. With you here, I finally have someone to share all of my discoveries with!"

Dad looked at me with such pride and affection. I never thought I would experience that again, but it felt so good. Never mind that I was still mostly in the dark as to what "discoveries" I'd actually stumbled onto. I just liked feeling my father's pleasure.

"May I?" Dad asked, reaching a hand out toward my sword.

"I don't know, *can* you?" I said, in light-hearted reference to the physical limitations he was experiencing in this world.

"Don't be silly," Dad bantered back. "Of course I can. It's just the collision between humans that I haven't accounted for yet."

Right, I mockingly chided myself as I reached to unclasp my sword. *Anyone would know that.*

Then I paused, remembering something. "I almost forgot," I said, reaching across to my other side. "I brought something for you." I unlatched the other weapon I had purposefully started carrying with me in hopes of someday sharing this very moment with my father.

"Oh?" Dad said curiously, taking the Veritas Sword I presented to him, examining its black, twisted metal.

"This one's certainly seen better days," he said, then attempted to hand it back to me. Noting the expectant look in my eyes, he asked, "Did I miss something?"

I turned the sword over and presented it to him with the pommel facing up. Dad's eyes lit up when he recognized the name engraved on the bottom: *Caleb Brown.*

"This was mine!" Dad exclaimed. "Where on earth did you find this?" He ran his fingers over its distorted features some more, "and what did you do to it?"

"Long story, but I recovered it from a certain Xin warrior named Xaul."

Dad nodded absently, apparently lost in reliving the haunting events that surrounded his rescue of the orphaned boy.

I had anticipated Dad inquiring more about Xaul, or feeling prompted to shed a little more light on the mysterious business on the Shard of Inire that kept him from ever returning to the young Xin boy he'd entrusted his sword to. But Dad seemed to be avoiding his past at all costs.

Holding his reclaimed weapon in front of him, Dad skillfully brought the unique, black-lighted blade to life. He seemed to be genuinely intrigued with his sword's altered design, muttering things to himself about how he'd like to reverse engineer it and what he could improve on. After a few distracted moments, Dad turned his focus back to me.

"What I intended to illustrate with the Veritas Sword," Dad said, not missing a beat, "is its clear relationship to the Code of Life as the source of power. That relationship is so beautifully displayed in this matchless weapon." The blade of light appeared and disappeared easily on command under my father's skillful handling.

"But as you might have learned," he continued, handing the sword back to me for safekeeping, "the Code goes beyond just empowering weaponry; it flows through everything, providing a language for description of all things."

"Yeah," I chimed in. "My science class back in Destiny described DNA sequences as being the code of life, like the letters in a sentence used to describe what we see around us."

"That's right. Ah, here we are," Dad said, pushing open a large glass door that led out onto an expansive balcony. "After you."

I stepped out into the warm, sweet-smelling air that begged to be breathed deeply. One of the richest fragrances came from potted fruit trees, artfully lining the balcony's interior. The sky was in the middle of transitioning from radiant pink to a vibrant hue of orange that complimented the ripened peaches hanging from the trees' branches. Dad pulled off a peach for each of us and tossed me one as we walked over to the railing. Leaning against it, I drank in the incomparable beauty surrounding me.

"You're on the right track with the DNA," Dad said encouragingly, taking a bite of the juicy peach. "It's a good start to understanding how the Code of Life is like a language woven together to create everything we see and experience. But that's still only dealing with the tip of the iceberg. I want you to think of DNA as being only part of a subset language, if you will—of the grander, more complete language of the full Code of Life. If we think about it, there are more than just the three dimensions of the physical world that DNA deals with. Why concede that the Code stops there? It would stand to reason that it should extend to describe the other dimensions as well."

"Like what? Time?"

"That's our fourth dimension, yes. But you're still only halfway there," Dad said mysteriously, taking another bite.

I stared blankly at my father. As much as I would have loved to continue impressing him, this conversation had now officially flown right over my head, like so many of the conversations I'd had with my scientific-minded best friend. This was Stretch's element, not mine. Wrapping my brain around the idea of dimensions outside space and time was just not going to happen.

"If my theories are correct," Dad continued enthusiastically, "the Code of Life can be tracked through all *ten* dimensions that I maintain define our complete existence."

"O…kay," I said slowly, trusting I hadn't missed his point entirely. "So…isn't that just a brainy way of saying that we believe the Author has control of all things?"

Dad screwed up his face, obviously less than satisfied at the simplicity of my interpretation. "While that *is* a true statement—one you most certainly were taught in your training—you'd be selling yourself short of the bigger reward if you just accepted that statement at face value and stopped there. The promise behind the truth is this: if we can correctly discern a Code exists by which all things are created and controlled, then what is to stop us from learning it for our own uses?"

"You're telling me that you cracked the Code of Life?"

"Is that too much to believe?" Dad asked, looking happily around at the world he'd already begun to author. He held out his half-eaten peach for me to see.

"If I wanted to, I could rewrite this fruit to explode on impact. Or make a feather cut glass. The sky's the limit! The Author's designs are all mine to repurpose and perfect however I choose."

"How?" I challenged.

Dad chuckled. "I thought you'd never ask. All right, let me make this as simple as I can."

He unfurled the collection of pages he'd brought with him from the table inside and smoothed them out atop a marble pedestal beside an ornately carved mahogany box. The pages revealed a new set of drawings, but the carving on the box was what caught my attention. The design on it looked vaguely like that of the Living Tree—the same one that appeared on the back of my Author's Writ. Dad ignored the box and pulled my attention back to the drawings.

"First, I take a known object…." He pointed to the top drawing, a fine series of sketches portraying a manta ray, one of his favorite subjects. "Then I examine its Code…." He pointed to the complex-looking set of cryptic notes, running in the margins and onto a second page.

"Using a little imagination, I do my work…." Dad took out

the third page—a beautifully rendered drawing of a manta ray-type creature with elongated, jointed fins. In the lower corner of the page, he scribbled the word *wingray*. He promptly began folding it at sharp angles. Something about the drawing looked vaguely familiar, but I couldn't place where I'd seen it before. Dad concluded his folding technique while saying, "…restringing the original Code with new combinations of other known Codes, thus assuming authorship of my own design and…*voilà!*"

He held up a finished paper airplane with a grin. "A wingray!"

Before I could voice my dissatisfaction at this juvenile exercise, Dad drew back and launched the paper vessel out into the open sky. It sailed an impressive distance before its folds began to loosen and pull apart. Then, in an instant, the simple little paper did the impossible, transforming before my eyes into the fantasy creature I'd seen outlined in my Dad's drawing. I heard Dad laughing as I stood slack-jawed, watching this tiny creature come to life and growing to extreme proportions at an alarming rate. Reaching a bank of distant clouds, the wingray made a wide turn to come soaring directly back over us in a dramatic fashion. I couldn't repress the urge to duck as it swooped by overhead. It had grown even larger than I'd imagined; its enormous wingspan nearly covered the entire dome of the tower.

After it disappeared, I turned back to my father who was still chuckling, enjoying this part all too much.

"The paper can do that?" I said in awe.

"Naw…the whole airplane was something I just thought up for you. I thought you'd enjoy the special touch since you appreciate magic tricks…or at least you used to when you were twelve."

He was right. I had somewhat outgrown that phase, but this was no ordinary magic.

"So, you can create anything?"

"A perfect sunset, a wingray…anything I want—just like that!" Dad snapped his fingers for effect.

"Yeah, I got that part, Dad. What I was really looking for was the deeper answer. Where does the Code you are using actually come from? How are you controlling it? *Nothing comes from nothing,* right?" I asked.

Dad was visibly pleased with my prowess, wagging a proud finger at my chest. "You really have a knack for this just like me, son… fantastic question. The answer lies in this."

As he said it, Dad opened the mahogany box that had captured my attention earlier and withdrew a hand-sized object, formed from silver rods in a unique scrolling pattern of branches. He slipped his middle fingers and thumb into the farthest-most loops, fitting it onto his hand perfectly. It looked something like a metallic glove. The device was certainly impressive, if for those features alone, but what commanded my attention the most was the brilliant red stone set in the middle of it all—a stone that could be confused with no other.

"The Bloodstone…" I whispered, breathing in sharply. Of all the mind-bending discoveries I'd been subjected to since arriving in my father's world, this one was hardest to comprehend. *How had it survived? Hadn't Aviad taken it from me and destroyed the cursed stone himself? If he had, then how could it be here now? Had he failed?*

"It's not *the* Bloodstone," Dad took it upon himself to correct me. "But you're right in identifying it as a "bloodstone"…of sorts. This little beauty is my own design, a vial, really. With it, I was able to capture a portion of the Author's Code of Life. Now all the secrets to commanding life itself are mine to hold." Dad fingered the dazzling jewel affectionately.

"But…at what cost?" I asked him, suddenly fearful for his life and mine. I could still feel the sting of searing pain I had experienced when I held the forbidden Bloodstone's power, and knew all too well its ultimate promise of death.

"What do you mean?" Dad asked casually, seeming oblivious to these threats.

"It's cursed! It says so in the Writ; the...."

"The Bloodstone Prophecy—of course I've read up on it," Dad interrupted. "It presented a dilemma at first—that's why I chose to make a copy instead of looking for the original. Besides, if I'm not mistaken, Aviad already took care of that little problem for me by taking the curse upon himself. As far as I know, there is no curse anymore."

"You're willing to bet your life on that?" I asked, surprised by his cold assessment of the matter.

"I suppose it's only natural for the Author to have put securities around something so powerful.

But the way I figure, even if some part of the curse applied to my new bloodstone, it's nothing I can't undo, given time," he added with a shrug. "I'll crack it, just like the rest of the Code. And when I complete my research here, I'll take what I know back to those still trapped in the confines of the Author's story and lead them into one they deserve."

"You really believe you can improve on what the Author created?" I asked with amazement at what I saw as shameless arrogance.

"I'm well on my way to figuring it all out. And once I have, it'll be the perfect world with true freedom, freedom from the curse of the Shadow and...."

"Freedom from the Author," I finished, recognizing the inevitable conclusion. "But why are you so set on cutting him out?" I asked skeptically.

"And why are *you* so set on keeping him?" Dad countered, acting flabbergasted that I'd even challenge the idea. "What has he done to gain your devotion? Can you say with any honesty that the world *he's* created in Solandria or the Veil is 'perfect'? Tell me, has it gotten any better since I was there last?"

"Well…no. It's not perfect," I conceded reluctantly. At the same time, I felt a growing need to defend what I knew to be true. I tried to make my point with some humor, passing my hand through Dad's midsection to illustrate, "but then, neither is this place, right?"

"Oh, grow up," Dad scowled, pushing away my hand with no effect whatsoever. "Of course, it's not perfect yet, but at least I'm in control. Stick around and I'll fix that too if it bothers you so much."

"That's just it, Dad," I said. "I can't stay here. I'm here on a mission…to bring you back."

"Bring me back? You can't be serious! You've seen this place. Why would I want to leave? Why would you?"

"The family needs us, Dad," I began to plead my case. "It's been hard enough not having a dad while you've been in here chasing your wild theories, but now some real trouble has come.…"

"Trouble? Don't lecture me like you know anything about real trouble!" Dad's words exploded like a grenade. "You sound just like your mother, moaning about me spending too much time away. Well, maybe one of *you* should ask yourselves *why* I left in the first place. Maybe answering *that* tough question will be worth it one of these days, you think? Or are you just like the rest of them—too gutless to ask 'cause you might not like what you find?"

By the time he'd finished his attack, Dad's face was red with anger. It was a frightening image. I'd only seen him riled up like this a handful of times before. All of those times, Mom had been the one to take him on. This had never been an arena I was allowed to fight in before. But this time I was the only one here to speak in defense of the family. I let the steam build up against his arrogant accusations before launching my verbal counterstrike.

"*I'm* the coward?" I shot back. "I'm not the one abandoning my family so I can run away and hide from the Watchers. *You* are!"

My choice words had cut straight to the heart of the matter.

"What do you know about that?" Dad asked fearfully, his red face turning pale immediately.

"Probably too much," I said with a sneer, feeling the guilty thrill of having won this round so swiftly. "You saw something in the Eye of Ends that Tonomis wants. That's why he came after us; that's why he took Mom and Emily."

Dad's eyes widened at the mention of the Watcher's name. "Th-that's impossible!" he stammered. "I thought I left him in the Eye, he shouldn't have been able to...."

"Well, apparently that wasn't enough," I said rather coldly.

I could tell by his wild expression that Dad was frantically searching for some kind of solution to this fresh nightmare. As I watched genuine fear and hopelessness overtaking him, I felt my own anger melt away, to be replaced by pity.

Dad began pacing nervously. "My research is not ready for this yet. I can't do anything from here," he said, giving voice to his internal battle of the mind. "What am I supposed to do now?"

I took a deep breath, letting it out slowly. "Come back with me," I finally said. "I need you to help me rescue Mom and Emily. You know what we're up against with Tonomis better than I do. You outwitted him before. Whatever he is, we can fight this together as a team: father and son."

Dad looked at me with a deep and lonely sorrow. "I wish I could," he said, his voice cracking with emotion.

"Then...why don't you?" I asked.

For a moment Dad looked as though he would change his mind, but a second wave of regret crossed his face.

"I...I just can't," he said at last, dropping his head in defeat.

"Can't...or won't?" I argued.

Dad looked visibly hurt by the barbed comment. He sighed. "It's not that simple," he said, not answering my question. "Hunter, you're my only son. I love you so much, but there's more at stake here than just your mother, Emily and you. If I go back it...it will only do more harm than good. You must believe me. It's true; I've seen things in the Eye of Ends, things I wish I'd never known. And I did things back there I wish I'd never done, things that can't be changed...or undone. I'm not the man I used to be."

"So that's it then?" I asked, hardly believing what I had just heard. "You're just giving up, content to stay here, cozy in your little world while your family dies out there?"

Dad looked away, unable to look me in the eye. "It's not like that."

"Yes...it is. I risked my *life* to find you because I always thought family was worth the risk. I thought you would understand that but, boy, I was wrong. You're nothing but a...a coward!" I said.

Dad locked eyes with me as if to challenge the statement, but the truth of it hit home and I saw tears welling up in his eyes.

"Son, please. I don't expect you to understand it all yet...." Dad was pleading with me but I wouldn't hear any more of it.

"No. I think I alrcady do," I replied bitterly. I shook my head in disgust and stomped off toward the door.

I was surprised to find Trista standing in the doorway and was embarrassed to think she might have seen my last interaction with Dad.

"Trista? What are you doing here?" I tried to fake a cheerful voice as I quickly wiped away any trace of the hot tears I'd felt slip out moments earlier. "I was just on my way back," I explained as I walked quickly by her.

"I got worried. Is everything okay?" Trista asked, shifting her worried glance from me to the stranger left standing on the balcony, not missing the visible tension stretching between us.

"Yeah, turns out I just found the wrong guy," I said loud enough for Dad to hear.

"Oh, I see," Trista said with a knowing sadness.

I was silently grateful for the stacks of worthless junk laying in the way for me to angrily kick at as I passed through them en route to the mirror's exit. By the time I reached the empty frame, Trista was standing by my side.

"Are you okay?" she asked.

I tried to quench the anger that had built up inside, but there was no way to keep it from boiling over.

"This isn't how it was supposed to go!" I said angrily. "He doesn't care about anything but himself."

"People don't always do what we expect them to," Trista offered. "I heard a little of what you said to each other," she admitted somewhat sheepishly. "For what it's worth, I think your father still cares for you. He probably just needs more time."

"Time for what?" I shot back. "He's had all the time in the world."

"I don't know. He's obviously running from something."

"He's running from me and from his family. You know what? I don't want to talk about it right now. You ready?"

Trista nodded. She went over to the mirror portal and with a touch, the surface lit up just as it had on the way in. As she did, I remembered I still had my father's sword, and I tossed it unceremoniously into a nearby pile, another piece for his prized research collection. Stepping up to join Trista, I took her hand, and with a deep breath leaned in toward the mirror.

"Hunter, wait!" I cringed to hear my father's voice calling

urgently behind me. Trista kept me from leaving before he reached me. He was out of breath from running.

"Before you go...I want you to have this," he said, removing something from his neck; it was a leather strap that held an iron key, the key to his Author's Writ. I took it and looked back at him with a questioning glance.

"Perhaps one day it will help you understand," he said sadly. "Always remember there are two sides to every story, two ways to read the Writ. Promise me you will keep the key safe. No matter what happens beyond that mirror, don't let anyone know you have it."

I shrugged and took the key from him.

"I want you to know I'm...I'm proud of you, son," Dad said finally.

I was still too angry to appreciate the sentiment. Instead, I shoved the key in my pocket and turned my back on him for good. Stepping through the mirror, I left the image of my father and my dreams of having a family behind.

"Good-bye, Hunter."

I heard Dad's final words reverberating through the streams of light as the portal did its job to erase me from his world...and him from mine.

Or so I thought.

CHAPTER 21
CHAOS IN THE CASTLE

O n the other side of the mirror, Desi was nowhere to be found. We left the hidden room behind and returned to the abandoned library. Desi was there, her back turned toward us, dimly silhouetted by the tall, arching library window and the setting sun behind it.

"Well," Desi said calmly, eyeing the world outside the window, "what did you find?"

"He's there," I reported, "but he won't come out."

"Not even for his family?" Desi asked, sounding disappointed.

"No," I answered, the sting of it still fresh in my memory. "He's not coming back for anything."

Desi pondered the situation in silence, her back still toward us.

"Pity," she said. "I was hoping to meet him again."

"So, what now?" Trista asked.

"We destroy the mirror," Desi said, turning around to face us. There was a darkness in her mismatched eyes I hadn't noticed before.

"But if we destroy the mirror, how will he get back?" I asked.

"He won't," Desi said. "I'm sorry, but it's the only way to keep your father's bloodstone from returning to our world and falling into the wrong hands. You wouldn't want that to happen, would you?"

Desi marched back across the room toward the hidden bookshelf door, her intentions set on destroying the mirror. Despite my recent fallout with my father, I couldn't bear the thought of losing him forever. I stepped in Desi's path, blocking her from reaching the passage.

"Step aside, Hunter!" Desi demanded, raising an eyebrow at me.

"No! We came to rescue my father, not bury him."

"You're wrong," Desi admitted. "Our mission was never about saving Caleb; it was about stopping Tonomis from getting the power of the Bloodstone…whatever the cost. Sometimes sacrifices must be made for the greater good." She forced her way forward again, nearly knocking me over in the process. I stepped back and raised my Veritas Sword at Desi's chest. She cocked her head at me, seemingly amused by my new aggressiveness.

"Trust me, you don't want to fight me, Hunter," Desi said, pressing her chest against the sword's tip. "I wasn't the one who left you behind. If you're angry, take it out on your father. Destroy the mirror yourself."

"How can you say that?" I seethed. Deep inside, I knew she was right. I was angry at my dad: first, for leaving my family, and now, for staying behind when he had the chance to come rescue them.

"Everyone calm down," Trista jumped in, trying to diffuse the bomb of emotions that was ready to explode. "Why don't we find Hope? She might know what the Author has in mind."

"The Author has already made his decision," Desi said. "That's what frightened your father into hiding in the first place. Do you know what he saw in the Eye of Ends? Did he tell you?"

I shook my head nervously, still aiming my sword steadily at Desi. She forced a bitter smile.

"Your father saw that Tonomis would kill him one day; he would steal the Bloodstone and use its power to bring an end to the Author's reign in Solandria. Is that what you want to happen? Do you want to see everyone in Solandria become Tonomis' slave?"

That was a silly question; of course I didn't want that to happen, but I also didn't want to kill my father. There had to be another way.

"You're lying," I said. "Simon said you didn't know what my father saw in the mirror."

"You weren't ready for the truth," Desi said. "We only told you what you needed to know so you would help us find your father. If you knew the whole truth, you wouldn't be able to do what has to be done—destroy the mirror and leave your father in the past. With your father gone, the future he saw will never happen. It is the only way to save Solandria, the only way to stop Tonomis."

Desi searched my eyes with her own, continuing her challenge.

"Think about it, Hunter. Your father is dead to you anyway. Finish him off and move on with your life. If you do, I promise we can help you find your family. It's your choice, destroy the mirror or abandon your family…just like your father."

For the briefest of moments, I edged my sword closer to Desi, wanting to get even for all her lies. The only problem was I couldn't bring myself to do it. I wasn't a murderer, not like this. I dropped my sword in defeat and ran my fingers through my hair, clasping them at the back of my neck and letting out a deep breath.

"I'm not my father," I said.

"Good," Desi said, slinking toward the stairway again.

"But I'm not about to abandon him either."

With a dash I lunged toward Desi in hopes of wrestling her to the floor. She moved quicker than I had anticipated, sidestepping my attack and tripping me with her left foot. I stumbled to the ground and jumped back to my feet, circling between her and the staircase.

"You won't win this," Desi said confidently.

"Yeah, well, I'm not going to make it easy for you, if that's what you want."

Desi lowered her stance and narrowed her eyes at me again. I raced toward her a second time. She squared up with me this time, grabbing my right arm and ducking under it. Before I knew what happened, she twisted it behind my back and forced me to the floor. Straddling my back, she pressed up on my arm to keep me from moving and lowered her face beside my own.

"Give up," she whispered, her lips only inches from my ear. "Face it, your father isn't who you thought he was. What I'm doing is for your own good whether you know it or not. You have to trust me."

"Why should I trust you, if you can't even trust the Author?" I said through gritted teeth.

"Because neither do you," she said calmly, cutting to the heart of the issue. She locked eyes with me and repeated. "Neither do you."

Her words pinned me to the floor harder than any wrestling hold could. Of course I trusted the Author; I had been down this road before. I had trusted him with my very heart when the Blood-stone had its death grip on me. I had trusted him in Dolor when we were prisoners of the Scourge, and I even trusted him when

Xaul stole Hope's last breath. Yes, I had trusted him in tough times before, but now I faced another challenge. Would I trust the Author with the one thing I wanted the most...did I trust him with my father's fate? Did I trust him with my family?

Before I could object, Desi leaned over and planted a kiss right on my lips. It was a quick kiss, a bitter kiss—one I hadn't asked for or wanted, but the taste of it would linger on my lips for several minutes.

The sight of Desi's kiss moved Trista into action. She threw herself at Desi and tackled her off my back. It wasn't a well-planned move, but it did give me enough time to retrieve my Veritas Sword and block the entry again.

In no time at all, Desi flung Trista off her back like a rag doll.

"You're making a mistake, Hunter," Desi replied. "It doesn't have to be like this. Just step aside, and nobody will get hurt."

Before I knew what happened, Desi pulled out her whip rods and swung the orange whip at my legs, a foot above the floor. I jumped over it and readied for her next move. She criss-crossed her lashes, stepping closer every time. She wasn't trying to hit me, she was making a point. Using my Veritas Sword, I tried deflecting her attacks, but the length and speed of her whips put me at a disadvantage. With my back against the bookshelf, I had nowhere left to go. I lowered my sword and locked eyes with Desi.

"That's more like it," Desi said, licking her lips and lowering her whip. She must have spotted Trista's gleaming arrow reflected in my eyes because she ducked before Trista could take the shot. Spinning around with her whip, she knocked the bow out of Trista's grasp, wounding her hand in the process. Trista's arrow fired across the room into the velvet curtains that hung on the windows. The curtains burst into flames, adding a sense of urgency to the already tense situation.

Trista huddled on the floor, clutching her injured hand. I ran to her side to see if I could help. The door to the hidden room was unguarded, but I knew there was no winning this now.

"Are you okay, Triss?" I asked, examining the cut on the back of her left hand. It was a deep gash, the white of her bones showing through. It had to hurt, but she didn't cry. She clinched her teeth and fought through the pain.

"I'm sorry, Hunter," said Trista. "Your father…."

"It's in the Author's hands now," I said, releasing myself and my father to whatever the outcome. Before she reached the passageway, Desi hesitated. She glanced over her shoulder unapologetically.

"You'll thank me later," she said, turning back to the hidden stairway. At that moment, the lumbering shape of a troll, ten-feet-tall, stepped out of the shadows of the passageway with a growl. Belac. Desi didn't have time to react before the beastly creature backhanded her with his powerful arm and sent her sprawling across the room. She collapsed on the floor and rolled to a stop near the doorway.

"Get out!" the troll growled. "Get out of my house!"

His words were a thunderous roar that seemed to shake the very foundations of the castle. Then he saw me. Behind his ugly yellow eyes I knew…he recognized me.

"We'd better go," I said to Trista, helping her to her feet. But it was too late. Belac boomed across the room and scooped me up in his arms.

"You should never have come back, slave," he grinned viciously, squeezing the breath from my body. "I'm going to enjoy crushing you."

There was a flash of orange and Belac released his grip, dropping me to the floor with a howl of pain. Desi had recovered and was on the attack. Belac spun around to face her. The gash that crossed his back looked sore, but not deep. His thick skin provided enough protection to spare him the full shock of the weapon, but it had been enough to hurt him, enough to make him shift his focus. He lumbered across the room toward Desi, who was holding the shackles we had retrieved from the prison.

"Come on, you brute," Desi demanded, having successfully averted his anger for the moment. Desi leaped forward, narrowly avoiding Belac's grasp, and locking one end of the shackle to his wrist in the process. He was too slow to avoid crashing into the wall beside the door. The wall began to crumble with the weight of his massive body—a crack starting toward the ceiling from where he lay. Belac got up and shook it off. In the commotion Desi latched the other half of the shackle to the iron ring, which had once held the torch.

"Over here, you big lug," Desi taunted the beast, continuing to keep his focus on her. In an impressive show of pure strength, Belac broke the iron anchor from the wall, bringing a massive piece of the stonework around the doorway with it. Swinging the heavy stone overhead like a weapon, Belac charged at Desi again. She dodged his first attack but the hunk of stone that was anchored to his arm crushed the wall behind her, causing the crack overhead to split and spread further.

With a major portion of the door support ripped out, the wall above it caved in, blocking our escape to the hallway before we could reach it.

"What now?" Trista asked, still holding her injured hand.

Before I could answer, the windows shattered into the room, bursting from the force of a hundred black birds now flooding in. They flocked together and spiraled to the floor, a clear sign that Vogler had found us and was about to appear.

"I can't hold them both off, Hunter," Desi shouted, swinging the whip wide at Belac. Belac returned the favor with a pummeling crash of his boulder.

"Come on, Triss," I said, running for the center of the flock. The birds scattered at my approach before regathering in another corner of the room. "If we keep them apart, Vogler can't form."

Trista joined me, running from place to place, delaying Vogler's arrival. Belac looked confused and distracted by the chaos and Desi added two more lashes to his back while he wasn't looking. This only angered him more. We were holding our ground against the double threat, but it wasn't going to be enough. The flames in the curtains had already started to spread through the room, setting the ceiling ablaze and weakening the already compromised structure.

"It's happening, Hunter," Desi shouted over the commotion. "Vogler is here for your father. You have to destroy the mirror so we can get out."

She was right. Regardless of what I wanted for myself, I had to stop Vogler from getting Dad's bloodstone, even if it meant never seeing my father again. I knew what I had to do.

"Scatter Vogler as long as you can," I told Trista, "but get out through those windows before this place falls down on you."

"What about you?" Trista asked, as I picked up my sword and cinched the straps of my backpack tighter.

"I have a mirror to destroy. It's the right thing to do. I know that now." Desi caught my eye and nodded in agreement before narrowly dodging one of Belac's boulder attacks.

With newfound purpose, I ran for the hidden room, leaping down the steps, two at a time. Facing the mirror, I raised my sword and made ready to hack it in two. My own reflection stared back, sword raised, daring me to try.

"Hunter, what are you doing?" a voice seemed to whisper in my ear. It sounded like my father.

"Giving you what you want," I said to myself.

I thrust my sword toward the mirror, but my own reflection countered the attack, magically blocking my sword from penetrating the mirror. I swung again and again; every time my reflection fended off my assault with equal power. I couldn't seem to win the fight, but I kept trying anyway.

"The mirror will defend itself," the voice whispered. "There is no way you can win."

I charged forward again. The result was the same as before; my attack was blocked by the blade of the Veritas behind the mirror. I mounted a series of volleys, building one upon another until I had exhausted every attack in my playbook. Despite my best efforts, I couldn't stop my reflection from countering my every move. It saw everything I saw and could react just as fast.

"You can't defeat your own reflection," the voice whispered with a cackle. "That is the riddle you must solve to break the mirror's link."

I had to find a way to keep my reflection from reacting to my attacks, to beat it at my own game.

"How do you defeat your own reflection?" I repeated to myself. The only way to do that, I figured, was to attack blindly. I closed my eyes and approached the mirror. Falling forward, I plunged my sword into the mirror. My blind reflection did not counter the attack. I was through.

A surge of power raced through my arms, jerking me and the blade forward like a powerful magnet. I wanted to pull the sword out, but I couldn't. Whatever power the mirror had over me was not letting go. I opened my eyes to find the heat of the blade melting the center of the mirror, smoldering with white-hot light. The mirror was cracking under the pressure of the sword, each crack revealing a bright white light behind it.

Finally, the mirror exploded from the sword's blade, shattering in every direction. Instantly, my blade was released and I was thrown across the room, landing on the floor near the steps. It was done.

My father was gone...forever.

I ran up the stairs into a library engulfed in flames. Black smoke filled the room, replacing the chaos of the fight that once filled it. Covering my mouth with my sleeve, I followed the smoke toward the windows.

"Trista! Desi!" I shouted. "Are you still here?"

"Ungh, ungh," a weakened voice grunted from behind the curtain of smoke.

"Hang on, I'm coming," I called out, crawling across the floor. "Keep talking so I can hear where you are."

"Ungh," the voice groaned.

Moments later, I spotted the shape of a single figure collapsed on the floor in a huddled, trembling lump. To my surprise, it wasn't Trista, Desi, Vogler or Belac. It was a man, wearing nothing but a loin cloth, and he appeared to be injured. His back was turned toward me and his arm was stretched over his face in an attempt to keep the smoke away.

"Gone, it's gone," the man said. This time I recognized the tone of his voice.

"Dad? Is that you?"

"Hunter..." he replied weakly, turning so I could see the right half of his face. His eye was red and swollen from the smoke. For the briefest of moments his expression seemed to brighten at the sight of me, but almost immediately the look faded. "Stay away from me...save yourself."

There was no way I was leaving him. Not like this. Guarding my own face from the smoke, I raced to his side and lowered myself beside him. If he was hurt, I wanted to help.

"You came back. How did you…?" I stopped, suddenly spotting the lashes across his back. The skin was cut open and black blood flowed from wounds that looked to have been inflicted by Desi's whip.

"Leave me…" he managed to say.

"I'm not leaving you, Dad. We're getting out of here together. The windows are just over here…. We can make it…just take my hand."

"I can't, Hunter," he said sadly. "I…I can't." He lifted his left arm, which had been hidden from view and I saw why. It was in horrible shape; the skin was yellow and starting to peel away from his arm, which was also swollen and larger than it should have been. His fingers looked like they had been melted together in places. My first thought was that he had been injured by the fire somehow, but when I saw the shackle latched to his wrist and a boulder attached to the other end, my concern began to grow. In my absence, some-one had tethered him to the boulder that Belac had been attached to.

"Don't worry, Dad," I said, still not fully understanding what I had just seen. "I can save you. I can cut you free."

"No, Hunter, you can't."

For the first time since I had found him, Dad lowered his right hand from his face and revealed an even more horrifying sight. His face was contorted and misshapen, as if a giant tumor had over-taken the entire left side. His eye was yellow, bloodshot and much larger than the right side, which still looked every bit like my dad. The sight took a moment to sink in. It was almost as if my father had been mutilated on his entire left side. He was starting to look like…Belac. It didn't make sense, unless…my father…was….

With a frightening groan, the ceiling of the library began to cave in, interrupting my thoughts. A giant section of it cascaded

down a mere twelve feet from where we sat. It would only be a matter of time before the rest came down as well.

"There isn't time, Hunter," Dad said out of the right side of his
mouth. The angry flames danced in his tear-filled eye. "Save yourself. Just leave me here."

"I'm not leaving!" I said boldly, though the sight of my father
sickened me. No matter what was happening to him, I couldn't
leave my father behind in this deadly blaze. There wasn't time to
think, I had to take action. Igniting my Veritas Sword, I severed the
shackle that anchored my father to the boulder and helped him to
his feet. He was weak, but he could walk.

"This way!" I shouted over the crackling flames, pulling him
across the broken glass toward the windows. We jumped through
them and onto the swampy ground outside. Moments later the entire ceiling fell, pushing a hot blast of air through the windows and
nearly knocking us over. I could only hope Desi and Trista had
made it out before us.

We hobbled a safe distance away and watched what was left of
Belac's castle...or my father's castle...burn to the ground.

"You should not have saved me..." Dad said. "You should have
let me.... Arrrgh!" Clutching his chest, he keeled over, collapsing to
the ground on his hands and knees. I leaned over to help him but
he motioned with his good hand for me to keep away. When the
pain subsided he rolled to his back and breathed deep, heavy gasps.
When he did, his left side—the deformed half—lay closest to me.
From here, he looked every bit like the monster Belac had been. I
shuddered.

"Hold on, Dad," I said. "You need help."

"It's too late for that," the deformed side of his face seemed
to say on its own. His voice sounded different...more bestial and
Belac-like. The large yellow eye examined me and a wicked smile

crossed the left side of his face. "Nothing can save your father now. You should have left him alone."

The sound of Belac speaking through my father sickened me.

"Dad? What's happening to you? What's wrong?"

"Hunter...I'm here," Dad's voice spoke softly, but from where I sat his lips didn't move. It was as if each half of his body were being controlled by its own personality. One half was Belac, the other was Dad. I moved around to the other side of my father's face, preferring to see it over the grotesque features of Belac.

"We need to find help, Dad. There were two girls with me. Did you see where they went?"

"Gone," Dad's side said, weakened by whatever sickness was coursing through him. He shook his head and struggled to fight through it. "Trista's gone."

I was both surprised and relieved to know he remembered her name from the other world. Until that moment, I didn't know if the man I met in the mirror was the same man I saw before me... or if it was some kind of trick. The fact that he knew Trista's name was evidence that he was indeed my father. Or at least part of him was.... It was the other half that frightened me.

"Gone?" I asked, "What do you mean? Where did she go?"

"After you...brought me back...I saw birds...they covered her...and she was gone," Dad managed to say. Every word was a struggle to get out. He gasped deeply for air and tried again, "They flew away...she wasn't...there."

Despite his broken description, I had heard enough to piece together a picture of the event in my mind. The news was not good. Raking my fingers through my hair, I let out a deep, anxious breath. Vogler had taken Trista and I blamed myself. A cloud of gloom hung over my head, my face reddened and my fists clinched. I was mad, but not at Vogler; I was angry at myself. *How could I have let this happen? You're an idiot, Hunter. You were so worried about keeping Vogler away from your father's mirror that you let him take away your only true friend. What were you thinking?*

Looking away from my father, I fought to hold back tears. My heart felt like a dead weight in my chest, as if it had stopped beating altogether. I closed my eyes and a picture of Trista jumped into view, Vogler hovering over her, his eyes hidden behind the mirrored glasses. He was smiling.

I wanted to do something about it—to run off and save her, but I had no clue where he had taken her. For that matter, I had no clue if she was even still alive. There was nothing I could do about it now; Trista was in the Author's hands. I pushed the thought aside and tried to refocus on my father but the wound of his message had left a hole in my heart. There would be time for regrets later. Right now, I had to figure out how to save my father; if I didn't I might lose him as well. I took another deep breath and tried to regain my composure.

"What about Desi, the other girl, did you see her? Did the birds get her too?"

Dad shook his head, and forced himself to speak again, "She's not…who you think…Graagh!"

The sound of Belac's growl cut my father short from saying all he had intended.

"He knows who she is," Belac interrupted. "He's working with her…. He's come to kill us both…to kill YOU! Just look at our castle…our sanctuary! It's ruined. EVERYTHING is ruined…and it's all…his…fault!"

Dad's eye followed Belac's gaze to the smoldering ruins. It was true; the castle was burning to the ground and there was nothing we could do to stop it.

"No," Dad answered himself. "He is a good boy…he is…a…."

"He's a fool! Don't you see? He's one of them, come to find the Eye.... He should not have come here! We should kill him before he finishes us both."

"Kill him?" Dad questioned. "But...but...he's my son...."

"Yes...but he's not mine," Belac answered with a sinister tone.

"No, I...I can't let you do it...I...."

"You have no choice; I do what I want.... We do what we want!"

"Belac, please...."

Dad's voice wavered and broke off with a sudden gasp. The pain was back. His hands shot up and he started clawing madly at his own chest as if he were trying to dig something out of it. The skin on his good arm began to crawl and lump around as if something inside him were trying to crawl out of him too.

"Dad?" I asked as he dropped his face into his hands. "Dad, what's going on? I came here to find you. To help save you.... Let me help you. What can I do?"

When Dad looked up, the expression on his face had changed to a determined stare. He looked right at me but I didn't like the look he was giving. Then, Dad said something I thought I'd never hear him say.

"You're right. We have to kill him.... It's the only way...."

"Dad?" I asked, completely caught offguard by how easily he had been swayed by the lies of Belac. "You aren't serious are you? I'm your son.... It's me, Hunter."

"Yes," Dad repeated. "He must be destroyed."

"Let's crush him like a bug," Belac said.

My father and Belac frantically searched the ground until they spotted a stone that was sticking out of the mud. The Belac side was much stronger and dug it up in almost no time at all. The stone was the width of my chest and probably twice my weight. Belac eyed me angrily as he lumbered forward with the stone in his arm. I fingered my sword and pulled it out in defense, but I couldn't decide what to do. Would I be able to kill my father if it came down to it?

Belac paused for a moment at the sight of the Veritas Sword, then grinned when he saw the look on my face. He knew what I knew…I couldn't kill my father. He continued forward. Dad's hand and Belac's held the stone together. I stepped back in fright as my father approached, but I slipped on the soggy ground, falling flat on my back. Before I could recover, my father and his stone were already overhead.

"Please, Dad, don't do this," I begged.

With a powerful groan Belac hoisted the stone up overhead; my father's arm held it with him.

"Let me do it," Dad said to Belac, closing his eye so as not to watch the result of what was about to occur. Belac smiled and eased his grip on the stone, giving full control to my father.

"Forgive me, Hunter…" Dad replied, as he raised the stone even higher. "But there is no other way."

He looked up at the stone and released his grip, letting it fall directly on his own head. With a horrific *crack* the impact of the boulder knocked him out cold. The stone rolled backward and fell to the ground with a thud. My father and Belac wavered for a moment, their eyes rolling back before they fell head-first into the mud beside me.

"Dad! Dad!" I said, scrambling to my knees and turning him over on the ground. "Dad, please be okay!" A deep gash on the back of his head was draining black blood from his body at an alarming rate. I grasped my Veritas Sword hilt and set it against the wound. The miraculous power of the Code of Life did its job, healing the cut and stopping the bleeding.

His eyes stared blankly at the sky overhead. He had done it; he stopped Belac from killing me, but at what cost? My father lay calmly on the ground now, so calm in fact that it made me uneasy. Was he dead? Was all my searching for nothing?

"Please don't die, Dad, not like this…not now. I need you…I need a family again, a real family."

There was no reply, just his blank skyward stare.

"Dad, can you hear me?"

Nothing.

A light rain began to fall. Just a few drops at first, splashing over his motionless form, but it began to build. In the distance the sound of rumbling thunder could be heard. In no time at all, it became a downpour. Dad's Belac-features slowly began to wash away under the rain until he was entirely himself again.

I felt so alone, so defeated. I started to cry. I lay my head against my father's bare chest and hugged him for the first time since I was a boy. It was then that I noticed he began to breathe. His chest rose and dropped in a silent sleep. My father wasn't dead…he was still alive.

"Dad, you're okay! You're alive!" I said, looking into his face. There was still no response. He may have been breathing but he wasn't okay. The rain continued to pound down on us. We needed shelter and we needed it now.

A flash of lightning silhouetted the hillside, revealing a stone stairway a few dozen feet away. I knew those stairs; they led to the Lost Refuge at the top of the hill. There wasn't much left of the place, but with the castle still burning it was our only hope of finding shelter. I removed my backpack and pulled it on backward, so it covered my chest. Then, I pulled my father's arms over my shoulders and hoisted his limp body onto my back. I would carry him with me…all the way if I had to.

It was a steep climb, a feat made twice as difficult by having to haul the weight of my father through the drenching rain. But inch by grueling inch I climbed upward, wondering what my father's last words about Desi meant. *She's not who you think she is.* The statement confused me.

Another angry flash of lightning lit the top of the hillside, which was still a long way off, and the storm was not easing up. If there was ever a time for the Author to intervene, this was it. I needed help.

CHAPTER 22

THE OTHER MAN

M y body was weak, especially my knees, by the time we reached the hilltop. It had taken every ounce of strength in me to half-carry, half-drag my father's limp body up the steep staircase. Every footstep presented yet another opportunity to slip and lose my balance on the wet rock and mud.

Though the climb was difficult, the weight on my heart strained me the most…the weight of having lost Trista. I couldn't get over it. I was only just beginning to realize how much she meant to me. I could only hope she was okay, that somehow Vogler had let her live. If not, I would never be able to forgive myself.

Cresting the hill, I scanned what remained of the Lost Refuge. Despite its title, the destination itself was anything but a refuge; it was little more than a scattering of stones. Every piece of the once massive structure lay strewn across the landscape. No two stones sat atop each other; there was no cover here from the storm. The only exceptions were a crumbling tower and a toppled doorway, which had once been a portal back to Aviad's bookshop. The doorway was buried beneath a pile of boulders now, a new touch probably erected by Belac after my last visit to ensure nobody else ever escaped through it.

The sight brought back a question that had been gnawing at the back of my mind ever since I had rescued my father. How deep did the connection go between Belac and my father? Would he remember my visit with Stretch? Would he remember what he had done to us? Did he remember how close he had come to crushing me under one of the boulders in these very ruins? The answers would have to wait until he recovered…IF he recovered.

Skreeee!

The night air and driving rain were accompanied by a distant haunting sound that seemed every bit like Vogler's birds. It was probably only the wind howling against the tower, but my imagination made it so much more. With Vogler on the loose, nothing was safe.

Skreeee, skreeeee!

The noise continued, but I tried to ignore it. With options for shelter severely limited, I stumbled through the field of rubble toward the ruined tower, carrying my father on my back the whole way. Once we arrived, I pushed my way in through what remained of its door and collapsed to the ground from sheer exhaustion.

The tower itself was still standing, but it was far from stable. I looked up the tower's shaft to the crumbling roof overhead. There were two levels to the tower—the lower ground level and a platform or loft of some kind, about a dozen feet up. A rugged wooden ladder with only three remaining rungs leaned against the edge of the wooden planks that made up the floor of the loft. Above that, a criss-cross of rotting wood beams stubbornly held their position, lending a false sense of stability to the structure. Finally, at the very top, whole sections of the roof had collapsed inward, leaving giant gaps where the rain fell in. As long as we steered clear of the drips, we might actually manage to dry ourselves in the space. The tower walls would provide ample shelter from the howling wind and driving rain. The place was as good as we could hope to find under the circumstances.

I sat up and surveyed the remainder of the space. In a stroke of luck, it appeared as though previous travelers had used the tower as a shelter before us and left a variety of objects behind.

The ashen remnants of a campfire lay in the center of the room, complete with a pile of scrap wood. There were other things strewn about as well, things we could use for survival: a collection of bottles (some broken, others not), some rope, a small pile of hay in the corner, (which someone had gathered together as a bed), along with some ragged, old clothes left hanging on a peg on the wall.

I lifted my father in front of me and dragged him across the room toward the make-shift bed. His legs slid across the floor, leaving a trail of black blood in the dirt behind us. Every time I saw it, I was reminded that my father was still infected. He belonged to the Shadow. As badly as I wanted to believe otherwise, there was nothing I could do to change the reality that he had never been rewritten. I could only hope the Veritas Sword would heal his wounds and buy us time to meet with Aviad soon.

As we neared the hay pile, a rustling movement caught my eye and I nearly dropped my father from the shock. As it turned out, we weren't alone in the tower after all; we had rodents. A decent sized rat-like creature scurried across the room and squeezed through a small hole in the wall. The creature peeked back out at me and hissed unhappily at my intrusion. It had a small piggish snout, teeth that stuck out like a wild hog's and cat ears that pointed straight up.

Before I could find something to throw at it, the rodent scurried back through the hole into the soggy outdoors in search of a more private home.

As I laid my father in the bed of hay, I noticed his skin was as cold as ice from the frigid rain and night winds. Without clothes to keep him warm he would soon freeze. For that matter, so would I. His physical wounds were easily healed by my Veritas Sword and I set to gathering some scrap wood for a fire. Luckily, there was more than enough laying about the tower. With a few sparks of my Veritas Sword, I had a roaring blaze in the center of the room in no time. The space warmed quickly and the fire brought a homey feeling to the otherwise drab place.

Next up was dry clothes, which former travelers had so graciously provided. I dressed my father first and then stripped my own wet clothes and pulled a tunic over myself. The sleeves were a bit too long for my arms, but it would have to do until my clothes dried. As I rolled up my sleeves I noticed that somehow in all the commotion of Belac's castle, the screen of the Symbio device on my wrist had shattered completely. Considering it useless, I pried the device off my wrist and tossed it into the corner of the room.

I strung the rope across the room and hung my jeans and T-shirt on the line to dry next to the fire. Things were starting to come together well.

A pair of broken bottles would make a perfect pair of cups, so long as we were careful to mind the sharp edges. I broke the stem of the bottles off completely and set them outside the door to collect rain water. As far as survival went, we were doing well. Water, fire and shelter—the three biggies were covered. Food would have to wait for now.

When at last I had nothing else to busy myself with, I slumped beside my father on the hay and let out a long tired sigh.

"Don't worry, Dad," I said. "We're going to make it."

How exactly we would make it, I didn't know. Dad's brow was wet, but it wasn't from the rain. He was sweaty from whatever sickness ailed him. He was still breathing, but at times it seemed labored and painful. I wanted to help, but I had no clue what to do next. So I just sat beside him, wiping his brow with my sleeve, counting every labored breath my father took.

So much had happened over the past couple of days I could hardly process it all. My family had been kidnapped, Trista was gone, my father was Belac, and Desi…I didn't know who she was. With my father nearly dead, I wondered if I would ever find any answers.

A sudden knock at the door pulled my attention away. I raised my sword to the ready and pulled the door open. I found myself face to frightened face with the bearded prisoner from Belac's castle. I had planned on going back to rescue him but in all the commotion I had completely forgotten him. The man looked like a drowned rat; his long, greasy, black hair hung limp in the rain, framing his scraggly beard, which was matted with mud from his climb up the hillside. He was wrapped in a green cape to keep warm. Despite his grubby appearance, something was familiar about him that I hadn't noticed at the prison. It was the look in his eyes…strong and determined. But his gaze softened instantly when he saw me.

"Hunter?" the man said weakly, still standing in the pouring rain. His voice was shaky, not the least bit as stern as it once was, but I recognized it immediately.

"Faldyn, is that you? What happened? What are you doing here?"

"Trying to keep dry at the moment," Faldyn replied simply, looking up at the sky, which continued to pour down relentlessly. "May I…join you?"

"Yes, of course, come in," I said, motioning him in.

He gladly entered the tower and removed his green cape. He shook the water from his hair and stepped up to the fire to get warm. I watched in stunned silence as the man who had once been a captain of the Codebearers, a man who had conspired against the Resistance to steal Hope, now sat huddled next to the fire I had made. Seeing him like this, I hardly knew what to think…or to say.

"It is a good fire," Faldyn said matter-of-factly. "Thank you."

The words sounded strange coming from his mouth. I had never known Faldyn to be a man who was thankful for much of anything. At least, he never showed it if he was.

"You're welcome," I said in return, but when Faldyn's eyes crossed the room to the place where my father lay, his face paled at the sight.

"It can't be…. Is that Caleb?" Faldyn asked, somewhat reluctantly.

"Yes," I answered. "You know my father?"

"Know him?" Faldyn asked excitedly. "He's the reason I came to this cursed swamp in the first place. I've been searching for him for some time. He has something I need…something of great importance to the Resistance."

"I thought you left the Resistance," I said, trying to avoid sounding like I had a clue what he was talking about. Truth be told, I didn't, but I had my suspicions that Faldyn might be after the new Bloodstone for himself. It only made sense. He had often used questionable means to gain an advantage over the Shadow. I had no reason to believe he had changed.

"Is that what they told you?" Faldyn asked. "In a way, I suppose they are right. But it's not exactly how I would have put it."

No surprise there. He always had his own spin for everything.

"What really happened then?" I asked, deciding to humor him.

Following a long silence, Faldyn began to tell his side of the story. "After Venator's fortress was taken, I found Hope. She was badly wounded by a Veritas Sword. Someone had stabbed her clean through."

"Yeah, I know," I said, not wanting to admit that it was my fault…that I had stabbed Hope. Faldyn shot a curious glance my way before continuing his story.

"Anyway, I took her back to the Resistance. We treated her wounds but as you know the wounds of a Veritas Sword cannot be healed except by the Author himself. All we could do was watch the life slowly drain from her body until I could stand it no longer. I knew that if Hope died, the Resistance would soon follow. We had to do something. Hope was not like the rest of us, she was something greater."

"You mean a Virtuess?" I asked, often wondering what the term meant.

"Yes," Faldyn replied, a look of surprise lighting his eyes. "How did you know that?"

"Petrov told me," I said, "the night before he died."

The news of Petrov's death seemed to come as a shock to the man. He had been away from the Resistance for so long he had failed to keep up with what had happened in his absence.

"Oh, I'm…sorry to hear that," he said in a distant voice. I didn't want to believe him but in reality I sensed the news had actually hurt him. He was being genuine.

"I had hoped to meet up with Petrov again soon. The two of us had a bit of a misunderstanding before. We didn't part on good terms, I'm afraid. When I heard they were transporting her to Obdurant for further care, I was worried. There were rumors that the Shadow intended to attack the transport but I knew that Petrov wouldn't believe me if I told him. I decided to keep my distance and do my part to ensure the transport made it to its destination. When the Shadow attack happened, I did the only thing I could think to do. I secretly stole Hope away, so the Shadow could not find her."

"That's not the way I heard it," I challenged. "I heard you mounted the attack with the Shadow…that you stole Hope."

Faldyn appeared visibly hurt by the statement, but I wasn't buying it.

"People believe what they want to believe," Faldyn said sadly. "They needed a villain and they felt I fit the part. But I can assure you that I did not work with the Shadow…. I would never do that again. I was trying to help. I was trying to save Hope from certain death."

"Then why didn't you just return Hope to the Resistance and prove your innocence? Why did you hide?"

"Because nobody would believe me," he said in remembrance. "They would just think it was the same as before…that I was… betraying them again."

His eyes searched the crackling flames as he spoke. Something had happened in his past that this man was not proud of. It was something that had scarred him and haunted him to this very day.

"You betrayed the Resistance?" I asked, not entirely surprised by his ability to do so but at the same time amazed that he had actually confessed to it so easily.

"Yes, I pretended to be one of them, but inside I didn't truly believe the Author had the best plan in mind. The Shadow used me as a spy within the Codebearer ranks. I would listen to their strategies and feed the Shadow the answers they needed. A lot of men died because of me. Eventually, I was discovered and I ran away. But once the Shadow realized I was no longer of use to them, I wasn't treated as one of them either. I was a man without hope. That is when I first met Aviad. For the first time in my life I believed that the Author did care. Everything I had learned about the Codebearers as a Shadow spy suddenly became real to me. The training, the Veritas Sword, the Author's Writ…all of it. I became a Codebearer in my heart that day, but I knew there was no way the Resistance would ever accept me…not after all I had done."

I found a lump growing in my throat. Was I actually feeling sorry for this man? Either he was an amazing actor or I had truly misjudged him.

"What did you do?" I asked.

"Well, Aviad had his own plan for me. He gave me a special gift and a promise to deliver to the Resistance—a child. Her name was Hope."

My jaw nearly hit the floor. I couldn't believe what I was hearing. Faldyn had brought Hope to the Resistance?

"You look surprised," Faldyn noticed.

"Yeah, I guess…everything I thought about you was…wrong," I answered.

"Not everything," Faldyn admitted. "I didn't exactly want Hope to go back to the Resistance. She was so weak and frail when I found her in Venator's chamber that I feared she was dead already. I knew that as long as Hope lived, the Resistance would be safe. After I saved her a second time, I kept her in the safest place I could think of and put her into hibernation with one of the Shadow's potions I had in my possession from when I was a spy. The cave protected by the dragon proved to be the perfect place to hide her."

"But then why did you leave her? If you truly cared, you could have stayed with her."

"Yes, I wanted to, but there was something else I felt I needed to do. I needed to recover an item I knew your father once had in his possession. I tracked him all the way here where I ended up being captured by that wretched troll. I've been his prisoner for longer than I care to know. Not a day has passed that I haven't thought of Hope and what has become of her."

I spent the next several minutes sharing what had happened during my previous visit to Solandria, how we found Hope and watched her die at the hands of Xaul. I told him how she had been rewritten by the Author and was marked as one of the Seven. The story brought tears to Faldyn's usually stoic expression. Wiping the tears away, he released a long, drawn out wavering breath of relief. The burden he had carried to save Hope had been lifted. Suddenly, his face took on a new expression. Despite all Faldyn had done, Hope had been rescued by the Author's own plan.

"It is good to know he has things under control, isn't it?" Faldyn said at last. "I should have known he was able to save her in his own way. I just let my emotions get in the way I guess."

"Hope has a way of doing that," I asked.

"Yes…yes she does," Faldyn said with a smile.

For the first time I found myself agreeing with the man. I too had nearly let my feelings for Hope keep me from allowing the Author's plan to unfold. In a way, I was no different than Faldyn. Both of us would have done anything to save her. We had both been too short-sighted to allow the Author's plan to unfold in his own time. Even as the thought crossed my mind, I was reminded of Trista and my father. I decided to trust the Author with their fate now, even as I had done with Hope's before. There wasn't much else I could do.

Faldyn's stomach growled like a lion that hadn't been fed in weeks.

"You don't happen to have anything to eat around here, do you?" Faldyn inquired. "I'm afraid that scab of a troll, Belac, didn't feed me too well when I was in his keep."

"I know," I said, remembering the leech mush I had survived on during my brief stay in Belac's prison. "I wish I did, but I'm afraid we're on our own."

"That's too bad," Faldyn sighed. "I could have used a good chunk of meat."

Out of nowhere, something fell to the floor between us—the limp body of a dead rat-thing that looked identical to the one I had scared away. A rustling sound overhead drew our attention up to the beams. A lonely black bird hopped from plank to plank, searching for shelter and a meal. The sight of it made my jaw tense. There was only one bird, but it reminded me of Vogler…perhaps it was still him.

"*Caw, caw,*" the black bird replied before flying away into the rainy night.

"Well now," Faldyn said, picking up the rodent by its tail, "it looks like the Author was a step ahead of me yet again."

"You're not actually going to eat that, are you?" I asked, contorting my face at the sight of the horrid little animal.

"Actually, they're quite good if you can get past their appearance," Faldyn replied. He scavenged the ground and found a length of stick which he pushed through the body of the rodent. He did what he could to remove the creature's skin and held it over the fire to roast.

"How did you find him?" Faldyn asked while he was waiting for his supper to cook. "Your father, I mean."

"It's a long story," I said.

"I have nowhere to go," he answered. "Might as well pass the time with the tale. It will give us something to talk about anyway."

I decided to tell him about my journey to find my father, leaving out the part about the Eye of Ends. It was good to have someone to talk to. I didn't fully trust Faldyn yet, especially after all that had happened with Desi. I was starting to wonder if there was anyone I could trust fully anymore, besides the Author. When I got to the part about my father being Belac, I hesitated, wondering how Faldyn would take the news. Seeing as I had once been a prisoner of Belac, I knew how much I had wanted to get even with the troll.

"When I came back from the mirror," I explained, "my father was lying on the floor and I saved him from the fire. Only he... wasn't really himself."

"How do you mean?" Faldyn asked, examining the smoking corpse of his rat meal.

"His face was all screwed up. He looked like...." I couldn't bring myself to say it. I was frightened by what Faldyn might think, which is why it came as a shock when Faldyn finished the sentence for me.

"Belac," he said knowingly.

"Yes...how did you know?"

"I figured it out some time ago. The longer I stayed with him the more I realized he wasn't a real troll at all. Trolls don't live on leech blood. Belac's what we call a Speculumbra, a Shadow of the mirror. It's a parasite really that transforms its host into something it most desires."

I didn't fully understand why anyone would want to live like Belac, especially my father. But one thing was good, it meant my father wasn't to blame for the things Belac had done.

"So, Belac wasn't my father after all, that's good."

"Well, yes and no. A Speculumbra feeds off of its host, living out its unhindered desire. Your father wanted to be free of the Author and free of the Shadow. He wanted an escape. The mirror offered him that chance, but what it offered was a lie...a trap. Caleb saw himself as powerful and great...and in his own way he was... but he was also a slave. Your father believed he was free, but he was a slave to himself...to Belac, a prisoner of the mirror."

Suddenly, it all made sense. The mirror was the connection between my dad and Belac. That's why it was hidden, because my dad's desire was to be hidden from the things he'd seen in the Eye of Ends.

"So when I destroyed the mirror…" I started to say.

"You destroyed the ability for Belac and Caleb to exist on separate sides. Belac and your father are united again."

"But my father stopped Belac—he's himself again."

"So it would seem," Faldyn said, looking my father over. "But the Speculumbra is a parasite that is not so easily eliminated. It can return at any moment; you never know when. It may have vanished for a time, but as long as he lives, the desire to feed the Speculumbra will live in him. It needs blood to survive."

"That explains Belac's fascination with leeches. It was the only way he could keep control of my father."

Faldyn nodded, "And we cannot let him have another drop…no matter how hard it is or how badly he wants it."

I was reminded of Gabby's tales of Gerwyn and how he had become dependent on leech blood as well. I wondered if this was anything like that.

"Gabby once told me there was a time when Gerwyn was transformed. He was always drinking leech blood too. She said they cured him by bathing him in a pool of some kind."

"Yes, the pools of Cornin," Faldyn said. "Sadly, the pools are dried up for the season."

"But it's raining."

"Ah, but the pools are underground and fed from a spring that only fills them three times a year. If my calculations are correct, we are still two cycles of the moon away. No, for now, we will just have to keep a sharp eye on him. The important thing is to make sure he never touches leech blood again."

Faldyn removed the rat from the fire and examined it again. Considering it done, he allowed it to cool and tore off a piece of meat. He offered me a piece and despite its ugly appearance, I discovered it didn't taste nearly as bad as I expected.

The night passed slowly. Even though the rain had let up, the wind did not. It whistled around the tower like a howling ghost in the darkness. Faldyn wasn't tired, but after twenty-four hours with no rest, I was. He offered to care for my father while I slept. I accepted and sat on the driest part of the floor, pulled my knees to my chest and rested my head between them. But I didn't go to sleep. Instead, I used the opportunity to silently keep an eye on Faldyn. I still didn't fully trust him. After all, he hadn't exactly been forthcoming about what it was he was after.

Peering through my legs, I watched the grizzly man as he tended to my father and stoked the fire. Every once in awhile, he'd cast a quick glance my direction. I'd close my eyes and count to ten before opening them again. This went on for about an hour before I could no longer fend off the lulling effects of fatigue. It came slowly at first, weighing on my eyelids and slowing my pulse to a crawl. I caught myself nodding off a time or two. Whenever it happened, I'd make sure my father was still lying in bed, that Faldyn wasn't up to anything suspicious and that Vogler wasn't anywhere to be seen.

Eventually, my plan backfired and I nodded off, this time for good. When I awoke, it was to a brilliant beam of morning sunlight streaming through one of the lower cracks in the tower walls. The bed of hay was empty and Faldyn was nowhere to be seen.

Chapter 23

A Change of Plans

Losing things comes natural to me. It doesn't really matter how big or small something is…if it can be lost, I'll manage to lose it at least once in my life. There was even a time when I managed to lose the kitchen sink (no, I'm not kidding, but it's a long story involving my Uncle Jim, a kitchen remodel and a trip to the dump in which I mistakenly loaded the wrong sink). But of all the things I've lost in my life, I never thought it would be possible to find and lose my father, all in one night. This had to be the biggest blunder of all time.

Storming across the room, I bolted out the door into the morning light. The air was crisp and cold…the moist ground steamed as the previous night's rainfall evaporated in the sun.

"Dad!" I yelled at the top of my lungs. "Dad, where are you?"

I spotted Faldyn wandering casually back toward the tower with a handful of rats dangling from his hand by their tails. I marched right up and laid into him.

"All right, Faldyn! Where is he?"

Faldyn gave me an indignant look. He could sense the accusation in my tone and didn't appreciate it.

"If by 'him' you mean your father," he said firmly, "then he is right over there."

Faldyn pointed across the misty hilltop to the edge of the hill crest where my father stood alone. I was happy to see him standing again. Surely, that meant he was going to recover.

"Oh," I said, feeling foolish for having assumed the worst of Faldyn. It was hard to change my picture of him. "What is he doing?"

"Your guess is as good as mine. He's just been standing there for the past hour; hasn't said a word since he woke up this morning. Perhaps you'll have better luck. I'll get a meal started while you talk with him." Faldyn raised the ugly rat-things even with my eyes. I scrunched up my face and looked away.

"Yeah, can't wait," I said half-heartedly before heading toward my father.

Dad was dressed in the simple beige tunic and leather belt I had borrowed from the peg on the wall. His hands were clasped together behind his back, and he was looking over the land below. In a way, he appeared almost statuesque in his stance.

"Hey, Dad. What are you doing out here?" I asked.

He didn't respond.

"Tough night last night, huh?" I asked, trying to break the silence. He sighed and glanced down into the swamp at the blackened ruins of the place that had once been his home. He seemed to want to say something, but held his tongue.

"Talk to me, Dad," I said. "What's going on?"

He eyed me sadly and finally broke his silence.

"It's happening," Dad said.

"What is?"

"The end," he said simply, letting the words hang in the air like a dagger over my chest. The way he spoke made it sound so deadly… so final.

"End of what? Is it something you saw in the Eye of Ends?"

He didn't say it but as Dad looked me over I knew he was determining how much he should share.

"What is it, Dad?" I asked again, pressing him for an answer. "Tell me what's going on. You can trust me."

"How much did she tell you?"

"Who, Desi?"

Dad nodded.

"She told me that Tonomis is after the Bloodstone, that he'll stop at nothing to gain control of it and use it to take over Solandria."

He shook his head.

"No, Hunter, it's much worse than that."

"How much worse?" I asked.

"Tonomis doesn't want to control Solandria…he's working with Sceleris now. Together they plan on destroying it—to bring the Author's story to an end."

"Can he do that?"

Dad nodded. "I've already seen it."

Of course he had; Dad had entered the Eye of Ends. He had navigated to the very center of the Maze. He saw the final images of the history of our worlds. He had witnessed it for himself.

"But why would he destroy everything? What good could that possibly accomplish?"

"He believes it is the only way to truly be free of the Author's will. He wanted me to join him. After destroying the Author's story, he plans to use the Bloodstone to birth a new one, a world without evil, free from the Author's control."

"You mean, like your world?" I asked.

Dad's face turned suddenly sour. He took offense at the comment, and only after I said it did I realize it made him sound like he was no better than Tonomis himself.

"No," Dad snorted. "Nothing like that. What I created was a sanctuary, a place of safety to hide in. I built my world out of necessity to escape the evil Tonomis was planning. I am not like him."

"I'm sorry, Dad. I didn't mean that you...."

"I know, I know...it's okay," Dad said, holding up his hand to halt my apology. "You know, Hunter, leaving you behind was the hardest thing I ever did. I never wanted to, but it was the only way I could save you from him, from what he was going to do to you... to our world."

He started to choke up as he said it, and looked briefly away so I wouldn't see. The toughness in him was breaking down as he realized his best laid plans had fallen apart. I put my hand on his shoulder to comfort him.

"Without my bloodstone," Dad said, staring blankly at the smoldering remains of his castle, "I can't hide anymore.... Tonomis will find us and kill us both."

He locked his icy blue eyes on me to make sure I had heard him correctly.

"Kill us? Why?" I questioned.

"Because we're the only ones who have handled the Bloodstone, Hunter," Dad said. "He is threatened by that. That's why I had to hide; I wanted to save you. I thought that if I could stop him from finding me, maybe we could save the rest of Solandria as well."

"We can get help, Dad. The Codebearers...and Aviad, they'll know what to do. The Author will help us stop Tonomis."

"The Author?" Dad scoffed. "The Author!"

I nodded weakly.

"Don't you get it? The Author's the one behind it."

"How can you say that?" I asked.

"Did you forget who created the Eye of Ends? It's the Author's story, Hunter. I've seen the ending he has in mind. I've been there. Tonomis will kill you…and me…and then Solandria will be destroyed. It is what the Author has written."

"But he wouldn't end our story that way; the Author is good."

"Is he?"

The way he said it made me uncomfortable. Of course the Author was good. I had met him. He had rewritten me…given me a new heart. Evil people didn't do that.

"We can trust him, Dad. I know we can."

Dad looked unconvinced. Obviously, he didn't share my enthusiasm and confidence in the Author and his ways.

"I used to believe that too, but I've learned he doesn't care. Good and evil is all the same to him, Hunter. He's writing both sides of the story, playing both sides of the game. He allows the Shadow to run free, promising to one day make everything right. But I've seen what he is up to—the Eye never lies. The Author may be good, but even if he is…he must be evil, maniacal and vindictive as well."

He sighed as he looked over the ruins of his former life—the castle of Belac. He was a man without direction, a man whose fate seemed sealed to usher in the very doom he had tried to escape.

"The Author always has the final word," he said sadly.

"But there must be another way. Tonomis doesn't have your bloodstone yet. You do, right?"

"I did," he corrected, "but I left it in the world of the mirror, a world you destroyed."

"So your bloodstone is gone, then," I said. "That's even better. If it doesn't exist, Tonomis can't find it…."

My father shook his head, cutting me short.

"It doesn't work like that," he said. "A bloodstone contains the Code of Life in it and can never be destroyed. By destroying the mirror, the power of the bloodstone will return to its point of origin—the center of the Eye of Ends. Whoever has the Eye has the ability to find the Bloodstone. That is what Tonomis has been after; it's what he was using me to retrieve. He told me we would change the world with it. I believed him at first, but when I saw the Bloodstone in the center of the Eye, it revealed the truth. That's when I ran. I had seen the destruction Tonomis intended to do with it."

"But we know where the Eye is! You left it with Simon. We can get the Bloodstone again. We just have to go back and use the Eye to...."

"Hold on a minute...who's Simon?" Dad asked.

I searched Dad's face for any sign that he knew what I was talking about. Apparently he didn't.

"Simon Ot, your friend? He helped you hide from Tonomis, remember?"

Dad's expression was a blank slate until a sudden thought crossed his mind and brightened his eyes.

"Clever," Dad said, smiling to himself.

"What?" I asked,

"What did you say his name was again?"

"Simon Ot," I said.

"Spell it backward."

"To Nomis...Tonomis," I said, feeling stupid for not having noticed it before. "Simon *is* Tonomis! But how? I thought Tonomis was really Vogler, the big detective with an attitude and the ability to form out of birds."

"He very well could be both," Dad explained. "Tonomis isn't exactly human, you know. There were many things about him that were quite unnatural."

Of course, Tonomis himself told me that he went by many names....Vogler was one; Simon must have been another. I was so caught up in the idea of searching for my father that I had failed to realize I had led my father's enemy right to him.

"You mean all this time I've been...set up?"

"I'm afraid so," Dad said with a frown.

"And Desi...she's been...."

"Working for him all along. She's one of Tonomis' favorite distractions. She's a Vicess, half human—half Shadow!"

I buried my face in my hands and wanted to beat myself for not figuring it out sooner. I hated being made a fool of...especially by a girl. She had played her part perfectly, pretending to be in trouble when Vogler attacked at the bookshop. She had probably set up the attack in the library and Belac's castle. I'd been so focused on Vogler as the threat I hadn't even considered that Desi was really the one leading me away.

"I don't get it. If Desi's working for Tonomis, then why didn't she just kill you and me when she had the chance?"

"Because they want to make sure they have the Bloodstone first. She must have known that by destroying the mirror the bloodstone's power would return to the Eye. Tonomis already knows how to enter the Maze of Rings on his own. I caught him doing it once before I escaped. It was then I realized he had been lying to me. He didn't need me to enter the Eye...he wanted something else from me. I was being used."

"We have to stop them.... I've been to his hideout; maybe we could sneak in and steal the Eye back."

"No, it's much too risky; he'll have Black-Eyes all over that place. We wouldn't make it past the entrance."

"Well, we have to do something."

Dad pondered the situation for a moment, stroking his chin in that thoughtful way he always had. He bit his lower lip and narrowed his eyes in search of an idea. When it came to him, it was like a light-bulb had been switched on.

"There is one other way…but it's pretty much a long shot and practically impossible."

"Sounds like my kind of plan," I said, leaning forward with anticipation. Dad couldn't help but smile at my eagerness. He cleared his throat and explained his plan.

"The Eye of Ends is said to be cut from the Living Tree that once fed life into Solandria, right?"

I nodded my agreement. I knew the story well; it was the centerpiece of the Author's Writ and the first story I had read in the book. Not only had I read about the tree, I had been there and lived the events that were recorded in the book. I had stolen the Bloodstone and as a result, Solandria had been broken. Dad continued his thoughts.

"Long ago, before I fled from Tonomis, I discovered a pattern in the layout of the shards. I wrote about it in my Author's Writ. The pattern, I felt, would lead me directly to the secret location of the Lost Shard—the original home of the Living Tree. If my theory is correct, there may still be some of the original tree left, lying about on the shard. It is possible that any part of the tree may provide a second entry point to the Maze of Rings. If Tonomis is inside the Maze, we can gain access as well."

The plan sounded reasonable. We had nothing to lose, and it was far safer than attempting to break into an underground bunker.

"Well, what are we waiting for? Let's go find this lost shard."

I started back toward the tower but Dad caught me by the arm before I got far.

"Hold up, Hunter. It's not going to be so easy. We need to find my Author's Writ first. That's where I kept all my notes."

"Already found it," I said confidently. "I have it with me back in the tower."

Together we hurried back. Faldyn looked up from a fresh batch of his ugly rat-on-a-stick meals as we entered.

"Good morning," he said. "I'm glad to see you are feeling better, Caleb. Would you care for some…?"

"Not now," I said, shoving my way past him in a hurry to retrieve my backpack. I opened the large pocket and pulled out the book…only it wasn't my father's Writ after all. Instead, I discovered I was holding a ragged hardbound copy of *Watchers: Myth or Mystery*, written by Simon Ot.

"Wait, how did that get there?"

Dad looked disappointed.

"Someone must have swapped it out when I wasn't looking… Desi," I said, gritting my teeth. Even now she was a step ahead of me. I threw the book across the room in frustration.

"Don't worry, son," Dad said, recognizing the look of disappointment on my face. "It was a long shot anyway. It's my fault for not remembering the silly riddle in the first place."

"Riddle?" I asked. "You never said it was a riddle."

"Well, more or less. I suppose for most people it would seem like a line of gibberish. But it's a pattern and a riddle."

"I think I know which one you mean. Trista and I deciphered a message from your drawings using a Caesar's shift," I said proudly. "When we transferred the letters, they spelled a phrase in the Noctu's Old Language."

Dad's face lit up. "Do you remember what it said?"

I strained to recall the phrase and etched it in the dirt as each word came back to memory.

IN GIRUM
IMUS NOCTE
ET CONSUMIMUR
IGNI

That's it!" he said excitedly. "The letter sequence I found in the Maze of Rings—the one that reveals the location of the Lost Shard."

"Xaul told us it means: *We Enter the Circle by Night and Are Consumed by the Fire*...or something like that," I said.

"Excellent, Hunter!" Dad said. "Well done."

"Thanks Dad, but what's the answer to the riddle?"

"Unfortunately, that's something I don't remember," Dad said with a chuckle. "I wrote that phrase down on a scrap of paper when I was in the Eye of Ends, but when I returned I didn't remember doing it at all. In fact, I don't remember much of anything inside the Eye, except seeing the final vision."

"So, we'll have to figure it out together," I said.

"Yes," Dad said excitedly. "Now, if we had a map of Solandria I could show you what I meant about the matching sequence in the shards."

"There is a map in the Author's Writ," Faldyn suggested.

"Yes, but we don't have the Writ anymore," I explained. "Somebody swiped it."

"Perhaps, you could borrow one," Faldyn said.

"From...? Do you have one you're not telling us about?"

"Nope, but I'm pretty sure *they* did," Faldyn said, pointing to a couple of skeletons sitting in the corner. At first I dismissed the idea. Clearly, the bones weren't going to talk, but upon second glance I noticed something dangling from one of their necks, a small chain with a key attached to it. It was a rusty old key that looked like it could dissolve into dust at any moment. The handle of it bore the

Author's mark…three interlocking *Vs*. It was clearly a key that belonged to an Author's Writ.

I moved across the room and pulled the chain off the skeleton's neck. Instantly, my fingers were covered in an orangey dust from handling the key.

"Well, we have a key…but where is the book?"

"The key will lead you to it," Faldyn said.

"What? Like a compass or something?" I asked. I hadn't known that about the Author's Writ before.

"Allow me," Faldyn said, reaching out for the key. I handed it to him and he moved toward the wall. "Watch and learn," he said before closing his eyes.

He took the key and with a firm tap, he rapped the triple *V* handle against the wall like a tuning fork.

TWING…Hmmmmmmmmm!

Despite the rusty appearance of the key, it produced a golden tone, laced with a chorus of heavenly voices. Faldyn held the key out at arms length and keeping his eyes closed, let the sound guide him. The key reverberated with a humming sound that seemed to grow louder and softer as Faldyn moved about the room. It reached its loudest pitch as he hovered over the hay pile my father had slept on. Excitedly, I tore the hay pile apart and found a cloth-wrapped book buried like a hidden treasure. It was the Author's Writ.

Faldyn opened his eyes and handed the key to me.

"Thanks, Faldyn," I said.

"You are quite welcome," he replied.

With hurried fingers I placed the rusted key into the lock on the book cover and turned it to the right. Like magic, the embossed design on the cover lit with a golden light as I turned the page. Words began to form on the pages, becoming visible where once they were not. I got goose bumps every time I watched it happen… the good kind of goose bumps.

I flipped through the book until I came to the page with a map of Solandria drawn on it. I stepped back and the map extended up from the pages like a holograph, lighting up the walls of the room and allowing all of us to look at the map from all sides. There were too many shards to count, but we began to identify collections of shards in formations—like the stars in the skies formed constellations. Almost immediately, my eyes fell on Inire. It was one of the easiest shards for me to spot.

"Here," my dad said, pointing his finger into the holograph not far from where Inire hovered. "These sixteen shards are part of the Nautilatian collection. I'll start from the outermost shard and read the names of the shards inward to the center of the spiral. You make a note of the first letter in the shard's name as I go."

"Okay," I said excitedly.

"Inanis," Dad said aloud, pointing to a small shard about a third of the size of Inire. I wrote the first letter of the shard's name on the ground with my finger, "I."

"Nebulya. Galacia," Dad said, pointing to the frozen shard I had visited on my last trip to Solandria. Again I repeated the first letter, writing it on the ground.

"Insula," he said, pointing to a smallish shard that looked almost like a speck in comparison to the others. Following this shard, there was a larger gap in the Nautilatian formation, but he moved past the space to the next in sequence.

"Rellim, Ut, Merula, Inire, Mihi, Uberian, Sophmalan, Noc, Obdurant, Cordova, Tepi, Eventu…"

By this time the shards had started to grow closer together and the spiral had grown considerably tighter.

"Well, what do you have so far?" Dad asked.

"IN GIRUM IMUS NOCTE," I said, reading the letters that also happened to make up the first phrase of the riddle.

"Amazing," Faldyn said, reading it over and double-checking my work.

"What about the second half of the phrase?" I asked.

"It's there, if you read it in reverse," Dad explained.

"That's cool!" I said, mouthing the rest of the phrase as I read it backward. "But what does it mean?"

"It's only a guess, but I believe at the center of that spiral there is another shard...a lost shard where the Living Tree is hidden."

"Unfortunately," Faldyn added, "it's not a very friendly part of the Void to fly into. The space you speak of is known as the Black Curtain. Many brave sky captains have tried to navigate through it, only to end up turned around or lost. Sometimes, entire ships come out of the Curtain...only the ships and no men. You'd have to have a death wish to go in there."

"Which is exactly why we're going," Dad said, eyeing the space on the map with courage.

"My thoughts exactly," I replied, but when I realized what he had said I paused. "Wait, we're going with a death wish? I thought...."

"What better place for the Lost Shard to be hidden, than behind an impenetrable curtain of darkness?" Dad asked.

"Well, yeah...but can we go back to the death wish part because I was pretty sure that we were trying to stop Tonomis from killing us...and destroying the world...not, you know, hurrying his plan along."

"We're not hurrying his plan along. We're going to change it. The only way we don't die is if we stop Tonomis, so we're not really at a loss if we do. We might as well die trying."

"That's comforting to know," I said, feeling rather sheepish.

"I'm not sure I understand," Faldyn said.

We quickly caught Faldyn up on what my father knew about the Eye of Ends and how Tonomis was going to recover the Bloodstone, if we didn't get to it first. In the end, he understood the weight of our mission and decided to warn the rest of the Resistance of the potential danger that was coming.

"I only hope the Resistance will trust me this time," Faldyn said.

"They will," I said. "Just find Hope and give her this." I pulled the medallion Hope had given me off my neck and handed it to Faldyn.

"Hope's necklace?" Faldyn said, grasping it in his palm.

"Tell her I found my father, and that we're going to try and stop Tonomis from getting the Bloodstone. We could use all the help we can get."

"I will," Faldyn said. "But how will you be traveling there?"

"Don't worry about that; I have it covered," Dad said.

"You do?" I asked. It was the first I had heard of it. In the distance the sound that had haunted me through the night returned.

Craaaaa, craaaaa!

"There she is," Dad said with a smile. "Come on, it's time you met Nowaii! I think you'll like her."

CHAPTER 24
INTO THE BLACK CURTAIN

O n the other side of the Lost Fortress, the hill dropped down into a ravine where a cave was carved out of the foothills. Just inside the mouth of the cave was a Thunderbird that had grown considerably larger than any I had ever seen. Her foot was tethered to the rocks, but she looked well cared for. Evidently Belac, or my father, had been good at keeping pets.

"Hunter, meet Nowaii," Dad said, "my Thunderbird."

"*Craaaa*," the mammoth bird responded.

"Hello there, girl," I said, reaching toward her neck and stroking her feathers. She lowered her head further and ruffled her feathers so I could feel the down beneath them.

Dad untethered Nowaii and together we climbed onto her back. With a giant leap, the Thunderbird took to the skies, carrying us over the terrain of the Shard of Inire and out to the open skies of the Void.

By midday we had already passed the shards of Mihi, Uberian, Sophmalan and Noc. By sunset Cordova, Tepi, and Eventu were behind us. We stopped only to gather food and water along the way, keeping each stop as short as possible.

As we traveled Dad told me stories of his adventures as a Codebearer, how he had fought dragons, Skrills and all kinds of Shadow creatures. Despite the hardness in his heart toward the Author, Dad seemed to genuinely like the Codebearers and had enjoyed his time serving with them. I tried to engage him about the Author, but he brushed the subject aside as if it weren't important.

Before the last sliver of sunlight faded into the murky mist of the Void, we arrived at our destination. A wall of black clouds rose before us, lit on its sides by the fiery red sun. Beyond the edge of the clouds lay the mysteries of the Black Curtain and quite possibly, the Lost Shard. After seeing our destination, I regretted agreeing to the journey. Breaking into Tonomis' underground lair would have been less intimidating than this.

"Are you sure this is the place?" I asked nervously, as we approached through the first layer of clouds.

"Pretty sure," Dad said. "It looks like a black curtain to me, don't you think? You aren't wimping out on me are you?"

"No, no....no...I'm just wondering if it would be better to enter it during the day because of all the sunlight that probably... can't...penetrate the...clouds....Oh, never mind." Before I could finish talking, we passed through the front of the curtain and were immediately swallowed in darkness.

"*Craaaaa!*" Nowaii called.

"Steady, girl," Dad said, stroking her neck and trying to calm her down. Even though I couldn't see, I felt her body tremble beneath me. She was scared.

"I fear nothing but the Author," I whispered to myself. The words lit up my Veritas Sword, but did little to lighten my heart because there was nothing to see. What seemed like a million minutes later we still saw nothing but black. I was starting to freak out.

Dad decided to whistle the familiar tune, *You Are My Sunshine!* He used to hum and sing it a lot when I was a kid, but somehow, here in the blackness it lost its ability to bring comfort. As a matter of fact, it only added to the creepiness of the place.

"Please stop, Dad," I begged. "Your whistling is freaking me out."

"Aw, come on, son. Where's your sense of adventure...your courage?"

"Maybe it will catch up to me when we're back on solid ground. I don't like being...nowhere."

"*Craaaaa!*" Nowaii squawked in agreement with me.

"Well, for what it's worth, I'm not too thrilled with it either," Dad admitted.

Suddenly, the wind began to pick up. Nowaii started to shift from side to side in the currents of the air. Once or twice she dropped so quickly I left my stomach somewhere behind me. Then, in the distance ahead, there came a great whooshing sound. At first it sounded like a waterfall or a great wind, but then it became something more.

"Do you hear that?" I asked. "It sounds like a train or something. What is it?"

"I don't know," Dad said calmly, "but I think we'd better hold on tight. I see movement ahead."

He was right; at the furthest reach of my sword's light the clouds began to move abruptly to the right. Something was stirring in the center of the Black Curtain...something big and powerful. There was a half-second of absolute stillness and then...*WHOOSH!*

In an instant Nowaii was pulled to the side by a massive gust of wind. The jolt was so sudden that Nowaii's wings nearly broke from the pressure of it. She tucked them close to her body and gave in to the will of the wind. All at once, we were tumbling through space with no control over our direction. Up, down and side to side, we were tossed about in the wild currents, riding an unseen airstream. There was no flying here, no fighting the constant pulling and twisting; we were completely at the mercy of the winds.

The sensation was disorienting, like a roller coaster in the dark. I clung to my father as long as I could, but eventually the G-forces pulled us apart. The only thing keeping us connected to Nowaii was a tether rope that was latched to her saddle. Soon, even that began to give under the pressure.

"Hunter, the rope is not going to hold!" Dad shouted over the roar of the wind. "Hurry, give me your hands, son! We have to stay together."

"Where are you?" I asked, unable to find him through the blackness.

"Here…I'm here!" he shouted back.

I reached out and felt his fingertips in front of me. I took hold of his wrists just before the tether broke loose and we separated completely from Nowaii. The winds were pulling even harder now, spinning us around the center of what seemed to be a massive cyclone. I couldn't tell for sure, but I sensed we were rising higher and higher through the middle of it. Eventually, the gusts of wind began to pry my father and me apart; my strength was failing and my hands began to slip.

"Hunter, hang tight!"

"I…I can't, Dad…I…."

Before I could finish speaking, we were torn apart by the wind and I was spinning away through the air on my own.

"Hunter!" I heard my father scream before the sound disappeared in the roar of the Black Curtain's fury.

The last thing I remember before losing consciousness was the sense that I was falling, dropping fast, like a comet bulleting toward the ground at break-neck speed.

This is why you should never pick a fight with a tornado, I thought as I fell. Then it was over.... Everything went black.

CHAPTER 25

THE LOST SHARD

I woke up feeling like I had just lost a fight. My body was sore and bruised. I was thankful to be alive, but at the same time I was worried about my father.

I saw a grey sky and black trees above me. The air was warm and still, with not even the slightest bit of wind. I heard thunder in the distance but the cloud cover overhead did not look anything like storm clouds. I tried to sit up, but my muscles felt like they were on fire.

"Easy there," a girl's voice said. "You haven't got the strength for that yet."

"Hope? Is that you?"

Her face appeared above me, as if out of thin air. Her lips curled in a sweet smile and her almond eyes searched my own and calmed my nerves. The medallion I had sent with Faldyn hung elegantly from her neck. It looked so much better on her than it did on me. It belonged.

"Here, drink this," she offered, bringing a cup to my mouth. "Be careful; it's hot. It will help you regain your strength."

The aroma of the foamy drink aroused my senses, the same juniper scent I first smelled when I awoke. I took a quick sip and almost immediately began to feel better. The sweet drink had a rich velvety texture, much like my favorite latte, only much…much better.

"This is good," I said, taking a longer sip from the cup.

"I'm glad you like it," Hope replied. "Feeling better?"

"Much," I answered. I wiped a bit of foam from my lips with my sleeve and sat up easily. Like magic, the pain was almost completely gone.

"Where am I?" I asked, taking in my surroundings. I was sitting in the middle of a grove of blackened trees that looked as if they had recently survived a forest fire. Their limbs and trunks were as black as soot, but what struck me most of all was what they held. Skeletons, hundreds and hundreds of skeletons lined the trees, some of them hanging from the branches and others scattered about the ground. I eyed the scene nervously. "Am I…dead?"

"No, you're on the Lost Shard," she said simply. "But I wish you would have waited for me. I could have made your arrival less… dramatic. Why did you leave Noc without me?" Hope asked.

"I was just anxious, I guess. Once I figured out where my father was I couldn't wait to get started. Then Desi arrived and I kinda got…carried away…."

I took another sip of the drink, but to my dismay I found the cup was already empty. I didn't realize how quickly I had downed it.

"I understand," Hope said. "Patience is one of the hardest things to learn. But good things come to those who wait."

"Is there any more?" I asked, handing the empty cup back to Hope and licking my lips expectantly.

"One cup is enough, trust me. You couldn't handle more."

I frowned at the news. Whatever was in her concoction was powerfully good stuff.

"I've brought you something," Hope said coyly, averting my attention from the empty cup.

"What is it?"

"A gift…from Aviad," she said, handing me a small package wrapped in simple brown paper. I tore open the wrap to find a small vial with a cork seal. It looked empty. I shook the jar and heard a light *tink* inside. Upon closer inspection, I saw the glass vial wasn't empty…there was a small speck inside it. The speck was so small I practically had to cross my eyes to focus on it. Hope looked amused.

"Not what you expected?" she asked.

"You could say that. What's it for?"

"It's a seed, the start of something new. It will help you repair what has been broken. It will bring life where once there was death."

"But, it's just a seed…."

"Not an ordinary seed; it has the power to change this world forever, Hunter. You just have to believe it."

"This seed?" I asked, looking at the tiny speck in disbelief. It was smaller than any seed I had ever seen. "So, what am I supposed to do with it—put it in a Styrofoam cup of dirt in my kitchen window and water it once a day?"

Hope laughed.

"You'll know, if you're listening to the Author."

"Right," I said, tucking the vial in my pocket. "Did he say anything else? Did you ask if the vision in the Eye of Ends was true?"

"I…I can't tell you that."

"Why not?"

"Because it isn't meant for you to know."

Of course, it wasn't. Aviad rarely let me see the whole truth. It wasn't his way. The truth was always wrapped in riddles or secret messages. *Here, have a seed Hunter. You don't know what it does but use it.* Stuff like that was starting to annoy me. I mean, why couldn't he just tell me what his plan was for once?

"What's wrong?" Hope asked, spotting the frustration on my face.

"I'm just tired of all the secrets the Author keeps. Sometimes I just wish I could see a glimpse of what the future holds."

"No, you don't…trust me."

"Why, is it that bad?"

Hope chuckled. "There you go again, assuming the worst of everything."

"Well, it's kinda hard not to when you're surrounded by a forest of dead men," I said, pointing to the surroundings.

"I see your point," Hope answered, "but it still doesn't mean everything ends in tragedy."

"So, it's good then?" I asked.

Hope sighed. "You really want me to tell you, don't you?" she asked, raising an eyebrow at me.

"Can you?" I asked.

She thought about it for a moment, and seemed to be genuinely considering the idea. After a short silence, she nodded her head and looked both ways before beckoning me to lean in closer.

"Come here," she said quietly. My heart beat a little faster in anticipation of what she was about to say next. I leaned toward her and she put her lips right up to the edge of my ear and held there for a moment or two before whispering her secret in a slow, hushed tone.

"Everything will be exactly as it should be," she said. As she finished, she started to giggle. She had played me perfectly.

"I should have seen that coming," I said dryly, shaking my head and trying to suppress a smile of my own.

"Oh, but that wouldn't be any fun," she replied. "You have to admit some things are better as a surprise."

"Maybe the little things," I said in agreement, "but it's the bigger things that worry me more."

"Listen," Hope said, putting her hand on my shoulder. "I know you're scared and concerned about what the future might hold. But you don't have to be."

"I don't want to be," I answered. "But the visions my father saw in the Eye…they…."

"Aren't important," Hope replied. "If you trust the Writ and what the Author has said about the story to come, you won't have to worry. Remember the words of the Writ, the ones that Gabby sang?"

"You mean the song about *finding joy that's hid behind?*"

Hope nodded and began to sing the tune. Her voice was sweet and heavenly as it rang through the air.

A greater story is being told,
Beyond the things you see and hold.
The pages turn in perfect time,
Leaving what we know behind.
Death is not the end, dear one.
Another chapter has begun.
So be not sad, oh heart of mine,
Find the joy that's hid behind.
Through darkness light will find its way,
While we await the dawn of day.

As she sang, my chest felt as if a giant, crushing rock had been lifted off. I was at peace. Just hearing her sing reminded me that the

Author knew what he was doing. After all, he had sent her to me, hadn't he? She belonged to the Codebearers.... She was a gift from the Author to all of us.

"Every page has its purpose, Hunter," Hope said after finishing her song, "even the difficult ones. We just have to believe that things are going to work out the way the Author has planned."

"But it's not as easy as it sounds."

"No, it's not at first. But like that seed, your faith will grow until it's as strong and unshakeable as a mighty oak."

I held the vial up once more and looked at the seed inside it.

"Hunter!" my father's voice yelled through the blackened woods. "Hunter, where are you, son?"

"Dad, I'm over here!" I yelled back. I started to run toward the sound of his voice but turned back when I realized Hope wasn't following.

"Go on," she said. "Your father needs you."

"But aren't you coming?" I asked.

"Not right now; there's something else I must do first," Hope said. "But I'll be back soon. Just remember, no matter what happens in the Eye of Ends, the future belongs to the Author. We're never alone."

I nodded in agreement at the familiar phrase the Codebearers shared. Hope's eyes shifted from mine to a movement in the woods behind me. My father had found me.

"Hunter! I'm so glad you made it!" Dad said as he bounded onto the scene. "That was quite the fall, eh? Are you okay?"

I turned to greet him. "Yeah, Dad, I'm...fine," I said, but when I turned back to where Hope had once stood, she was gone.

"Good! From the looks of things we lucked out. We could have easily ended up like one of those poor souls," he said, pointing to the tree full of bones. "That would have been a nasty ending, wouldn't you say?"

"*Never alone,*" I whispered to myself. Clearly, the Author had been watching out for us. But for what purpose?

"And that's not all," Dad continued excitedly, "you'll never guess what I found!"

"What is it?" I asked.

"Come here; I'll show you."

He led me through the grove of blackened trees to a clearing, not far from where Hope had found me. The ground darkened as we approached, and it was dry and cracked in places. In the center of the clearing, a massive tree stump remained. Despite all the differences in the landscape, I recognized it at once.

"The Living Tree," he said in a theatrical voice.

"Or what's left of it," I added, noting how dead it was. There was nothing left but the stump and even that seemed to be rotting away.

"Ah, but its rings are still intact, see?" Dad pointed out. "That's the important part."

I glanced over the intricate pattern of the circular grain of the tree. I had never noticed it before, but it actually looked quite a bit like a maze, complete with dead ends and backtracking paths that led toward the middle of the tree and the eye-shaped center.

"So what do we do now?" I asked.

"We sleep, of course!"

"Sleep?"

"Yes, you have to be asleep in order to enter the Maze of Rings."

I vaguely recalled Simon saying something to that effect in his explanation about the Eye of Ends. It only made sense that the tree stump would require the same thing.

"Wait a minute, don't we need a Watcher to enter the Maze?"

"Not if Tonomis is already in the Eye himself. Remember, the

Eye is a cross section of this tree. The rings will be the same as these. If my suspicions are correct both will lead to the Maze of Rings. The only way to know for sure is to get some sleep."

"Sleep? But I'm not really tired," I said. The potion Hope had given me made me think I might never sleep again. I felt more awake than any time in my life.

"Oh, you will be," Dad replied with a mischievous look in his eye. He knew something I didn't. He set to work, gathering a collection of small sticks that were lying on the ground here and there. I didn't question him, I just watched. He had obviously done this before and knew what he was doing. When at last he had a decent handful, he motioned toward the tree stump. "Go ahead. Touch the rings."

I reached out toward the tree and paused for a moment before my fingers touched the surface. Dad nodded his encouragement and reached out with me toward the rings. The moment my fingers connected with the tree, I felt like every ounce of energy in my body drained through my fingertips and was pulled into the tree itself. My knees gave out and I fell forward onto the stump like a limp ragdoll.

Before I knew what was happening, I opened my eyes and found I was standing on the edge of a cliff, overlooking a vast crater that stretched out for what seemed like miles. Several hundred feet below, a winding labyrinth of stone walls circled inward…and in the center of it all, a pillar of fire streamed upward like a bright column of light. There was no doubt about it; this was the Maze of Rings.

CHAPTER 26

THE MAZE OF RINGS

The view from above was breathtaking, but I couldn't enjoy it. The ledge was far too narrow for my liking and the drop was… dizzying. A tunnel led down the side of the hill, giving access to the floor below. I started to edge my way toward it, but Dad held me back.

"I wouldn't go down that way if I were you," Dad said.

"Why not? How else will we get down?" I asked, backing away from the ledge.

"Not easily," Dad replied, peering over the edge. "But getting there is half the fun."

"Fun?"

"Hey, nobody promised you it would be a cakewalk. The Maze of Rings is a dangerous place without a Watcher to guide you. We aren't exactly here as guests. Only the smartest and toughest make it to the middle, which is why nobody has done it but me," Dad bragged. He pointed back at the tunnel and continued, "If you want to go that way, by all means be my guest, maybe say 'hi' to a Crag Spider or two along the way. But as for me, I prefer to limit my risk…. I'm climbing down."

He peered over the edge at the canyon floor, which was hidden in the darkness far below. He tried calculating the distance in his head and pulled the rope we had collected in the tower ruins from my backpack. Next, he began bundling together the pile of twigs he had gathered on the Lost Shard and wound the rope around it.

"Let me get this straight. You'd rather climb down that cliff than face a few ugly, little spiders? I didn't know you were arachnophobic."

"I'm not," Dad said, taking offense at my ribbing. "They're Crag Spiders. You wouldn't be able to squash any of those big daddies with your shoe," Dad explained.

"Come on…how big can they possibly be?" I challenged.

Dad held his arms out in a hoop shape, roughly the circumference of a manhole cover.

"For real?" I asked, stunned at his gesture.

"And those are the little ones," Dad said, nodding. "They hunt in packs; trust me, you don't want to meet one. It's not a fun way to die."

I rarely admitted to it, but avoiding any eight-legged thing, especially one you could look in the eyes, had always been a good idea in my book. I wasn't about to break that rule.

Under Dad's direction, I used my Veritas Sword to help him carve out a section of the rocky ledge to fit the bundled "log" of sticks.

"This here is what we call a 'dead man's anchor,' Hunter," Dad explained as we finished digging.

"Because we're dead men?"

"No. The sticks are the 'dead man.' This hole I made is like their 'grave.' So I just loop our rope around the 'dearly departed' like so and…." Dad handed the doubled rope to me and said, "Go ahead, give it a tug; low to the ground like this."

I pulled. The bundle of sticks held the rope in place.

"Hey, cool," I said, surprised at the resourceful simplicity of it all. It felt good to have someone as experienced as Dad leading the mission—someone who had scouted this out before me, who could point out the pitfalls. In other words, it felt good to have a father in my life again.

"You ready, kid?" Dad asked.

"Yes, sir."

"All right. Then watch how I use the rope to lower myself down the cliffside to the next ledge down there. I'll wait for you to follow after me. That way I can coach you on your technique and be there to stop you if you slip…or join you in falling."

"Nice," I said, swallowing hard at the thought of it.

Scooping up the rope in two coils, he heaved them out over the side. The separate lengths snaked their way down until gravity stretched them taut. Dad straddled the doubled lines, looping them up and over his shoulder so they crossed over his chest. Then, gripping the paired ropes with one hand in front and one stretched behind him, he slowly leaned back into the cavern and began walking down the steep bank toward the next ledge. Once he secured his footing at the base, he waved for me to follow. It all looked easy enough.

Doing my best to imitate his technique, I managed to loop myself into the makeshift harness as he had done and rappelled down to join him. Despite my best effort though, I lost my footing once or twice along the way, triggering miniature avalanches of loose pebbles to tumble into the gaping void below me. Thanks to the rope and Dad's coaching, I didn't join their fate.

Once I was standing safely beside him, Dad winked at me and said, "And now for the fun part." With a quick flick of his wrist, he released the anchor above us, letting the rope slither its way down to our feet.

"Hey! How are we going to climb back out?" I asked, upset at having lost our lifeline.

"If our mission is successful, we won't need to climb out," Dad said, as he set about reanchoring the rope. Satisfied with his work, Dad motioned for me to join him in straddling the newly tethered rope. He pulled me close up against him and started feeding the rope across my chest, looping around his back and over his shoulder. I noticed this time the rope wasn't doubled up like before. Instead, Dad had tied it off in one massive knot at the anchor; we would be leaving the rope behind.

"We'll need every inch of it to reach the ground," Dad explained. "Should be long enough."

Should? I gulped. Looking back up the steep slope we'd just rappelled, I quickly calculated it had to be around one hundred fifty feet from the top anchor to this point. Doubled-up, the rope had barely covered a third of the distance. That meant at its full length the rope would be somewhere around three hundred feet. I shuddered to imagine we'd be descending further than that in one drop!

"It's going to get dark down there. The walls of the Maze are over a hundred feet tall. We'll need your Veritas Sword for light. Keep the rope snug, and so long as you stay leaned into me you should be able to manage a free hand for the sword."

I nodded and shifted my sword so I could access it more easily.

Dad slowly edged us backward over the second ledge and leaned back. I felt the rope slide across my body. For a moment, my feet couldn't touch the ground and I was left helpless, looking straight up at the top of the cliff. My back faced the suffocating darkness of the deep unknown.

What on earth am I doing? I couldn't help asking myself.

It took a minute or two to get the hang of coordinating our footsteps, but soon we were well on our way into the darkness of the labyrinth below.

"By the light of truth all things are revealed," I recited aloud, holding my Veritas Sword out to the side. The comforting glow of the blue blade shone brightly, providing a ten-foot radius of light to plan at least a few steps ahead.

We reached the end of the rope before we reached the ground. Dad kept his cool, but I could tell he was more than a little concerned. I cut a few rocks from the side of the cliff and tossed them down. The sound of the stones hitting the rock floor seemed to be just beyond the light of my sword.

"We're going to have to free-climb the rest of the way," Dad said. "It can't be more than fifteen or twenty feet."

I slipped carefully out of my backpack and dropped it ahead of us. It landed with a *thud*. Before I could take hold of the wall and release the rope, there was a crumbling sound where I had just cut the stones free. The side of the wall had repaired itself just like the Tempering Stones did when we practiced sword fighting in Sanctuary.

"Dad, look!" I said excitedly. "The stone is healing itself."

"So it is...."

"Hang on, that gives me an idea!" I said.

I plunged my Veritas Sword into the stone, all the way to its hilt, and held on tight.

"Grab on," I told Dad. He wrapped his arms around me and we let our weight pull the sword down the side of the cliff, leaving a sizzling trail in the rock wall as we went. The wall healed itself almost as quickly as we cut it and in no time we were at ground level.

"Nicely done," Dad said as he let go and stepped onto the cold stone floor. "Ingenious, just like your old man."

"Yeah, well, we're not out of the woods yet," I said nervously, thinking of what lay ahead of us.

"No, we still have to get lost in them first," Dad corrected. "Come on, the tunnel ends this way. That's where the entrance to the Maze begins."

I retrieved the backpack I'd dropped and followed my father into the darkness ahead. We were between two rock walls: one the towering cliff face, the other the outer wall of the Maze of Rings. The ground was gritty beneath our feet, like a smooth, solid slab of rock that had been sprinkled with sand. Each crackling step echoed off the grey stone walls. It gave the space a certain, creepy ambiance. The good thing about hearing your own footsteps is that you can't easily be followed by anyone else. You know when you're alone.

Eventually, we came to an arched hole in the wall to our right, the entrance to the Maze. An inscription was carved overhead that read: *WHAT THE EYE REVEALS, IN FATE IS SEALED.*

"That's a cheerful thought," I muttered, remembering what Dad had said about the visions. Was the end truly coming? Would Tonomis win?

The floor was scattered with the bones of those who had met their end, searching for a glimpse of the future. They hadn't made it far; the Crag Spiders had finished them before their journey began.

I knew this because the lifeless remains of one of the spiders was curled atop the bones of one of the dead, a spear having penetrated its abdomen, but not before it had dealt a death blow to its victim. I gasped, seeing the creature for the first time. Dad had been right…. These were not your ordinary household spiders. The black, rock-encrusted body lived up to what I'd thought were Dad's exaggerations in size. This killer arachnid was perhaps even bigger; its jagged, bulbous body as imposing as a wrecking ball. I shuddered at the two skeletal forms, locked in an eternal battle like a sign posted at the Maze's entrance, serving as a warning to all visitors: This was dangerous ground.

Dad wasted no time scavenging the fallen. Like clockwork he moved from body to body, gathering whatever items had been left behind. A swarm of moths, hidden in one of the remains, fluttered out as Dad rummaged for items. The undersides of the moths' wings were black, but the backs were an entrancing, incandescent gold, which glowed in the darkness as the swarm of moths entered the mouth of the Maze and turned left. Dad gathered a pair of curved knives, a velvet pouch that seemed to be full of sand, and a spear, which he took for his own personal protection. He tucked the knives in both sides of his belt and pointed the spear out in front of him.

"Beyond this point anything can happen, so keep alert, and stay on your toes. Don't forget, Tonomis may be here already—could be waiting around any corner. Most importantly, if you see a vision forming, look away. If you don't, your visit here will be over and it's *poof*, back to Solandria."

"Got it," I said, feeling the excitement building in my chest. A low howl of wind escaped the gaping mouth of the Maze, hitting me in the face. The first thing I noticed was that the labyrinth had bad breath; it smelled of sulfur. The second thing I realized was that it sounded hungry—ravenous even. It had been a long time since a mortal had wandered into its throat and it was ready for another visitor.

"So how exactly will we know if we're going the right way?" I asked as we stepped through the archway and into the first ring of the Maze. Dad glanced to the left, then to the right. The passageway seemed to disappear into the inky blackness in both directions.

"I'm kind of hoping it will come back to me as we go," Dad confessed. "It's been so long and my memory of this place isn't exactly all there."

"How much do you remember?" I asked.

"Pretty much everything up to that arch we just passed through," Dad said, pointing his thumb over his shoulder.

"You mean you're just…winging it now?"

"Yup! From here on out, we're going on instinct."

My own instinct told me to panic, but I did my best not to show it. "Okay then, to wherever the Author leads us," I said, hoping to inspire him (and myself) with Hope's words.

"Something like that," Dad replied. His message was clear: he knew the Author was in control, but he didn't have to like it.

After considering the branches off the entrance, Dad finally made the decision to head down the passageway splitting off to our right. For the next half hour he led me through a series of twists and turns that seemed to move us closer to the center of the rings, and then back out. At times, it felt like we were wandering aimlessly. The only good thing was that our wandering had been fairly uneventful to this point—no Shadow monsters. Considering all of the stories Dad had told about the dangers of the Maze, I was glad nothing had shown up…yet.

The further we went, the stronger I felt that each step forward was another step closer to, not just our quest's end, but ours as well. I knew what Dad had seen in the visions. If we didn't get to the Bloodstone first, this very well might be my last adventure ever. Remembering Hope's advice, I tried harder not to dwell on those thoughts.

Instead, I decided to engage my mind with repeating to myself the riddle my father had written from his original quest through the Maze. *We enter the circle by night, and are consumed by the fire.* I even made a rhythm of it and marched to the beat of the words as we walked. There had to be some reason he wrote that....

As we continued down the passageway, I began to hear soft fluttering sounds, like bats or small birds darting about in the darkness behind me. Every time I looked, nothing was there, but the near-silent noise made me uneasy nonetheless.

"Why is it I get this feeling we're being watched?" I asked.

"They don't call it the 'Eye' for nothing. Down here, you're always being watched." Dad pointed up at the column of fire piercing the darkness high above us...always constant, never wavering, never blinking.

Thanks, Dad, I thought. *Way to calm a guy's nerves.*

I decided to chalk up the unsettling feelings and sounds to my overactive imagination, forcing myself back into step with my silent rhythm. *We enter the circle by night....*

"Hunter! Watch out!" Dad shouted to me, waving wildly at the floor.

Too late. I felt something shift beneath my foot.

"Don't move a muscle," he cautioned, pointing down at the place where I had just stepped. I slowly looked down to see what I'd stepped on. A thick thread had been stretched across the passageway only a few inches from the floor.

"What is it?" I asked, more frightened by my father's reaction than by the actual threat. "A booby trap?"

He nodded intently, getting down on his hands and knees next to me for a closer look at the thread. "The deadliest kind—a Crag Spider made this."

I suddenly got this image of an enormous spider hidden in the shadows, with one foot resting on this very thread, waiting patiently for the vibrations that would signal its next meal had arrived... namely, me.

"Whatever you do now, don't panic," Dad coached me. "We're going to take this slowly."

Easy for him to say! He wasn't the one with his life literally on the line. I felt like every pounding of my heartbeat was pulsing down the line to ring the "dinner bell."

"I'll need your sword for light," Dad said, taking it from my hand. He started walking away. "I'll be right back. Just…wait here."

What else was I going to do? As Dad quickly disappeared down the tunnel, so did the light. For a tense moment I was left alone in the dark, trying to master my fears.

By his fear, a man appoints his master, I breathed over and over to myself, drawing upon the strength of the Code.

Even so, Dad could not have returned soon enough. The blue light from my Veritas Sword was just as much a hero as my father was, chasing away the lurking nightmares in the shadows. Holding as still as I could, I peeked through the corner of my eye and saw he was carrying something.

"Okay, here's what we're going to do," Dad said calmly. "This rock is going to take your place. The important part is that once the line is stretched, we can't let it up. From what I know, the spider doesn't strike until the line goes loose."

I gulped and waited patiently as Dad pushed the line down with a hand on each side of my foot. Then, he instructed me to roll the rock over the middle. We both held our breath as he slowly lifted his hands off the line.

The line held tight. Not hearing anything, Dad breathed a sigh of relief and tried to wipe off the oily substance that came from the spider's thread. He made a face and held out his fingers to me. "Weird smell, isn't it?"

I leaned away from the offer. "If you know so much about these Crag Spiders, don't you think you could have said something about watching out for the trip lines sooner?"

"Cut me a little slack," Dad said. "I'm still trying to remember everything. But, no harm done, right?" He patted me on the back, and not waiting for my reply, said, "All right then. Let's get back to it."

Dad handed back my Veritas Sword and led us on up the trail. We had only gone a few yards up the path when we both heard the sound.

TWANG!

The sound was like…a note being plucked.

We both stopped dead in our tracks.

"It knows we're here," Dad whispered. The way he said it, I didn't need to ask what "it" was.

"What do we do?"

"Stay alive," Dad said simply. "The trap is behind us, but the spider can approach us from any direction. They're not stuck down in the Maze like us."

Gripping sword and spear, Dad and I positioned ourselves back to back to defend against both fronts. After a few minutes of silence, we decided the best course of action would be to keep moving. So, with Dad leading the way, I walked backwards to protect against a rear attack. This went on far too long.

After nearly half an hour, we'd still not seen or heard any response from the tripped Crag Spider line. By now we were well away from the original site. Feeling convinced we were past the danger, I decided to turn around and walk forward again.

Big mistake!

As soon as my back was turned, I heard a hissing sound from behind me. I whirled back around and came face to face with a Crag Spider, hovering about six feet from the ground. The black exoskeleton shell covering its body and legs glinted like polished steel in my sword's light. Its long pinchers were only inches from my head.

The spider made a strange hissing sound as it spread its jaws and readied for the kill. My feet felt like lead and I froze in place.

"Get down!" Dad shouted behind me.

I did, just in time to miss his spear, which planted itself right between the spider's fangs. The stunned creature howled and shook its head, trying to get free from the spear. Dad launched himself into the fray, grabbing hold of the spear and shoving it back further into the spider's head.

"Don't just stand there!" Dad shouted as he struggled to hold on to the spear. "Cut it down!"

"Where?"

"The legs," Dad grunted. "Go for the legs!"

I ran past the spider and severed all four legs on its left side with a single swipe of my Veritas Sword. The unsupported body fell lopsided to the floor and squirmed in circles. Dad finally freed his spear and delivered a death blow to its face, piercing its forehead.

"Wh-where did it come from?" I asked bewildered. "I'd only turned around for a second…."

"From above," Dad said, looking up into the darkness. "It must have been following us for some time, waiting for the opportunity to present itself."

I suddenly felt horrible. I'd nearly killed us by neglecting my post. "I'm sorry, Dad."

"We're just lucky this one was so big," Dad said, wrenching the spear free from the motionless foe.

I looked at him like he was crazy.

"I'm serious," Dad explained.

"How did it find us?" I asked, noticing something odd about the creature's face for the first time. "It doesn't have any eyes."

"You're right," Dad agreed, leaning in for a closer look. "Whoa! Do you smell that?"

I did. It was the same scent we'd discovered on the spider's thread, only much stronger. It seemed to be coming from the oil-like liquid pooling up under the dead creature.

"They probably hunt by smell," Dad observed. "Maybe coat the thread with their own scent and use that to track their prey…or just make a claim on them."

After Dad convinced me that we were free from the Crag Spider's threat, we set back off down the passage. That didn't stop me from keeping a wary eye to the sky, though. In my opinion, we couldn't get out of the open Maze soon enough. Imagine my relief when we discovered a doorway cut into the end of one of the Maze's passageways.

Dad seemed just as excited, but for a different reason.

"A decision point," Dad said, motioning me to shine my light into the opening. The roughhewn door led into a large rectangular room with white limestone tile on the floor.

"What is this place?" I asked.

"It's coming back to me now," Dad said, choosing to leave the Maze's path to enter the room. "The Maze presents various decision points that can alter the path of the Maze."

"Is it safe?"

"It's at least worth exploring," Dad said.

As soon as I stepped inside, the passage behind us sealed shut, blocking any chance of escape. The stone wall itself had closed up in the same way the Tempering Stone had healed itself. Unlike the open passageways that had led us here, this room had a ceiling twenty feet high.

"Oh yeah," Dad said, his voice echoing off the walls, "and every decision we make in the Maze is final; there's no going back."

"I kind of got that point," I said, glancing nervously across the room. The light from my sword cast a dim blue light on the scene. We were standing near the middle of the room, which stretched out twelve feet in either direction. There was a chandelier of unlit candles, hanging from the center of the ceiling. The walls were solid dark stone on all four sides, and the tile floor was a ghostly white. The stark contrast of the two created an eerie effect that the floor was floating in space. The illusion was only heightened by the fact that the white floor tiles reacted to the glow of my sword like a black light.

"It's our first test," Dad said thoughtfully. "Each room has one entrance and one exit…assuming it isn't a dead end, of course."

I really didn't like the use of that phrase, "dead end," in context with our current situation.

"So, where's the exit then?" I asked anxiously.

"That's the test," Dad said, as he continued to eye the space.

"A hidden passageway?"

Dad nodded, "Except, not quite that easy."

With a puffing sound, the candles of the chandelier flickered to life on their own, causing our shadows to dance on the walls behind us in the warm light of their glowing. A golden sparkle of light I hadn't noticed before reflected off a tile near the center of the room.

"Hello, what's this?" Dad wondered. He strode to the place and bent over to examine the golden inset.

"There seems to be some kind of inscription here," Dad said, clearing his throat and preparing to read it aloud:

One door is Truth, the other one Lies.
Which one can you trust? Only Truth leads to life.
This key you are given: one question you ask.
Knock, then discern through which door you must pass.

"Might make a little more sense if there *were* any doors," I complained, looking around at the empty room.

"Like I said, these tests are tricky," Dad said. "Look for anything that might symbolize a door. It's not always clear."

Glancing around the bare-walled room, I happened to notice a strange movement along the floor to our right and left. A pair of rectangular shadows danced in time with the candlelight, just like our shadows. The only difference was that unlike ours, these shadows seemed to have no source.

"Check this out," I said, pointing to the flickering shapes on the floor. "Does that look right to you?"

Dad cocked his head and investigated the shadows with childlike curiosity.

"Well, I'll be," he muttered, reaching out above one of the cast shadows. With his palm outstretched, he connected with the front of an invisible object. Rippling out from his touch, an ancient, wooden door appeared. The rotten frame almost looked as if it would fall apart at any moment. Over the door frame a single word was written in red letters: TRUTH.

"Well, that was easy," I said, reaching out to open the door.

"Not so fast," Dad said, grabbing my arm. "There are supposed to be two doors, remember?"

"Sure, but this one says TRUTH," I pointed out. "What more do we need to know? This is the one we needed to find."

"Still, we might as well see what our options are."

I couldn't imagine why he wanted to, but I figured it couldn't hurt. Dad walked over and touched above the second shadow and a second door appeared, identical to the first: old, wooden, and a sign over its frame that read (you guessed it), TRUTH!

"Well, that's confusing," I said, pondering the situation.

"I think that's the point," Dad said, glancing between the newly revealed exits. "One of them lies."

"Great. So how are we supposed to know which one is the real door of truth?" I wondered.

"*This key you are given: one question you ask,*" Dad repeated. "I think we're supposed to ask the doors a question of some kind."

"How about just asking the door if it's the door of Truth?" I suggested.

"The door of Truth would say 'yes' and so would the door of Lies. Won't work."

Dad was right, and now that I thought about it, asking which one was the door of Lies wouldn't work either; the door of Lies would lie and say "no," just like Truth.

As the riddle rattled around in my head, a thought struck me. "Did the riddle mean we only get to ask *one* question? Or one for each door?"

"It's not very clear," Dad admitted. "To be safe, we better come up with a question that gives us the answer we need no matter which door we ask: the perfect question."

It was true. We couldn't risk counting on two questions; our wording would have to be very specific. We might only get one shot at this.

"No pressure," I muttered.

I ran through at least a dozen questions in my mind, but every combination seemed to come up short of a precise answer that eliminated any doubt as to which door was really the true exit. Given enough time, I'm sure we could have figured it out, but that's when things got a little, shall we say, interesting.

A gritty, grinding sound came from the wall to our left. The wall was lowering down, and something was spilling into the room. Sand…and lots of it.

"Oh great, who flipped the hourglass?" I whined. At the rate it was coming in, the sand threatened to bury us in only a few minutes. Already, it had reached my feet. "Tell me you remember something, Dad."

"I don't; the Maze is always shifting…. This is a different test than before."

"Well, we'd better think of something quick because we've just been given a deadline."

Just when we thought the situation couldn't get any worse, a second grinding noise added to the first. The wall to our right was lowering and a second batch of sand came spilling in. While Dad and I scrambled and bounced potential questions at each other, the sand in the room reached to our ankles.

"Dad! What was it that the riddle said about 'Truth' and 'life'?" I asked, fighting to keep on my feet.

"Only Truth leads to life," he answered.

"Only Truth…" I murmured, before shouting excitedly, "that's it! Then we know there is only one true way out!"

Dad looked at me in confusion.

I explained hurriedly, "We have to ask either door if there's only one true way and if a door says 'no'…."

"Then we'll know it's the door that lies," Dad finished the thought. "The perfect question…. Brilliant, Hunter!"

The sand was growing deeper by the second, now almost to our knees. Wasting no time, I knocked on the door nearest me. It was the first door, the one I had almost entered before. Nothing happened.

"Go on," Dad urged. "Ask the question."

I rehearsed it once in my mind then in my loudest voice I asked, "Is there only one true way to life?"

In response, the door answered with two red letters, writing themselves on the face of the door: NO. It was the wrong door. Knee-deep in sand we worked our way over to the other door, which was no easy task. By the time we arrived, we realized we had another problem.

"It's still locked!" I shouted, pushing against the face of the door with all my strength. "The riddle didn't say anything about a lock!"

"It's no good anyway. The door is surrounded by sand; you'll never open it," Dad said, his face turning pale.

"We have to try," I begged.

Together, Dad and I shouldered the door, hoping it would open. It didn't budge.

With the sand level rising to my chest, the words of the riddle came to me with new revelation. *This key you are given...knock... ask.*

Pounding on the door, I shouted, "Will you please let us pass?"

Three letters painted themselves near the top of the door: YES. With a final push, the door swung open and we spilled out through the opening, riding a river of sand.

CHAPTER 27

THE EYES HAVE IT

We weren't buried in it anymore but there was still sand everywhere. It was in our hair, our ears, our clothes. I even found myself spitting the stuff out of my mouth and trying not to bite on the grit it left between my teeth. It was one of those "wish I could take a shower right about now" moments that I often found myself in. I shook my head and did my best to brush myself clean.

While Dad poured piles of sand from his shoes, I tried to figure out just exactly where in the labyrinth the door had dumped us. When I looked up, I saw that the door itself had disappeared completely.

Staring up through a gap between the walls of the Maze, I caught sight of the Eye's cavernous ceiling high overhead. It was bathed in an orange glow that emanated from the center of the Rings. We were still well off-center.

"Why does it feel like we're even farther away than when we started?" I asked, feeling a wave of discouragement wash over me.

"We may very well be," Dad replied, shaking the sand from his hair. "But the Maze doesn't work like an ordinary linear one. Things don't connect like you might imagine. It's always changing. At any moment, we could come across another challenge that transports us straight to the center of the Eye."

Or we could get stuck in an infinite loop of random traps and never find our way back out again, I thought.

A pair of the golden moths suddenly passed into my view, fluttering away down the long tunnel and disappearing behind some new branch in the Maze. Theirs was a hopeless, wandering flight through the Maze, in my estimation…not unlike our own.

I sighed. "So, which way do we go now?"

"Your guess is as good as mine. Why don't you pick?" Dad suggested.

Checking first to make sure he was serious, I glanced up and down the length of the passageway to weigh our options. Either way looked the same, with no distinguishing features to base a decision on. I'd have to go with my gut.

"Hmmm…that way," I finally said, pointing to our right.

Dad didn't object, motioning for me to lead on. I lifted my Veritas Sword higher to light our way and set out in the direction I'd seen the moths fly.

Before long we reached the turn I'd thought the moths had taken. Sure enough, a pair of tiny flickering orange lights were dipping and drifting far off down the passage. With nothing else to guide me, I decided to follow their chosen path a bit further.

"You know, Dad, I've been thinking. Have you ever noticed that the moths always seem to stay down in the trenches of the Maze. They can fly. So why don't they just go up and over the Maze walls?"

"Interesting observation; maybe they've got predators up there," Dad suggested, "or have an aversion to the Eye's light."

"But they've got that whole, 'as a moth is drawn to the flame' reputation going for them," I contested. The predator idea sounded bad too. I had enough to be nervous about without entertaining the idea of new threats from above.

"Yeah, they do love light, don't they?" Dad admitted. He chuckled to himself and said, "Remember camping with that bug zapper we got from my uncle Jim? We'd put it out at night and all the bugs would just come right over and...."

"They were consumed by the fire!" I blurted out dramatically.

"It was electricity," Dad reminded me, having missed my point entirely, "but that's a fun way to put it."

"No. I mean the answer to the riddle you wrote, Dad. *We enter the circle by night and are consumed by the fire.* The answer is 'moths.' Don't you see?"

Dad was all over the idea. I could almost see the wheels in his head spinning.

"Entering the circle *by* night…as in by the *cover of night*, darkness, shadows."

I nodded enthusiastically. "Staying low in the Maze passages; there's your 'cover of night.'"

"And we think they're still drawn to the center flame?" Dad threw the question out, poking at the integrity of our blossoming theory.

"Why not? They're obviously going somewhere," I answered. "Haven't you noticed how they never turn around? It's like they're on a mission."

"If you're right, then we just found ourselves our own natural GPS to the center of the Eye!" Dad said, breaking into one of his signature, crooked smiles. "I can't believe you figured all that out, son. Incredible!" He gave me a friendly punch on the shoulder and messed up my hair a bit like he always did when I was a kid.

"Hey," I objected, wriggling out from under the affectionate gesture. I had forgotten how much I missed these simple moments together. "You were the one who figured it out the first time through the Maze. That's why you wrote the riddle.... I was just following the clues."

"Yeah, well, enough with the clues," Dad said. "We've got some moths to follow!"

We both broke into a run, chasing down the passage after our distant newly appointed guides. They must have been able to sense we were following because they sped up too, staying always a good ten yards in front of us. My sword's light didn't provide us with enough view of the path to make a full-out run, limiting us to a tentative pace. And then there was the trick of tracking them when they made a sudden turn down a side passage and disappeared momentarily from view.

The last turn opened into a circular room with over five different branch-offs to choose from.

"Where'd they go?" Dad panted, making a frantic turn in search of the golden lights from their wings.

"There," I pointed to a particular path. "I see lights reflecting off that wall."

The light was growing dimmer by the second. I dashed off down the path in pursuit with Dad playing catch-up a few yards behind.

"Hold up, Hunter," Dad tried to say, falling farther into the shadows. I heard him trip over something and stumble to the ground, but I didn't stop, for fear we'd lose the moths' trail around a potential secondary turn.

Reaching the corner, I came to a dead stop. There was no sign of the glowing guides anywhere. Even stranger yet, there was nowhere for them to have gone.

"What is it?" Dad asked from out of the darkness.

"It's a dead end," I replied. I swung my Veritas Sword's light from side to side, but couldn't see anything but the three solid walls.

"Figures," Dad sighed. "If I didn't know better, I'd say they were trying to give us the slip."

Confused, I turned to head back toward where Dad was still fumbling about in the dark, but before I could leave, something caught my eye. A patch of surface on the dead-end wall began to glow softly and out of its light, a milky constellation of twinkling lights appeared.

"Hey, come on back here with that light," Dad complained. "I can't see a…ouch…blessed thing."

"Just a sec," I said, not wanting to pull my eyes away from the phenomenon. The lights became brighter, spinning around until they formed into a shape…the shape of a person. For some reason, the face was blacked out. A second faceless person appeared beside her. I squinted, trying to make out the blurry features.

"Hunter, what's going on?" Dad's voice called out, sounding concerned.

I didn't answer, but continued to watch in amazement as a pair of hands reached over and yanked what looked like black bags from the two heads. The faces revealed were my mother and Emily. They were crying and scared and…so very real I could almost reach out and touch them. Mom turned and seemed to look right at me. She smiled.

"Mom?" I said, reaching toward her. She reached back, our fingers only inches apart when my father's scream broke the moment.

"Hunter, don't!" Dad shouted as he dove headlong from out of the shadows to tackle me. The image vanished the moment we hit the ground.

"Dad, what are you doing?" I argued, trying to push him off me. "It was Mom, she's in trouble and…."

"It was a vision, Hunter. We can't look at them, remember?"

Truthfully, I didn't remember. In fact, I was actually angry with him for pulling me away from them. I was confused.

"But she could see me. Emily was there too, and they need our help. They might be...."

"It doesn't matter," Dad said sternly. "We can't change what we see in the vision unless we have the Boodstone. You have to look away."

I searched his eyes for any sign of sympathy for what Mom and Emily must be going through. Did he even care about them anymore? How could he say it didn't matter? They were in pain, and he didn't seem to be worried at all. He must have known how I was feeling because he answered my thoughts directly.

"Hunter, listen to me; you have to trust me. I've tried chasing visions and it doesn't do any good. All it does is steal your future from you. I still care about your mother. I love her, Emily and you more than you could possibly know. We're going to save them, but the only way we're going to be able to do that...the only way we defeat Tonomis is if we...."

"Get the Bloodstone, I know."

Suddenly, I remembered what he was talking about and why we were here. The vision had been so powerful it had almost led me out of the Maze.

"You're lucky, son. That was close. Another second or two of that vision and you'd be gone."

"Thanks, Dad," I said, as he helped me to my feet again. "I'm sorry I...."

"Ahhh, forget it," he said, waving me off. "We've got a lot of road to cover so we'd better get back to it, right?"

He was right, but without the moths to follow, we were going to be back to navigating the Maze blindly again.

"Dad, do you suppose the moths were trying to lead me into that vision?"

"Like a trap?" Dad asked. "I'd be surprised. I really believe we were on to something with our idea that they are on a migratory path to the center fire."

"Then where did they go?" I held my sword light back up to the dead end to let my dad see the problem for himself.

"Where, indeed?" he asked, walking closer to the end wall to run his hand over it. He picked up a loose rock from the ground and used it to tap against the solid stone wall in random places. It sounded as thick and unmoving as it looked.

"Hey. Did you just feel that?" I asked, becoming aware of a cool sensation on my right arm. I held my hand out to the side and tried to pick up the source of the gentle breeze. Dad moved in front of me and picked up the trail easily.

"Here," he said, brushing his hand over a small fissure in the side wall of the dead end. He lifted his stone and tapped the wall near the crack. This time, the wall didn't sound so impenetrable, just hollow.

"You think they went in there?" I asked, amazed that the moths could have squeezed through the sliver of an opening. To do so, they would have had to slide in sideways with their wings folded flat.

"Stand back," Dad commanded. He squared up to the wall and then delivered a well placed kick centered on the crack. Thin sheets of rock broke away from the wall, creating a wider opening. After busting out as much rock face as we could, we found ourselves staring down the throat of a naturally formed tunnel, an open vein running through the rock. It was certainly big enough for the moths to have flown down easily. A man? Not so easily.

That didn't stop Dad from attempting to stick his torso into the tunnel, testing it out for size.

"You're not actually thinking of going in there, are you?" I asked nervously.

He wiggled his way back out and instructed me, "It looks *just* big enough for us. The technique is simple: keep yourself as flat as possible. When it starts to get real tight, hold one arm in front, one behind you."

"And think thin," I teased, patting Dad's belly.

"Just for that I'm sending you in first," Dad threatened. "Actually, since you are the smallest, you should go first. If it gets too tight for you, then we'll know I won't fit and can back out."

"Oh great," I said. "So now I'm the guinea pig? Remind me why I'm doing this."

"For Mom and Emily," Dad said, removing my backpack and thrusting it ahead of me into the hole. I thought of their frightened faces. There was no question I would do whatever it took for them. But there was something more.

"You mean, for our family," I added.

Dad looked embarrassed, "Oh, right…yeah."

Taking in a deep (and potentially final) breath, I plunged head-first into the hole, my Veritas Sword held in my leading hand. From what I could see, there was no sign of where this tunnel might end. We started at a shallow crawl, eventually settling into a belly-slither, and finally inching along on finger and toe power. The tighter the passage got, the more I felt like a rat being ingested by a snake.

As bad as all that was, the worst part didn't come until I needed to scratch my itching nose. Or maybe it was at the point when I realized that I'd never actually seen one of the moths use this tunnel, meaning we could be on a fool's errand.

Just when I thought I would crack from the weight of the world pressing down on me, a small, golden light ahead gave me hope.

"I see…one," I said, squeezing the words out. "A…moth."

"Uh-huh," Dad grunted. I could only imagine how tight things were getting for him. I forced myself to keep pushing ahead. After all, the moths weren't likely to wait and even if they did we were running out of time if we wanted to beat Tonomis.

"Al…most…through," I gasped, forcing myself to the other side. "It's too tight…. I'm stuck!"

"Stuck?" Dad asked. "What do you mean, stuck?"

"Can't…move…" is all I could manage to say.

"Can you come back toward me?" Dad asked.

I tried but found that I couldn't. In all my struggling I had apparently managed to wedge myself literally between a rock and a hard place. There was no budging.

"No…" I gasped, unable to refill my lungs with a sufficient amount of air to speak more than one word at a time.

After two minutes of intense struggling, I managed to break my way out of the crack and onto the other side. There was no way Dad was going to make it without a little help. Using my Veritas Sword, I enlarged the hole so Dad could fit through.

We followed the flittering moths as fast as we could as they navigated through a seemingly never-ending series of twists and turns. As we continued in our pursuit of the moths, the light radiating from the pillar of fire became noticeably brighter and more intense. It was an encouraging sign that we were moving closer and closer to the center of the maze. But the knowledge that Tonomis was most likely still roaming the maze overshadowed any excitement with a looming sense of doom.

Then, all at once, the corridor turned and opened into a wide circular courtyard crowned wth a towering pillar of swirling flame. It was the center of the Eye of Ends. We had reached the Inmost Circle.

CHAPTER 28

THE INMOST CIRCLE

The mesmerizing swirl of light and fire that rose from the center of the Maze now stood directly in front of us, coming to rest atop a stair-stepped pyramid of black stone. An inexplicable sense of awe fell over me. I was in the presence of something great, something far more powerful than I. The cyclone of fire was as wide as a house at the top and as narrow as a finger at the base where it met with the pyramid's tip. Surrounding all sides of the structure was a pit of indeterminable depth, which gave the impression of a fortress' moat. Only a slim stone pathway, no wider than a balance beam, crossed from our side of the pit to the pyramid in its center, a design that was hardly meant to be forgiving of missteps.

Encircling the moat, seven jagged-cut boulders, twice the size of a full-grown man, were erected as monuments, watching over the scene like silent guardians.

As we stepped into the circle of the sacred flame, a powerful gust of wind blew out from the center of the room toward us. Bits of rock and sand rippled outward across the floor toward our feet. It served as a warning that our presence here was known.

The whole space carried an emotional weight with it, a feeling of reverence. Somewhere deep inside, I knew I didn't deserve to be here. I wasn't meant to see this place. I was trespassing, and I felt very afraid. Dad, on the other hand, seemed to be unaffected by the scene. Whatever knowledge he had about the Author and his ways had not been allowed to leave his mind and reach his heart. He saw only the science of it—the miraculous was not an option.

The pungent, sulfuric smell of the Maze was suddenly laced with a sweeter smell, a familiar scent that I couldn't quite place. I didn't know why exactly but all at once my excitement faded away. Something was wrong.

"We shouldn't be here," I said, my voice rife with awestruck wonder.

"Don't be silly," Dad replied. "This is why we've come. It is time to seize the prize. The end is within our grasp."

"That's kind of what I'm afraid of," I confessed, backing away a couple of steps.

"Look, there it is! Just like I told you," Dad shouted, pointing toward the tip of the pyramid. Hovering and spinning just below the tip of the fire was a crimson red stone. I knew in a heartbeat it was the Bloodstone—the dreaded stone that had caused so much chaos was dangling and spinning in the fingertips of the flame. In a way the flame itself looked like a giant pen tip, writing its story into the very heart of the Bloodstone.

"Don't do it," I said nervously. I was growing more and more uncomfortable with the plan. Dad looked over at me and I could see it in his eyes. He was hungry for the power of the Bloodstone again. I too had once felt that hunger before I realized that it was the lust for the Bloodstone that had kept me in bondage to the Shadow…to Sceleris and his ways. Now, seeing that same greed mirrored in my father's expression brought a sudden clarity to this entire mission. We were not supposed to be here at all.

"Hunter, what are you talking about? If we don't recover the Bloodstone, Tonomis most certainly will and we will all be doomed. We have to take matters into our own hands. We have to get the stone before him."

All at once things became clear to me; I had brought my father on the wrong mission.

"No, Dad, we don't. We should be looking for Aviad, not the Bloodstone. I made this mistake before, trust me. We don't need the Bloodstone, or the Eye or anything like that. We just need to find Aviad."

"Bah! He can't help us," Dad dismissed my anxieties. "Tonomis is probably in the Maze right now making his way here. It's a wonder he didn't beat us to it. If it's a sign from the Author you want, that's it!"

"I don't know," I said, still unable to shake the uncertainty.

Dad had heard enough. His patience was wearing thin.

"Fine. If you won't go with me, then I'll go alone," he said. "Just stay here and keep an eye out for Tonomis, will ya?" With that, he headed toward the narrow bridge.

The width of the bridge couldn't have been more than four inches at its thickest point. Dad slid his right foot out onto it and gently pressed his weight down on it. He spread his arms out on both sides to balance himself as he raised his left foot and placed it on the narrow way. Once he was sure his body weight was centered over his left foot, he lifted his right foot and continued forward like a slow-moving gymnast. Twice he nearly lost his balance and quickly countered his fall with the circular movements of his arms. Despite the close call, he continued forward, undeterred by his brush with death.

After several painful moments of suspense, he set foot on the far side of the pit with a triumphant hop. He flashed a nervous smile my way and gave a thumbs-up before scaling the twelve steps that led to the top of the pyramid. Each of the steps (if you can call them that) were waist high and required Dad to hoist himself up the steps one at a time. When at last he reached the top, I held my breath as he stood before the spinning Bloodstone in the clutches of the flame.

He approached the stone as if it were merely a trinket to be had or something of interest he collected on his travels. It wasn't that he was oblivious to its power; he had created an entire world with it. No, he knew what it was capable of, but he had lost his fear of it. The object itself was of no consequence to him anymore…it was just a means to an end. For that matter, he seemed completely un-fazed by the power of the raging whirlwind of fire, which rose over his head and held the Bloodstone.

Despite the fact that Dad was standing only a foot away from the fiery blaze, he seemed to feel no heat. Clearly, this was no ordinary fire.

With eager hands he reached out and grasped the stone. I looked away as he touched it. Part of me expected something powerful to happen, a surge of light maybe or a smoldering heat that burned in my father's grasp…something dramatic. There was nothing.

Dad smiled. I sighed in relief.

He stepped down from the pyramid, and crossed the chasm with incredible speed and confidence. With the Bloodstone in hand he felt almost invincible.

"We've done it, Hunter!" Dad said excitedly, as he raised the stone between us. "The power to defeat Tonomis is back in my hands."

Before I could reply, a wiry, grey-haired man with a hooded cloak stepped out from the shadow of his hiding place behind one of the boulders. A black pipe hung from the corner of his mouth. "Then what are you waiting for?" the man asked. "I am here, and I have been waiting for this moment for a long…long time."

All at once it came to me. The scent I had smelled earlier was Tonomis' pipe. The smell of juniper hung sweetly in the air just as it had the day of our first meeting in his office long ago. Of course, back then I knew him simply as Simon. Now I knew he was so much more than that. He was a deceiver, a traitor to the Author himself and an ally of Sceleris, who was plotting to unravel the very fabric of Solandria.

"Tonomis!" my father growled. The old man blew a ring of smoke and lowered his hood to reveal the face I had known as Simon, only now it looked different. His eyes were dark and his smile was twisted.

"Yes, Caleb," Tonomis replied. "You have done well. I couldn't have found the Bloodstone without your help. You are to be commended for a job well done. You have made a most excellent student."

My father didn't look too convinced.

"You're losing your grip, old man," Dad replied. "I'm not your student anymore. I'm my own man."

"It doesn't work like that, I'm afraid. You see, as the guardian of the Eye, it is my job to protect its power and see that it does not fall into the wrong hands—hands that would keep the Author's future—my future—from coming true."

His statement shocked me. Did Tonomis actually think he was the Author?

"I've seen your idea of a future, and I'm not interested," Dad challenged, holding his palm out toward the man who seemed unfazed by the threat. "I've escaped from you before, and I can do it again."

"Yes, you did and you could, but you won't…not this time."

Dad looked dumbfounded by the man's boldness. Tonomis was calm and in perfect control. His hands were tucked behind his back and he rocked back and forth on his heels.

"We are not so different, you and I," Tonomis chuckled. "Deep inside, you believe what I believe."

"No, I don't," Dad said, locking eyes with the man.

"Ahhh, but you do. Like me, you doubt the Author's purpose. You believe you can do better and you are willing to do anything… and I do mean anything…to get what you want…even at the cost of your family."

Dad shook his head, "That's where you're wrong. I would never do anything to hurt them."

"You already have, and you will do it again."

Dad couldn't find the words to disprove what Tonomis had just claimed. He looked at me, and then back to his accuser.

"Perhaps a demonstration is in order," Tonomis said. With a snap of his fingers, Desi stepped out from behind one of the other stones that surrounded the pyramid, followed by two guards on opposite sides of the pit. They were the same guards that had monitored the entrance to Simon's secret lair: a man and a woman, the Black-Eyes. This time the effects of the Quell had been removed; I recognized them as the medics who had captured me after the school fire. Tonomis must have been the one who sent them to find me. He had been searching for me. Once he knew I was Dad's son, he probably planted the Quell to make me forget what he had done.

But it wasn't Desi or the black-eyed thugs that I was most interested in. It was the pair of prisoners that were being held in front of them. The prisoners' heads were hidden under black bags, and their hands were bound, but even before the bags were removed I knew who they were....

"Watch it, buddy!" the girl beneath one of the bags said, as the guard pushed her forward. "I don't know who you think you are, but if I'm so much as five minutes late for my track meet you'll be sorry you ever laid hands on me. I've never been late for anything in my life and...I'm not about to...oomph...ouch...hey!"

"Easy there, princess," the male guard said, handling her a bit more roughly in response to her struggle.

The guards removed the prisoners' masks, revealing the perplexed faces of my mom and sister, Emily. The adjustment from complete darkness to light was blinding; their faces were all scrunched up to protect their eyes from the brilliant light of the fire.

"Janet? Em? What are you doing here?" My father's voice cracked when he saw them. Mom couldn't bring herself to say anything in reply. She just stared at my father...or rather, glared at him. I could tell she was upset. In her mind she had already painted him as the villain. He was to blame for all of this. Dad knew the look all too well; he looked away.

"Daddy!" Emily's face brightened. "Daddy, I can't believe it's really you! Tell these...these...brutes to get their meat hooks off of me."

"Hang on, sweetie," Dad said to her. "I'm not going to let anything happen to you."

"You already have," Mom muttered under her breath. I could tell by the pained expression on my father's face that he had heard her too.

"It wasn't supposed to be like this, Janet," Dad said. He searched her eyes for sympathy, but found none. "I was trying to make a better life for you...for our family."

"Yeah, well, I'm glad it's working out…for you."

Her last words embedded themselves in his heart like a dagger. For the first time Dad was seeing the pain his decisions caused. His family was in trouble, and it was his fault.

The guards covered both Emily's and Mom's mouths with their hands. Emily squirmed and tried to yell at the guard from under his smothering grasp but it just sounded like *mmph, mmph mmm mmph* to me.

"Let them go, Tonomis," Dad said. "They have nothing to do with this…. This is between you and me."

"Actually," Tonomis said coldly, "I can't do that. You made a deal with me, remember? We were going to change the world… together. You and I were going to rewrite the future, to create a better ending."

Dad's face paled. "That was before I realized who you really were and what you were capable of. You want to destroy Solandria and everything in it…. I've seen it."

"A necessary means to a greater end. Don't be so short-sighted, Caleb. You and I both know this story is not worth saving. We can do better. Together…we will make all things new."

"But my family…they'll die."

"A temporary problem," Tonomis said, "but we can rewrite them in our new world. You can do whatever you want. Without my immortality, you will never unlock the full potential of the Blood-stone. You will die like the rest, just another pawn in the almighty Author's game. Is that what you want?"

Dad didn't reply, just hung his head and sighed. Was he actually considering Tonomis' words?

"You can't do this on your own, Caleb. You need me to control the Bloodstone, just like I need you to hold it. We were meant to do this…together, as one life force. This is the way it must be."

"Let them go, Tonomis!" Dad demanded a second time.

"Let them go, Tonomis!" Dad demanded a second time.

"Oh, I intend to," Tonomis replied, "but only after you hold up your end of the bargain. Allow me to unite with you in the Bloodstone, and there will be nothing that can stop us. Together we will write a new beginning…a new story."

"And if I don't?"

Tonomis nodded to the Black-Eyes and they forced Mom and Emily to the very edge of the bottomless pit. Emily's eyes widened with fear as loose gravel cascaded over the side. We never heard it hit the bottom. Emily screamed beneath the smothering hand of her captor.

"I believe this is what you call a checkmate, Mr. Brown. So, what will it be? Allow me to make you the Author you were born to be and save your family from the end of this world, or selfishly try to horde the power for yourself and they die?"

Dad pondered his options in silence. I could only imagine what he might be thinking at the moment. In a way, it was not unlike my own fight with the Bloodstone. Venator had offered me the world on a platter.

"The Bloodstone will never bring you what you want, Dad," I said before he could speak his mind. "It's nothing but trouble, trust me. Put it down; you don't want it…you don't need it. You just need to trust the Author."

"I'm sorry, Hunter. But I…can't," Dad said. "Tonomis is right; the only way to save my family is to work with him. I have to write my own ending to the story."

Before I could object, he walked toward Tonomis and held the Bloodstone out between them. Tonomis greedily reached out but Dad pulled it away before he could grasp it.

"Let them go first," Dad said. "I don't want them to see what happens."

Tonomis motioned for the guards to release the prisoners. They obeyed, stepping away from the pit and letting Mom and Emily go free.

"Get them out of here, Hunter," Dad said. "Go, and don't look back, no matter what happens."

"But Dad…what about you?"

"Forget about me. Sometimes sacrifices must be made…for the greater good."

"Dad, I…."

"I said, go!" Dad shouted angrily. "I'm still your father! Take your mother and Emily and get them out of here, now! That's an order!"

The look he gave me sent shivers down my spine. He looked more like the monster I had seen in Belac than the friend I had come to trust in the tunnels of the Maze.

"Yes, sir," I said, but I wasn't doing it because he told me. I was doing it because I realized he was not the father I had once thought him to be. A real father wouldn't abandon his family like this…no matter what the cost. I locked my jaw and started to turn away.

"Don't take it so hard, son," Tonomis chuckled. "Your father is doing the right thing. He's a very brave man."

"That's funny," I said. "All I see is a coward who won't stand up for what he knows is right."

"Hunter, I…I don't have a choice…."

"Yes, you do, Dad. We always have a choice. We may not be able to change the future, but we can choose who we spend it with, and who we trust with it. You made your choice…you only trust yourself. You're no better than he is…. You and Tonomis are the same."

Dad had nothing left to say, and neither did I. I turned my back on him and led Mom and Emily out of the circle and back into the Maze. After all of this adventure, I couldn't believe it was ending like this. I was still the boy without a father; we were still a broken family. I had failed. What's worse, Trista was still gone and I had nothing to show for it but a futile quest. At the moment my life felt like…a dead-end.

"Hunter, where are we going?" Emily asked, as we zigzagged through the Maze.

"Home, Em. I'm going to find our way back home."

"But I don't understand. Where are we? What's going to happen to Dad? We can't just leave him behind."

"Why not?" Mom said bitterly. "He's never done anything for us. He made his choice…he doesn't need us."

Just then, a heart-wrenching scream echoed through the halls of the Maze. It was the voice of my father. He was in pain…horrible pain.

"Was that…Dad?" Emily whispered.

None of us answered; we all knew it was. We froze in our tracks. It was one thing to lose your father or to have him leave you, but it was an entirely different thing to hear him suffering and not do anything about it. Before I could stop her, Emily turned and ran back to see what had happened to her daddy.

"Emily, no!" I shouted, chasing after her. She was too quick; she was a track star and I was…well, not. By the time I caught up to her, she was standing at the entrance, peeking back into the center of the Maze. What we saw froze us in our tracks. Tonomis was nowhere to be seen; in his place stood a being that was unlike any I had ever encountered. The inky black thing had the shape of a man, and a pair of devilish, red eyes glowing in the place where its face might have been. The inkform and my father both had a hand on the Bloodstone, but neither seemed able to release it. The Bloodstone was in control now, searing itself into my father's hand and connecting him to the black thing before him. Then, the voices began.

"We are of one mind, one will, one being," the thing and my father said in unison. "Immortal and man, in one combined...." The black being had no mouth, but its eyes flashed hotter with each word. At first, its voice sounded like Tonomis, but soon was joined by a third voice...a hissing voice I recognized immediately. Sceleris.

"All the powerssss of the Author will be ourssss. It issss our desssstiny."

Like a vacuum, the Bloodstone consumed the black being as if it were nothing more than smoke. The blackness swirled like a storm inside the stone.

"Now, complete the sssacrifice and become one with ussss."

Entranced by the voice, my father raised the now blackened Bloodstone in front of him and with closed eyes plunged it deep into his own chest where his heart should have been. The implanting of the Bloodstone was painful and frightening to see. Dad screamed at the top of his lungs and nearly collapsed from shock. He pulled his hand out and looked down at the black hole that remained in his chest. The hole healed quickly...sealing the stone within him. The stone was now his heart.

Emily gasped and looked away. A black oozing substance began to bubble out from his chest wound. It spread across his body like some sort of strange skin disease. The blackness covered everything. Starting with his chest and torso, it traveled like wildfire across his arms and legs until all that remained was my father's face. In the end, that too was consumed by the entity that now owned his body—the black inkform of Tonomis.

The hissing voice of Sceleris echoed through the cavern. "Risssse, my ssservant. Risssse and be one."

My father stood, and the glowing red eyes that once belonged to Tonomis flashed open over what was likely his face. The eyes burned with a fire that could only be fueled by the power of the

Bloodstone itself. The voice of Sceleris commanded his next move.

"It is time," the inkform said to Desi and the black-eyed goons that remained. "Today we destroy; tomorrow we restore."

"Sir," said the Black-Eye woman, her voice as lifeless as the way she moved, "the enemy has already been alerted. The entire Resistance force is headed toward the Black Curtain."

"Good," the inkform chuckled, "let them come. Shadow warriorssss are ready to fight acrossss every shard in Ssssolandria. When the Codebearerssss arrive we'll have plenty to keep them dissssstracted. We will give them the epic battle they have been waiting for."

"They outnumber our forces two to one," the male Black-Eye said dryly.

"It does not matter. The battle issss only a diversion anyway. While they are busy fighting a pointlessss battle, I will bring the realm to its kneessss by erassssing each shard into oblivion one by one, until there issss nothing left to fight for."

"What about the boy?" Desi asked, pulling her whip rods from her belt and fingering them. "I was hoping I might get to…enjoy his company for awhile."

"Do what you want. Just make sure none of them leave the Maze. I want to ssssave them for last."

Desi smiled deviously, and with a quick flick of the wrist she ignited both of her whips. "I won't disappoint you."

Having seen enough, the inkform roared and grew into a massive form several times its original size. It sprouted black dragon wings and launched itself into the air over the labyrinth. The dragon circled the pillar of fire several times before sending a stream of red light out of its eyes and into the center of the flame. The flame reacted by turning red and shifting erratically above the center of the ring.

"Free ussss," the black dragon commanded the flame. Submitting to the dragon's word, the red fire split in two and created a portal to the world beyond the Maze of Rings.

The inkform dragon flew through the rift, and the red flame thinned until it was no more. I had seen enough. We needed to move quickly to warn the Codebearers of Tonomis' true plan and his alliance with the Shadow. Emily tiptoed with me on our way back into the Maze where Mom was waiting. Unfortunately, before we were free and clear, one of the moths that had been wandering the Maze fluttered straight into Emily's eye, catching her by surprise.

"Ew, gross!" Emily screamed. She swung her hands at the hapless creature and batted the insect away, causing more than enough commotion to draw attention. Desi was the first to notice us and locked eyes with me from across the inner circle.

"Fetch him for me," Desi said to the Black-Eyes, pointing our way and smiling maliciously. The two Black-Eyes turned their heads mechanically to see what she was pointing at.

"Run!" I shouted, pulling Emily away by the arm.

The Black-Eyes removed a handful of fire darts from their pocket and flung them at us as we ran. The darts flew with incredible speed across the expanse of the inner circle and embedded themselves in the floor beneath our heels.

"Wait for me!" Mom replied, ducking behind the wall and throwing her high-heeled shoes behind her.

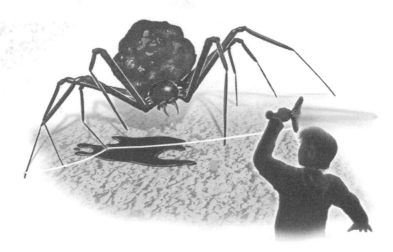

CHAPTER 29

THE SCENT OF A SPIDER

Actually, being chased through a maze is really quite exhilarating, so long as the things you're running from aren't trying to kill you.

With the dart-tossing Black-Eyes hot on our trail, I did my best to guide Mom and Emily on a winding chase through the Maze of Rings. Mom did her best to keep up, but she was constantly falling behind. It wasn't entirely her fault though. After all, she wasn't exactly dressed for the occasion. She was wearing a business skirt and blouse, and had been running barefoot the whole time.

"Slow…*huff huff*…down…*huff huff*," Mom gasped. We doubled back through what must have been the twelfth passageway. The Black-Eyes moved quickly.

"Quick, let's hide in there," I said, dousing my Veritas Sword and ducking into a small cave-like room that was connected to the passageway. We sat in absolute darkness for what seemed like an eternity until a pair of hurried footsteps passed us.

We sat still for a few minutes longer, waiting out the second Black-Eye pursuer. In the meantime, I did my best to catch Emily and Mom up on where we were and what had happened. I explained about Solandria, the Shadow and the Resistance known as the Codebearers. I told them how Dad used to be a Codebearer and that he had found the Eye of Ends…how the visions he saw within it were predictions of the future and ultimately were the reason he left us for fear they would come true. I told them of Tonomis and his desire to become the Author.

"I can't believe," Mom said quietly, "that all this time your father's stories were so real…and I didn't believe him."

"What do you think happened to Dad?" Emily asked. "Is he… you know…."

"Dead?" I asked.

"Yeah, that." I couldn't see her face, but I could hear a slight sniffle coming from where she sat. I had rarely heard Emily cry over something genuinely important. She usually cried only when she wanted something.

"I don't know. Maybe a part of him is still in there. If we ever get out of this place alive, I hope to find out."

Mom sighed. "Hunter, you know more about the Author than we do. Do you think he can help us, even here?"

I couldn't believe my mom had asked the question.

"Yeah, I'm sure he can," I said. "You know, the Codebearers have a saying about that…."

"What is it?" Emily asked, sounding genuinely interested.

"*We are never alone,*" I said. "The Author is always watching over us."

There was a long silence in the dark.

"Well, I sure hope he knows what he's doing," Mom said.

Watching the Author's plan unfolding, I was beginning to wonder just how things might end. I knew the Author was in control, but if Solandria was destroyed...what would happen next?

"He brought us back together, didn't he? I don't think that was an accident." The more I thought about it, the more I realized that there had to be a purpose in all of this.

"Well, enough sitting around in the dark. Let's go find a way out of here," Mom said.

After lighting my Veritas Sword, I kind of wished I hadn't. The room we were in was crawling with Crag Spiders—so many in fact, that Emily couldn't find her voice to scream! She was petrified, as was Mom. Thankfully, the spider horde was both deaf and blind. Each one of them remained still, focused blindly on the task of managing their complex network of threads.

Remembering what Dad had told me about the smaller ones being more dangerous as pack hunters, I tried to settle both Mom and Emily down before we triggered a feeding frenzy.

"Don't freak out," I cautioned. "They won't know we're here as long as we keep clear of the lines."

Mom seemed to appreciate the assurance and gave a frightened nod.

"On three," I said, "I want us all to move slowly and carefully toward the cave entrance."

"One...two..." but before I could say "three" Emily made a wild dash for the mouth of the cave and out into the passageway screaming. She narrowly missed triggering one of the lines that passed by the door. That was the good news.

The bad news was that our pursuers most certainly would have heard Emily's screams. Sure enough, as soon as Mom and I exited the spider's den, I heard a telltale shout come from somewhere further in the Maze. They were coming for us. We didn't have much time. I had to think of a plan…and quick!

Fearfully, Mom ran toward where Emily had stopped, shuddering just at the edge of my sword's light. I could hear the pounding footfall of our three pursuers growing louder. They would be on us before we could make any effective escape. Suddenly, I had a brilliant idea!

"Wait here," I told Mom and Emily. To their horror, I then ducked back into the Crag Spider's den. They both nearly freaked when I came back out moments later, dragging the dead body of a spider, a thin trail of its purplish oil leaking out behind it.

"What are you doing?" Mom gasped.

"No time to explain," I said hurriedly. "Grab a leg, Em!"

My sister looked at me with a "you've got to be kidding me" expression. Mom pushed her aside and took hold of a shiny leg, pulling along with me.

"Where to?" she asked.

I looked back at the den door and focused on the direction I'd seen the majority of the spider's threads leading. "This way!"

We ran to the right, heading for the turn just up ahead. As soon as we reached it, I dropped the creature and told the girls to stand back. Using my Veritas Sword, I sliced open the area where I figured the spider's oil gland was, letting the smelly liquid spill out freely, covering the floor.

As I did, I caught sight of a flashlight beam dancing across the other end of the passage.

"Go!" I told Emily and Mom, sending them on up ahead. If my plan was going to work, I'd have to let the Black-Eyes see me. A distant figure suddenly came racing into view, swinging the wide beam of the flashlight across my face. Immediately a fire dart flew at me, missing me by a few feet. They'd seen us, all right…perfect.

Climbing up and over the dead spider, I ran on as fast as I could to catch up to my family.

"Keep going!" I shouted. "Faster!"

Behind me, the Black-Eyes were shouting too, having fallen prey to my slippery trap. *That should slow them down.* I grinned, imagining the smell that would be covering their pretty little suits.

We raced through a few more turns in the Maze before Mom and Emily came to a screeching halt. They had recognized the nearly invisible threads weaving across the floor from our visit to the Crag Spiders' den. From the sound of the shouting coming up behind us, the Black-Eyes were catching up. There was no going back...or forward.

"We're trapped!" Emily shrieked, squeezing Mom's arm tightly.

I looked down at the trip lines, and thought of the hungry horde waiting on the other end. It was time to finish my plan.

I sure hope Dad's theory was right. Lowering my Veritas Sword to the ground, I aimed it at the first thread.

"Follow me," I said boldly.

"Hunter, no!" Mom shouted.

It was too late; I'd already cut through the first one and wouldn't stop until I'd sliced a clear path for us through the rest. If we could get through this without the deadly scent marking us, we'd be home free. I hadn't counted on being outwitted.

"Stop right there!" the female Black-Eye demanded, having suddenly appeared to block the path in front of us. She brandished a fistful of fire darts and shined her blinding flashlight directly in our faces.

Part of me wanted to take this threat head-on. I was a trained Codebearer, after all. But a voice from behind convinced me otherwise.

"Put it down, Mr. Brown," the man's voice said. I glanced behind me to see the second Black-Eye advancing toward us from the other side, darts at the ready.

"That's right...nice and slow," he coaxed, watching as I squatted to lay my weapon down. As soon as I let go, the blade of light disappeared, leaving mostly darkness, except for the light from the two flashlights.

"Kick it to me," the woman commanded, glowering. I caught a strong whiff of the spider oil soaked into her clothes. Smelling it made me want to gag because the scent was horrid, yes, but also because I feared what was coming. I'd set a deadly game in motion and now we had no way out of it.

"I said, kick it to me!" the woman yelled angrily. When I kicked it, the metal on the sword hilt scraped noisily across the ground. The unpleasant sound seemed to echo off the stone walls, bouncing up and down the corridor, but strangely never fading. Instead, it crescendoed into a loud chorus of hissing.

Emily looked up to where the noise was coming from and screamed. The Crag Spiders had come to dinner...every single one of them.

The Black-Eyes looked up at the army descending on us and immediately started firing their darts into the swarm, killing a good number of them...just not enough. For every one that fell, two more surged forward in their place.

"Stay close to me!" I shouted to Mom and Emily, hugging them tightly. Terrified, Mom and Emily buried their faces in my shoulder as the horde finally closed in around us. When I'd imagined this part of the plan working, I hadn't expected being there to watch.

Drenched in the spider's oil, the Black-Eyes didn't stand a chance of survival. It was only a matter of time before the Crag Spiders got their prizes, claiming the man first, then dragging the woman under. The two fallen flashlights were kicked around, providing an eerie effect to the whole grizzly scene.

Amazingly, Dad's theory about the Crag Spiders' hunting by scent held up. More importantly, the scent I'd been marked with from the larger, elder spider acted like a repellent to this smaller horde, keeping them a safe distance away.

"They're not going to harm us," I said to Mom and Emily, once I'd realized this truth. "We're free to go."

Still shaking, Emily started to pull away, but I held her tighter. "Don't let go yet," I said, walking us together as a unit toward my Veritas Sword. "We've got to stay close. It's my smell that is protecting us."

How many times does a little brother get to say that? I wondered.

"Ew! You can be so gross," Emily groaned, wiping away the tear streaks on her face.

Using the light from my Veritas Sword, we quickly navigated safely around the bend in the Maze, free from the threat.

"Where to now?" Mom asked the obvious question.

"We've got to find a way out," I said. "We're not safe in here."

"Now, *there's* an understatement," Emily groaned.

Admittedly, it was kind of a silly thing for me to have said. And knowing what I knew now about the Maze, it was a pointless thing to say. There was no escape from the Eye of Ends unless… unless we found a vision! I'd found one before; we'd find one again. I quickly explained the plan to Mom and Em as we jogged through the twists and turns of the Maze.

"Just keep your eyes open for anything unusual," I said, "especially any kind of light. The last vision I saw was hidden around the corner of a dead end. You might see these luminescent moths… those can be helpful too."

"What about birds?" Emily asked.

"Birds? What birds?"

I looked in the direction my sister was pointing and suddenly stopped in my tracks. The silhouette of a raven could be seen set against the fiery cavern ceiling, gliding above the towering Maze walls.

"*Caw! Caw!*"

The solitary raven turned toward us and was soon joined by more of them on all sides.

"Those are no birds!" I shouted. "It's Tonomis. We can't let him find us. Go back! Go back!"

We started to run the other direction, making it back around our previous curve before something like a lightning bolt flashed across our path. We skidded to a stop. The orange light cracked loudly; then sizzling, it fell limp to the ground. A lone figure stepped into view—Desi!

"What's this?" she taunted, twirling her weapons playfully in front of her. "Leaving so soon? But the night is young…and I've so enjoyed playing with you. How about we have a little fun first?"

She started marching straight at us, snapping one angry whip after the other, laughing at the fear she instilled. With nowhere else to turn, I prepared to do battle with the evil Vicess.

"Ahhh!" Mom called out fearfully. I felt a gust of wind as the passage behind me filled with a flurry of a hundred wings. I whirled around just as the angry flock took its imposing shape, a step behind me.

"Get down!" Vogler's voice bellowed. He didn't give me a choice, throwing me to the ground and firing his silver gun at Desi in a single motion.

Desi successfully deflected the round with her shield whip and scrambled down a side passage for cover.

"Looks like you could use a friend about now," Vogler said stoically. "Let's get you out of here!"

Mom and Emily looked wide-eyed at the intimidating black man they'd only seen as a detective on the news. Sensing this was no time for introductions, we hurried to follow our new-found bodyguard through the Maze. He kept a keen eye trained behind us, while directing us with mission-driven efficiency until we reached a dead end.

"This is it," Vogler said, nodding toward the wall.

"It's what?" Emily started to ask, but then became quiet when the milky light of the coming vision began to appear.

The transformation didn't intrigue me as much as the man standing next to me. A man, or being, I had completely misjudged. As intimidating as he was, I felt compelled to speak to him.

"So…you're a Watcher."

"Yes."

"But you're not Tonomis."

He pursed his lips and raised an eyebrow. "No."

"And all this time you've been trying to protect me from him and Desi?"

He didn't need to answer that. And he didn't.

The last question was the hardest to ask. "My friend Trista…."

"Is waiting for you," Vogler interrupted, pointing toward the vision that was coming into focus now.

Emily squealed with delight, recognizing her best friend, and started babbling to Mom about what it might mean that we were seeing Triss, flying on the back of a giant parakeet. It was a Thunderbird, but who cared? As quickly as the picture had come into focus, it blurred again, this time from my own tears.

He had saved her! I suddenly felt the overwhelming urge to hug the man, which I did.

Vogler took it like a man, a rather big man who didn't have much practice with hugs. He cleared his throat. "You've still got a mission to complete…Mr. Brown," Vogler reminded me in his cool manner.

Mom and Emily had already instinctively touched the vision, their bodies wavering between physical and light. The full vision now included an intense aerial battle between many Shadow and Codebearers, besides Trista. The sky was an ominous gray. It wasn't exactly an inviting picture. It was a darker part of the Author's plan, but one I knew I could face. I reached my hand out to touch it as well. As the vision exited me out of the Eye of Ends, I heard Vogler's parting words:

"Even the dark things will become like light if you learn to see with the Author's eyes."

CHAPTER 30

LIKE A MOTH TO THE FLAME

If there had been anything to hold onto, I would definitely have had a white-knuckled grip on it. My body felt small and stretched thin as I was carried, along with Mom and Emily, in the black current that had engulfed us. Helpless and blind, except for the occasional glimpse of some fractured image flickering between the beating wings, we rode the chariot of Vogler's winged forms through the Eye's vision at a terrifying speed, propelled onward toward our impending doom. There was nothing I could do now to stop it. Oddly enough, I didn't want to.

Vogler's words echoed loudly in my head, "*Even the dark things will become like light if you learn to see with the Author's eyes.*" Those words challenged me, daring me to hope beyond the fear-filled future. They dared me to stand and fight in spite of the odds. The longer I flew in the wake of this mysterious Watcher, the more I felt as if his strength and resolve were becoming my own.

Then we landed and the good feelings were gone.

A blast of wind and rain pelted my face as Vogler's wings dispersed to reform his body, leaving us struggling to maintain our footing aboard the violently pitching deck of a Resistance Sky Ship. The wide deck of the elite attack vessel was alive with crew members, rushing about to keep the ship airborne amidst the brewing storm. Some were firing weapons out into the angry gray sky. All around us, the howling winds were pierced with the screams of a raging battle being fought between Codebearers and Shadow. Turning, I found the distant axis of the swirling storm just as I'd expected: a wild, red column of fire shooting up from a distant shard. The vision was here. The future was now.

"We've got them on the run now…hold her steady and keep the pressure on. The battle is ours," a confident voice shouted from the helm of the ship. The commanding voice carrying easily over the chaos of the fight belonged to none other than young Philan. He was dressed in full Codebearer armor and looked every bit the part of the commanding captain he had become. I was amazed at how quickly this faithful young man had risen through the ranks. It seemed like only yesterday he was a nine-year-old boy, challenging me to a foot race at the training rounds. Now, here he was a man of twenty years (Solandrian time) and already the commander of the Codebearer's Resistance, a position he had been given by Aviad himself. He led with authority and power and his men respected him. He was not afraid.

"Philan!" I shouted, racing up the stairs in excitement to see my friend again.

"Hunter! Is that you?" he asked in shock. "I was told you were coming but…how in the world did you get on our ship?"

"I had help," I said, glancing back to introduce Vogler but he was already gone.

Philan's eyes were focused on my mother and sister who were being blasted by the rain. Handing the helm over to his second in command, he quickly brushed past me to greet them. "This is no condition for two lovely ladies to be left in."

After quick introductions Philan chided me for leaving my family in the elements. The look of delight in Emily's eyes betrayed an obvious attraction to the chivalrous young man, but before any further conversation could be exchanged, the Sky Ship shook abruptly to one side and began to drop. Philan steadied himself against a railing in time to catch Emily and keep her from falling over.

"She's losing air, Captain!" a deck hand shouted. "Raptling off the port side."

Philan looked up at the balloon overhead and spotted the trouble immediately. A small dragon-like creature with two legs and a forked tail had collided with the balloon, managing to tear a hole in the side with its razor-sharp teeth.

"Archers, get that thing before it sends us to the Void!" Philan shouted, pushing Emily back to her feet and pulling his Veritas Sword out in an attempt to regain order on his ship. Before any of the archers on deck could steady themselves enough to take aim, a mighty Thunderbird with a Codebearer riding it dropped from the sky and pried the Raptling off of the vessel with its talons, shaking it like a ragdoll. I immediately recognized Faith, the Thunderbird that had carried me across the Void in my first Solandrian adventure. With a vicious toss Faith flung the Raptling into the air and her rider fired a well-aimed arrow into the creature, dissolving it into a black mist before it knew what had hit it.

With the threat removed, two of Philan's men scaled the ropes and set to work, mending the tear in the balloon, while the other deckhands released the counterweights to return the Sky Ship to its rightful course. The repairs were made quickly and the ship was back in action. The Thunderbird rider who had saved the day circled back around and landed on the deck, dismounting and removing a hood to reveal the blonde locks of hair beneath it.

"Triss...is that really you?" Emily shouted excitedly, rushing over to greet her best friend and pummeling her with questions. "I can't believe you're here! How did you learn to fly like that? You never told me you could shoot an arrow. You wouldn't believe what we've been through...."

I was thrilled to see Trista again, but as usual my sister was hogging all her attention. The barrage of questions Emily was throwing at Trista would keep her busy for a very long time. I just smiled from a distance, grateful to know that Trista was safe. Then, while Emily was right in the middle of one of her questions, Trista broke away and strode across the deck to where I stood.

"Hey there," Trista said as she neared. "Did ya miss me?"

"You have no idea," I said. "I'm so glad you're safe!"

"Me too," Trista said with a smirk. Then without any warning, she leaned in and pulled me into a giant hug. I savored the moment, wrapping my arms around her in return and letting my cheek rest against the top of her head. When I looked up, Mom winked her approval from across the deck. I rolled my eyes and let her gloat in the fact that she had seen this coming. With all the chaos around us, it was good just to be still; I didn't want the moment to end but finally Trista pulled away again.

"So, I guess you saved your family after all," Trista said, looking back toward a confused Emily and my overly happy mother.

"All except Dad," I answered. I told her about my father's connection to Belac and how Tonomis had overtaken him in the Eye of Ends.

"Where is he now?" Trista asked.

My eyes searched the skyline but I saw no sign of the monstrous figure we'd seen obliterating the shards in the vision. It appeared the ultimate destruction had not begun…yet. An explosion of extreme emotion hit me—both of dread *and* hope—ratcheting my stomach into an impossibly tight knot.

"I'm not sure he even *is* anymore," I answered sadly. "Even if some part does remain, I don't see how we could ever save him. We might not even be able to save Solandria."

"What do you mean?"

Before I could explain, Philan stepped in.

"Sorry to interrupt, Hunter, but there's someone in the captain's quarters who wants to meet with you. I was told to take you to him as soon as you arrived."

From Philan's reverent demeanor, I knew immediately who "he" was. Trista gave me a knowing look and turned her attention to assisting Mom and Emily to safer quarters. Falling into step behind Philan, I willingly followed him to the Sky Ship's command quarters. The door opened, revealing a noble figure standing in front of the room's rear windows, overlooking the surrounding battle.

"Hello, Hunter," came the man's warm, familiar voice, though he had not yet turned to see me. Apparently, no announcements were required. Not that this was surprising, considering who I knew him to be.

Though I recognized him, he looked younger and stronger than when I had last seen him. No longer was his appearance that of a helpless prisoner or a feeble old man in a bookshop. No, Aviad now stood dressed in warrior's armor and ready to do battle. He was the very picture of a mighty leader. "Aviad," I said in reverence, bowing my head as he finally turned his face to me.

He smiled broadly through his neatly trimmed beard. His unmistakable blue eyes sparkled with ageless life; yet, there was something new in their regal depths—a deep sorrow.

As he held my gaze, a million unsaid thoughts and emotions passed effortlessly between us. If I had held out any hope that the end vision might somehow be averted, our silent exchange completely erased that.

"Yes, I could stop it," Aviad finally spoke in answer to my silent pleas. "You must understand, Hunter, that I wanted to spare your father from this end even more than you have. But I cannot. Even more, I desire the Author's way above all. What you have seen of the vision in your father's drawings cannot be changed, for this is what the Author has written. The Titan rises even now to destroy everything in its path." Aviad closed his eyes and in that silence I heard one shout, followed by another and another as the crew outside raised the alarm of a new threat growing up out of the Void. Neither Aviad nor I needed to look to know what was transpiring beyond the cabin walls.

I tried to swallow the lump in my throat, but it would not ease.

Stepping closer, Aviad put his arm around me and spoke with deep passion. "Do not let this knowledge steal away your courage, great warrior! For you know as I do, that the Author's ways are *always* good…no matter what comes."

I knew what he said was true. I had seen the Author's careful handiwork in my own life. It was the Author who rescued me from my enslavement to the Shadow. He provided Aviad, who gave his own life to rescue me from my desire for the Bloodstone.

The stakes were greater this time—the fate of the entire world rested on the outcome of this battle! Still, at the heart of it all *was* the Bloodstone and another man—my father. A thought suddenly came to me.

"The Author allowed you to save my life once," I said boldly. "Why not my father now? Is there anything I can do to help him see you, so you can give him a new heart like you did for me?"

Upon hearing my words, Aviad's eyes lit up. "Spoken like a true son. Come, I have something to show you."

Following Aviad's lead, I walked across the room to where a full-length mirror hung on the wall.

"Do you recognize this mark?" Aviad asked, pulling down his shirt collar just enough to reveal the glowing, golden mark of a three-tongued flame alive beneath his skin. I did recognize it—the mark of the Flame, the same one given to the Seven, including Trista, from the prophecy of the Consuming Fire.

"This mark," Aviad continued, "is the sign of the power of the Author's Code of Life living in its bearer. I have borne this mark from the very day the Author wrote me into his story. It reveals his power in me. You have seen the Seven marked with it when the prophecy of the Consuming Fire was fulfilled. But what you have not seen until today is this…."

Aviad reached over to my own shirt collar and pulled it down. I blinked. There, burning beneath my skin was the golden light of the Flame!

"You see, Hunter, when the Author rewrote you, he prepared you to receive his mark. The Author's Code of Life is at work within you and all true Codebearers—ready to work *through* you as it has through me. You are the Author's son—with all the rights and privileges that title entails."

I couldn't get over the thought of being the Author's son anymore than I could pull my eyes away from the mark alive within me. The longer I looked, the stronger its light seemed to become.

"And you will certainly need his power to do what I am sending you to do," Aviad added.

Those last words snapped me back to attention. "What do you mean, 'sending me'?"

Before he could answer, the door to the cabin flew open and a breathless Philan stood before us. "Something big is happening out there! We need your help!"

Without saying a word, Aviad calmly followed his concerned commander out onto the deck. The faces of the crew we passed were marked with panic. Knowing what they had seen, I didn't blame them.

We didn't have to look far. Though it was still a great distance off, the massive form of the Shadow Titan filled much of the sky-line. Its enormous body seemed to move in slow motion as it lumbered closer to one of the distant shards. A cry went out among the shipmates as it raised a fist to the sky and brought it crashing down on the shard with deadly force.

"Grab hold!" Commander Philan shouted, not a moment too soon. A shockwave of the shard's explosion rocked the Sky Ships across the battlefield, sending everyone, both Shadow and Resistance, into instant chaos. Even the sky seemed to panic, striking out with purple lightning bolts at random.

By now, Trista, Mom and Emily had returned to the deck to witness the cause of the commotion. Their faces were wet, and not just from the rain. They knew who was behind the Titan, and they knew what was coming.

"What is this that has come upon us?" Philan asked Aviad. "How can we do battle against something so great?"

Aviad turned away from his fearless commander and looked directly into my eyes.

"You have told me how much you want to save your father, but how far are you really willing to go?"

The intensity of his piercing stare communicated that my answer could not to be given lightly. What was the true measure of my devotion? I rubbed the place over my chest where the mark had been revealed to me and considered Aviad's words. *You are the*

Author's son, with all the rights and privileges. If that were true, as I believed, then....

"How far *can* I go?" I finally blurted out.

Aviad smiled. "How far did I go for you?"

Turning to Philan, Aviad gave the urgent command. "Hurry! Prepare a Thunderbird for flight. Hunter leaves immediately."

"But..." I began to protest, "I don't even know what I'm going to do!"

Aviad slapped my leg, and I felt an object in my front pocket. "You've been given exactly what is needed for such a time as this: our greatest weapon." I'd completely forgotten the little bottle Hope had given me.

"A seed?" I asked, amazed that it could ever be described as a weapon. I hadn't given the Author's seemingly insignificant gift a second thought until now. I suddenly felt more than embarrassed, remembering how Hope had expressed the need for me to be listening to the Author to know its purpose.

"It's not just any seed. What you have been given is *the* seed of Truth," Aviad explained. "Pure Truth has the power to preserve, to restore."

I was starting to get the picture.... Uh, no. Who was I kidding? This mission to pit a seed, with special powers or not, against a Titan seemed ridiculously out of scale.

Aviad hadn't given up on me yet. "I am sending you to deliver it into the heart of the storm—the heart of your father...if you are willing."

By now Philan had returned with the saddled Thunderbird, my friend Faith. Two other crewmen handed me a leather helmet and goggles, and assisted me in buckling on a harness. A growing crowd of Codebearers were leaning in now, looking anxiously to me, awaiting my decision. All around, the storm was whipping almost as fast and furious as the questions spinning through my head.

"Where is his heart now?" I asked before a sudden, terrifying inspiration came to me. "The Lifestream…" I whispered. "The Bloodstone's power is in the Eye's Lifestream. That's the heart of the storm, isn't it?"

Aviad nodded approvingly.

Philan, noting my nervous expression, tried to petition Aviad. "Permission to take his place, sir."

Aviad shook his head "no." "The Resistance needs you here, Commander. This seed has been given to Hunter…no on else can carry it."

Catching my anxious look, Aviad added, "But I never send you alone. Go, Hunter. I have already sent others before you."

Stepping into the cradled hands Philan offered, I mounted Faith and clipped my harness to her saddle.

"*Via, Veritas, Vita!*" Philan said, grasping my forearm in a warrior's grip.

The crew around us echoed his battle call as Aviad looked on. Urged on by their words, Faith took the initiative to hop up onto the Sky Ship's railing, waiting there for my command.

I looked back over my shoulder at Trista. She smiled supportively and hooked arms with my mom and Emily. They looked so worried and lost, not understanding the full depth of all that was unfolding around them. Even though I felt nervous, I still had the knowledge of the Code of Life to steady me—they were left on their own.

"It's going to be all right," I called back to them. "You can trust the Author." The words were meant as a reminder for me as much as an encouragement for them. After all, I was the one heading straight toward a raging column of supernatural fire—a certain suicide mission if ever there was one. Just how far would this mission to save my father take me? How far had Aviad gone to save me?

Gripping the saddle's handle, I nudged Faith with my knees and the giant bird launched out over the Void and into the deadly mix of war and storm. I sensed an extra burst of speed behind each flap of her wings as we darted between the Shadow and Codebearer attacks. It was almost as if she already understood the urgency of our mission.

Faith carried me quickly across the Void toward the insatiable fire that consumed what remained of the shards the Titan destroyed. It was in many ways like a black hole, erasing all things from existence and giving nothing in return. To enter the heart of it was certain doom, yet here we were flying straight at it like an ill-fated moth to the flame. I clutched tightly to the vial that held the strange seed, then tucked it into my pocket for safe-keeping. My only consolation was that it might provide some means of escape from the pillar of fire. The purpose of the seed still eluded me, but I knew it had to be planted in the heart of the storm. So, with my destination fixed and my heart in my throat, I guided Faith toward the brilliant flame.

The aerial battle that surrounded us was as thick as the fog in the Void. Over us, beneath us, beside us and before us, the battle raged on in an epic struggle between good and evil. The Codebearer forces continued to strike the Shadow forces down. The Resistance fleet was numerous and strong but the Shadow were putting up a good fight. For every Codebearer Sky Ship, for every Thunder bird that flew into battle, there were as many Gorewings, Treptors and dragons that took to the skies to engage them. Other creatures darkened the bloody sky as well, playing to neither side. There were untamed beasts and massive sky serpents that devoured Codebearer and Shadow forces alike, without discrimination.

As we made our way skillfully through the fray, I began to notice one friend after another, fighting within the Resistance ranks.

A squadron of reptilian bird-like creatures carried Noctu warriors, among whom I identified Xaul. Captain Samryee and his cousins, the Thordin brothers, Ven and Zven, were part of another Sky Ship's crew, catapulting netted missiles into the Shadow ranks, dropping many into the Void.

As I raced by them, one after the other, I took strength in knowing that they were fighting alongside me, even though they didn't know the mission I was on. I truly was *Never Alone*.

It was only after catching a glimpse of Stone-Eye Sterling's Sky Ship, *The Bridesmaid*, engaged in direct combat with one of these ghastly creatures that I considered breaking from my mission to help. Stoney and his crew were desperately fending off the long beast with flaming harpoons, but the creature threatened to coil around the ship's balloon and puncture it, if something wasn't done to destroy the sky serpent quickly. My fears were put to rest when a pair of Thunderbirds swooped in from above and distracted the creature long enough for Stoney and his crew to break free. I couldn't be entirely sure it was them, but I thought I'd just seen Rob and Kim Bungle, soaring into the midst of the chaos just in time.

How long the distraction would last was anyone's guess, but it was enough time for me to focus on the task ahead. I had to reach the Lifestream at the center of the storm. Unfortunately, this also meant that I'd have to make it past the monstrous beast undetected. The creature stood guard beside the flaming cyclone, smashing every shard that neared it into hundreds of pieces. So far, three shards had been destroyed…two more were being drawn in toward the blazing fire.

I decided my best bet was to keep low to the ground on one of the shards. I would have to keep out of sight until its attack on the shard was inevitable. At the last minute, while he was focused on the destruction of the shard, we'd fly out of hiding toward the

Lifestream. If the Author was with us, I'd pass by unnoticed, just another loose piece of the broken shard.

With my plan set, I lowered myself against Faith's back and let her dive in a dizzying spin toward the surface of a nearby shard. I didn't recognize the terrain; it was a land I had yet to explore, a beautiful and lush jungle world, rich with deep foliage and teeming with animal life. What a pity it would soon be erased.

Faith leveled out her descent and dodged through the tangled web of giant banyan trees in search of a place to perch and wait. I failed to notice that we were being followed by a stealthy black dragon and its bloodthirsty rider. Just as Faith approached a broad tree branch for her landing, the leathery wings of the dragon ripped through the air behind us and passed overhead. As it passed, the rider of the dragon jumped free and landed on Faith's back behind me—Desi.

"You again," I stared, caught offguard by her abrupt arrival.

"Going somewhere without me?" Desi asked, a challenge in her eyes. Before I knew what to expect, she landed a powerful blow to my chin and knocked me clear off of Faith. The only thing that kept me from falling was a simple leather strap, connecting me by harness to the Thunderbird's saddle. I dangled upside down, watching helplessly as Faith banked left and right through the twisted jungle. Things were not going as planned.

"Creeee!" Faith warned as she dropped further to her left from the shift in weight. Her wing tips brushed the tops of the trees and even Desi nearly lost her balance. She dropped to her stomach on Faith's back and hung on for dear life as the massive bird began to adjust its flight in response to my dead weight.

The dragon's talons lashed out at Faith from behind, determined to bring her down out of the sky. Faith slowed in response and did her best to avoid the dragon's attacks with well-timed shifts in direction. As the dragon turned around and came back for a second attack, Desi somehow managed to sit upright in the saddle again and began to work at loosening my only remaining lifeline... the leather strap that connected me to Faith.

"Faith, do something!" I shouted, feeling more than a little light-headed from the ride. As the last of the tether buckle slipped loose, Faith responded with a barrel roll and caught hold of my arms with her feet. Somehow, Desi managed to keep hold of the saddle too while Faith leveled out. For the moment, I was hanging below the Thunderbird and Desi rode above, as the black dragon returned for its second attack. Faith's taloned toes were busy holding tightly to me, leaving her no way to retaliate. With the odds stacked against us, Faith resorted to dropping below the tree line for cover, hoping to lose the dragon in the maze of trees. She moved quickly through the jungle, the trees a blur of motion beside me. Faith dodged left, then right with masterful navigation. The dragon was too big to follow us and had to settle for watching from above, waiting for another opportunity to strike.

Tree after tree whooshed by in a rush. Faith slowed to make a turn and dropped abruptly, nearly colliding with a low-hanging branch in the process. Something was wrong.

"*Cra...Cra...Cree...*" the bird gargled above me. I could tell by the sound in her voice that she was choking on something. A second later, I saw why.

"Put us down, you wretched thing!" Desi demanded. Somehow, during the commotion of the chase, Desi had managed to wrap her whip around Faith's neck and was choking the life from the bird.

"Desi, stop it!" I begged, knowing full well my plea fell on deaf ears.

"Not until this dumb bird lands," Desi said through gritted teeth, pulling tighter on the fiery whip, which burned into the Thunderbird's neck. Faith's grip on my arms weakened as our flight continued.

"Hang on, girl…just don't let go!" I shouted, staring down past my feet to the forest floor as Faith's grip on me weakened. Her movement was more erratic now and she seemed to be actually targeting the tree branches instead of trying to avoid them. The maneuver was meant to shake Desi off her back, but it wasn't working. Desi clung viciously to Faith, her blazing orange whip singeing the beautiful feathers and into the skin beneath them in an attempt to force Faith to the ground. Unable to steer herself, Faith smashed headlong into a tree, losing her grip on me as we spun out of control through the branches.

Tumbling down through the brush and limbs, I fell, until at last my bruised body landed with a dull *thud* on the muddy jungle floor. The force of the impact knocked the wind out of me and for a moment I lay paralyzed. When I could stand, I stumbled wildly about, searching for my crashed Thunderbird. If any hope remained of getting to the Lifestream before this shard reached the Titan, I would have to move quickly. I needed Faith to be safe and alive. There was no telling what Desi might do to her.

Fighting through the brush, I discovered a small clearing in the trees ahead. When I broke through, I found the magnificent creature I had come to love and cherish laying helpless and unmoving on the ground as Desi casually released the whip from her neck. Her wing was bent unnaturally below her body, broken from the fall. I rushed to Faith's side, ignoring Desi. I stroked the bristling feathers of Faith's neck softly as she labored to breathe, but I could tell these would likely be her final breaths. She flinched slightly, and shuddered in pain.

"Easy girl, we're safe now. You saved me. Everything is going to be okay.…"

The words were meant to be a comfort for the bird, but I knew she would not be long in this world. She knew it too. Faith's sparkling yellow eye stared back with the knowledge of her demise. She nuzzled me with her beak and blinked slowly, accepting what love I could offer through the warmth of my touch. With one final shudder, her body fell limp and her life slipped away.

"It's your fault, you know," I heard Desi taunt as I stood beside my fallen friend.

"You!" I growled, clinching my fists and glaring at her. "You did this! You...you murderer!"

Desi smirked at the accusation, a trickle of blood trailing from a cut on her lip. "Don't kid yourself. Killing her was your idea."

I glared back at her. What was she suggesting?

"You had already sentenced her to death, taking her on whatever suicide mission you were on," Desi said. "Or didn't you realize what you were doing?" She shot a glance up through the trees at the deadly flame of the Lifestream's funnel, looming ever closer as our shard was sucked in.

"So what? The dumb bird just got what you both had coming a little early," Desi continued. "Lucky for you, I stopped you before you ended up dead as well."

As she said this the dark form of her dragon passed by overhead, circling down to land behind her. It looked hungrily at Faith's limp form. I was thankful Desi grabbed her sharp-fanged creature's reins.

"Now, come with me before you do something else stupid," Desi commanded.

"I'm not giving up," I said firmly, taking a step back from her and drawing my Veritas Sword, "and I'm *never* going with you!"

A terrifying look of anger flashed across Desi's face. Before I could even think of how to counter her attack, her blazing whip flew out, wrapped itself around my arm, and yanked me face-first to the rocky ground. The violent fall caused my sword to fly away, clattering across the stoney soil.

"You *will* come with me!" Desi demanded, dropping her knee painfully into my back, pinning me in place. "I've got orders to take you and your family into the Void and I'm not going empty-handed. Tonomis and your father have big plans for your family in their new world—an Author-free world—just like your father always wanted."

My arm throbbed from the fiery whip's cut. I grimaced, fighting back the urge to scream.

"What my father wants…" I grunted between labored breaths, "…is not what he needs."

"Oh, and you have what he *needs*? Is that what this little mission was about?" Keeping her weight pressed on me, Desi did a quick pat-down, finding the vial in my pocket.

"Ooo, what's this?" She shook the bottle and laughed wickedly. "Some secret formula? Is this the best your futile Resistance could come up with? And you were willing to go along with it…. You know, you really are pathetic."

Shoving my face roughly into the ground, Desi stood up, examining the fragile container more closely. I twisted around and looked at her in time to see an evil grin curl across her lips.

"Since you seem to be having a hard time getting the picture…." She threw the vial to the ground and stomped on it. The glass shattered instantly; the tiny seed it had protected lost forever among the slivers. Twisting the toe of her boot into the glass, she ground it down further for added effect.

"It's *over*!" Desi said with finality. "You lost. Move on."

She grabbed my wounded arm roughly, dragging me to my feet. Despite the pain, I couldn't take my eyes from the shattered vial, the perfect symbol of the Resistance's fragile hope, now completely destroyed.

"The Author's days are over…our future is with the Titan now," Desi added, pointing up through the tree line to the furious red sky darkened by the massive shadow of the Titan. It raised one of the neighboring shards from the sky and brought down its mighty fist. The larger mass of land broke into smaller pieces, which the Titan crushed in its hands. The end was playing out exactly as had been foreseen. What would be the purpose in fighting it? The Titan was in control. Once he destroyed the last of Solandria, he would reign supreme.

That's when the thought struck me—the conclusion I'd dreaded was all of my own making, fashioned from my fears. The Eye had never shown anything beyond this moment. Though all seemed lost, it wasn't—not yet. I resolved, once and for all, not to let my fears rule over me. I was a Codebearer, saved by the Author and marked for his purposes, not the Titan's. I would never give up! A burning in my chest seemed to strengthen me from within.

"No!" I shouted, wrenching my arm free of Desi's grip. "My future begins and ends with the Author…. I'm not coming."

"Enough!" Desi roared in frustration and grabbed for her whip. "I'll take you back in pieces if I have to!"

I had no weapon beyond my words to even attempt to stop her this time. Instinct kicked in and I ducked, avoiding the burning cord as it lashed high at my shoulders. That didn't account for her other whip. The second, blue-flamed cord swung at my ankles, catching me off-balance and knocking me down. Twirling the orange whip over her head, Desi brought it down with deadly speed at my face.

It happened so fast, I'm not even sure how I did it, but somehow I managed to catch hold of the fiery whip. It neither burned, nor tore off my skin as I'd expected. My arm was glowing all the way from my hand back to the place on my chest where the mark had been given. I felt supernatural power flowing through me in that moment.

Gripping the whip tighter, I pulled it back with all my strength, wrestling it from her hands. I threw the cruel device away and locked eyes with Desi. Her eyes reflected an expression I'd never seen her wear before—fear.

Unsure of her next move, Desi backed off. As she did, the storm winds seemed to increase, pulling harder at the branches around us. The sound of a sharp crack from a weaker tree, snapping under the strain, broke our stare-down. Desi looked quickly skyward. Our shard was closer than ever to the Titan and the Lifestream was picking up speed dangerously fast, which apparently was enough to settle things in her mind.

"Stick around if you want," she said, retreating to her dragon, "but dying ain't my thing."

In one quick motion she swung herself up into the saddle and dug her heels into the dragon's scales, shouting her urgent command. The beast snorted then took to the angry skies. Despite its strength and Desi's screamed threats, the powerful creature was no match for the raging wind above. Its leathery wings flapped mightily, but it succumbed easily to the Lifestream's current, dragging both dragon and rider straight into the vortex ahead of them. What I hadn't acknowledged before was deathly clear now. There would be no escape.

Alone at last, I dropped to my knees and desperately fingered through the bits and pieces of what remained of the glass vial Desi had crushed into the ground.

"Please be here, please, please be here," I whispered to myself as I searched for the lost seed. I brushed my fingers gingerly across the trampled dirt, but no matter how hard I looked, the seed could not be found. I had failed. The precious seed Aviad had entrusted to me was gone.

Already the trees began to sway back and forth with the powerful windstream that was pulling everything closer to the pillar of fire. The Titan's monstrous silhouette was visible against the fiery red blaze, his flashing eyes set in the middle of his featureless face like a pair of crescent moons at midnight. The color of the flame bathed the landscape in a stark red light and harsh black shadows.

There was nothing left for me to do now but sit and wait for the inevitable end that would come to this shard and everything that lived on it. In one powerful blast, the Titan would certainly crush the land mass as he had the other shards, fracturing it into a thousand smaller pieces better suited in size for the column of fire to consume. The Lifestream that had once fed the Author's code into this world through the Living Tree now served a new master, erasing everything that existed in this world.

I bowed my head and closed my eyes in a silent prayer to the Author. As I prayed, I listened. I listened to the wind in the trees, the roar of the flame and the stirring of my own soul.

"Do you have nothing left for me here? Is this the way you meant things to end…at the hands of those who would rob your very signature from this great world? Please, pick up your pen and write again. Use me to bring your truth to the very heart of darkness. I am willing…I am yours."

It was subtle at first, so subtle in fact that I dismissed it as a mere trick of the wind. But soon a particular sound rose out of the noise and the chaos—the sound of a song. A soft and beautiful song rose from the very ground beneath me.

When I opened my eyes I noticed something that hadn't been there before. A tiny, green stem curled out of the ground where the seed had been crushed. It was glowing green, like a spark of strangely colored flame about to grow, the first signs of life the seed had ever shown.

It was strange to think of something new being born in a moment when everything around it was about to be destroyed. But as the seedling began to grow, so too did the song. It became louder and more refined, encircling me with its entrancing melody. The music erased any doubts or fears that remained in my mind. There was no room for anything like that now…only the song mattered. I felt new again.

The trees surrounding me began to sprout with new life. Flowers budded and blossomed on their branches in a matter of moments, as if a second spring had fallen on the land and everything in it. Then the best thing of all happened—Faith began to move. The song that brought life to the world around us was restoring Faith to life as well. Her eyes flickered open and my heart nearly burst with the joy of seeing her alive.

"Faith! You're alive!" I shouted excitedly.

"*Creeee,*" the Thunderbird replied.

In a moment she was standing again, her broken wing completely healed by the presence of the song and the simple seedling growing from the ground. Clearly, it was no ordinary seedling…. There was something magical about it, something so incredibly precious that I regretted how casually I had treated it before.

"*Creee, creee!*" Faith said in warning. The Titan was on the move, nearing the shard and threatening to bring an end to our joyful reunion. With courage and purpose reborn in me, I set my mind and my heart on the task I was called to do.

"I know, I know, hang on…. There's something we have to do." I dug the seedling up from the rocky soil and cradled it in my palm as if my very life depended on its survival. In some ways, perhaps it did…maybe all of our lives did. I mounted Faith, who was eager to be airborne again.

"Okay, girl," I shouted. "Let's fly!"

With a powerful leap Faith took to the skies, but unlike Desi and her dragon we didn't fight the winds that pulled us toward the all-consuming flame…we rode them. We flew toward the fire with purpose and determination. We had to get the seedling to the center of the flame…it was our only hope. There was no turning back.

The Titan brought his mighty fist down on the shard below us, breaking it in two. The shockwave from the impact pushed us forward like a mighty wave on the sea might push a surfer. The wave pushed us past the Titan and for the briefest of moments he caught a glimpse of me. Perhaps it was the song still resonating from the seedling that caught his attention. Whatever it was, he wasn't pleased and he covered his ears in pain.

"You!" the Titan groaned. "What are you doing here? I am master of this world…. Take that thing away. Stop…now!"

But I couldn't stop, and I didn't look back. My eyes were fixed on the flame before me, which now seemed more like a giant wall of fire because it was so close. Never before had we flown so quickly. The winds were with us and nothing could stop us now. Without the slightest fear, we passed into the column of fire and were swallowed in its light, like a moth to the flame.

In my mind I had imagined the Lifestream to be a raging inferno of consuming fire all the way to its core. Surprisingly, it wasn't… at least that wasn't what I was seeing. The fire was actually a cylindrical wall meant to protect what lay inside, a single shard of land, floating under a radiant beam of white light that seemed to reach to infinity. There were no other shard fragments in sight; no Desi or dragon either. We were alone.

With nowhere else to go, Faith instinctively carried me up toward the well-lit shard of soft meadowland. There were no trees or landmarks on its surface whatsoever. Upon landing, Faith tucked her wings and I dismounted to explore the small island. It appeared to be about three-football-fields-wide. I carried the seedling across the meadow to the place where the shaft of light was most concentrated and the seed's song seemed to be the loudest. We were near the center of the shard.

A stone marker lay in the soft soil, engraved with the Author's mark. I had the feeling this was the place I was supposed to plant the seedling. Bending down, I carved a small trench out of the golden soil with my hands and placed the seedling in its new home. Almost instantly, it began to grow. In a matter of seconds it grew from a few inches to several feet and showed no signs of stopping.

I backed away from the sapling and watched as the wall of the Lifestream began closing in and feeding into the ground of the shard, causing the seed to grow even more rapidly. Fed by the fire of the Lifestream itself, the tree became as tall as any skyscraper I had ever seen, and its branches spread out as wide as the shard itself. I suddenly recognized what was happening—this was a brand new Living Tree.

As the whole force of the wall of fire was poured into the tree, the fire thinned and finally disappeared. The world of Solandria was no longer hidden behind the firewall. Then the tree's roots began to stretch out. They broke out of the sides of the shard and reached across the sky toward the neighboring shards of Solandria that the Titan had not yet destroyed. The roots connected several shards together and new shards started to form on the roots where there was ample room to grow. The Author had done it; Solandria was being restored.

I wasn't the only one watching the tree take root. The sight of the tree angered the Titan, who suddenly realized he was losing control of the world. He was standing in a spot that offered a clear view of the once-hidden shard and the massive tree that was now growing on it. With a sinister glare, the Titan headed toward where I stood on the shard. Before he could make his way over to destroy the tree, another root shot out from the underside of the shard and wrapped itself around the Titan's waist. Undeterred, he raised a fist in angry protest and prepared to smash the small shard to pieces. Before his havoc could be unleashed on the tree, two more roots shot out from the shard and bound his wrists, pulling both of them behind his back. The tree roots strengthened their grip and began to choke the life from the Titan's body.

As I watched, the Titan's frustration grew as his vision of the future unraveled before his eyes, and it struck me. Somewhere inside of that giant mass of a beast, my father might still be alive. Maybe I could communicate with him and save him yet. After all, Aviad had asked me how far I'd be willing to go to save my father. Perhaps he meant for my father to be saved from the Shadow's clutches even now.

It was only a hunch, a hairbrained idea but it was worth a shot. Racing back to Faith, I mounted the bird and took to the skies once more. This time, I was heading straight for the Titan, hoping beyond reason that my father might be able to hear my plea and do something.

When we were within ear-shot, I shouted for my father's attention while Faith circled in place.

"Dad, are you still there? Can you hear me?"

The Titan just growled his ugly, bestial roar in response. He was so busy struggling against the tree roots he hardly had time to notice a boy on a Thunderbird. To him we were little more than a stray gnat in the air, if he even saw us at all.

Just then one of the roots from the tree shot straight through the Titan's chest, ending his struggle and pulling him down into the Void. But just before he fell, his arm swung across the sky and the gust of wind from it knocked me clear off the Thunderbird's back. Before I knew what was happening, I was falling, tumbling down into the blackness of the Void. I thought perhaps Faith would catch me, but she didn't even notice I had gone. I was falling fast. The last thing I remember before blacking out was the sudden realization that I might never see daylight again.

CHAPTER 31

THE VOID

The first thing I sensed when I awoke was the fog. It was a black fog…full of evil and a life force of its own. I knew it was there even though I could not see it—I felt it all around me.

Instinctively, I reached for my sword, but it wasn't there. Neither was my backpack. Without them, I felt almost naked.

My memory was intact, all the way up to the point where I fell from the sky. The visions had all come true, but despite the horrors of what my father had seen in the Eye of Ends, the Author was victorious. Solandria had been saved. The Titan had been defeated and with him Sceleris' plans to bring an end to the Author's story had been foiled.

But if that were true, then what had happened to me?

As my eyes adjusted to the darkness, I realized there was a light in the distance, a soft reddish glow pulsing in the dark. I stood with arms outstretched and felt my way through the mist toward the pulsing light. To my shock, the light was coming from the chest of my father's limp body. He was lying on his back, looking up at the emptiness through the mist swirling in the red light. The source of the crimson light was the Bloodstone, which was pulsing like a heartbeat in his chest.

Moving closer, I saw that Dad's legs were twisted in unnatural ways. An open wound bled profusely, adding to the pool of black, inky blood beneath him. He was a broken man, barely holding on to life.

Sensing my presence, Dad struggled to focus his eyes on me. With a deep raspy breath, he gasped, "Hunter, why did you follow me? After all I did…all the mistakes…."

"Because I couldn't let you die alone," I told him.

Though he could hardly bear the pain, he raised his hand to take mine in his own. His breathing quickened and the Bloodstone flickered erratically. I stroked his hand and tried to calm him as he lay there. He was dying. I knew it would not be long.

When his breathing eased, he spoke again. "What about Solandria? Did he…is it…?"

"It's safe, Dad. A new tree is growing in Solandria, and it's uniting the shards. Solandria is going to be whole again, a new world."

Dad's expression darkened at the sudden realization that the Author had come through after all, and he had been on the wrong side of the battle.

"I'm sorry, Hunter. Everything I thought I knew…everything I did…was wrong. The visions I saw, they weren't the Author's fault… they were mine. I became the very thing I was trying to stop…a murderer. I would have made a pretty awful author."

"Yeah, you would. But it's not over yet; maybe the Author can still…help."

Dad smiled at the thought. "No, my story is over. People like me don't get a second chance. I'm not the hero, Hunter. I'm a lost life that will hopefully serve as a reminder to the hero of what not to become."

"I'm no hero either, Dad," I said.

"You are to me," Dad replied with tears in his eyes.

My chest swelled with the knowledge that despite our differences, my father was proud of me. Even though it felt good to hear the words, I knew they weren't true. I knew myself all too well.

"But a real hero has things all figured out. He has a plan; he's strong. I…I still doubt the Author at times. No matter how many times he's saved me, I still have a hard time seeing his purpose."

"Son, if there is one thing I've learned from all of this, it's that we're not supposed to have things all figured out. Life isn't about what we control…it's about having faith."

He gasped for another breath before continuing.

"I lived my life in fear of something I had no control over, and I let that fear steal my life from me. I destroyed the very thing I loved, and became the enemy I thought I could defeat. If I could have it to do over again, I'd choose to put my hope in the Author… not myself."

He looked deep into my eyes and squeezed my hand tightly

"You don't have to have it all figured out. You have hope…and that's the sign of a true hero. You have something worth fighting for. Knowing the future, having it all worked out, will only steal that from you."

Dad's words rang true in my heart. This was a real father and son moment, the kind I had longed for while he was gone.

A sinister chuckle echoed in the black fog, coming from everywhere and nowhere all at the same time. The voice of someone I had come to know all too well was taunting us—Sceleris, the serpent.

"Bravo, bravo! How touching. Father and sssson, reunited again for the lasssst time. A fitting end to your pathetic existencccce."

The fog pulled back from where my father lay, retreating through a tunnel behind me like a vacuum. With the fog gone, we discovered we were in some kind of underground cavern, trapped on a small island of stone and surrounded on all sides by a lake of iridescent green water. How we had come to be here was beyond me.

The pool of black blood beneath my father streamed away from his body and wound across the stone floor to the base of a throne. As I watched, it began to rise into the shape of the serpent. The black snake coiled himself around the throne and stared back at me. If ever a snake could smile, Sceleris was.

"What do you want, Sceleris?" I challenged, standing to my feet.

"It's not what I want—it's what I *have* that amuses me."

"Oh yeah, what is that?"

"I have YOU!"

His red eyes flashed brighter as he said it, and he laughed again at the look of confusion that crossed my face.

"Sorry to burst your bubble, but I belong to the Author. I'm here to get my father and bring him home."

"Oh, foolissssh boy," Sceleris chuckled to himself, "there issss no going home. Not from thissss placccce."

A dreadful moan rose from the green waters, sounding like a chorus of voices…ghostly voices.

"You are beyond the door of death, a placccce of no return. Only the dead can enter here, and here you are. My prize."

Sceleris' voice always gave me the shivers, but this time it froze me stiff. What he was saying made no sense at all. Surely, the Author hadn't sent me on a suicide mission, had he?

"The door of death…but that can't be. I'm not dead. There must be some mistake."

"That'ssss what they all ssssay when they firsssst arrive. But the Author himsssself has promisssed to send the dead to me. They all belong to me. You…belong to me."

That couldn't be true. How could it? Sceleris was lying! I had given my heart to the Author, and he had rewritten me. I didn't belong here.

"I mussst admit," Sceleris said, "it took much longer to claim you than I thought. You put up a good fight, but the time for fighting issss over. I have a proposssssition for you."

"I'm not interested," I said, searching for an escape. The tunnel across from the lake was my only hope, but there was no way to get to it unless I swam, and I swam like a rock. There had to be another way.

"How far you are willing to go to ssssave your father, hmmmmm?"

His words were an echo of what Aviad himself had said to me before I took the plunge. But how could Sceleris know them? Had he heard what was said between us a while ago?

"What do you have in mind?" I asked, weighing each word as he said it.

"I'm willing to make you a deal that will buy both you and your father a little more time in the land of the living, a deal that ensures your family will be together."

It sounded too good to be true. I knew there would be a catch.

"Go on," I said. "What do you get out of it?"

"Nothing really, a mere token of…."

"What…is…it, Sceleris?" I asked harshly.

"Sssssilence," he said slowly and clearly.

"Silence? Is that all you want?"

"Yesss…that issss it. Do not ssssspeak of the Author; don't carry the Writ…and don't ever…ever…tell anyone about Sssssolandria. Do all thisssss, and I will give you the life you have alwaysssss wanted in Dessstiny. You will be popular in sssschool, get good gradessss and your family…your family will be whole again and the Shadow will leave you alone. It'sss everything you alwaysss wanted…with no downssssside."

The request seemed simple enough. After all, speaking of Solandria usually got me in trouble in the Veil. My friends thought I was weird because of it. I could keep it a secret, couldn't I? But then, I would be living a lie. I wouldn't be who I really was.

"I don't know," I said at last. "It doesn't seem right."

"Then your father will die like the rest of the doomed souls in the lake."

Out of nowhere a pair of white-fleshed water banshees lifted themselves from the green lake and slid across the stone floor on their bellies like seals with arms. They were the ugliest things I had ever seen. Long pointed noses, large yellow eyes and the teeth of a shark. Behind them they pulled a black chain, which they latched onto my father's ankle, using it to pull him back toward the water's edge.

"Wait!" I shouted, causing the banshees to stop short of the final pull. Sceleris smiled at my sudden willingness to listen.

"Let me get this straight. All I have to do is stop talking about Solandria. I can still believe in it and come here whenever I want?"

"Yesssss…all you want, but you musssst keep it hidden. A ssssecret world that only you know exisssssts."

"What about Trista and the others in Destiny who already know?"

"You cannot talk about it with them," Sceleris said.

"But what if I accidentally say something…?"

"You won't. I will sssssteal the wordssss from your lipsss."

I pondered the options that had been set before me. It sure would be nice to be popular at school, and I certainly wouldn't miss the Shadow causing trouble in my life anymore. I'd have a family again and a father. It was my chance at a new beginning. But how could I keep the truth about the Author a secret—a secret of the Shadow?

"Sssso, do we have a deal?" Sceleris asked.

For the briefest of moments I thought I'd say "yes," but even as I opened my mouth, I changed my mind. My father meant a lot to me, but Solandria and the Author meant so much more.

"Wait a minute. What am I thinking?" I said aloud. "I cannot accept your deal and return to your bondage now that I am free. I am a son of the Author…and you have no power over me. I can't stop talking about Solandria any more than I can stop talking about myself. Solandria is a part of me; it's my home…where my family is. It's where Aviad has called me."

Upon the sound of the name, Sceleris coiled so tightly around his throne it began to crack under the squeezing pressure of his muscular tail. His eyes lit with fire and he bellowed out his final orders with an intensity that rattled the room.

"Pull him in!"

"Please, no!" Dad begged, but even if they heard him, the water banshees paid no attention. With a horrid splash my father's body slipped over the edge and sank below the surface.

"And to think, your father thought you were hissss hero," Sceleris laughed. "You are nothing but a zero—a nobody with nowhere to go."

"No, it doesn't end here…not like this," I said, eyeing the water with determination.

How far are you willing to go to save your father?

Without a second thought I dove into the green abyss. The

shadowed form of my sinking father was directly below me, being pulled to his watery grave by the weight of the chain that clasped his ankles. His was not the only form here; thousands of bodies floated in the water, all of them chained to an invisible anchor beneath the shadow of the deep, but I couldn't afford to take my eyes off of my father for fear of losing him.

The wailing and moaning of the dead seemed to drown every good thought from my mind. I focused my sights on Dad and dove further and further down until the water darkened around us from green to grey. It was tougher to keep swimming; the bodies of the dead were everywhere and their arms and legs kept grabbing at me.

My lungs began to burn, nearly bursting in need of a breath of air. If I didn't head back to the surface soon, I would die. Still, I forced myself to dive further; I had come too far to let him slip away now. With the weight of the chain pulling him down, Dad was just out of reach when the water banshees began to attack, encircling me. Their razor-sharp claws tore through my skin. I did my best to avoid them, and in all the commotion, I forgot and inhaled the horrid, green water into my lungs. Surprisingly, I found this water had the same effect as air. I could breathe here. The waters of death had no effect on me.

The screaming banshees came around for another attack, but this time I felt my strength return. I caught them both by their hair and tied them together in a knot so they couldn't swim straight. They struggled, screaming like little girls on a playground.

I searched for my father and headed down to where he was chained.

"Dad," I said, my voice gurgling under the water.

His face looked lifeless, but I didn't lose hope. I found the chain that had been shackled to his leg and pulled at it, hoping to break it off. I pulled and pulled but it was no use.

Then, a pair of arms reached past me and took hold of the chain. Hope was here. I didn't know how she got here, but I was grateful she had. She made a ball of fire in her palm and melted the chain from my father's leg. When his leg was freed, I started pulling him up toward the surface once more.

Hope shook her head and pointed downward into the deep blackness. Unsure of where she was going, I followed. Together, we pulled my father down with us. Eventually, the murky water began to lighten again. Somewhere overhead, the flickering of the water's surface beckoned us closer. My lungs began to burn, begging for air…real air. As we approached the surface, I spotted the underbelly of a small row boat. We headed for it and broke through the surface of the water, gasping for breath.

"Grab the rope!" a familiar voice shouted. Faldyn was in the boat and anxious to pull us in. Hope and I sprawled out on the floor of the boat while Faldyn tended to my father.

"You're crazy, you know that?" Hope finally said once she had caught enough breath. I chuckled, still trying to catch my own.

"What were you thinking?" she asked. "Raiding the Void is… well, it's not supposed to happen."

"I guess I just thought if Aviad was willing to give his life for me, I wouldn't be his son if I wasn't willing to do the same for someone else."

"That's a pretty good excuse, I guess." Hope elbowed me in the arm. I pretended to complain, but I didn't mind. Unfortunately, when Faldyn turned around, his expression wasn't as cheerful as ours.

"Faldyn, what's wrong?" I asked.

"Your father…" he said grimly, "he didn't make it."

"What?" I asked, unwilling to believe it. "After all of that? But I thought he'd…."

"I'm sorry, Hunter," Faldyn said.

Hope put her arm around my shoulders. "It's not your fault; you did everything you could…and more."

"We need to see Aviad," I said boldly. "He can fix this."

Faldyn nodded and started rowing us back to shore in silence.

We carried my father's body through the woods to the portal of the twisting trees. We arrived at Sanctuary in the midst of a grand celebration. The entire town had been rebuilt; it was alive again and looked as good as the first time I had seen it.

The entire Resistance seemed to be there, celebrating the defeat of the Shadow and the return of the Living Tree. While singing, dancing and fireworks were happening all around me, I carried my father's limp body though the cheerful chaos to the Temple where Aviad and the captains of the Resistance sat at a long table, overlooking the festivities.

Trista was showing Emily her bow and how she had learned to use it. Mom was listening to Gabby's latest story about her grandson, Cranton, and how kids these days need to use their imaginations more. Xaul and Stoney were sitting at a table to the side, sharing stories from the battle. The Bungle family took up an entire table by themselves, and Evan and Vogler stood behind the table of captains, watching…. The Thordin brothers and Samryee were slapping each other on the back and laughing extra loud. Even Boojum was scurrying about, followed by a family of baby sharks as he stuffed his face with all kinds of food. The atmosphere was alive and full of joy; it was so surreal I almost thought it was a dream.

But the crowd began to hush as we moved through the activity toward the head table. The whispers and murmurs turned into an uproar as we laid my father's body down before Aviad and knelt in reverence before the man I had come to know as the Author's son.

"See here, what is the meaning of this?" one of the Codebearer captains complained.

"Indeed, this is highly irregular. Most uncalled for," another declared.

Aviad raised his hands and the crowd began to calm.

"Hunter, you've returned."

"Yes, sir," I said. "I've brought you my father."

"So I see," Aviad said calmly.

"He's…he's dead."

"Yes, I know," Aviad said, his eyes pooling with tears as he spoke. It was the first time I had seen him cry. Suddenly, I began to wonder if I had been mistaken. Perhaps Aviad couldn't save my father now…maybe it really was too late.

"You asked me how far I would be willing to go to save him…" I said. "I've gone as far as I could go…. I need you to heal him like you did me."

"It doesn't work that way, Hunter," Aviad said.

"What do you mean? I thought you sent me to find him."

"I did."

"I risked my life to save him because I thought that you could… make him live again."

Aviad peered over my father's lifeless form and shook his head. He closed his eyes and began to weep. The tears that fell were genuine tears for a man he clearly cared for.

"Oh, Caleb," he sighed, speaking directly to my father as if he could still hear. "Why was it so hard for you to trust me? I could have saved you from yourself a thousand times over if only you had been willing…but you would not let me. You were so zealous for independence, so driven to know what *would be* you passed over the one gift that would have given you the freedom you sought. And yet…even this was written so that you might serve a higher purpose."

A tear dropped from the eyelashes of Aviad and fell onto my father's face. The tear held more power than all the forces of Sceleris combined. It was the tear of the Author falling on his own story. A final tear dropped on the Bloodstone buried in my father's chest. I watched in awe as slowly the Bloodstone began to glow again. Dad's lungs filled with the breath of life reborn and his eyes opened with sudden awareness of his surroundings.

The crowd gasped and my family gathered around the table. Mom, Emily and even Trista stood by my side, watching as my father awakened before Aviad, who had restored him.

"Well, Caleb, do you trust me now?"

"I do," Caleb said, oblivious to anyone but Aviad.

"Then there is something I must take back—something you've been keeping from me."

Caleb looked down at his chest. The Bloodstone was shining through, throbbing to the beat of his heart. He knew what Aviad wanted—his heart. The Bloodstone WAS his heart.

"Yes, but if you do, won't I...die again?"

Aviad nodded.

"Isn't there any other way?" he asked.

"No, but if you trust me, I have a new story where a hero like you is needed."

"Me? I'm no hero; I ruined everything," my father said solemnly, remembering the destruction he caused when united with Tonomis.

"Yes," Aviad replied softly, "you did. But if you trust me, things can be different this time." I could tell my father was thrilled with the idea of an adventure all his own, but when he looked at the faces of his family around him, his excitement waned.

"But what about my family, will they be able to come too?" Dad asked.

"Someday," Aviad said plainly, "but not yet."

Emily threw her arms around our father in a giant hug. "Oh

Daddy, please don't go. We've missed you so much."

"I have to, Em," Dad said. "If I don't go, this…this thing in me will kill me just the same and we'll never be together. Be strong… you'll always be my princess."

Mom was next in line to approach Dad. The years of tension between them left so much to be said, but there wasn't much time to heal the rift. "Caleb, I'm sorry I never trusted you with all of this. I guess I just never knew how real it was."

"It's okay, honey. I didn't really trust it myself until just now. I never meant for it to end like this. I only wanted to help save our family.…"

"You did, sweetie," Mom said. It was the first time I had heard her call him that in a very long time. "You gave us something to believe in."

Without another word, she leaned in and gave him a kiss, a simple kiss filled with baggage from many years of misunderstandings. But it was also a hopeful kiss, the start of something new, a bridge between hearts that had been torn apart.

When she was finished, Mom stepped back and let me and Dad have the final word.

"Hunter, my boy, what's left to say?" Dad asked. "I'm sorry I can't be there for you."

"It's okay, Dad," I replied. "We've had a pretty good adventure."

"We have…haven't we?" Dad smiled.

"Yeah, not many kids get to beat their dads in a wrestling match in the sky."

We shared a teary smile at the memory. I knew that wasn't exactly how it had been, but it was how I would choose to remember it.

"And not many dads have a son as brave as you. Thanks for believing in me…even when I didn't believe in myself."

I hugged my dad for the last time and squeezed harder than ever before, so that I would remember it for a lifetime. If I had my way, I never would have let go.

Dad broke the embrace and looked me in the eyes.

"I'm a bit scared," he admitted.

"It's going to be okay, Dad," I said. "We're never alone."

"No...no, we're not," Dad said, looking back to Aviad.

"It's time," Aviad said, nodding to my father.

Dad closed his eyes and let Aviad do the rest. With a careful hand, Aviad reached into my father's chest to remove the Bloodstone. My father arched his back and drew in a deep painful breath. Aviad took hold of the Bloodstone and pulled it free. All at once, my father's form fell limp and he began to fade like a ghost. He couldn't move, but in his eyes I thought I saw a smile. Then he was gone.

A moment of solemn silence hung in the air. With a heavy heart I stared at the empty space where my father had once lain. The crowd was hushed. The only thing that stirred was the faintest breeze, which rustled the leaves in the trees around Sanctuary.

Then, with a sudden gasp, the crowd began to come alive with excitement. I overheard one of the men mumble to those around him, "Do you see what I'm seeing?"

The murmuring grew quickly, though I had no clue why. I spun around to see what all the commotion was about and spotted a movement in the sky. Something was happening overhead...something big.

Like a paper being torn in two, the clouds pulled apart, revealing a crack of light that stretched across the sky. The rift in the sky grew wider until it was evident there was something hidden behind it...something lost in the blinding light. It looked as though it were a portal to another world entirely.

I saw my father standing beside Petrov and Gerwyn, waving at us and smiling down from the beginning of his new adventure. I waved back and watched as my father turned around and faced the city of light that rose before him. As we watched him climb a stairway, Hope captured the moment in song as she repeated the second half of the refrain I had come to cherish:

Death is not the end, dear one.
Another chapter has begun.
So be not sad, oh heart of mine,
Find the joy that's hid behind.
Through darkness light will find its way,
While we await the dawn of day.

Mom put her arms around Emily and me, squeezing us closely as we watched the window between worlds close. With a loud cheer from the crowd, the festivities resumed as a double celebration—a celebration of victory and a celebration of life—the new life of my father.

When the celebration was over, Aviad led my family and Trista back into the Temple where he presented us with a gift, my father's Writ and key, the ones Desi had stolen from me.

"But I don't understand," I said. "How did you find it? I thought Desi…."

"I have my ways," Aviad smiled. "Let's just say that being the Author's son has its privileges."

He motioned for me to open the book. I placed the key in the lock and gave it a quarter-turn to the right. Just like magic, the book came alive with an unworldly light. The pages flipped open to a passage near the end of the book. The passage was about Destiny and would lead us home once more. Led by Trista, Mom and Emily touched the words first and vanished from Solandria.

Before I joined them, I had to ask Aviad one last question that had been bothering me. Even before I spoke, he sensed I was going to ask.

"What is it, Hunter?"

"Before I go…I just have to know…." I started.

"Of course, what is it, Hunter?"

"What happened to the Eye of Ends?" I asked.

Aviad smiled, "Don't worry. It's safe. Vogler took care of it. I can assure you it will not fall into the wrong hands ever again."

Satisfied, I touched the lighted words of the Writ and left the world of Solandria behind.

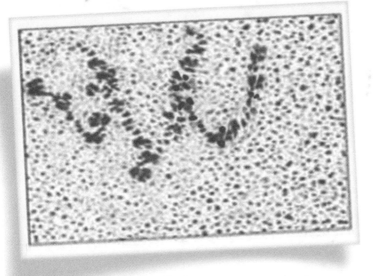

CHAPTER 32

ANOTHER NEW BEGINNING

"**H**unter! Emily!" Mom called up the stairs. "We're going to be late for the meeting if you two don't hurry up. The car is nearly defrosted."

"Beauty can't be rushed, Mom," I reminded her from my bedroom desk, fully expecting my sister to be practicing her usual monopoly of the bathroom mirror for another couple of minutes. I needed that time to finish getting an e-mail written and sent out.

"Nice try, but this 'beauty' is all ready to go," Emily announced from my doorway, bundled up for winter, but still looking stylish. "What's holding you up? You've been holed up for the last hour."

Ignoring the question, I stood while giving my e-mail one last read over.

Emily took the opportunity to sneak up next to me and spy out my desk's current "paper jungle" for herself. "Research notes?" she asked, sounding surprised. In a lowered, mocking voice she added, "Who are you and what have you done with my brother?"

"It's not like that," I said. "I've just been going through Dad's research. You know, for all the mistakes he made, he also made some pretty amazing discoveries about how the Code of Life works. I've been passing along the highlights to Stretch for the last week or so."

"Yeah?" Emily asked. "Any progress on that front?"

"A little," I replied. "At least it's given us something in common to talk about again. He seems to like the intellectual stimulation. But I think this next piece is going to blow his socks off! Want to see?"

Intrigued, Emily nodded and glanced at her watch. "Better make it quick though. I give us thirty seconds before Mom leaves without us."

I quickly scrolled back up to the top of my e-mail message to where I'd inserted a black and white photograph.

"That's the Author's mark," Emily said, immediately recognizing the identifiable three *Vs*. "But why is it all…smooshy?"

The grainy photo showed a series of irregular blobs connected by dark veins of lines, creating an undeniable resemblance to the Author's mark—even if it was a "smooshy" one. If I hadn't known what it was, I might have seen it as some kind of stained-glass window that had melted.

"It's a micrograph of the proteins designed to hold our body's cells together," I explained.

"Micrograph? Proteins?" Emily looked impressed at my depth of proficiency on this subject. "You got this from Dad's notes?"

"No, I found it online," I said, showing her the journal's Website where I had found and copied the image. "Dad's notes in his Author's Writ talked about a theory of how the Code was an integral part of every living thing. When I mentioned it to Rob the other day, he suggested I check the science journals. That's when I came up with this gem."

"Impressive work for a former slack-off," Emily said in a round-about compliment. "Think it will be what finally convinces Stretch that the Author is real?"

"Probably not," I said honestly. "But the way I see it, convincing him has never been my job anyway. I'm just planting another seed."

Timed perfectly to Emily's prediction, the front door could be heard swinging open and Mom shouted up the stairs, "Last call! I'm putting the car in reverse and driving away. So unless you plan on walking…." The front door closed.

I clicked the *Send* button, grabbed my coat and Writ and followed Emily downstairs and out into the wintry weather that had blanketed Destiny.

The car was already backing out into the street as we raced across the snow-covered lawn to wave Mom down. Even though I got there first, I let Emily "steal" the front passenger seat from me. After all, she was the first-born. That and getting to share the backseat with Trista when we picked her up wasn't such a bad deal either.

"Playing it a bit close tonight, aren't we?" Mom asked as we finally drove off. "I'm sure Kim could run through another training session on 'timeliness' if you wanted."

She was referring, of course, to Mr. Bungle and his infamous session involving egg-timers, dodge balls and floor wax—a strange but effective demonstration on the Code of Life and always being prepared. Tonight's weekly Codebearer meeting at the Bungle's promised to be equally as memorable and challenging.

I was still amazed by how eager both Mom and Emily had been when Rob's dad first approached us with the idea of joining their newly formed Codebearer home group. After returning from their traumatic introduction to Solandria as hostages, Mom and Emily naturally had a lot of questions about the Shadow, the Author, the Codebearers, and about where Dad was now. I did my best to answer, but was more than grateful for the assistance.

We were just one of a handful of families the Bungle's now hosted at their house each Tuesday night. Each member was different from the next—young, old, newbie, veteran—but we all shared one thing in common: our deep desire to learn about the Author and his ways. There was something so refreshing about being around others who, though different, understood you and also challenged you.

One remarkable development in our group was the addition of none other than Cranton. When he finally helped set the record straight on our involvement in the school fire, he was promptly expelled from the school district for his part. That was a big blow to Cranton's grandmother, Gabby, who was already struggling to care for this troubled teen. When Rob learned of the expulsion, he somehow got the crazy idea to reach out and offer Cranton and his grandmother help in finishing off Cranton's schooling from home. Homeschooling wasn't exactly a popular idea with Cranton, but Rob's parents embraced the challenge of incorporating another kid into their family life, and he eventually went along with it. Naturally, Gabby was delighted to discover the Bungle's home group and over time convinced Cranton to come along too.

Considering all of the amazing twists and turns my life had taken of late, it was peaceful just watching the snow lightly falling outside the car window, transforming Destiny into a city of white. Picturing the pure whiteness of the ground as a blank page, I imagined the Author sitting down, thoughtfully dipping his pen and preparing to write another chapter. Who knew what he might write next? Some of the plot might be difficult, some of it might be too mundane for me to even notice developing, but all of it would be good. Never wasting what might have come before, I knew he would continue weaving every line together toward his story's eventual climax—another new beginning.

CHAPTER 33

EPILOGUE

"**S**o what do we do now?" I asked eagerly, attempting to search out the depths of the murky black water beneath our rowboat.

"We wait," Hope replied with a hint of amusement.

I knew she was going to say that. Obviously, patience was a lesson the Author never tired of finding time for…and one I still needed to practice.

Watching my reflection ripple across the Lake of the Lost, I shivered, knowing that not all that long ago, I had been counted among its silent numbers—one of a million chained souls locked away beneath its shadowy surface, numb to the life that awaited them in Solandria.

Remembering made me all the more excited to have been sent by the Author to rescue one more out of the depths. Every awakening was special, Hope had told me, but this arrival was particularly important to me. I gave the surrounding water another thorough scan, looking for signs of life.

"Do you think he'll be ready?" I asked.

Hope laughed. "Honestly, Hunter, could you say that you were 'ready' when you first came?"

She had a point. Nothing could have prepared me for what was waiting to be discovered on the other side of the Veil in Solandria—a world filled with truth, both terrifying and beautiful.

"And that's why I had you," I teased.

Hope smiled, her eyes sparkling with the reflections of a million dancing flames. I turned around to look back at the now-familiar sight—Solandria's new and vibrant Living Tree—its every golden leaf a flame of light. What had started as a small seed now loomed mightily above its shard, its roots reaching out across the Void to every disparate shard, drawing them back to unity—the promise of a restored Solandria.

But the tree meant so much more to me. It reminded me of my purpose—to plant seeds of truth in those who had not yet seen their lives through the Author's eyes. I would do whatever it took to make sure that the Secret of the Shadow was never kept.

Hope's voice suddenly recalled me to the moment at hand. "Time to get wet," she said, tossing me a rope. My heart leaped as she grabbed the oars and moved us closer to the rising patch of bubbles she'd just spotted.

I held my breath. The wait was finally over. A new soul had been awakened. A new adventure was about to begin.